In 2016, Phelan published his first fiction novel, *The Beech Tree,* voted No. 1 on Goodreads' '2016's Best Summer Reads.'

Phelan has also published non-fiction, short stories, and poetry.

To Tammy, Jen, and Katie.
Thank you for your support.

Don Phelan

THE GOD PARTICLE CONSPIRACY

AUSTIN MACAULEY PUBLISHERS™

LONDON · CAMBRIDGE · NEW YORK · SHARJAH

Copyright © Don Phelan (2019)

Ordering Information:
Quantity sales: special discounts are available on quantity purchases by corporations, associations, and others. For details, contact the publisher at the address below.

Publisher's Cataloging-in-Publication data
Phelan, Don
The God Particle Conspiracy

ISBN 9781643782843 (Paperback)
ISBN 9781643782850 (Hardback)
ISBN 9781643782867 (Kindle e-book)
ISBN 9781645367383 (ePub e-book)

Library of Congress Control Number: 2019938271

The main category of the book — Fiction / Thriller / Espionage

www.austinmacauley.com/us

First Published (2019)
Austin Macauley Publishers LLC
40 Wall Street, 28th Floor
New York, NY 10005
USA

mail-usa@austinmacauley.com
+1 (646) 5125767

James Conlan – Editor, Story Consultant
Kevin and Jennifer Landino – Concept Developer
Lucy Kubash – Editor, Creative Advisor
Kaitlyn Phelan – Editor

1

Sarah's plan was simple: find her mentor, Dr. John Logan, stay ahead of those trying to kill them, and save the world. It was a simple plan—just not an easy one.

She rushed down the steps of the Greyhound bus, dug into her backpack, pulled out the blood-smudged manila envelope, and hurried into New Orleans Union Passenger Terminal. She found a row of rental lockers and stuffed the envelope, plus a roll of hundred-dollar bills, into locker number 2852. The French Quarter was a half-mile away. Before crossing Canal, Sarah glanced over each shoulder, praying her pursuers weren't in sight.

Standing at the intersection of St. Anne and Bourbon Streets, Sarah checked the sticky note she held in her hand once more before approaching the fortuneteller.

Queen Esther's Tarot Readings, $10 read the chalkboard sidewalk sign beside a rickety card table. Before sitting on the metal folding chair in front of the table, Sarah's head spun 360 degrees, scanning for God-knows-what. She wasn't sure that she'd recognize something out of place if it bit her in the ass.

"Are you Ruby?" Sarah blurted once she faced the Tarot card reader again.

The Tarot reader didn't look up as she chanted incantations and swirled the cards around the table in front of her. Nodding at the sign, she stopped long enough to reply in a pronounced Jamaican accent, "Dat what de sign say?"

"Ah, I see. I'm sorry. My mistake, Queen Esther." Sarah's heart sank and her mind raced. She was sure Dr. Logan's clues led her here. She was sure of it. Or was she? Adrenaline seared her nerves as it shot up her spine. She was alone. She was afraid.

She checked the note and street sign again before turning to the fortuneteller, "Can you tell me—"

"What else de sign say?" Queen Esther interrupted, still chanting over her cards.

Sarah reached into her purse for a twenty and pushed it across the table. She shifted in her chair as the soothsayer held the bill up to the light, then stuffed the money into her cleavage. "Close enough."

Sarah didn't protest. Finding Logan was worth an extra ten-spot. She pulled a photo from her pocket. "Have you seen this face?" She pushed a wrinkled photograph across the table toward Queen Esther. The priestess's eyes were yellow as an eagle's or a pit viper's. She wasn't sure which.

Queen Esther's squinted. "Dis face? I cain't say I seen dis face—"

Sarah panicked. She didn't know where she'd gone wrong, but she knew she had just exposed herself to immediate danger. She jumped from the chair and spun full-circle, studying the faces of tourists to see if any were staring back. She hoisted the backpack from the sidewalk and turned to run, then she heard Queen Esther begin to speak slowly. Peering hard at the photo, Queen Esther said, "Seen a face *like* dis. Not so round as dis, though."

Sarah stopped, studied the viper-eyed Tarot card reader for a moment, then plopped back down into the chair. She leaned in close to the voodoo priestess and whispered, "You have? You've seen him?"

Queen Esther leaned back and closed her eyes as if in a trance, facing the blue New Orleans sky. He hands ceremoniously shuffled the cards around the table, babbling incoherently as she conjured voodoo spirits.

She stopped chanting long enough to say something.

Sarah understood: "Mebbe I has. Mebbe I hasn't."

Sarah scrambled to find another twenty. She handed it to Queen Esther, who opened one eye long enough to tuck it into her bosom beside the first one.

Beads of sweat rolled down Sarah's spine as Queen Esther made a show of shuffling the cards. Snap! The priestess's head jerked forward, and her snake-like eyes bulged in horror. She flipped over the Tower Card and threw her hands toward the heavens while she spoke in tongues.

Sarah had seen the Tower Card before; it forecast destruction and chaos.

"You're telling me," Sarah muttered, then repeated her question, "have you seen him?"

Queen Esther stood quickly and snatched up her chair, cards, and cash box, and tucked them under her heavy arms. At six-foot-four and three hundred fifty pounds, Queen Esther was a formidable presence. She glared at Sarah before she stomped down the sidewalk toward Marie Laveau's House of Voodoo.

"Wait! Where are you going?" Sarah pleaded. Queen Esther ignored her.

Sarah's eyes followed Queen Esther until she ducked into Madame Laveau's shop. Checking over each shoulder again, Sarah followed her. Queen Esther was the only lead she had to finding Dr. Logan.

Peeking through the open-air doorway, Sarah realized Queen Esther had disappeared. She moved slowly through the store, dodging security cameras as she navigated past shelves of ceremonial dolls and incense.

A commotion behind her spun Sarah around. Queen Esther burst into the open doorway, her gold lame slippers pounding the shop's wooden floor and rattling the merchandise on store shelves. With a quick jerk of her head as she passed, she summoned Sarah to follow her through a beaded curtain at the back of the store.

How did she do that? Sarah wondered. Within seconds, Queen Esther had entered, somehow exited, and re-entered the same front door of Madame Laveau's. Sarah had no time to satisfy her curiosity.

"Sarah!" the priestess shouted into Sarah's face as she gripped the young woman's shoulders. Under normal circumstances, Sarah would be terrified of this large, black-skinned woman with a curious accent.

These circumstances were far from normal. "Yes?" Sarah said.

Despite a steady stream of sweat flowing down her back, Sarah felt oddly safe. "You in trouble, girl." Queen Esther nodded back toward the curtains. Sarah peeked through the curtain. Two tourists wearing souvenir shirts from the Margaritaville gift shop across the street looked under counters and around shelves as they worked their way toward the back of the store. A white price tag dangled from one of their shirts.

"You bein' followed," Queen Esther blurted.

"I know," Sarah replied. *Real tourists don't wear earpieces*, she thought. Sarah turned to Queen Esther and whispered, "Who are they?"

Fully a head taller than Sarah, Queen Esther looked down at Sarah and said, "Seriously, girl. Do it matter?" Queen Esther tugged Sarah's shoulder and yanked her away from the curtains. "Come. Dis way."

Sarah was wary of this odd woman who seemed to be protecting her. Nevertheless, she followed the Queen's bright-blue muumuu through a passageway in the storage room of the shop. The voodoo queen pulled her into a dark tunnel of brick walls and formaldehyde-soaked timbers. "Where are we?" Sarah asked.

"Underground Railroad," Queen Esther panted as she rushed ahead of Sarah. "Truth is, ain't nothing underground about it. Least-ways, not here in New Orleans, see-ins' how everything's at sea level. Hurry!" Ahead, a sliver of light slipped between buildings. Sarah clung to Queen Esther's muumuu as they rounded a corner.

Sarah never saw it coming—the sharp sting in her neck an instant before her world faded to black.

2

Eight Months Earlier

Behind the limousine's black-tinted windows and isolated from the chauffeur by a bulletproof glass partition, two passengers watched Dr. Logan stride across campus toward his next class. Despite receiving anonymous threats intended to silence him, he continued lecturing and writing about the Higgs boson particle, his hypotheses on the increasing anomalies, and the role humans may be playing in the strange events.

"He's not getting the message, is he?" The man in the limo scowled, his bushy eyebrows and bulbous nose were pressed against the one-way window.

"The message, sir?"

"He didn't take the hint. He's not getting the message that he needs to shut up; to keep what he knows to himself. We're secure here, right?"

"Secure, sir?" The aide sat beside her boss in luxurious leather seats separated by a console. The boss swirled a rocks glass half-filled with expensive Russian vodka as he waited for her answer. "Yes, sir. The vehicle has scramblers, encryption—the works."

"Nobody can eavesdrop on what we're saying?" His question seemed redundant to her but that was nothing new.

"That's what I'm saying, sir." Her nose twitched again as a waft of his cologne found its way to her nostrils. He always wore too much, especially when he was nervous. When he sweated, the combination of cologne and sweat turned the odor sour. Lately, he'd been sweating a lot.

People rarely defied him; instead, they cowered. Anyone who failed to recognize his directives as orders must have misunderstood him, he believed; it was as simple as that. To make sure he was understood, the portly man often re-arranged sentences as if they weren't clear to the listener the first time. "We've warned him, haven't we? We have, right? Haven't we warned him?"

He fidgeted in the leather seat. "Some people are going to be very upset. Some very upset people." He pushed out his jaw, stretching the sack of flabby flesh beneath it.

"Yes, sir. I understand, sir."

He turned and snarled, "No, I don't think you do. People, I won't say who, certain people, these people can be very dangerous. Bad people, you get that? When they don't get their way, they hurt people. People like you, and your family, and your family's family."

A chill ran through her as she saw the fear in the eyes of this man of immense wealth and power. He was accustomed to getting what he wanted. Now he was sweating profusely as he spoke. The car smelled like vinegar. She could see he was terrified.

"What would you have us do, sir?"

"Do we have eyes in his classroom?"

"Yes, sir. The gentleman from Brooklyn, sir."

"Send him a text to call me ASAP."

The assistant pulled out her phone, punched ten numbers, and sent a message. Two minutes later, his phone was ringing. He grabbed it and shouted, "One hour. I'll meet you at the restaurant." Handing her his phone, he ordered, "Throw it away. Get me a new phone."

One hundred yards down the block on the opposite side of the street, a young man aimed a long-range listening device at the black limousine from the back seat of a Buick Enclave. He wore earphones and spoke into the mic positioned in front of his lips. "You getting all of this?"

"Roger that, Commander Maycroft. Your signal is coming in wall-to-wall."

3

"Here," Beth Logan leaned over and kissed her husband, John, on the forehead, then refilled his coffee cup from the insulated carafe. "What are you working on?" she asked, watching him sit across the low table from her in his Adirondack chair. Minutes ago, the New York Times Sunday Edition was delivered by an enterprising college student, along with several bagels smeared with cream cheese, four small bottles of orange juice, and coffee.

Fat-bellied robins had returned to New England from their Southern nests. The morning was sunny and warm. Dirt beyond the home's wraparound front porch smelled of renewal and the begonias had started to bloom. Beth sipped her coffee and bit into the sun dried tomato and basil bagel as she browsed the Times headlines. She knew her husband well enough to know he wouldn't answer. Lost in thought, nothing short of an explosion would get his attention.

"I'm not sure," he mumbled to Beth's surprise. "I'm not—" His voice trailed off as he alternately stared at his laptop and thick textbook opened on the arm of his chair. "Something," he paused. "Something about Hawking's theory. It's possible, I suppose, but there are parts of it that just don't make sense."

"Do you mean the part about the Higgs boson particle?" Beth knew that her husband, Dr. John Logan, a preeminent Astrophysicist and Cosmology Professor at the nearby university, had lately been examining Hawking's theory of The God Particle, in part due to inexplicable events occurring throughout the world. He nodded, checking the textbook against what he saw on his monitor.

Their daughters, Lisa and Lucy, dug with spoons in the flowerbed surrounding the porch.

"I'm getting the dirt ready to plant petunias," Lisa announced. Seeing her sister's excitement, Lucy clapped her hands together and laughed.

"Hamilton is now in the top ten longest-running plays in history," Beth reported from the Times' entertainment section. She perused the Op-Eds and said, "Looks like there's another scandal going on at the White House." She looked at her husband to get his reaction. Nothing. "In World News, an entire Russian town was swallowed into a sinkhole. All 7,000 residents are missing and presumed dead."

"That's nice," he replied absentmindedly. Several minutes passed before he stopped, turned to his wife, and said, "What did you say? A sinkhole in Russia? Here, let me see that!" He grabbed the paper and found the article Beth was citing.

"Aha!" He jumped up and strutted back and forth along the porch. "Aha! I knew it! I knew it!"

"You knew what?" Beth asked sweetly.

"Shhhhh! Shush!" With his hand, he motioned her to lower her voice.

"I believe I'm not the one shouting, dear."

Logan stopped, looked up and down the street, and then sat back down into his chair. "You're right. I'm sorry. I was—I am—so excited to see this."

"You're excited to see that 7,000 people disappeared and are presumed dead?"

"No, no, of course not. No, that's tragic. Horrible. What I meant was: it's typical of the weird events I have been talking about. They seem to be happening in China, the U.S.A., the Middle East and Africa, South America, and even Australia. But this is the first I've heard about one in Russia."

"The article says they can't confirm if it was actually in Russia or Ukraine," Beth clarified.

"Yes, I see that. That's typical. Russia prefers to keep its bad news secret, like when its leaders denied that a Cosmonaut died in space. The article says the story was leaked to the Times by a young woman who grew up in Bilieva, Belarus. She attended the Lomonosov University in Moscow. On holidays, she traveled by train to visit her family in Bilieva. She took the train because she enjoyed traveling through the small towns along the way, especially one named Liozna. After dark, the flame atop the petroleum refinery flare stack would cast its reflection across the Moshna River and Liozna's downtown buildings, some of which had stood since the town was founded in the 1600s."

Beth leaned toward her husband to listen to the story.

"One day, the train was rerouted to the south, adding several hours to her journey. Nearly two years had passed before the train resumed its shorter route through Liozna. As the train approached the small town, she became both excited and confused. When she looked out the window, she saw the bridge was new but it had been built across an empty gulch; the river was gone. The town's main street and all of its buildings were gone, replaced by lush, green crops. There was no flame rising from the flare stack. In fact, the whole refinery had disappeared."

"That seems very strange. Did she ask anyone about it?" Beth replied.

"Yes, she asked the train's conductor, and her professors at the university. They all told her the same story; that nobody knew the refinery had been leaking crude oil and petroleum into the town's soil and ground water for decades. The pollution had even contaminated the river. When a farmer's barn filled with hay caught fire, wind blew the burning hay across a small field and to the refinery. The refinery caught fire and resulted in a massive explosion. Fireballs of flaming fuel caught the town's buildings on fire, burning them to ashes. Apparently, it happened so fast, none of the nearly 7,000 people who lived in the town survived. They vanished in the blaze."

"That's tragic," Beth said, then paused before adding, "nobody, not a single person, survived out of 7,000?"

"That's just it. The student didn't believe the story. It didn't make sense. The refinery burning down, the town catching fire, sure, that could have happened. But how does a river disappear? She took her questions to the Russian media and was stonewalled. She sent the story to the Times, who started asking the Kremlin and the Belarus government for answers."

"Did she find out what happened?"

"No. Now she's missing. The Times believes she has been imprisoned or murdered. What in the world is going on?" Logan muttered.

"That is horrifying. Is anyone trying to find out what happened and where she's gone?"

Logan studied the article again, looking for an answer. "No, it doesn't appear so. This is the first article published on the matter, and even the Times has hit a roadblock trying to find out more."

Beth joined their daughters in the front yard flower garden, working the soil with a claw, giving the dirt a breath of fresh air and waking the soil's nutrients. "So, you want to plant petunias this year?" she asked Lisa and signed to Lucy. They both nodded their heads eagerly and giggled.

"What do you think?" Beth tossed the question over the porch railing in his direction. She knew it was a futile attempt.

"This, this could be the proof I need..." Logan's voice trailed off again. His pace quickened, punching the keys on his laptop, then turning back to the astrophysics textbook book, and examining the Times' article. Beth truly believed he had wheels inside his head and, today, they were spinning off their axles.

"I was thinking about taking the girls to the new Disney movie this afternoon. Do you want the three of us to go or do you want to come with us?" Joyously, Lisa and Lucy hugged each other; they'd been waiting for the movie for months now.

"Sure, that would be great."

Surprised, Beth asked again, "You mean you want to go with us to the new Disney movie?"

Dr. Logan looked up, "Huh? What? You're taking the girls to see the Disney movie? They'll like that. You'll have fun."

Beth shook her head. "I see. Come on, girls, let's go wash this dirt off our hands and go see a movie." She turned to face them so she could ask them both the question: "Who wants popcorn with lots of butter?" They jumped up and down and gave each other a high five. Beth kissed her husband on the forehead as she passed his chair. "Figure it out, honey. I know you can." Beth and Logan's daughters disappeared into the big house in Borough Center where doctors, lawyers, executives, and other Princeton faculty lived.

His eyes darted from his laptop monitor to the Times' article, to his textbook and notes. He was so focused he didn't see the entrepreneurial newspaper and bagel delivery girl standing in front of him.

"Dr. Logan?" she asked, straddling the crossbar of her bike. He didn't seem to hear her. "Dr. Logan?" Still, no response. "John!" she yelled his first name, something only his wife and few close friends called him.

"Huh? What?" He looked up. "Oh, I'm so sorry. Did we forget to leave the envelope out with money for the newspaper and bagels?" he asked, digging into his pocket for a twenty.

"No," the delivery girl replied. "No, you paid me. It's not that." Manila envelope in hand, she walked slowly, nervously, toward the professor. "A man stopped me at the corner a few minutes ago. He paid me a hundred dollars to bring this to you. He looked kind of scary." 'John Logan, PhD' was scrawled on the envelope. Logan offered five dollars to the girl as a tip. She pushed it back, saying, "I just got paid $100 to give you this; I think that included the tip."

"Yeah, sure, okay," Logan agreed. "Thank you." He held the envelope on his lap as he watched her ride away before bending the metal clasp to open it. With his right hand, he retrieved the contents of the envelope. Tucked inside the envelope was a photo of Beth and the girls digging in the dirt while he sat on the porch in his Adirondack chair. In the picture, today's New York Times headline blazed across the newspaper lying beside him on the low table.

He shivered as he raised his head, panning the windows and rooftops across the street. Calculating the approximate angle from which the picture had been taken only minutes earlier, he guessed the photo had been taken from Professor Berens' house several homes to the south. The vantage point was from a second floor window or the roof above the garage.

Professor Berens and I are friends, he thought. *Why would he do such a thing?* Professor Berens had lived in the neighborhood for decades, long before Beth and Dr. Logan. The retired head of the Economics Department, he had spent an illustrious career advising numerous presidential administrations. Logan couldn't fathom that his friend and neighbor would betray him by allowing someone to photograph Logan's family from his home.

Cautiously, Logan shut the laptop down and folded the newspaper to hide the envelope. On rubbery legs, he entered the house and made his way to his and Beth's bedroom. He glanced at the photo once more before stuffing it beneath his rolled-up socks in the dresser drawer, the photo still wrapped in the Times' editorial section. He wandered back along the hallway till he found Beth and the girls readying themselves to go to the movie.

"Going somewhere?" he asked dully.

Beth kissed his cheek and laughed, "Always the joker. Did you decide to come with us after all?"

"Yeah, yes, I did. I'm coming with you." Wherever they were going, he was going to be with them.

"We're going to the new Disney movie, Daddy!" Lisa shouted, "I'm so-o-o-o-o excited! I can't wait."

Ah yes, the new Disney movie, Logan thought. He remembered Beth saying something about that now. Thoughts and images collided within his brain as he drove to the movie house.

Dr. Logan paid for tickets while Beth ordered popcorn with an unhealthy dose of fake butter for everyone, a box of Raisinets, and Junior Mints.

Sitting in the dark theater with his beloved family, he couldn't get the photo out of his head. His hands trembled as he grasped a few tufts of buttery popcorn. He tried to force them into his mouth but gagged instead. Even his favorite candy, the chocolate-covered raisins, tasted foul.

"Are you okay?" Beth leaned across their two daughters, noticing his uneasiness.

"I'm not feeling so great," he admitted, "but I'll be fine." He reached across the girls to pat his wife's hand reassuringly. Beth stared at him for several seconds before turning back to watch the movie.

On the drive home, the girls giggled in the back seat and re-enacted the movie characters. Beth examined her husband's face; the strain was noticeable.

"What's going on?" she asked.

"Oh, it's probably nothing. I'm sure I am worrying unnecessarily. Someone pulled a sick prank, that's all."

"A prank?"

"Somebody delivered a manila envelope with a picture of our family in it."

"When?"

"This morning, after you and the girls went in to clean up from digging in the dirt."

"No, I mean when did someone take a picture of us?"

"This morning, when you were digging in the dirt."

Beth stared straight ahead. She felt sick. Her hands turned numb and trembled.

Dr. Logan turned onto their street and slowed. A black station wagon was parked in front of Professor Berens' house with the word 'Coroner' in block letters on the back. Two men pushed a gurney loaded with a body bag toward the hearse.

Beth's head snapped toward Dr. Logan. "That picture. Where was it taken?" Dr. Logan didn't answer. He didn't need to. Blood had drained from his face, and his complexion told her everything she needed to know.

Dazed neighbors milled about on the sidewalks, watching the retired and now-deceased Professor Berens being hoisted into the hearse. Logan pulled alongside his neighbor, Bill Lybarger, an investment banker. "What happened?" he asked.

"Sounds like they think he might have had a heart attack. He had dinner with us last night. He said he was tired from running a

5K in the morning and went home about 7:30. That was the last anybody talked to him."

"He always seemed to be in good health," Beth said blankly.

"The autopsy will tell more," Bill replied. "Just goes to show you die no matter how hard you try to prevent it."

Dr. Logan pulled away slowly.

"I want to see that photograph," Beth demanded. Dr. Logan wished he kept secrets from his wife.

He didn't want her to see the contents of the envelope, especially the blood-red 'X' smeared across the photo of Dr. Logan and his family.

4

Four Months Later

Princeton's campus was beautiful in autumn. Today would be Sarah Carmichael's last good memory of the university.

October's morning air was cool and crisp. Sunlight danced off dew, wetting the ivy as its tentacles gripped the university's red brick walls. Cloudless, the sky was bright blue as Sarah crossed the carpet of yellow, red, gold, and brown. Squirrels raced from tree to tree, grabbing acorns till their cheeks bulged, as they scampered to their nests.

Nearly skipping, Sarah was eager for her next class. Two years earlier, she had been awarded a fellowship at Princeton's Department of Astrophysical Sciences. Today, a lecture by her favorite instructor, John Logan, PhD., would be attended by twice the number of students enrolled in Dr. Logan's class.

Department Chairperson for one of the world's most respected schools in Astrophysics and Cosmology, Dr. Logan was well-known, not only for his captivating lectures but for his unparalleled knowledge. Word had spread throughout campus that, today, Dr. Logan was going to speak on the topic of The God Particle. Students from all curricula—Math, Theology, Biology, and Marketing—gathered in the university's largest lecture hall. They were eager to see Logan's presentation made up of equal parts of science, controversy, and showmanship.

Sarah understood science was a male-dominated field where women are rarely perceived as equals. Unlike other young women who yearned to be accepted in science and math, Sarah refused to comport to the science-geek stereotype by wearing flannel shirts and rumpled jeans. Instead, she walked through campus in tailored slacks and low heels, resembling a marketing major more than an astrophysicist.

Growing up, Sarah's father had told her, "Being someone's bootlicker won't get you respect." It wasn't her fault, he explained, that she got both brains and beauty. At 5'9", she was 135 pounds of lean muscle. Long, chestnut hair framed olive skin and bright blue eyes.

She'd heard the catty whispers too long; that she should spend her time competing in beauty contests instead of studying the Cosmos. As a scientist, they suggested, she was simply too pretty to be taken seriously.

Predictably, rumors swirled that she must be sleeping with the teacher to pull the grade point she did. Gossip, though, wouldn't stop her from accepting Dr. Logan's invitation to the Small World Coffee Shop on the second and fourth Tuesday of each month.

There, she would match wits with others in the field who had far more extensive credentials than Sarah. Logan, his faculty peers, and a few PhD candidates who soared in rare air, challenged one another's hypotheses while sitting around a long table at the back of the campus coffee shop.

Sarah quickly gained the respect of these seasoned astrophysicists and cosmologists. In the coffee shop, her gender and appearance didn't matter. In the world of astrophysics, Sarah was twenty-eight going on thirty-five.

For most of the semester, Sarah had looked forward to today's lecture: *The Higgs Boson Subatomic Particle: The God Particle.*

"The Higgs boson subatomic particle," Dr. Logan began as he held forth in the coffee shop, "is the glue that holds everything together—your body, the metal in your car, the planets, even the sun. Without it, everything would collapse and, in a sense, melt into an indistinguishable blob of subatomic goo."

"It's not quite as simple as that," he admitted to his colleagues, "but for the purpose of an example, that's pretty close."

Logan was fifteen years Sarah's senior. His rosy cheeks, round face, and stocky build fit well with his weekend passion—playing in Princeton's amateur rugby league. The teams were made up of a ragtag group of retired first-string players from local colleges, current second-stringers who had given up hope of seeing varsity playing time, and a few who, like Dr. Logan, were wet-nursed on the sport in their British homeland.

This morning, the auditorium was filled with those eager to hear Logan's theories about The God Particle, especially as they related to the theories of Stephen Hawking, a mentor of Logan's.

Sarah had arrived twenty minutes before the lecture's 10:00 a.m. start, but she spotted just one empty seat in the middle of the center row about halfway up. Running a gantlet of hard, pointed knees and stubborn thighs, she apologized as she struggled past. "Excuse me, pardon me. Sorry."

Sarah managed to accidentally hit five of those already seated with her backpack as she struggled to reach the vacant chair. She could feel the scowls burn into the back of her neck as she bent over to rest her backpack at her feet. "What a bitch." Sarah's face turned bright red as someone behind her added, "Homewrecker."

This is not the time or place to lose your temper, she told herself.

"You made it. Congratulations," said a friendly voice sitting to her right.

"You're just saying that because I stopped before I had to climb over you." Straightening up, she looked at the young man speaking and forgot what she was going to say.

"Hi, I'm Aedain." The young man smiled and stuck out his hand. Sarah gripped his hand in return.

"I'm Sarah." Later, she would remember how good he smelled—as if he'd just stepped out of a soapy shower. Sarah clung to his hand longer than she had intended. His eyes were bluish-grey and his smile was genuine. She shook his hand beyond what good manners required.

Their clumsy silence broke when Aedain asked, "Do you come here often?"

"Yes, I'm afraid I do," Sarah laughed at the lame pick-up line delivered in the presence of science geeks surrounding them.

They passed the minutes waiting for Logan to take the podium by talking and smiling. Later, she remembered smiling… and talking… about something; she just couldn't remember what. She caught herself twisting her hair around her finger like she did when she was fifteen. It had been a long time since she twisted her hair.

He reminded her of someone; she wasn't sure whom. He was easy to talk with, not brash or boastful, but confident. Minutes passed quickly until the auditorium's wall clock indicated it was 10:00 a.m.

Waiting in auditorium's wings, Logan appeared relaxed but excited. He showed no outward signs of the terror he felt a few months earlier when the Times' delivery girl handed him a manila envelope with a picture of his family. If he had any lingering worry that the incident was anything more than a sick prank, he didn't show it.

The university's department head approached the lectern and the room went politely silent, "Good morning and thank you all for coming. This is quite an impressive turnout—" Sarah tuned out Dr. Logan's boss while he relished his moment in the spotlight, droning on about the university's commitment to Astrophysics and Cosmology, blah, blah, and the esteemed Professor Logan, blah, blah, until she finally heard, "Please welcome Dr. John Logan." Beaming and waving to his audience, Dr. Logan nearly sprinted from the wings toward the podium.

She straightened in her chair as he adjusted the microphone. From the corner of her eye, she noticed Aedain shift in his seat as well, giving the instructor his full attention.

"Thank you all for coming. For those of you who are in the graduate studies program in astrophysics and cosmology, please understand that many who have joined us in our audience today are not. Please bear with me when I attempt to translate some of our complex theories of physics into layman's language for our guests. Will that be okay?"

Heads nodded 'yes' throughout the auditorium. "In 2012 or so," Dr. Logan began, "Stephen Hawking proposed his theory on the potentially catastrophic outcome of a quantum fluctuation in the empty space in the Cosmos between numerous galaxies. To use layman's terms, he is talking about a 'vacuum bubble.' Hawking proposed that such a vacuum bubble could grow in space and expand at the speed of light, or possibly even faster. In fact, there may be a vacuum bubble somewhere out there in the Cosmos which has already begun expanding. We just don't know it yet."

Dr. Logan paused as he watched numerous heads in the room tilt in confusion.

"We can only see what light has delivered to us, isn't that right? For example, if we are looking at Mars, we can only see the reflection of the sun's rays against Mars' surface. If a cosmic event has its own source of light, we will not be able to witness it until the event travels at light speed to the photoreceptors in our retinas. We can see light from distant stars only after it has traveled billions of miles to our eyeballs. Are you with me so far?"

Half of the audience understood what the professor had just said. Others looked bewildered.

"So, if the vacuum bubble expands fast enough and far enough, it could, conceivably, grow to become powerful enough to suck the entire Milky Way into it. The suction of the vacuum bubble would be so strong the light from our sun could not escape it. In short, our Earth, sun and planets, our entire galaxy would cease to exist. Poof. Gone."

Silence fell on the room while Dr. Logan stood at the front, waiting for the audience's reaction. A hand rose in the front row.

"Yes?" Dr. Logan pointed to the student.

"I think you lost me at vacuum bubble," the perplexed look on the student's face was evidence his statement was true.

"Ah, yes, well," Dr. Logan paused. "For now, to illustrate the theory, let's use a black hole for comparison, shall we?"

The student simultaneously nodded and shrugged. Dr. Logan resumed, "How do you describe a hole?

Most people would describe one as an area with nothing in it; a hole is devoid of matter. If you take a shovel and dig a hole, you leave an empty space behind, right?"

The same heads nodded.

"When we talk about a black hole, the opposite is true. Black holes are filled with mass and light, as well as dark energy and dark matter. Let me explain: from a scientific standpoint, we're not one-hundred percent sure black holes exist. But we do know that there are inexplicable gaps in the Cosmos which many theorists believe are black holes.

"These theoretical black holes occur when the center of a galaxy collapses—a solar system's sun, for example. In the example of digging a hole with a shovel, most people who are not astrophysicists—lay people—believe a black hole is like the hole you dig in your backyard; it is devoid of matter. It is just empty space. On the contrary, astrophysicists believe that the implosion of a galaxy's sun causes a massive gravitational pull. If, for example, the galaxy's sun implodes, the vacuum it creates will suck everything into it, even sunlight. That's right; the black hole does not allow even light to escape it. That is why, to our earthling eyes, it appears as a blank spot in the Cosmos. It is everything *but* that; it is jam-packed with matter. We just can't see it because light's reflection is not permitted to escape from it.

"The larger a solar system's gravitational center—its sun—the greater the gravitational pull when it implodes. Many of us believe there are certain suns in distant galaxies which could create gravitational energy strong enough to pull other galaxies into its black hole, including ours."

"Professor?" The hand in the front of the room popped up again. "Yes?"

"So, this thing you're talking about? Is it Hawking's vacuum bubble idea, or it could be a black hole, too?"

"Well, since you ask, yes, in my opinion, it could be either one. Hawking focuses on the vacuum bubble idea—a vacuum which keeps expanding and drawing matter to it, including entire galaxies;

an event which could occur at the speed of light or even faster. That means that we wouldn't see the front edge of the vacuum bubble coming, at least not with enough time to do anything about it. We—our galaxy—would disappear instantly."

Logan watched as mouths in the audience fell slack.

"But it could also happen as the result of a gigantic sun imploding. Take Canis Majoris, for example, nearly five thousand light years away, it is an intensely red giant sun and center of its universe. If Canis Majoris implodes, it could create a gravitational pull powerful enough to suck all of its planets into a black hole. More than that, it could create a quantum fluctuation—a vacuum bubble—beyond its own galaxy. The gravitational pull could be powerful enough to suck our entire Milky Way into it."

Logan panned the blank stares before him. "But let me be clear, there is far more about the Cosmos that we don't know than what we do know. We only know about 5% of what happens in our universe, including within Earth's atmosphere. We are completely ignorant about 95% of the Cosmos."

Another student raised his hand. "Are you referring to dark matter and dark energy?"

"Excellent question. In part, yes. We're still working on exactly what makes up dark matter and dark energy. We suspect that black holes make up some of dark matter, but it also contains hot and cold gases, subatomic particles we have not identified, neutron stars and more. When it comes to dark energy and dark matter, we are in the infant stages of exploration. What we have found so far is this: dark matter and dark energy are everywhere. They're in our atmosphere, in our own solar system, in the air we breathe, and in the spaces we travel. Dark matter and dark energy are not just something 'out there in the universe'; they are right here with us on earth. In the fifteen feet between you and me right now, there is both dark matter and dark energy which we cannot measure, and about which we know nothing."

The student raised his hand and spoke at the same time, "So how is your theory different than Dr. Hawking's, Dr. Logan?"

"First, let me say that Dr. Hawking's vacuum bubble is a plausible theory, although he himself says it probably won't happen, at least not right now. The Cosmos is a new frontier. We know dark matter and dark energy exists but we don't know how it interacts with other energy and matter. There are questions about the methodology we use. Why do we measure speed by the velocity of light? Is there a faster speed than light speed? Could a cataclysmic event in the Cosmos occur at faster than light speed?" Logan stared at blank stares staring back.

"Think about it this way, if a speed faster than light exists, there is a greater possibility that the implosion of a distant sun would create a massive, powerful black hole capable of sucking other galaxies into it. We'd be gone before we knew it."

A few students shifted uncomfortably in their seats as they tried to comprehend the earth simply disappearing with no warning.

"Professor?" a weak voice several rows behind Sarah asked.

"Yes?"

"With all due respect, why wouldn't we know it was coming? I mean, like, if we saw, you know, like, Jupiter disappear?"

"Actually, no," Logan answered. "Everything we see—you, me, the wall, the trees, and Jupiter—is only visible because the light of our sun is reflecting from it and bouncing back to our eyes at the speed of light, right?"

A few heads nodded.

"If the suction of the black hole was speeding toward Earth faster than light speed, our visual reception of the actual event of Jupiter being sucked into another galaxy's black hole would not have reached us yet as the speed of light."

The weak voice was getting weaker and seemed to be negotiating for a more palatable scenario. "How could that be possible? How could there be a speed faster than light speed?"

"Is there a reason there couldn't be?" Logan challenged the minds in the room to think differently.

The weak voice persisted. "Okay, so, what if it happened at light speed but not *faster* than light speed. I mean, we can see Jupiter. It's right up there in the sky. It is closer to the imploded sun, so we would see it disappear before it sucked Earth into it, wouldn't we?"

"No. The sun's reflection of the catastrophic event would land on the back of your eyeball at the same time the suction hit you in the face." Logan paused to let that sink in.

"Hawking's theory," Logan resumed, "suggests it may happen at faster-than-light speed, which means the giant sucking sound would reach the earth before the most recent reflection of light from Jupiter arrives on Earth. Earth will have ceased to exist before Earthlings could witness Jupiter disappearing."

The weak voice was beginning to tremble. "I don't get it. I mean, how could we just disappear and not see it coming?"

Dr. Logan stopped for a moment, grasping for a way to explain it so the student could understand. "Let's pretend you are driving on the interstate and you see an accident. What would you do?"

"Call 9-1-1?" A few students laughed uneasily, then stopped.

"For this illustration, let's say nobody has cell phones. The only way to report an accident is to drive to the nearest police station. Are you with me so far?"

The vacant faces in the audience answered his question. On an old overhead projector, Dr. Logan sketched lines to symbolize a highway and a rectangle to symbolize an exit sign.

"You witness an accident and you're on your way to the police station at the next exit. We'll call that next exit 'Earth,'" he explained. "You are driving a 4-cylinder Ford and you represent the sun's reflections of the Jupiter disappearing into a black hole. You are racing at 90 miles an hour toward the exit 'Earth' to report the event but a mile from the exit, a red Ferrari doing 175 goes screaming past you and gets to Earth first. What is the Ferrari?"

The student with the weak voice asked, "Really fast?"

"Bingo! The Ferrari is really fast. The Ferrari is the vacuum bubble expanding at a rate faster than the speed of light!" Dr. Logan's scanned his audience. Their brains struggled to comprehend. "The Ferrari would travel so fast we wouldn't have any warning. We would cease to exist before we knew our own extinction was imminent. What would it matter if you had even thirty minutes' warning, what would you do? What planet could you escape to? If you were lucky enough to have a spaceship parked in your driveway, where would you go? The planets within our range to reach them would already be gone."

Silence blanketed the room, even the trembling, weak-voiced young man behind Sarah.

"That sucks," a student blurted from across the room.

"Yes, it does," Logan laughed. "It sucks. Figuratively and literally. It totally sucks."

"So, how do we know? I mean, like, how will we know?" the trembling voice spoke again.

"That's just it. We won't." Dr. Logan paused, then added, "Maybe."

Sarah spoke up this time, "Maybe? Will you elaborate on 'maybe,' Dr. Logan?" The weather was too chilly to be sweating, she knew, as a bead of perspiration rolled down her spine.

"Some theorists have suggested we may have some warning. We might witness spotty events which we cannot explain—a quake-like tremor which happens to one half of a room but not to the other, objects moving mysteriously across a table. Things disappearing before your eyes when there is no magician in the room. Anomalies, I call them. Gravitational anomalies. Remember, the Higgs boson particle—The God Particle—holds things together; that's its job." Dr. Logan tapped the lectern. "Imagine, if you will, that a cosmic event occurs which disrupts the Higgs boson particles holding this lectern together. What would happen to the lectern? Would all of its components disassemble? Would it cease to exist as matter in lectern form? Would it turn to dust? Or would it—poof!—disappear?"

Sarah spoke. "My guess is that it would disappear. If matter is not being held together in any form, I say it would go 'poof.'"

Sarah saw several heads in the auditorium nodding in agreement.

"Dr. Logan, what about an earthquake which occurs on the other side of the world," Sarah continued, "but not here? Or an object moving without a force propelling it? How would the Higgs boson particle be responsible for that?"

The professor smiled. "Excellent question. Excellent. We know The God Particle exists but we don't have all the answers on how it interacts with every form of matter. For example, consider your earthquake example. It is possible that the Higgs boson particle plays some role in the way dark matter and dark energy behaves in our Cosmos. If we agree that is possible—for the moment, let's say it is true—then every cosmic event which is capable of disrupting the Higgs boson particle in matter which is visible and tangible, could just as easily disrupt the particle's function in matter and energy that we cannot see. Wouldn't you agree?"

Sarah surveyed the room and saw faces whose expressions ranged from wonder to confusion.

"Does that explain some of the weird things happening, Doctor? Like all the sinkholes we hear about now? When I was growing up, I never heard about city streets and towns disappearing, swallowed by a hole in the ground."

"Possibly," Dr. Logan said. "Scientists who subscribe to the theory that gravitational anomalies exist further suggest those anomalies may also be predictors of something worse. Think of a volcano; it sends out warnings, little blasts of ash and smoke before it unleashes its full fury. If you follow this logic to its ultimate conclusion, these gravitational anomalies could be precursors to an imminent apocalypse. They might be on a path to increasing in intensity and frequency until the invisible suction of the black hole arrives and completes the job."

"Could that be possible in Dr. Hawking's vacuum bubble theory, too?" Sarah followed.

"Yes, absolutely," Logan answered. "The challenge is: when you know only 5% of something, there is a great deal that could be possible about the 95% which we don't."

The weak voice spoke again, "Professor, not all volcanoes' minor eruptions lead to major ones. Some of them settle back down for centuries. Is that possible?"

"Let's hope so," Dr. Logan replied softly. "My most recent research suggests that such anomalies may be the result of yet another possibility, one that has nothing to do with Hawking's theory and provides evidence that, once more, man is his own worst enemy."

Dr. Logan glanced at the round clock on the lecture room wall. "But we'll need to save that for Thursday's lecture. I'm sorry, class, we've run out of time. On Thursday, I'll present how propulsion experimentation may play a role in causing these weird events being observed throughout the world. But here's a hint: if anyone tells you it's just swamp gas, don't believe them! See you Thursday."

He turned on his heel and strode from the lecture hall, leaving a roomful of raised hands and dazed expressions.

Aedain leaned toward Sarah and muttered, "I'm so glad I came to class today. Next time I'll just cut my wrists and skip class."

"They are theories," Sarah replied, "nothing more—at least for now."

"For now? That doesn't give me a lot of reassurance."

"I wasn't trying to reassure you."

Sarah stood and offered her handshake to Aedain. "It was nice to meet you." He shook her hand, smiled as he added, "I'll be here Thursday if you'd care to share an armrest again."

Sarah couldn't control her physical tick—a non-committal head tilt—as she replied, "We'll see." She bit her lip and wished she could reel her words back into her mouth but it was too late.

"We'll see, then," Aedain replied politely. Sarah watched him deftly navigate the auditorium's row of seats and leave through its double doors.

Five months later, Sarah remembered that morning as particularly beautiful, possibly because she had counted so few beautiful days since.

5

On Thursday, Dr. Logan reached the lectern and ignored the dazed expressions and raised hands. It appeared as if the stunned students had remained as statues in their chairs since Tuesday. Arriving just in time, Sarah spotted Aedain in the same seat he had been two days earlier. She struggled past the row of knees to take the seat beside him.

"Hey," she nodded and half-smiled, "is this seat taken?"

"It is now," Aedain smiled as he spoke. Sarah felt comfortable with him, mostly. Yet, she found him puzzling. Wearing jeans and a long-sleeve Henley, he dressed the part of a student. His medium brown hair appeared strategically tousled but neatly shaved at its edges. A Rolex chronograph wrapped around his wrist suggested he grew up wealthy. Or it was fake? Sarah couldn't tell. He didn't seem shallow enough to pretend to be rich. But something seemed off.

Dr. Logan sprang from the wings of the stage like a thoroughbred bolting from the starting gate. That was his style. He'd run at full gallop run for fifty minutes straight. He'd take a ten-minute break and do the second leg of the lecture with the same energy. "The only limitation humans have in exploring the Cosmos beyond our Milky Way is the speed of travel. Think of this, in July of 1969, it took more than two days to reach the moon's atmosphere, only 238,000 miles away."

"Only 238,000 miles away," a voice toward the front of the lecture hall sneered.

"Yes, I said *only*. By comparison to the voyages we've made to Mars and Saturn, 238,000 miles is like jumping over a puddle. If we intend to explore exoplanets—planets beyond our Milky Way—we must be able to travel more than 100,000 light years away. So, by comparison, Earth's moon is our next-door neighbor.

In the past fifty years, we've cut travel time to the moon down to just over eight hours. That is roughly one-sixth the time it took the Apollo astronauts to reach the moon. What is the next closest planet to explore? Mars. Yet Mars is at least fifteen times the distance from Planet Earth to our moon.

As you know, the distance between planets varies as the planets orbit the sun. Travel time to Mars ranges from five months to a year, depending on how close the planets are in relation to one another during their respective orbits. Mars is the second-closest planet to Earth. How far away are rest of the planets within our universe? The distance varies. How can we make space exploration beyond our universe possible if it takes so long to travel to other planets and galaxies? If you believe in UFOs and extraterrestrial beings, how have they traveled through hundreds of light years in space within one lifetime? Do they have longer lifetimes than humans?"

Dr. Logan paused and waited for someone in the audience to offer an answer. Nobody did.

"Ah, yes, lots of questions but the answers are hard to come by. Why? Let's start with propulsion theory. Until now, the Saturn 5 rocket has been the propelling force behind many of our travels into space, but the Saturn 5 will never be able to generate the velocity necessary to escape Earth's atmosphere and thrust a spacecraft into the universe at speeds sufficient to get to the edge of the Milky Way and back in one lifetime. In fact, if we could propel a spaceship through the Cosmos at light speed, it would take 100,000 years to reach the ice crystals which surround our Milky Way."

Sarah heard a commotion in the row behind her. Struggling past the obstacle course of bony knees, a man in a yellow sport coat struggled toward the exit. Once beyond the auditorium seats, he plopped a porkpie hat on top of greasy hair and pushed open the auditorium door.

Struck by the man's appearance, she felt a chill. He didn't belong here. Not in this class. She stared at the auditorium door, now closed, for several seconds before she realized she wasn't the only one who noticed him.

"Maybe he wasn't interested in a vacation on Mars," Aedain whispered. Sarah was surprised Aedain had noticed the man but even more shocked by the look on his face. Aedain's brow was creased with concern and Sarah noticed his thumb rubbing against his forefinger. Sarah's dad did that when something didn't look right.

"He didn't seem like someone who was really interested in cosmology, did he?"

"No," Aedain agreed, his eyes turning back toward the closed door. Sarah forced her attention back to Dr. Logan at the front of the room.

"Even though Pluto has been downgraded from its status as a planet, it is still part of our solar system and, right now, we have an exploratory spaceship on its way to Pluto. The trouble is this: using conventional technology, Pluto is 4.67 billion miles away, more than 19,000 times the distance from Earth to Moon."

"Consider how rudimentary our propulsion methods are today. Currently, we propel things into space by putting stuff in the front and pushing it out the back, thereby propelling an object forward. Take a jet, for example. You force jet fuel and oxygen into the front of the engines, explode it, and channel it out the back, thrusting the plane forward. With this type of conventional propulsion, it will take nearly 18 years to reach Pluto. It will take another 20 years to return, provided you can create the same propulsion conditions to return that NASA used to launch the spacecraft. There is no guarantee this is possible. Add five years for exploring the demoted planet, and you've got a 45-year round trip. Show of hands, who's ready to leave Earth when you're 30 and not return till you're 75? Who is ready to spend their adult life flying through space to a destination you may never reach?"

The audience squirmed in their seats as they hung on their instructor's every word. But not Sarah; she glanced repeatedly at the auditorium door.

"Furthermore, Pluto is still within our own galaxy. Exploring beyond our galaxy to stars and planets which are hundreds of light years away will require inventing new, more advanced propulsion methods which do not depend on pushing from behind but rather pulling a spacecraft through the Cosmos, essentially sucking it into space at faster and faster speed."

"You mean like a vacuum bubble sucking planets and light into it?" Aedain blurted.

"Almost. Hawking's theory talked about quantum fluctuation—the vacuum bubble—as a type of black hole," Dr. Logan acknowledged. "However, if the spacecraft was pulled at light speed into a black hole, we would lose it completely, along with the astronauts and all of the data they had collected. That's not exactly the outcome we're looking for, is it?"

The class collectively shook their heads 'no.' Scribbling illustrations on the overhead projector, he continued. "Imagine this, imagine that we could create a gravitational wave of energy which is capable of traveling at light speed. Let's say we could sling it into Earth's orbit like we can cast a fisherman's net across the surface of the ocean. Then imagine that beyond Earth's atmosphere and gravity, there is a spaceship waiting, orbiting until the moment it could intersect with the net of gravitational energy. The spacecraft would, essentially, hitch a ride on the accelerating gravitational wave like a surfer catching a wave off Oahu. In theory, the spacecraft could ride the wave of gravity infinitely, without using up any of its own energy."

A hand in the crowd rose. "But, Professor, wouldn't it need to have power to stop and explore planets along the way?"

"Yes, of course. NASA could build a self-contained space capsule on board the larger craft—the spacecraft's own satellite of sorts. I don't know how NASA would configure a space exploration vehicle exactly; that's not my point. My point is this: the technology exists right now, today, to launch a gravity-based propulsion system into space which could transport one or more spacecraft near light speed through our universe. The technology exists *now*. Right now!"

The weak, faltering voice was in today's audience. Today, though, his voice didn't tremble. "Doctor, if this technology is possible now, why aren't we using it for space exploration?"

"Who says we're not?" Logan replied, then added, "If we have that technology today, then it stands to reason that we also have developed a self-contained, perpetual source of energy and food to explore planets along the way. That is, unless we think they're going to stop at a Piggly Wiggly."

Logan's jokes were never very good but a few in the audience laughed dutifully.

"What's more," Logan continued, "this perpetual energy source could be used to push the gravity blanket faster and faster, to the speed of light and beyond." He glanced at the round clock and said, "We'll talk about that after the break. Let's take ten minutes, shall we?" Logan held up both hands with all fingers and thumbs extended. "The second half of the lecture starts in ten minutes, sharp."

Sarah took the break as her opportunity to investigate.

"Excuse me, sorry, excuse me," Sarah apologized as she bumped along the row of knees and made her way to the exit. She opened the door and walked straight to the ladies room. From the corner of her eye, she spotted the man in the yellow sport coat and pork-pie hat standing with his back to her, hunched and sputtering into his cell phone. She heard him say, "Yeah, right now. He's shootin' his mouth off about it right now. I'm tellin' ya."

Sarah hurried into and out of the rest room, the pork-pie-sporting man's words replaying inside her head. *He's shootin' his mouth off about it right now.* As Sarah returned toward the auditorium, the man glanced over his shoulder and scurried toward the building's exit. Sarah felt the eerie chill again as she re-entered the auditorium and bumped through the row of knees toward her seat.

Logan had returned to the podium and had resumed his lecture.

"Think of this theoretical wave of gravity as Aladdin's magic carpet. Where does it get its energy? Most likely, it would come from a magnetically based, perpetual-energy source. Stay with me—I'm going somewhere."

Logan held up two magnets. "Have you ever tried to attach two positively charged magnets to one another? It doesn't work, does it? No. They repel one another. Imagine, for a moment, if we could create a propulsion mechanism based on that principle—a propulsion source which not only *defies* gravity, but *uses* gravity to propel material *away*, rather than attract material toward it? Imagine this gravitational blanket as a host ship being nudged by an on-board perpetual energy source within the parasite spacecraft, pushing it faster and faster? Try to comprehend the outcome: it would be possible to travel at light speed through the Cosmos, maybe even beyond light speed. That's right. If this technology exists, we could hitch a ride on a blanket of gravity to reach the outer limits of the Milky Way in days rather than decades."

A hand rose from the middle of the audience. "Yes?" Logan pointed at the student.

"How do you—I mean—what—how could that even be possible?"

Logan paused. The student's question was a good one. "Start by re-thinking gravity itself. We have always looked at gravity as a magnetic force which holds objects to the ground. Everything that goes up must come down, remember? What if that is only half of the story? What if we have unwittingly ignored the *other* side of gravity? What if there is an equal, opposing force of gravity which pushes objects *away* from Earth?"

Dr. Logan opened his mouth to continue when he was distracted by commotion coming toward him. Charging through the lecture hall's side door, Princeton University's Dean of Students was followed closely by Dr. Logan's Administrative Assistant and two Campus Security officers.

Shaking their heads and speaking low, the Dean took Dr. Logan aside. The Dean said barely three words before Dr. Logan's knees buckled and he collapsed to the floor. The campus officers helped him to his feet and rushed him out of the room.

"I apologize," the Dean steadied himself with the help of the lectern and leaned toward the microphone. "Due to recent developments, the remainder of Professor Logan's presentation must be postponed until a later date. We appreciate your cooperation as you safely exit the building." Dr. Logan's assistant helped the trembling Dean down from the podium and to stage's exit door.

Sarah felt numb. Something was wrong. Something was very, very wrong. Dazed, she followed Aedain out of the lecture hall. Neither of them spoke until they parted at a fork in the sidewalk.

"I'm headed this way," Sarah pointed toward the path she had taken in the morning.

"I'm this way," Aedain replied blankly and pointed in the opposite direction. He paused, then added, "Do you want me to walk you to your bus stop?"

"No, but thank you." Sarah was so numb she didn't question why Aedain knew she rode the bus to campus. When the question eventually occurred to her, he was gone.

The campus' layer of leaves didn't seem as colorful now, and she looked down at the dull, grey sidewalk instead of the bright, blue sky. She reached into her backpack for her cell phone and pulled up her list of frequent phone numbers. She clicked on 'Dr. Logan.' It rang until it went to voicemail. Ten minutes later, she tried again.

She tried every half hour and, each time, the call went to voicemail. When she turned the television on, a somber-faced anchor opened with the network's lead story, "A popular Princeton University professor's family was found brutally murdered in their home. Police are investigating."

The news video cut to a photograph of Logan's wife, Beth, and their two daughters, Lisa and Lucy. A video clip showed Dr. Logan in handcuffs and being loaded into a police car outside this morning's lecture hall.

Sarah bolted for the kitchen; she knew she wouldn't make it to the bathroom before she threw up.

6

Sarah insides were gone. Someone—she didn't know who—had taken a big, dull spoon, scooped her insides out, then dumped them onto the floor. She was certain of it. That's how she felt.

Inside the church, she sat in the eighth row from the front, in the middle of the pew. She wasn't surprised when nobody sat beside her. It was okay; she wanted to grieve alone. The organist softly played a medley of funeral songs.

Once the funeral processional arrived at the church's entry doors, the organist raised the volume and switched to a British dirge. The cross bearer led the procession into the church, flanked by two altar boys with their prayer hands pointed skyward, followed by the priest waving a polished brass censer with pungent smoke rising through its vents. The smell usually made Sarah sick. Today, she was just numb.

The caskets will come next, Sarah knew, and her throat tightened till she was sucking hard to get air.

Beth's casket was first, followed by Lisa's, then Lucy's.

Sarah prayed their last moments were mercifully brief.

She remembered how her mentor's face beamed when he spoke of 'his girls,' and he seemed to share a special connection with Lucy, who was born deaf.

Behind them, Dr. Logan's familiar, jaunty step was reduced to a clumsy, faltering gait. Struggling to stay upright, he forced one foot ahead of the other. His shoulders slumped and tears had carved paths through his once-rosy cheeks.

"Dearly beloved, we are gathered here today to honor the memory—"

Sarah's flashback came without warning. She no longer heard the priest's words but instead the screams of her father. It was twenty years ago. She remembered watching her Dad's face twist in agony. As if in slow motion, he ran toward Sarah and her mother, his arms reaching out for them. The look of horror on his face said everything; he knew wouldn't reach them in time. He knew he was powerless to stop the horror he was witnessing. Sarah remembered her mother's arms wrapping tightly around her; she didn't know why. She heard popping sounds. Like firecrackers but different. Sarah didn't understand why Mommy was suddenly lying on top of her but her arms no longer hugged her. She couldn't understand why the family car was driving away without them. Before that day—a day like any other day the family went for ice cream—she'd never heard the word 'carjacking.' As Daddy paid the clerk, Sarah and her mother walked to the car. Each day for twenty years, she wished they'd waited for him.

In the days after her mother's murder, her father appeared as Logan did today. Her Daddy held her hand as they walked behind her mother's casket. Her aunt told Sarah that Mommy wasn't coming home.

Sarah didn't understand why.

For months following the carjacking, Sarah watched her father spiral into depression. Sitting in the corner of the couch, he stared out the picture window of the brick bungalow. He seemed to be waiting for her to walk up the sidewalk and into the house. Every night around ten, he snuffed out his last White Owl of the day and found his way to bed.

By the time puberty hit, Sarah had grown accustomed to his routine.

It's my fault, she thought. *If only I had waited while he paid for the ice cream. If only I had resisted when Mommy took my hand and led me to the car. If only.*

With each day, Sarah felt more and more powerless to help her father.

School and her studies became her refuge. Her teachers were her confidants. Mrs. Ruiter, her sixth grade Science teacher, introduced her to the stars and planets. She was smitten. "You can devote your whole life to understanding the universe, and you will have only begun to ask questions," Mrs. Ruiter told her. Her fascination with the stars grew into determination. From that moment forward, she would be the best. She would learn from the smartest people she could find. In doing so, she regained some power.

Growing up, she left her father behind, sitting on the couch smooshing White Owl butts into his ashtray. As he had felt on that tragic day, she felt powerless to reach him in time to save him. The only time they connected was when the former sniper took her to the shooting range with him. "Aim small, shoot first," her dad taught her.

She was a junior in high school when she showed him her acceptance letter to Princeton. She hoped he would be pleased, even if she had no money to accept their offer.

Sitting in the compressed corner cushion of the couch, her father held the letter in his hand as he peered over his reading glasses. His eyes welled with tears. "I'm proud of you, Sarah," he choked. "I'm so, so proud of you. I'm sorry I haven't been a very good father to you. You've done this all on your own."

Sarah sat beside her dad and cried with him. "It's okay, Daddy," she said. "I always thought it was my fault. We should have waited for you."

It was the first time in more than ten years her daddy held her tight, hugging her as if he would never let go. "I'm so sorry," was all he could say.

"Well," Sarah regained her composure, "I'm happy to get this acceptance letter from Princeton. Maybe I'll frame it. Someday, maybe I'll save up enough money to go."

Her dad stubbed out the White Owl burning at the edge of the ashtray, lifted himself from the couch, and disappeared into his bedroom. He returned with a large, white envelope which he handed to Sarah. "Your mom had a life insurance policy. I could never bring myself to cash it in. But there's plenty for Princeton, probably even grad school if you want to go that far." Sarah sat speechless on the lumpy couch.

"Whatever you do in life, Sarah, whatever happens, good or bad, don't let it take *living* away from you. A man took your mother's life but, while she was alive, she always *lived,* do you understand that? That's why you and she didn't wait for me; she wanted to hold hands and swing them together as you walked to the car with your ice cream cones. That last moment of her life, with you, she was *living*."

Sarah's eyes were nearly swollen shut as she wrapped her arms around her father's neck and pressed her cheek against his. Tears flooded their faces as they poured out years of heartache to one another.

"Don't do like me," he told her. "Don't give up on life. Don't quit on the people you love. Don't give someone else power over you. Never. Never. Never give someone else your power."

Sarah pulled back from her father's face and pressed her palm gently against his cheek. She wiped his face as she spoke. "That goes for you, too, you know."

"I suppose so," he answered. "I suppose it does." Now, twelve years later, Sarah sat in a church pew, feeling as if someone had scooped out her entrails.

She couldn't make sense of the murders any more than she could make sense of her mother's murder.

Sarah's attention was drawn back to the funeral ceremony to the strains of 'Just a Closer Walk with Thee.'

She watched the procession return up the aisle. Logan looked more haggard than he did when he entered. Her heart ached when she saw him grip Lucy's casket to steady himself. Waiting her turn to exit the row, she followed mourners toward the back of the church and through the tall, wooden doors to the outside.

The sky was suitably grey. She squeezed the handrail as she walked down the church's steps, passing a small group gathered at the bottom. She could feel their collective scowl.

"I bet you're happy. Now you don't have anyone standing in your way." The voice was that of the person who had made the home-wrecker comment in the lecture hall last week. Her gut ached, knowing that, in the days and weeks ahead, the taunts wouldn't stop. Ignoring the catty comments hadn't worked. Today, she would take her power back.

Sarah turned toward the voice's scowling face, clenched her fist, and landed a roundhouse hook squarely on the girl's nose. Blood spurted from the girl's face as she collapsed, barely conscious, to the sidewalk. Leaning over the girl, Sarah whispered, "You want a war? Bring it." Sarah turned and walked away.

Digging into her purse, she switched on her cell phone and dialed.

Her call was answered with, "How are you doing?"

"I'm doing okay," Sarah lied.

"You don't sound okay."

Sarah's voice cracked, "They killed them, Daddy. They killed Dr. Logan's family. I know they did. I'm sure of it."

"Not on the phone, Sarah. Come see me."

"I can't right now. I need to find some things out."

"Sarah, you are in grave danger."

Sarah remembered Jack Nicholson's line in *A Few Good Men*. "Is there another kind?"

"Don't put a target on your ass. You understand me? Keep your head low. Watch your back. Pay attention to the hair standing on your neck. Remember what I taught you."

"I will," Sarah gasped between sobs. "Thanks, Daddy. I just needed to hear your voice." She clicked off the phone and shoved in into her purse, keenly aware of her surroundings as she walked.

7

A week before the funeral, Dr. Logan and Sarah were the only ones left at the Small World after Tuesday's big brain session. The other professors and Teachers' Assistants had gone home to their wives, partners, or cats.

"Sarah," Logan confided, "I'm scared. Seriously. I'm not kidding. I'm scared." She had never heard this tone in his voice before; he was always so sure of himself. Usually, he was confident to the edge of cocky. As Sarah's eyes locked on his, she knew it was true; he was afraid. He checked over one shoulder then the other, then faced Sarah again.

"Why?" Sarah asked.

"This theory I've been talking about. You know, the one challenging Hawking's theory that the Earth might disappear in a cataclysmic event with no warning?"

"Yes." Sarah nodded.

"Give me your phone," he stopped, opening his palm. Sarah reached in her purse and handed him her cell phone. He powered it down completely and handed it back, "Damn things won't let you take the battery out. You know it's so they have a way of tracking you and listening in on your conversations."

"That sounds a little tin-foil hat to me, Doctor Logan."

"Suit yourself," he moved his chair closer to Sarah and leaned in. "The people I am talking about don't wear tin-foil hats, Sarah. They are people—real people in powerful places—who want to silence me about my theories on the Higgs boson particle, and more importantly, about the real reason proton accelerators are being built throughout the world."

"You mean supercolliders? Like the one in Lucerne, Switzerland? The Hadron Collider?"

"Yes, exactly. But the Large Hadron Collider in Switzerland is small potatoes compared to the ones being built in Russia, China, Iran, and even the United States."

"We have a particle accelerator in the United States?"

"Well, we did. The Fermi Lab in Batavia, Illinois, outside Chicago, had a particle accelerator named the Tevatron. Sounds like an amusement park ride, doesn't it? I assure you, it isn't. Its stated objective was energy research. Stop. Think about that. Its stated objective was energy research. It closed in the early 2000s, but don't forget what I told you—energy research."

"So we don't have a particle accelerator in the United States now?"

"I didn't say that. I said Tevatron closed. I didn't say we don't have another one somewhere. The United States government was building one in Waxahachie, Texas—the Superconducting Super Collider, or SSC, they called it. It would have been two and a half times the size of the Hadron Collider in Lucerne but the multi-billion dollar project was abandoned in 1993 because Congress didn't care jack-shit about science, especially science which could replace fossil fuel energy. Politicians were, and still are, in the pockets of Big Oil. Most of our elected officials don't want to explore new forms of energy because those who profit from coal and oil are stuffing money into the politicians' re-election campaigns. The only reason they supported space exploration in the first place was to put on a dog-and-pony show for their constituents; to show them pretty pictures from the Mars Rover or the Hubble Telescope. The concept of creating a new propulsion more powerful than a Saturn rocket is of no use to them. Every time scientists suggest expanding space exploration, we get a collective 'duh' on the floor of Congress."

"You said 'most of them.'"

"Yes. There are a few key players in the Departments of Defense and Joint Chiefs of Staff who have kept their eyes on the ball. They pushed though funding by burying it in legislation which expanded military spending on bombs, ships, planes, and such. 'National security' is a very emotional phrase. You know, God, country, family, apple pie, and Chevy trucks. In politics, if you say it's for national security, you can pass a budget to sell ice to Eskimos."

"So you think there is another one built—or being built—in the United States? Am I hearing that right?"

"Yes, I think the United States is building its own massive supercollider. It could be anywhere—upstate New York, Michigan, Colorado, or Tennessee. They had a whole list of sites when they picked Waxahachie."

"Why don't they want you talking about your supercollider theories?"

"Simple. Most legislators are too lazy to learn why supercollider research is essential to world peace. The bad guys know what supercolliders can do, and they intend to exploit politicians' ignorance. If they play their cards right, one day they will gain control of the world's largest supercolliders and the energy they produce."

Sarah stared at her mentor as her mind raced with possibilities.

Before she could respond, Logan continued, "There's more. I believe the gravitational anomalies which people are witnessing are the result of these particle accelerators—supercolliders—being out of control. Their output in energy has exceeded man's capability to control it. Many of the scientists running these supercollider projects don't know, or refuse to accept, that their particle accelerators are having an impact on Earth's gravity as well as dark matter and dark energy within our universe. Nobody wants me to go public with this information, not the bad guys trying to corner proton collision energy nor the politicians, not other astrophysicists, not even the media."

"Why not?"

"Simple. If my suspicions are correct—that the anomalies are caused by man—politicians would need to stop it. They don't want to spend their time fighting for a cause they don't understand. The media doesn't want to educate the public; they'd rather keep the news simple, easy to understand and good for ratings."

Sarah added, "Governments throughout the world would find out that their economies are vulnerable to collapse if a new form of energy exists."

"Exactly. When the word gets out, it will put civilization on the brink of world war. There are too many countries with weapons of mass destruction. They will empty their arsenals to protect their nations' economic viability. We could not stop them from unleashing The Apocalypse."

"You're scaring me," Sarah replied. "So, they want to kill you to prevent the annihilation of Earth?"

"Pretty much."

"You keep calling them 'the bad guys.' Who are they?"

"Ah, that is the million dollar question. Who are 'they'?"

Sarah paused as she remembered his upcoming lecture just two days away. Sarah checked over one shoulder, then the other. "Aren't you—isn't that what you're presenting on Thursday?"

"Yes. Yes, it is. I have been warned. I've been warned not to give the speech."

"Warned?"

"Threatened, actually. They told me if I went through with the speech, the consequences would be regrettable."

"Regrettable?"

"Yes, it an odd turn of phrase, don't you think? Regrettable?"

"Who threatens with a word like 'regrettable'?"

Sarah thought aloud.

"Only two kinds of people I can think of. People who speak English, for one."

"And the second—?"

"People who don't."

Sarah let Dr. Logan's statement sink in; she recalled her British friends teasing her about her Americanized English. Logan was right: Sarah could hear the Brits making a threat with the word 're-grettable.' Then again, she could hear her Russian friends using the same word.

"At least we can rule out Americans," Sarah joked.

"Exactly. Americans wouldn't bother to threaten. I'd be dead already."

"But why? What are they afraid of? Are they really afraid of you telling the truth?" Sarah posed the rhetorical question.

Logan explained, "Of course. Look at it this way, if I tell you that you are going to die next week—it's a one hundred percent certainty—you'll probably drop to your knees, confess your sins and ask for forgiveness, right? You know, just on the chance you might be standing at the pearly gates before your next birthday?"

"I suppose."

"But if the media causes mass hysteria by talking about some theory they don't understand, people will scramble to get off this rock. They will kill anyone who gets in their way. Humans will think they'll be safe if they reach the Moon or Mars."

"But that won't be true," Sarah replied. "If the anomalies are signs that Hawking's vacuum bubble is happening, it could be only days or, at most, months before our entire solar system is sucked into the quantum fluctuation—Mars, Jupiter, our Moon. They will all disappear. There will no place to run."

"Ah, yes, that is true of the planets in our solar system," Dr. Logan wagged his finger as he explained. "However, in August, 2016, scientists discovered an exoplanet orbiting its sun, Proxima Centauri. They named it Proxima b. It is about one and a half times larger than earth, and it is approximately the same distance from its sun as Earth is from our sun."

Sarah cocked her head as she whispered, "This planet, Proxima b, would potentially have similar characteristics to Earth in terms of its ability to sustain life—the same temperature ranges, water, oxygen, possibly sources for food?"

"Exactly. It has that *potential*. But potential is not certainty. We don't know if it has everything necessary to sustain life. For example, what if the inhabitants of this planet thrive on hydrogen rather than oxygen? What if it has everything we seem to need but when we get there, we discover there is one essential element missing?"

"*If* we can get there," Sarah clarified. "That's a big 'if.'"

"Yes, it is. It is 4.2 light years away. About 25 trillion miles."

"That's one helluva' commute."

"It is that. As of now, we earthlings don't have a propulsion method or space vehicle to transport us far enough or quickly enough to reach the boundary of the Milky Way in one lifetime, let alone an exoplanet more than four light years away. It would be far more risky than Columbus crossing the Atlantic. In spite of the danger and slim possibility of success, millions of human beings will eagerly take the risk if they believe The Apocalypse is imminent. Regardless of what they believe—whether The Apocalypse is God's intent for man or mankind's self-destruction—people will do whatever is necessary to escape."

"Civilization will collapse into anarchy."

"That is an understatement."

"What about the ones who don't try to escape?"

"Most will choose not to believe. They will believe that liberal elites are conjuring up another global warming debate. They don't believe scientists because they don't understand science. To them, science is nothing more than hocus-pocus. They would rather spend their time choosing a fantasy football team than trying to understand the universe. It's not a bad way to live. They don't worry about it and, before they know it, *poof*, it's over."

"Ignorance is bliss."

"To some it is," Logan continued, "that is the reason people choose the news source that reinforces what they already believe. If they choose to put their faith in science, it means they might be required to change their thinking. Do you remember when the world was flat?"

"No," Sarah replied.

"People didn't want to believe Christopher Columbus, either. They saw what they saw, and that was proof enough. The world, to them, appeared flat. Remember when people believed tomatoes were poison?"

"They were?" Sarah asked. "When?"

"That's not the point. The point is: it is human nature; it's easier to stay the way you are than to change. Can a leopard change its spots?"

"Umm," Sarah pondered, "no?"

"Well, that's what most people think. But, what if we humans are wrong? What if, someday, scientists discover that leopards have always had the ability to change their spots, but leopards think they look good the way they are? Do you think people will believe science or what they have always believed about leopards?"

Sarah leaned within inches of Dr. Logan's face. "So, someone out there is afraid that one of the networks is going to break your story about gravitational anomalies and propulsion theories. When they do, the others will jump in with their own political spin to attract viewers who share their perspective?"

"Precisely. Once the big news organizations grab onto the story, it will be like tossing chum into the water. The more chum, the more sharks circle and make the water bloodier. More blood brings more sharks. Worldwide hysteria will become a feeding frenzy."

Sarah sat in silence, realizing that what her mentor was saying made sense, and why someone was threatening him if he shared his theory.

"Dr. Hawking's findings caused barely a blip on the media radar when he proposed them back in 2012. For the most part, they remain relatively obscure but—who knows why?—*my* theory scares the hell out of them."

"But you have only shared your theory with a handful of fellow scientists."

"So far, that's true. I feel the need to share it with the public, though, and soon. You see, Hawking was quick to downplay the possibility of it actually happening, based on the current level of energy in the Cosmos. Some aspects of mine, on the other hand, appear to be coming true. Every day, humans are experiencing events in their lives which they cannot explain. These events go against everything they know, everything they've learned, everything they believe. They will attribute it to God's will or Satan, when, in reality, it is simply the result of old-fashioned greed."

Greed. Sarah got it. If Hawking's quantum fluctuation theory happened, there would be no happy ending or divine intercession. We, as a civilization and collection of planets would become extinct.

Logan was right; his theory would be easier for people to believe because they were already witnessing strange events. If Logan told them it was fixable, that if human greed is to blame, the possibility of salvation might exist. *Yes*, Sarah thought, *Dr. Logan is very dangerous to the people causing the anomalies.*

The sound of glass breaking interrupted their conversation. A barista shrieked in pain. "What the faaa—?" her expletive trailed off without a finish. "How did that coffee pot fall off the shelf? It was on the back of the counter, for God's sake! Sonofbitch, that burns!"

Dr. Logan stood up, appearing to stretch even as his eyes carefully scanned the room. He was curious what had just happened but also wanted to make sure nobody was within earshot. Only two others were left in the Small World Coffee Shop; one wearing earbuds and feverishly typing on his keyboard; the other reading a paperback and sipping coffee.

Once he sat down, Sarah squinted and leaned even closer to her mentor. "Was that an anomaly?"

"I can't say for sure but the barista sure looks confused."

"If we're not the only ones witnessing these strange events, why are people keeping them secret?"

"People tend to blame themselves first. Right now, that barista is questioning whether she accidently bumped the coffee pot with her elbow and knocked it off the counter. Human nature tries to make sense of events according to our present body of knowledge. Or they chalk it up to swamp gas."

Sarah shook her head, "Swamp gas?"

"For decades, NOAA and NASA dismissed UFO sightings as swamp gas, which seems especially bizarre in those instances they were reporting about a sighting above a wheat field in Kansas. The authorities blame all manner of inexplicable events on swamp gas when they know better, but the public shrugs their shoulders and accepts their explanations."

Sarah nodded. "The public doesn't want truth. They just want to know the government is going to keep them safe."

Logan laughed, "How ironic. The public wants to believe the government is going to keep them safe when it is that same government who is telling them lies to keep them from knowing the truth. All I know is they want me to shut up."

"Who are 'they'?"

Dr. Logan whispered, "'They' could be anybody; any number of foreign governments come to mind. A good bet would be someone trying to gain control of the supercolliders. Follow the money. People kill for money."

Sarah leaned back in her chair to see if the other customers had left The Small World. The baristas stood with their arms crossed, glaring at the two of them. Glancing at her watch, Sarah realized she and Dr. Logan had been whispering nose-to-nose for nearly two hours. She was sure tonight's conversation would find its way to the campus grapevine.

"We'd better go," Sarah suggested as she reached for her backpack. "Are you going to share your theory on Thursday or just talk about Hawking's?"

"I don't know. I haven't made my mind up yet. But watch your back. If I am being watched, so is everyone around me—my family, my colleagues, my students. Everyone."

Now, a month after Dr. Logan buried his family, Sarah sat on the stoop of her townhouse in the crisp autumn air. She reached into her sweatshirt pouch for her phone and scrolled through photos of Dr. Logan, Beth, Lucy, and Lisa, an old, wrinkled photo of her mother she had scanned, and a recent one of her dad.

8

Sarah had never watched a human being disintegrate before her eyes. She knew, too, that her anguish paled in comparison to Dr. Logan's. Most of the undergrad students had left for home for the holidays. Today's lecture would be the last until after the New Year.

"Hey," a familiar voice caused Sarah to turn, "long time; no see. Mind if I sit next to you?"

"No, of course, please do." Sarah smiled as she motioned toward the chair beside her. "Aedain, isn't it?"

"Isn't what?"

"Your name. Aedain, right?

"Oh, yes, sorry, yes, it's Aedain." The good-smelling young man settled into the seat. "I wasn't sure you'd remember. The last time I saw you, well, we both left the auditorium in shock."

"I remembered your name is Aedain."

"I'm flattered," Aedain replied, before adding, "I'm sorry about what happened to Dr. Logan's family. What I'm trying to say is: I'm sorry for your loss. I heard you and Dr. Logan are close."

Sarah bit her lip. "I'm sure you've heard that," then turned toward the front of the classroom.

Logan stood at the front of his classroom. His swagger was gone. His confident bounce as he moved around the podium had been replaced with heavy legs. There was no holding forth on the secrets of the Cosmos. He no longer commanded the stage as an entrancing lawyer commands a courtroom.

Before his family's murder, his teaching style resembled a Gatling gun unleashing a blazing stream of bullets. His students understood, despite Dr. Logan being a grown-up, when it came to the Cosmos, he still brimmed with childlike wonder and excitement.

He was different now; his dull monotone was as boring as other professors'. He wandered the stage aimlessly, appearing lost and confused, checking his notes, and repeating large sections of his lecture. Logan had a reputation for never using—never needing—notes. He knew his material so well he could talk about the cosmos for more than an hour with nothing more than a follow spotlight and a Wi-Fi mic.

More than anything, Sarah felt empty. One month had turned to two and two months turned to three. She didn't expect his grief to be over; she understood how much he had lost. It was more than that, though. He wasn't just wallowing in grief; he was trying to destroy himself.

Twelve hours earlier, Sarah's phone rang. "Sarah," Logan slurred, "Sarah, can you come over? I need somebody to talk to."

It wasn't the first time he'd begged her come over. It wasn't the second, the third, or the tenth. Patiently, Sarah sat and listened to him lament for hours as he finished a third of the round-domed bottle, then half.

"I'm the one to blame for their deaths. If I had kept my mouth shut, my family would still be alive." After the booze took effect, he forgot what he had said before and repeated it, each time slurring it more.

Sarah sat on the living room couch of her mentor's home. Pictures of Beth, Lucy, and Lisa hung on every wall and sat on every shelf. Sarah had visited their home often enough to know that there were more pictures now than before they were murdered. It was clear Logan had dug into storage to find photos to add to his shrine of self-flagellation. She watched Logan's head turn toward one photo, then another, and another, as he sipped cheap Bourbon. Once an aficionado of Kentucky's finest distilleries, his numbed palate could no longer distinguish a boutique Bourbon from a ten-dollar fifth of blended whiskey distilled in Peoria.

Sarah placed her hand gently on her mentor's. "Listen to me. This—the booze—it isn't helping you. It's not the answer to your pain. It's just making everything worse. You need to stop. You need help. Let me call someone."

Logan ignored her as his glassy eyes labored from one photo to another. Before his family's murder, Logan's eyes sparkled and danced like stars in the night sky. Today, his eyelids were nearly as swollen as a boxer's after twelve hard rounds.

"It's been two months. I know that climbing into that bottle dulls the pain for a little while; I get that, and I'll be the first to admit that I don't know what you are feeling. I can't know. If you don't get help, you will lose whatever you have left."

"And just what is that, Sarah? What more do I have to lose?"

"The people left on this earth who still love you, who still admire you, who still believe in you."

The skin below Logan's eyes sagged into dark shadows. His cherubic countenance had deteriorated into that of a sad clown. He tried to pour another glass but the bottle was empty. Sarah stood, slung her backpack over her shoulder, and let herself out. When she left his house, she didn't expect to see him standing in front of the class today, steadying himself on the lectern as he spoke.

"He doesn't look good, does he?" Aedain leaned in, interrupting Sarah's recollections of the night before.

Sarah just shook her head. No, he didn't look good and Sarah knew she was powerless to help. As much as it crushed her soul, she knew she had to let go. She needed to distance herself from his downward spiral or she, herself, would get sucked into its vortex. No, she would not answer another late-night call from Dr. Logan. Never again.

The fifty-minute class hour passed painfully and the few students who had remained shuffled out of the auditorium. Sarah stayed in her seat, realizing she hadn't heard a word of her mentor's lecture.

"It was good to see you again." Aedain stood and gathered his backpack.

"You, too," Sarah blurted. "I'm sorry, I wasn't—I guess I was lost in my thoughts."

"No problem. I understand."

Sarah realized how alone she was. Right now, she needed someone. As much as Logan needed to talk with someone, so did Sarah. She desperately needed a moment of sanity.

"Aedain?" Sarah stammered, "Would you…? Do you want to go…? I know a place around the corner. It's called the Small World. Have you heard of it?" Sarah stammered, then blurted, "Would you like to join me for coffee?"

"Yes."

"Yes you've heard of it or yes you'd like to have coffee with me?" Sarah had her talents but asking a man out wasn't one of them.

"Both."

Their walk across campus was awkward. Neither could think of words to say. The last time they walked this path, Logan's family had just been murdered and a beautiful fall morning had twisted into horrifying reality. Today, the colorful carpet of autumn's leaves was covered by a blanket of snow, and Sarah suspected the squirrel was curled in its nest above them.

Thankfully, the coffee shop was nearby and the barista service was quick. Looking at Aedain from across the table was better, easier. She felt calmer.

She spoke first. "Have you taken a class from Dr. Logan before?"

"No, this is my first."

"Really?" Sarah's eyes grew wide. "Usually grad students have taken his courses in undergrad, or another class in their Master's curriculum."

"Oh, I'm not a PhD candidate. I am taking this class as an elective."

Sarah's eyes opened even wider. "An elective? Wow. That's very ambitious."

"How so?" Aedain sipped on the steaming cup of latte.

"This class is very advanced. Students with undergrad degrees in Cosmology and Astrophysics are struggling with it." Sarah looked around the Small World and remembered her Tuesday evening big brain coffee nights.

Aedain explained, "I suppose the Cosmos has been a bit of a hobby for me since I was little. Santa brought me a telescope one year. I've been pretty fascinated with the solar system ever since."

"Santa, huh?" Sarah chuckled, "Please tell me you don't actually believe he travels around the earth at light speed in a sleigh pulled by reindeer. Never mind. Don't answer that." The idea that this ruggedly handsome man still believed in Santa made her smile. "I'm curious. You took an advanced course in Cosmology because it's a hobby? How did you pass the prerequisites?"

"I took the waiver exam." Aedain's nonchalance was both impressive and disconcerting.

"You passed a waiver exam?" Sarah wasn't even aware such an exam existed. More than that, she had never heard of anyone with enough cosmology and astrophysics knowledge to qualify to skip classes necessary to enroll in Logan's advanced curriculum.

"Well, I guessed at a few answers." His eyes twinkled and the outer corners of his eyes wrinkled as he smiled.

Sarah remembered her phone conversation with her father, *Pay attention to the hair standing on your neck*, she recalled. Here in front of her was an exceptionally handsome man who acted like it was no big deal that he passed one of most challenging exams in science. Her neck hair stuck straight out.

She remembered meeting with Dr. Logan two nights before his wife and daughters were murdered. She remembered Dr. Logan telling her about the threats on his life. She suspected it was more than coincidence that this curiously intelligent young man happened to be seated next to her in the auditorium—twice.

An hour ago, she felt desperately lonely; she needed to talk with someone. Now, her signals were telling her to run. But she didn't.

"So, if Astrophysics is your hobby, what is your major? Neuroscience?"

Aedain tossed his head back and laughed, "No. Criminal Justice."

Sarah's skin prickled. Criminal Justice, a curriculum whose students find their way into military, law enforcement, and intelligence organizations. Dr. Logan had warned her. The night before Beth was murdered, Dr. Logan told her 'they' would be watching her, too. Was Aedain a 'they'? Of course it was possible. Still, if he was a plant, would he tell her his real major?

"What made you decide on Criminology?"

"When I was growing up, my dad was a cop in Brooklyn," Aedain explained. "He worked undercover vice in Bedford-Stuyvesant and Brooklyn Heights. He infiltrated the Mob, and from what I've been told by his fellow cops, he was instrumental in busting a huge racketeering operation. Two days later, he didn't come home." Sarah watched Aedain's eyes well with tears.

"I'm sorry."

"Yeah, well, shit happens, you know?" Aedain's voice cracked. Sarah watched his pupils to see if they dilated. They didn't; it appeared he was telling the truth.

"Were you close?"

"As close as a 14-year-old can be with someone he despised. My dad looked like everybody else in Little Italy. Back then, and for as long as I could remember, his name was Tommy Varisco. I thought my name was Tony. He could pass as Italian because he was black Irish, wavy black hair and olive skin, you know?

I was embarrassed. I thought my family was connected, part of the mob. Every time he came to school for Parent-Teacher conferences, I shrank as small as I could get, trying to hide. The looks we got from the teachers—"

"That must have been hard." Sarah's gaze remained locked on Aedain's pupils. If this was an act, Sarah thought, he was one hell of an actor. Or he could be real. She couldn't be sure.

"I just wanted to crawl under the desk. I always walked ten steps ahead of him, hoping people wouldn't think he was my dad. He knew it. It must have broken his heart."

"When did you find out?"

"After he was dead. Too late."

Sarah felt a pain in her heart as if someone had plunged a dagger into it.

"Hell, I didn't even know he was a cop. My mom would say to me, 'Your dad is a good man. You respect your dad.' But I hated him. I treated him like he was a monster. Then, after he was murdered, I looked out the window of the mortuary's black limousine at a sea of blue. Men and women in NYPD dress blues lined the street, every one of them standing at attention, saluting in their white gloves. It was too late for me to make peace with him."

Sarah's eyes welled up and the lump in her throat blocked her windpipe.

"Wow. Yeah. I'm sorry." Aedain struggled to compose himself.

"I didn't see that coming. I've never told anyone that; the part about seeing his fellow cops saluting."

Once she could breathe again, Sarah asked, "You think that's why you went into Criminal Justice instead of Astrophysics?"

"I suppose. I'm sure it was some sort of penance, compensation, cleansing of the soul, who knows?"

Aedain reached for the check.

"I've got this," Sarah interrupted. "I invited you, remember?"

"Yes," Aedain said, nodding. "Thank you."

Sarah stuck out her hand. "I'm Sarah Carmichael. You're Aedain. Aedain…?"

"Maycroft. Aedain Maycroft." He gripped Sarah's hand firmly in return.

Together, they left the Small World Coffee Shop on Washington on a cold January day. Sarah wondered what she would find when she searched the internet for an undercover NYPD cop killed in the line of duty ten years ago. She wondered if the news had even covered it. She knew, too, that a cover story about a cop's murder a decade earlier could have been planted in news archives as recently as two days ago.

Despite her misgivings, Sarah hoped it wouldn't be the last time they would see one another.

9

Wearing heavy sweatpants and a hooded sweatshirt, John Logan hiked along New Jersey's Round Valley Reservoir Trail until he reached a thick stand of bulrush. Carefully treading his way over twigs and sharp-edged rocks, he worked his way a hundred yards from the marked hiking trail to the edge of a muck pond. It was clear nobody else had the poor judgment to walk this path recently.

Logan checked his watch. It was 12:59 p.m. If Charlie was anything, he was punctual. Five minutes passed. He'd never known Charlie to be late but he saw no sign of him. He reached for his phone to call him, then remembered Charlie told him to take the battery out of the phone and leave it home.

Don't go home. Whatever you do, don't go home, Charlie's voice resonated in his brain. There would be no sentimental good-byes to the house in which he and Beth had raised their daughters. It was just as well. The home's memories turned out to be more tragic than joyful. There would be no tearful send-offs from his co-workers and friends who met at the Small World Coffee Shop. Before he found a place to hole up till his meeting with Charlie, Logan made sure to take care of one important piece of business.

"Hello, Johnny." Dr. Logan jumped at the sound of Charlie's voice, no more than six feet away. He spun around to see him but he was camouflaged in a stand of bulrush beside him. Slowly, Charlie emerged from the wetland grass as if an apparition.

"Damn, Charlie! I hate it when you do that." Logan shivered from the chill he felt throughout his body.

"You're like a damn ghost."

Today, Charlie was just as when Logan saw him ten years ago—lanky and thin. "I'm sorry for your loss, Johnny. I expected I would hear from you."

"Why? Why did you expect to hear from me?"

"Because Beth's and the girls' deaths wasn't the result of a burglary gone bad."

"You think so, too, huh? I wish I could prove who did it but I don't know where to begin. Besides, I don't have the luxury of time to investigate who killed them. The shit is going down fast, and I know I'm a target."

Charlie held his finger to his lips, "Shhh. Not now. Not here." Charlie reached into his pocket and pulled out a black plastic electronic device, aimed it toward the cattails and traced a path along the muck edge of the lake. A green, flat-bottomed duck boat moved past the cattails to the water's edge. Other than two oars, a remote controlled motor, and small black duffle bag, the boat was empty.

"Get in," Charlie ordered. Logan clambered over the gunwales of the shallow boat. Charlie grabbed the small bag and retrieved a radio and a palm-sized spiral notepad. He turned up the volume on the radio and reached into his pants pocket for a pencil. He didn't look at Dr. Logan when he asked, "Why are you running, Johnny?" Only three other people in his life had ever called him Johnny or dared to. His mom, his dad, and Beth. "Lean in close. The radio will mask our conversation if anyone is listening in."

"Who is listening in? And how?" Logan looked in all directions as he spoke.

"The real question is, who isn't? If they think you know as much as you do, I promise you that they are listening with satellites, long-range listening devices, drones and whatever other technology they can get their hands on. Hell, for all I know, somebody planted a transmitter somewhere here on the boat."

"Really? On the boat?"

Charlie peered through his eyebrows at Logan, "No, Johnny, I'm not *that* careless. Now, again, why are you running?"

Logan leaned over from his seat in the bow toward Charlie.

"I'm scared, Charlie. In my most horrifying dreams, I never imagined that teaching my theories about the Cosmos would get my family killed. Every morning when I wake up, Beth is not in my bed. The girls are not in their rooms. My home is empty. My life is empty. If God ended my life right now, I would be happy to have the pain in my chest stop."

"I believe you." Charlie waited for his former roommate to go on but Logan sat silently in the boat, staring across the water at nothing. His heart was gone. The former spy asked, "Are you afraid they will kill you?"

"Kill me? No, I'm not afraid of that. Torturing me into giving them answers I don't have? Yes, I'm afraid of that."

"Mm-hmm," Charlie muttered as he placed the boat's wooden oars into the oarlocks on the gunwales. He began rowing gently and in no particular direction.

"There's more, Charlie. It's Sarah. I'm scared for Sarah's safety, too."

"Sarah?"

"My Teaching Assistant and Research Team Leader. Brilliant student."

Charlie rowed and listened.

"I invited her, as a second-year grad student, to join our Tuesday-night discussions at the coffee shop. All but two of the others were tenured professors and the two who weren't are Doctoral candidates on the last lap of finishing their PhDs."

"And male."

"Huh?"

"The rest of them—the two students and the professors—they were all male. Am I right?"

"Well, yes, as a matter of fact, they were. How did you know that? What difference does that make?" Logan felt his blood pressure rise.

"It was just a guess, and it makes all the difference," the spy said calmly. "It explains why you are worried for her safety and it explains why you should be."

Logan tilted his head, as if he was a dog waiting for his master to speak.

"There was talk, wasn't there? Talk about you and her? About how she got invited to your big brain discussions, how she pulled a 4.0 GPA every semester and how she got the Research Team Leader job? How am I doing?"

"Sure, there was talk. I ignored it. I figured it was just a bunch of sour grapes."

"That's the problem."

"What?"

"You ignored it. You shouldn't have. Listen, Johnny, I don't give a rat's ass if you and this brilliant student of yours did a monkey dance under the telescope at midnight, you understand? What I want to know is why you're worried for her safety."

"It wasn't like that—"

"Why, dammit? Why? Tell me why you are worried for her but didn't say you were worried for the other professors or students in your coffee klatch." Charlie was growing impatient. "We don't have time for this. I need answers. Now."

Logan whispered, "She knew more about my work than anyone else; more than the other professors and a lot more than the grad students. I told her my suspicions about what might be causing these strange gravitational events."

"Damn! You told her you believe they are man-made. I was afraid you were going to say that." Charlie reached for binoculars from his pack and stared at the shoreline.

"More than that. Not just that they are man-made but that I have an idea which men and why."

"Quiet! Shush!" Charlie's rowing became unusually clumsy, the oars clunking loudly against the boat's aluminum hull. He continued his awkward rowing for several minutes before gliding the oars gently through the water again.

"What was that all about?"

Charlie nodded toward the shoreline. "There. At the edge of the lake. The guy from the white pickup truck launched a drone a few minutes ago. Pretty sure he was listening in. After my little percussion solo, I saw him yank his headphones off and grab his ears. The sound of these oars clanking against this aluminum hull must have hurt. He landed the drone and now he's driving away." Charlie stared at Logan then asked, "Now, who is causing these anomalies and why?"

"All I can say for sure is that I believe there are two very powerful people in the world trying to corner the world's energy. If they succeed in capturing the majority of the world's proton accelerator energy, they could destroy the global fossil-fuel industry and the economies which depend on it. Coal, oil, natural gas; their prices would collapse. The economies of major industrialized nations would follow and anarchy would reign."

"Which countries?"

"China, both Koreas, Russia, all the OPEC countries, the United Kingdom and all their protectorates, Australia, Venezuela." Logan took a breath, "You want a list?"

"Just one more."

"Yes, it would destroy the United States' economy and we would experience a depression the magnitude of which would make the Great Depression look like the Roaring Twenties."

Small waves lapped the side of the boat. Logan wasn't sure if Charlie's head was nodding in agreement or bobbing to the rhythm of the waves.

"Sarah knows these things, too?"

Logan turned his face toward the far shore.

Charlie warned, "You're right; you need to disappear. She does, too."

"She won't. She'll stand and fight."

"I hope not, for her sake. She'll wind up dead. If you disappear, maybe she'll wise up. Maybe, but not likely."

Charlie tore the page out of the spiral notepad and handed it to his friend. "Memorize this note," he ordered. "Then burn it." Charlie held the remaining notebook in his hand and touched it with a lighter. He dropped it to the aluminum bottom of the boat and watched it burn. "Any questions?"

Logan shook his head no.

"One more thing," Charlie said. "Lay off the booze and the pills. You need to keep your head out of your ass if you want to stay alive."

"How did you know—?" Logan said weakly. "For God's sake, Johnny, I'm a spy."

Logan hung his head. "I'm trying, Charlie."

"Trying ain't shit," Charlie retorted, "*doing* is all that matters." He started the motor and turned the boat toward the stand of bulrush.

Charlie left the same way he came. Like a ghost.

10

At 6:00 a.m., Sarah awoke to her clock radio blaring the morning headlines. The news wasn't good.

"Princeton Police are looking for Dr. John Logan, a professor of Astrophysics at Princeton University. Today, police issued a BOLO—be on the lookout—for Dr. Logan. If you have any information about his whereabouts, please contact the Princeton Police."

Sarah sat bolt upright. "Oh, my God. Oh my God, oh my God!"

The reporter continued, "Logan's wife and daughters were murdered last October, and the investigation into their deaths has not resulted in any arrests. Princeton Police say that Logan is not a suspect at this time but describe him as a 'person of interest.'"

Sarah knew better; she knew somebody was trying to frame him for conspiracy in his family's murders.

One week ago, he begged her to come over. She refused at first, assuming he'd be halfway through the bottle of Bourbon by the time she got there. She had plans to meet Aedain for dinner, and she wanted to keep them.

There was something different in Dr. Logan's voice this time, though. He sounded scared.

"Aedain, I'm so sorry," she explained in her text message. "Something has come up and I need to cancel. Will call you tomorrow."

Logan's door was open when she arrived. Completely ransacked, the home's living room couch was overturned. The couch's lining underneath had been slashed open. Pillows were gutted and the contents of the kitchen cupboards had been dumped onto the counters and the floor.

"They were looking for something," Logan stated the obvious. "My desktop computer is gone, and all of my CDs, my thumb drives, everything that might contain information they can use. Burglars would steal the computer but not the CDs."

"To frame you?"

"Maybe, maybe not. It may be they are setting me up or trying to see how much I know."

Sarah touched Dr. Logan's face to get his attention, then moved her fingers in sign language as the girls had taught her, "Where is your laptop?"

Logan looked up at the ceiling and around the room, then signed, "The trunk of my car."

Sarah signed, "Is there more?" Logan motioned for her to follow him to the 100-year old stone basement. Half of it had been ransacked like the upstairs but the other half was untouched, just as he had left it before leaving in the morning for the university.

"I think they got spooked," he whispered. "Something scared them off. It may have been the lawn guys or the doorbell. Who knows?" He returned to sign language, "Thank God they didn't find this." At the base of the abandoned chimney flue, Logan opened a small metal door used in the days of coal to clean out ashes from beneath the furnace. He reached behind the brick and pulled out a small brass plate with what appeared to be three letters or numbers etched into it. Sarah wasn't close enough to read the small numbers. Logan signed, telling Sarah to stay close behind him as he moved deeper into the basement.

He led her to the home's coal storage room. He jiggled a stone until it loosened and revealed a small safe installed behind the home's foundation. He spun the dial around, from one number to another, before he twisted the handle down. The safe door creaked open. He pointed to papers inside the safe.

"Remember this," he signed. "If anything happens to me, get these papers out of here. Don't let anyone get them. Not anyone."

Sarah signed, "Are these your findings?" Sarah winced at the sight of a dark brownish-red smudge on the manila envelope.

Logan nodded as he placed the envelope back into the safe and returned the metal plate etched with numbers into the flue. He motioned for Sarah to follow him upstairs to the living room. He whispered over his shoulder as he ascended the stairs. "The police questioned me, of course, but as you know, I was teaching at the time of the murder. I remember getting to the house, ducking under the yellow tape and pushing my way past the police. They grabbed me before I reached their bodies but there was so much blood." Tears filled his eyes as he pressed on, "There was blood everywhere—the floor, on the furniture, everywhere. I guess I got some on my hands and didn't realize it until later."

Now, as the news of the professor's disappearance spread over the airwaves, Sarah had no idea whether he had taken the secret documents with him, if he had made a copy, or if he was dead. All she knew was she had to get to the house. She had to find the brass plate, open the safe, and retrieve the envelope if it was still there.

"Aedain," she spoke to his voice mail, "I need to see you. Can you call me? Better yet, can you come get me?" Sarah grabbed her purse and sat on her front stoop until Aedain arrived. She checked her key ring to make sure the key to the back door of the Logan family home was on it. It was.

"Thanks for doing this," Sarah said, as they drove toward the Logan home. I didn't know who else to call."

"I'm glad you called *me.*"

The sun was rising over the rooftops of Logan's neighborhood lined with brick Tudors and Federal style two-stories. Crime-scene tape surrounded the house, and a half-dozen cars were parked at the curb.

"Feds," Aedain announced.

"Feds?" Sarah echoed. Aedain nodded.

"How do you know?"

"Local PD—the local police—would have a few patrol cars, maybe a detective car or two like those by the cul-de-sac. But there are no cruisers anywhere. Those are Feds."

"Patrol cars? Cruisers?"

"Patrol cars, sometimes called cruisers, have 'Police' decals on the side, like the ones that stop you for speeding. Those you see in front of the house are plain wrappers."

"What is a plain wrapper?"

"A car painted just one color, like the light green Dodge Charger there. It's a Police Pursuit version. They intentionally make them look boring so they don't attract attention but I can tell by the wheels."

"How so?" Sarah asked.

"The wheels are wider and taller to accommodate bigger tires and give them better traction. You won't see those on a Charger straight off the showroom floor."

Sarah paused, noticing Aedain's attention to details non-law enforcement people would miss. Then again, she thought, anyone studying Criminal Justice would have been trained to observe seemingly insignificant details.

"What kind of Feds?" Sarah had heard acronyms like FBI, ATF, and CIA. She wasn't sure what they all did but had heard them mentioned on the evening news and TV shows.

"Hard to say," Aedain replied as he circled halfway around the block then stopped. "They could be CIA or the FBI. Maybe several different agencies, but I doubt it. The different agencies don't work and play well with others. They wind up bumping into each other like the Keystone Kops. My guess is it's the FBI's BAU—Behavioral Analysis Unit."

"Behavioral Analysis Unit?" Sarah repeated. "You mean like the TV show? Criminal—something."

"Minds. Criminal Minds. The one with Penelope and Rossi. Yeah, that one."

"I thought they investigated serial killers and kidnappers."

"Oh, they still do. But they've branched out. They have divisions for Cyber Crime, Terrorism, Counterintelligence, just about everything. They even have a group specializing in weapons of mass destruction—chemical warfare, dirty bombs, nuclear capabilities, you name it."

"You think they might all be from the FBI? The BAU?"

"It's a good chance. That makes the most sense of all. They might be bringing all of their resources together to see if they can piece together a theory."

"What about the local police?" Sarah looked over her shoulder as she spoke, peering into the cars lining the street to see if anyone was peering back. Her hands were clammy as she rubbed the Logan's house key as a touchstone.

"Oh, the Feds will give Princeton PD a cover story to release to the media. They'll release it about 6:15 p.m., just before the opening credits of the national networks' evening news programs. All the stations will get sucked into the ruse. It will go something like this: 'Breaking news! Missing Princeton professor is being hunted by the FBI!' They'll all be so afraid the other networks are going to scoop them, they'll air the story with no corroboration. Once they put it on the air, neither of them—neither the PD nor the stations—will want to walk it back. They'll stick with it until they decide to divert the storyline in a different direction."

"You know a lot about this, don't you? I mean, for someone still in school, you seem to know the inner workings of law enforcement pretty well."

"I do."

Sarah's skin prickled again. Instinct told her to bolt, to escape from the car and run between the brick houses until she couldn't run anymore. She needed the envelope, though.

Aedain's voice was steady. "After my father's death, his vice squad partner eventually made Captain in NYPD. He is good friends with the head of the FBI's Cyber Crimes Unit. When I finished undergrad, my father's former partner got me an internship there for six months. Interesting group of people."

"Interesting?"

"Scary is more accurate."

"So what kind of story might they plant?"

"About the murder? Or the disappearance?"

"Let's start with the murder," Sarah said.

"Gangs. Drug cartel. Random serial killer. It could be any of them," Aedain explained. "Whatever story they decide on, they'll have plenty of evidence to prove it. Some of it might even be true." Aedain looked into his rear view mirror, then each side mirror, then back to the front.

"Gangs?" It seemed odd to Sarah that Dr. Logan's family would have been murdered by gangsters or a drug cartel.

"Sure," Aedain explained. "It could have been a local gang menacing the neighborhood with daytime break-ins. They weren't expecting the Logan family to be home; it was a robbery gone wrong. But that doesn't explain the break-in after their murders. So they might go with drug cartel story. The Good Doctor was trafficking coke and heroin to students and he was skimming. They killed his family as a warning to other dealers."

"Skimming?"

"The street dealer takes a little extra off the top before he gives the cartel its split. They torture and kill dealers who skim. They'll say the cartel tossed his place looking for money and drugs."

"But Dr. Logan would never be a drug dealer!"

"Tell someone that after the Feds and the media get done with him."

Logan's disappearance made sense to Sarah now. The Feds knew Logan was aware they were tracking his every move. Logan was certain the Feds would plant the story about gangs or a cartel, or that he was a serial killer the BAU had on its radar for years. Then they would arrest him. Whatever the ruse, it would be enough to take Logan into custody and interrogate him. That would be the last time anyone would see him. With the story they would plant, it would be the last time anyone would ask, 'Whatever happened to Dr. John Logan?'

A terrifying realization hit Sarah just as Aedain put it into words. "For all we know, he didn't disappear at all. The Feds may have arrested him and are interrogating him right now. They may be telling the media he's disappeared, on the run, kidnapped by a cartel, and nobody will imagine that the government already has him."

"The government, huh?" Sarah listened to the words as she said them. *The U.S. Government*, she thought silently. *U.S. citizens? Gangs? Drug Cartels? Foreign nationals?* Strangely, Aedain had a knack for putting into words Sarah's worst fears precisely at the moment she was feeling them.

"The thing is," Aedain continued, "you don't know who is who. Maybe Logan was smart enough to not trust his colleagues. Or maybe his trust was his undoing. They are the first people they'll interrogate. People he worked with, his students—" Aedain turned toward Sarah, "—like you. But you won't know who is asking you questions."

Sarah nodded. Inside her pocket, she squeezed the key Dr. Logan had given her.

"Did he tell you anything?" Aedain asked. "Anything the Feds might want to know? Did he give you anything to keep for him?"

Sarah looked straight through the windshield and down the street, "No. Nothing."

Aedain pulled slowly away from the curb. Sarah peered between each house, looking for a path to sneak back to the Logan house. Later, after dark, she thought; she'd come back alone and hope the crime lab investigators were gone. She didn't tell Aedain her plan.

Neither one spoke as they drove to Sarah's apartment.

"Thanks for doing that. I just wanted to see his house. I don't know why. I guess just so I could believe it was real. He's really gone. I didn't get to say goodbye."

"I know."

Aedain pulled up to Sarah's townhouse.

"Would you walk me up to the door?" Sarah asked. "I have to admit, I'm a little nervous. Actually, I'm a lot nervous."

"Of course." Aedain popped open the console and reached for a black nylon holster custom-fit for the Smith & Wesson M&P 9 millimeter it held. Aedain unsnapped the holster, slid the handgun out of the holster, and pulled back the breech to load a round into the chamber. "C'mon," he said. "Let's go check it out." He stopped, looked at Sarah, and said, "You weren't shocked when I opened the glove compartment and you saw a gun, were you?"

"No, not really," Sarah replied. "I figured someone in Criminal Justice would have a license to carry a gun."

"You're full of surprises. Seems like most of the women I meet hate guns."

"I'm not like most women," Sarah assured him.

Aedain wrapped his free arm around Sarah and she felt herself lean in against him. Strangely, she felt safe. Aedain searched Sarah's apartment before he returned to the door. "There's nobody here. No monsters under the bed or goblins in the closet. I'll stay if you like."

Sarah smiled. "I'm sure you would." She opened her arms to give him a hug and clung to him longer than she planned. Eventually, she pulled away and kissed his cheek, resisting her urge for more. She wanted to trust him, she did. She just didn't. Not yet.

Aedain nodded toward his holstered semi-auto on his belt. "Do you shoot?"

"I've been known to," Sarah replied as their eyes connected.

"Maybe we could go to the shooting range together someday."

"Maybe. We'll see." Sarah reached her hand behind his head and guided his face toward hers. She parted her lips and invited his mouth to hers. Aedain brushed her hair aside and caressed her face as they kissed.

"Oh, I, um, that was…wow," Sarah muttered as she pulled back, "I… did not see that coming. Maybe you should go." She hoped he would refuse.

"Uh, yeah," Aedain stammered, "I'd better go. Yes, I should go." Aedain moved toward the door before turning back. "You want me to go? I mean—"

"Go," Sarah said softly as she kissed his cheek once more.

Locking the door behind him, Sarah watched Aedain drive away. She poured a glass of wine, turned the lights off, and stared out her living room window. She sat, numb, mostly from shock and a little from the wine, through the rest of the day and into the night. She sat waiting for a strange car to pull up—a plain wrapper, maybe—and park across the street. By three a.m., she was fairly sure that wasn't going to happen. At least not tonight.

Her mind raced with questions. *How would she get into the Logan house? What would she do with Dr. Logan's research when she retrieved the envelope? Where would she keep the envelope once she got it?*

Using her phone's flashlight, she made her way upstairs and down the hall to her bedroom. When she saw her bed, the hair on her neck stood straight again. Sarah was compulsive about making her bed each morning. Now, though, a corner of her bedspread covering her pillow was mussed. Despite the recent chaos, she knew she hadn't left her bed like that. She pulled back the spread and lifted the pillow.

Beneath it, a piece of brass with three numbers scratched into it lay beneath the pillow.

Sarah sat down on the edge of her bed and stared at the brass plate she had last seen in Logan's basement. She stared at the numbers as a triumphant smile spread over her face. She knew exactly where Logan had left the blood-smeared manila envelope.

"Well played, Doctor," Sarah whispered as she slipped under her covers and clicked the bedside lamp off. "Well played."

11

Sarah walked briskly across the Washington Street Bridge, not breaking stride as she held her hand over the railing. Halfway across the bridge, she dropped Dr. Logan's house key into the water below. She had no use for it now. Nobody would find the key in Carnegie Lake and, even if they did, they wouldn't be able to connect it to her. She maintained her pace the rest of the way to the Small World.

"Latte, please. Grande," Sarah ordered, "and a blueberry scone. To go." She remembered Aedain's advice: "Keep your daily regimen. The more normal you look, the less attention they will give you. Eventually, they'll get bored and decide that surveilling you is a waste of time." Sarah had repeated her morning routine for two weeks.

Today, she would find out if two weeks had been long enough. She would find out if the envelope was still where Dr. Logan had left it.

Each morning, between 7:00 and 7:10 a.m., with her latte and scone in hand, Sarah made the short walk to the university's art museum. Her favorite bench outside the museum faced Henry Moore's *Oval with Two Points.*

Since the deaths of Beth and the girls, art seemed to soothe her. This New England winter morning was mild, and she sucked in each cool breath slowly and exhaled it in stages. Her heart pounded hard inside her chest. It was Tuesday; she didn't need to be to the lab until 9:00.

"Hey," a familiar voice said, as a man approached her.

"Hey, back," she answered. She patted the bench beside her, inviting him to join her.

"I think you're the only person on campus who likes this piece," Aedain said as he sat down. "It's calming, don't you think?"

"You surprise me again, Aedain Maycroft," Sarah answered. "I didn't expect a Criminal Justice major to appreciate art."

"Be careful judging books by their covers," Aedain admonished gently, "would you be surprised to know that I like music, too, as well as theater and ballet?"

"Yes, I admit, I would," Sarah admitted. "Do you play an instrument?"

"Piano, although I'm a bit rusty," Aedain said, "and guitar." He paused, then added, "I've always wanted to learn to play the banjo. I don't know why. It just fascinates me. Do you play?"

"I was in my high school band but I'm more of a dancer. Ballet, modern, tap. I spent a lot of time at the barre."

Aedain laughed, "Sounds like a few binges I've had myself."

"The barre, not the bar."

Aedain turned to look Sarah in the eyes, "I know what a barre is."

Sarah stared at Aedain, not sure what to make of him. "So you're a hard-drinking, rootin' tootin', gun-toting piano player. Who is your favorite composer?" Sarah knew she was testing him. Aedain knew it, too.

"I'm not sure I have a favorite composer but I do have favorite compositions. Chopin's *Polonaise*, for example, and Puccini's *La Boheme*. The most moving performance was when I watched Luciano Pavarotti perform *I Pagliacci* at the Kennedy Center. It was unforgettable. I like music that tells a story, I suppose."

If he is a plant, Sarah thought, *he's been well rehearsed.* Sarah hoped he actually played the piano and loved classical music. Sarah moved her hand to rest on his, saying nothing as they sipped their coffees and stared at Moore's masterpiece.

At 7:40, she abruptly stood up and announced, "Time for me to go." She slung her backpack over her shoulder, kissed Aedain on the cheek, and began her trek from museum concourse to Dillon Gym. Thirty minutes on the elliptical would trigger her endorphins and numb the anxiety, at least for a while.

"Bye, Sarah Carmichael," Aedain said as he watched her walk away.

She stood in front of her assigned locker at Dillon and looked both ways as she recalled the numbers on the brass plate. She spun the dial from one to the next, looking over her shoulder with each spin of the dial. She tugged the door open. The blood-smeared envelope Logan had shown her in his basement was still there. She pushed her backpack into the locker and stuffed the envelope inside. Tonight, she would learn its contents. Sarah fought the urge to grab her pack, race out of the building, and run home. "Stay chill," she repeated. She closed the locker's latch and spun the dial.

Half an hour later, sweat was streaming down her body. Some of it was caused by exercise but most by terror. After her morning workout, Sarah grabbed the backpack and headed across Washington and down Ivy Lane. *Keep looking straight ahead*, she repeated to herself. *Today is just like any other day.* She was conscious of every bounce in her step; if her step was listless, it could cause suspicion. Too much enthusiasm would get the same result. She forced herself to appear relaxed as she entered the Department of Astrophysics building. Inside, she was everything *but* relaxed.

It was Tuesday Lab. Sarah perched on a stool in front of the classroom to monitor the students. Grad school babysitting, she called it. She prayed nobody had questions today. A few did, and she forced a smile when she answered them. Minutes ticked by into hours and hours ticked by until it was time for her half-mile hike back across the bridge and a two-mile bus ride home. She'd walk up a flight of stairs to the safety of her apartment, lock the bolt, close the blinds, and open the envelope.

Inside her townhouse, Sarah searched every room, under her bed and behind her clothes in the closets before she dumped the packet from her backpack onto the living room floor.

"Now, my good Doctor, what is it you want me to see?"

Daylight turned to darkness as Sarah pored over more than a hundred pieces of paper, from sticky notes to lined loose-leaf paper and cocktail napkins. A wrinkled Tarot card, scribbled notes, mathematical equations, and theories were attached with paper clips and stapled to others which may be relevant. There were photos taken on family vacations. She paused at one, a picture of Dr. Logan, Beth, Lisa, and Lucy. Lucy was holding her favorite doll, Dorothy, from The Wizard of Oz. The pictures seemed out of place with all of Dr. Logan's mathematical formulae and theories.

As a youngster, Sarah bought 1,000-piece puzzles and dumped them into a paper bag before tossing the box and its cover picture into the trash. It was more challenging that way. Today, looking at the pile of paper scraps on her floor, the childhood puzzles seemed easy.

Sarah knew the professor well, though. Every piece in the envelope was part of the puzzle. They all meant something. She just didn't know what.

At quarter past nine, Sarah was still focused on finding links in the clues. Her head felt as if it was clamped in a vise. She was jolted from her scrutiny by the sound of Aedain's ringtone. Her heart pounded; she let it ring four times before she was calm enough to answer it.

"Hey," she answered.

"Hey." Aedain paused before asking, "Did I say something wrong?"

"Why would you think that?" Sarah dodged. She'd been both hoping for his call and praying it would never come. She was curious about the handsome man who suspiciously fell into her life when everything seemed to be falling apart.

"I don't know, it just seemed like you jumped up from our conversation this morning when I talked about studying music. It seemed I had upset you."

"No, of course you didn't say anything wrong. I was enjoying our conversation. I'm sorry. I looked at my watch and I realized I had to leave. To keep my routine, you know," Sarah explained, not sure she was telling the whole truth. "I guess I'm a bit rattled by all of this. I hope you understand. My mentor and friend has disappeared, his wife and daughters are dead, the FBI, CIA, or God-knows-what acronym is looking for him, and you show up, a Criminal Justice major who just happens to dabble in astrophysics and classical music."

"It must look suspicious," Aedain acknowledged. "But think about it, if I was sent by a government agency to get close to you without you suspecting it, I've done a piss-poor job gaining your confidence, haven't I?"

"Maybe so," Sarah conceded without saying the rest of her thought, *unless that's exactly what you intended.* She wanted to see him, to look him in the eyes when they spoke. Sarah had street smarts; she would know if he was lying.

"Meet me in twenty five minutes," Sarah blurted. "We can't talk on the phone."

"What? Where?"

"You know where."

Sarah hung up, jammed the papers back inside her backpack along with her laptop, and locked its zipper. She knocked on Mr. Landon's door across the hall and asked if she could leave her backpack with him for a couple hours. Mr. Landon adored Sarah, mostly because she baked soft brownies sprinkled with confectioner's sugar for him just like Sarah's grandmother had made for her as a child.

"Of course, Sarah." Mr. Landon was always kind. He rarely asked questions and, when he did, she handed him a gift to divert his attention—something baked fresh, preferably with chocolate.

Sarah jogged, then ran, three and a half miles to her favorite bench facing the museum. Aedain was waiting.

Sarah kissed him on the cheek and gave him a quick hug. "Aedain, I need to ask you something." Sarah asked. "Honest answer?"

"Of course."

"Look at me," she ordered as she pointed to her face, "here. In the eyes. Look at me. Do you know what happened to Dr. Logan's wife, Beth, and his daughters?"

Aedain was speechless.

Sarah believed he knew more than he was telling her, and she wanted to know why a news blackout seemed to be avoiding any mention of his death. "There is a big blank when it comes to news stories about it," Sarah said. "No network exclusive interviews, no Facebook posts with conspiracy theories. Nothing."

"You want the gory details? Really? I suppose I could find out."

"No!" Sarah held up her hand. "Stop! I don't want to hear how bloody they were. I've heard that already. Dr. Logan told me over and over. I don't need more nightmares. I want to know if the police know who did it."

"Why would I know that?"

Sarah stared hard at him. "Don't bullshit me, Aedain."

Aedain paused, sucked in a deep breath, and began. "The word on the street is, the perps were some local gangbangers, the Tray Outlaws or one of the Crips' gangs—they won't say. Some even think it was the Latin Kings brought in from Chicago or the Hondurans—MS-13—flown in from L.A. They're being very tight-lipped about who actually committed the murders."

"Street gangs? Why street gangs?"

"Gang members are hard to trace. They move around a lot. They're a lot more streetwise than most law enforcement agencies give them credit for. They don't leave evidence behind. No fingerprints, no DNA, nothing."

"Who hired them?"

"They think whoever committed the murder was connected."

"Who are 'they' and who are they connected to?"

"'They' are the law enforcement teams conducting the investigation. They believe the gangs may be connected to organized crime—a crime syndicate. A Columbian cocaine cartel. The Italian

Mafia. Bratva, the Russian mob. Hell, the Mickey Mouse Club, for all I know."

"But that's not where it ends, is it?

"No. It's very possible a foreign government is spearheading this thing."

"Which foreign government?"

"I don't know. I'm not sure they know. Some of the possibilities are Russia, China, Iran, and North Korea. It could be any one of them. Or none of them."

"What do you mean 'or none of them'?"

"I mean, it's not necessarily a *foreign* government behind it."

"Are you saying what I think you're saying?" Sarah peered into the shadows of the buildings surrounding the museum's plaza, looking for anything out of place.

"Yes. It would be easy to get Americans to believe one of our favorite enemies committed the crime but there are plenty of folks right here in the United States who wanted Logan to keep his mouth shut."

"Why? Why would they be more worried than if he was talking only about Hawking's theory?"

"Because Hawking almost immediately dismissed the possibility of his theory actually happening; he dampened hysteria before it began. Dr. Logan proposed a doomsday scenario; everybody dies and it is man's own fault. People want to keep believing what they already believe. But Logan takes Hawking's theory, puts his own twist on it, and starts telling people it's beginning of the end, that the anomalies are proof that Hawking is correct: Earth's annihilation is imminent."

"What if he's right?"

"What if he is? What good will it do? The only outcome of global panic is world war. Those who can afford it will be hunting down Elon Musk and Richard Branson to catch a ride on the next rocket to Mars."

"Elon Musk? Richard Branson?"

"Musk is using rockets to send satellites into space toward the goal of humans traveling to Mars. For all we know, he's already invented a spaceship capable of traveling beyond our solar system. Branson made the first hot air balloon flight across the Atlantic in 1987 and is now experimenting in human space travel."

"So they believe space travel to and from distant planets is possible?"

"More than possible. They both believe it is only a matter of time and technological development. So far, they have not developed the technology to propel a manned spacecraft beyond the ice crystals surrounding our galaxy. But Musk, I think, has figured out how to get humans to Mars already."

"He has?"

"Yes, but Mars won't be a safe haven if it gets sucked into a quantum fluctuation or a supernova implodes and the black hole it causes sucks three neighboring solar systems into it. Even if intergalactic space travel is possible, there is no planet you could reach quickly enough if Hawking's quantum fluctuation has already begun. The show will be over before the fat lady sings. Hell, the fat lady will still be sitting in the dressing room when the vacuum bubble reaches Earth. Flying to Mars or Saturn won't save you; those planets will be gone before Earth is."

Sarah's skin felt hot, then cold, before it crawled over her arms and back. Aedain was repeating Dr. Logan's predictions verbatim.

Aedain paused. "Your life is in danger, Sarah. If you follow Logan down his scientific path, they will come for you, too. You understand that, don't you?"

Instead of answering, Sarah asked, "Have you ever heard of a planet called Proxima b?"

"No. Is it a new one somebody just discovered?" She wasn't sure why but Sarah felt relieved to learn that Aedain didn't know about Proxima b.

"No," she explained. "It's a planet 25 trillion miles away which may have an environment that humans need to stay alive. You see, I believe you are right; the hysteria you predict will happen. There will be riots in the streets—civil war, world war."

Sarah reached to hold Aedain's face while she made her point. "Look at me. Do a few wealthy, powerful people already have a place to go and a vehicle to get them there?"

"Did you hear me about your life being in danger?" Aedain's tone was edgier now than she had ever experienced before. Aedain didn't answer her question.

"I know my life is in danger, Aedain, but I can't focus on that right now. I need to focus on what is causing these strange events. Is it the beginning of the end of life as we know it? Or is it something else?"

"Does it really matter, Sarah?" Aedain replied. If the answer to your questions is yes, what could we do about it?"

Sarah snapped back, "So, is that what you intend to do? Sit here and do nothing till we die? Is that your plan?"

"Who said I had a plan, for Christ's sake?"

Sarah wasn't so sure Aedain didn't have a plan—or at least know people who did. She was scared. For the first time, she understood Aedain was scared, too.

"Hold me," she leaned toward him. He pulled her close and wrapped his arms around her. "Tell me it's going to be okay."

"It's going to be okay," Aedain reassured her.

"Liar."

"Probably."

Together, they sat silently till the Grover Cleveland Tower's carillon chimed midnight. Sarah hoped that this would not be the last time she would see Aedain.

She wanted to get to know him better but she knew that doing so could get them both killed.

"Need a ride home?" Aedain asked.

"If you wouldn't mind, and if you'd be so kind as to stop at the coffee shop. Mr. Landon loves my grandma's brownies and The Small World's brownies are almost as good."

"No problem. Do you think he'll still be up this late?"

"Maybe. If not, I'll give them to him in the morning." Sarah noticed Aedain didn't ask why she was buying brownies for her elderly neighbor at midnight. The ride to Sarah's townhouse was short, and she kissed him on the cheek before she turned to get out of the car.

"Are you sure you don't want me to come up and check your place again? Make sure no bogeymen are there?"

"Thanks, I'm sure I'll be fine."

"You're welcome." Aedain pulled her back to him for another, longer kiss. Sarah didn't object.

Sarah watched Aedain pull away and waved a kiss before turning toward her townhouse. Mr. Landon's living room light cast shadows on his sliding door drapes. She knocked on his door and he answered. "They're not my grandma's recipe," she apologized. "They are the best I could do on short notice."

"Well, how perfectly lovely," Mr. Landon beamed as he spoke. "Perfectly lovely! Oh, here you go. Here is your bag." Mr. Landon handed the backpack to Sarah and turned his attention back to the brownies. He pivoted and added, "There was a couple who stopped by earlier for you."

"A couple?"

"Yes, a lovely young couple, about your age. They were knocking on your door. They seemed nice. I told them you were out for the evening. They thanked me and left."

Sarah's neck hair bristled as she turned and carefully crossed the hallway. She nervously slid her key into the lock of her apartment door. It was unlocked. She pushed against the door and stood in the outside hallway as the door swung open.

Her home had been violently ransacked. The living room couch was upside down and, just as Dr. Logan's living room couch had been, was slit open with a lengthwise gash. Couch pillows were slashed and their stuffing dumped onto the floor. Kitchen canisters were emptied onto the counter and floor, and white flour footprints crossed the apartment's carpet.

"A lovely young couple, I'm sure," Sarah muttered as she pulled the door shut, locked it from the hallway, and left.

Sarah looked over her shoulder as she walked slowly to her car, peering into the back seat before opening the door. She inspected beneath the car, under the seat and around the ignition, searching for anything which looked out of place. Carefully, she climbed into the driver's seat and prayed it didn't explode. *Get a grip, girl*, she told herself. *Think about it. Nobody wants you dead... yet. Not before they get hold of what you have in the backpack.* Sarah held her breath, gritted her teeth, closed her eyes, and twisted the key. The car's motor sputtered to life, and Sarah exhaled a sigh of relief.

She peered into every darkened car as she drove out of her townhouse parking lot, looking for someone—anyone—who didn't belong. She checked her rearview mirror as she drove, and she punched a number on her speed dial list.

"Hey," she said, "is it too late for you to keep me company?"

Sarah listened for an answer, then replied, "No, not my place. I'm on my way to yours. I'll be there in ten minutes."

Then, she pushed another speed dial number and waited through the answering machine message. "Hi," she said, "I need your help. Tomorrow. I'll see you tomorrow. Late."

12

Sarah stared at the pink Post-It note. It made no sense; it appeared as nothing more than a jumble of scribbles, child-drawn pictures, and a fraction. Sarah knew Dr. Logan better than to think they were random scrawls. It was code for something. Dr. Logan knew she would figure it out. Sarah knew their lives depended on it.

"What do you make of it?" Sarah asked the gray-haired man with a ponytail hunched over the engine compartment of the late '60s muscle car. She sat on a grimy wooden ledge in a garage behind a brick bungalow built in the 1950s in Southgate, a Detroit suburb. The man's given name was Walter but his closest friends called him Tuffy. He'd earned the nickname on the streets of Lincoln Park as a teenager and cemented it for life fighting on Hamburger Hill in Vietnam. After he came home from Nam, he spent the better part of forty years in Ford's River Rouge Plant in Dearborn making Ford trucks.

"Not sure yet."

"I've run every algorithm I can think of."

"Algorithms, huh?" Walter—Tuffy—tapped the head of a ball peen hammer against the alternator, nudging it into place. His teeth were clamped down tight on an unlit White Owl cigar stub stuck in his mouth. He stopped lighting them when he got the news from his doctor. Agent Orange and forty years of tobacco had taken their toll. The doctor told him he had eight months to live—tops. That was five years ago.

"Algorithms," he grunted and held out his palm. "Hand me a nine-sixteenths box end."

Sarah reached into the worn toolbox, dug around till she found the 9/16th-inch box-end wrench and placed it in Tuffy's open palm. Her feet still dangled over the side of the workbench just as they had when she was a child, watching her dad work on his latest restoration. Today's project was a black-and-gold 1969 Chevy SS. "Give me the BFH," he ordered and stuck out his palm again.

Sarah remembered being eight years old and asking what a BFH was. "It's a Big f—" Tuffy caught himself. "It's a Big Funny Hammer." She was fifteen when she realized the F didn't stand for 'funny.' Sarah handed him a two-pound sledge, and with two hard whacks, the alternator fell into place.

"There, that oughta' do it." Tuffy handed the BFH back to his daughter.

"It's what I do, okay? I use mathematics to figure things out."

"Well, that's one way. Here, pull back on this pry bar while I tighten 'er down. Be gentle, though, don't yank on it. Just hold it in place. So, you like math problems, story problems, figuring stuff out, right?"

"Yes." Sarah watched her dad's forearms bulge as he bore down on the wrench.

"What if it's not that?"

"What if it's not what?"

"A math problem; maybe it's something you can't figure out with a calculator and a bunch of decimal points."

"Dr. Logan is a scientist. His life is math. He would have known that's how I would find the answer."

"You and everyone else."

"What do you mean?"

"He knew that if he created a code based on mathematics, you would be able to solve it, but so would everybody else. It's what they are expecting."

He punctuated his statement by slamming the broad-striped hood of the Chevy SS down and wiping his shop rag across its metal-flake paint job to remove his fingerprints. He reached deep into a steel cabinet beside his workbench and removed an item wrapped in a clean, dry shop rag, placed it gently beside the spare tire of the SS and closed the trunk.

He turned to Sarah and reached for a wad of wrinkled, scribbled paper in her hand. "Here, give me those notes. You and this Dr. Logan, are you close?" He shuffled through them slowly, studying each of them carefully before moving to the next one.

"If by close you are asking if we confided in one another, then yes, we are close."

"You ever confide in him anything about me?"

"I mentioned, you, yes. I talked about you. I told him that I wish I hadn't moved away, that I wish was able to see you more often, and," Sarah gulped, "that I didn't know how much more time I would have with you."

"Your professor there is one smart boy. He knew how to send everyone else on a goose chase while he sent you right to me."

"How so?"

"You see this?" He pointed to numbers scrawled on the Post-It note.

"Yes, I've tried to make sense of them but they don't fit into any algebraic formula that I know."

"Of course not. He knew they wouldn't."

"Why?"

"Because they are not math. Anybody looking at these, a math geek like you, well, they'd go down the same squirrel trail you did. Your professor knew they would. He knew you would, too, until you couldn't figure it out. He knew, eventually, you'd come to me."

Sarah was baffled. How could two men who'd never met know exactly how she would react under a certain set of circumstances?

"These numbers? I used them all the time in Nam. Logan was smart enough to leave out the symbols. Those would have given the code away. I know where he is."

"Where? Please tell me!"

"You're in danger, honey. Listen," Tuffy choked as he reached into his toolbox. "I got this for you. They call it a burn phone. A burner, something like that. I saw it on TV. I paid cash for it at the Walmart so it can't be traced. At least not until you use it once or twice. Don't even take it out of the blister pack or put the battery in until you need to use it. Then dump it right after you've made your call."

"Dump it?"

"Beating it into pieces with a hammer might work but dropping it in a river is even better. If you don't destroy it, the authorities can ping the number after you've made a call and home in on your location. You might want to buy a couple more to have them handy. Anyway, back to these numbers. Watch what happens when I plug those numbers into my phone's GPS app."

"Holy shit."

"You can say that again."

"Holy shit," Sarah repeated.

Tuffy stuck a drain plug into his garage workroom sink and turned on the water. "Like I said, it wasn't math. They are GPS co-ordinates," Tuffy plugged four different, random GPS codes into the app before he removed the phone's battery, reached for the ball peen hammer and beat the phone into pieces. He dropped the remaining skeleton of a smart phone into the sink filled with water. "There, that oughta' do it."

"You, you just destroyed your phone," Sarah said in amazement.

"Yep, I sure did," Tuffy replied. "But it won't take long before the people chasing you figure out what I did. You need to move fast and stay below the radar. This Logan, he's smart, see? He knew you'd figure it out even if it meant driving all the way to Detroit. If you need me, call me. I don't know what I can do, but I promise, I'll do whatever this ailing body can."

"I know, Dad." Sarah wrapped her arms around her father and held on tight.

Tuffy handed her the keys to the black and gold metal-flake Chevy SS. "Here, take the car. No doubt they have GPS tracking installed on your car by now. This way, they won't see you coming."

"But I haven't let my car out of my sight—"

"Sure you have. Every night it sits in your townhouse parking lot. Tracking devices are small nowadays—the size of a bus token. Once you fell asleep, they tucked it under your bumper or attached it to the frame. They've had a lock on you for days, probably weeks. They know where you've been, the routes you taken, stops you've made, miles per hour. The whole megillah."

"Seems like an invasion of privacy."

"Oh it is. But who's going to stop them? Besides, satellite radio tracks you every day. Cell phones, laptops." Tuffy pointed up toward the ceiling joists. "Even things that fly."

Sarah listened. The low hum of a distant neighbor's lawn mower was all she heard.

"Drone," Tuffy explained. "It's been flying overhead nonstop since you called me and told me you were on your way here. They probably had another one follow you all the way from New Jersey."

Sarah felt her blood turn cold mixed with searing adrenaline spiking down her spine at the same time. She changed the subject.

"How've you been, Daddy? You know—"

"I have good days and bad. The soldiers they dumped that poison on, it just wasn't right. I've lived longer than most. Those of us that are still alive, well, most are feeling the effects now. All types of cancer, liver failure, kidneys shutting down, you name it. We're dying faster than the rest of the population. But, like I said, I have good days and bad. There's only so much they can do. I see Mary every week or so."

"Mary? Who is Mary?" Sarah's face brightened.

"It's what I call the hospital in Ann Arbor. UMCCC—University of Michigan Comprehensive Cancer Center, I think that's what it stands for. It's where I go for treatment. But the name's too long. If I tell people I'm going to the cancer center, they look at me like a sad puppy. I hate being pitied. If I tell them I'm going to see Mary, they react like you did. They think I've got a hot date."

It was Tuffy's turn to change the subject. "Do you remember how to drive a stick?"

"Of course," Sarah rubbed her eyes and stood up straight. In those moments when he wasn't consumed with pain, Tuffy taught Sarah skills most teenage girls never learned.

"No, I mean, do you remember how to *drive* a stick?"

"Yes, I remember," she smiled, recalling days she and her dad drag-raced together, one behind the other reaching speeds of more than 100 miles per hour through the winding roads of southwest Detroit. Sarah turned on the ignition and heard the motor's 400 horses roar to life.

"They might not see me coming but I think they'll hear me!" Sarah yelled.

"Maybe so. Take I-75 South. Hit it hard through the curve south of town. Jump off on Toledo road and cut southwest to US 24. The drone won't be able to keep up with you and if you're weaving through traffic, they might not be able to tail you on the ground."

Sarah's eyes welled as she stepped out of the car, wrapped her arms around her dad, and held him tight. Minutes passed before their eyes cleared and they released their grip.

"I'd better go." Sarah didn't want to go. She wanted to stay wrapped in her father's protective embrace. But she knew he couldn't protect her from the people who were hunting her.

"Do you remember what I taught you?"

Sarah nodded. "Aim small, shoot first."

Tuffy nodded as he held her tightly. "Listen to the hair on the back of your neck. One more thing, I put a couple of things in the trunk you might find useful. Remember, if you need me, you call me. You got that?"

"But what about Mary?"

"She can do without me for a few days if need be."

Sarah rumbled into the southbound lanes of I-75 and quickly merged with the Detroit traffic cruising at 80. She pressed the accelerator to the floor and buried the speedometer, weaving between cars, travel trailers, and semis. She tucked in between two school buses caravanning on a field trip and waited for anyone following her to catch up and fly past her in the left lane. Nobody did. Even though she knew she could outrun the drone, she also knew the drone could go higher and search a fifty-mile radius. She needed to hide till the sun went down.

As she exited I-75 on the Dix Toledo Road exit, she remembered a do-it-yourself car wash was once there. Today, it had been abandoned and left to decay. It was the perfect hiding spot. She slid into one of the vacant bays and, shutting the motor down, she listened for the sound of a drone until darkness settled.

Once it was pitch dark, Sarah coaxed the throaty motor alive, cruised through a nearby neighborhood before returning to Dix Toledo Road, following it to US-24 just like her dad had told her. She'd stay on US-24 till she was south of the Michigan-Ohio state line, avoiding the turnpikes and their license-plate recognition cameras. She'd find a less popular route to head east.

Through the night, she planned her trip, right down to the coordinates the pink Post-It note provided. But what then? What was she looking for? And whom?

It was past midnight when Aedain's ringtone startled her.

"Hey," she answered.

His calm voice steadied her. "Hey," Aedain replied. "I called you twice and I stopped by your place today. You didn't answer the door. Are you okay?"

"I'm okay," Sarah paused, then added, "I just needed to get away for a few days. You know, to do some thinking."

"I get that," Aedain said, pausing before adding, "so, are you back in town now? May I see you?"

Yes, yes, she wanted to see Aedain desperately. But she couldn't. She was 400 miles from Princeton. "No, I'm in... umm... Charlotte."

"Charlotte? You're in North Carolina?"

"Yes, North Carolina. I'm passing through it right now," Sarah said as she passed under a sign, 'Welcome to Pennsylvania.'

"What made you decide to drive to North Carolina?"

"I was in Georgia, actually. I'm on the way back now. Just needed to clear my head and a road trip sometimes helps."

"Did your muffler go bad?"

"I think so. It's been really loud for that last couple hundred miles. I'll take it into the shop when I'm back in town. Honestly, it's a little hard to hear you right now. May I call you when I'm back in Princeton? After I've had some sleep?"

"Sure," Aedain replied, "of course."

Sarah wished she could listen to his voice as she drove through the night. It just wasn't possible right now. "Goodnight, Aedain. Sleep well."

"Stay safe out there."

She'd only known Aedain for only a month but she felt close to him—closer than any man besides her dad. Right now, though, she didn't have the energy to explain why she was 400 miles from home and 500 miles from where she told Aedain she was. Aedain would ask why her dad would know how to help her. She wasn't ready to tell Tuffy's story.

She ruminated on her father's words as she rolled through the night: "What if it's not a math problem?"

Sarah flicked on the overhead light and rifled through the mess of papers on the passenger seat beside her. Sarah found the picture of Dr. Logan, Beth, Lisa, Lucy, and Lucy's doll. She recalled happier times. The girls were patient with her, teaching her how to sign—first one letter at a time, then phrases. Lucy would sign and Lisa would translate as the three of them sat on the floor in the girls' upstairs bedroom.

Before long, Sarah was fluent with her letters but sometimes faltered with phrases or uncommon words. Her favorite phrase was 'I love you.' Sometimes she substituted 'I love you' whenever she didn't know the right answer.

"No!" Lisa would giggle, "That's not the sign for 'Oz,' this is! I showed it to you yesterday! Do you remember Lucy doll's name? I'll give you a hint: her name is the color of her shoes."

Sarah's hands froze to the steering wheel for a moment, then pounded the wheel gleefully with both hands.

"Ruby!" The photograph in Dr. Logan's secret papers had meaning—nothing was there by chance. "Ruby!" she shouted in triumph. Her elation ebbed as she paused and mumbled, "Ruby what? Or Ruby who?"

She knew what she had to do. She hoped Aedain would understand. Someday, maybe he would. Whether he did or not, though, wouldn't change her course now.

Sarah rolled down her passenger window and threw her cell phone over the side of the bridge over the West Branch of The Susquehanna River, just before catching the exit for southbound I-180. She'd be in Harrisburg by morning.

New Orleans was a hard 24 hours away.

13

More than a day later, the Chevy's dashboard clock displayed 2:00 a.m. when Sarah rolled into the Mobile Regional Airport. She looked in both directions before lifting the spare tire. A thick roll of hundred-dollar bills rested beside a .40 caliber semi-automatic Glock, wrapped in a clean, dry cloth. For now, she'd leave the gun and most of the money in the trunk.

She left the car in the airport's long-term parking lot, then boarded a Greyhound bus to New Orleans' Loyola Street Station.

Once she reached New Orleans, she dug into her backpack and pulled out the tattered, bloodstained envelope. She stuffed it into the terminal locker along with the Trac Phone and a few hundred-dollar bills. She shoved the Post-It note into her pocket; she would need it later. The French Quarter—the center of New Orleans' tourism—was a short hike across Poydras Street from the station.

That was the last thing she remembered—crossing Poydras and searching the Quarter for Ruby. She had no idea how much time had passed since she met the Tarot Card reader on the corner of St. Anne and Bourbon Street. She was still groggy from the tranquilizer jabbed into her neck.

Drifting in and out of consciousness, Sarah strained to hear voices nearby. One sounded like Queen Esther, the voodoo priest-ess, and the other, a man's voice she didn't recognize. Registering only pieces of the conversation, she didn't understand why these two people were talking about her as if she was unconscious. She could hear them. Didn't they know that?

"Of course she's clean," the priestess asserted. "You think I'm so dumb that wasn't the first thing I checked? No bugs, cell phone, GPS—"

"Wait. What? No cell phone?" the male voice interrupted. "I've never seen a millennial without a cell phone. Are you sure she's who she says she is?"

"Pretty sure. She fits the description Logan gave about some-body who might come looking for him," Queen Esther said. Sarah felt cool metal brushing over her bare arm. "The scanner says she doesn't have any transmitters on her. She's startin' to rustle. You better go."

Sarah struggled to open her eyes in time to catch a glimpse of the strange man before he left. Inside her brain, she screamed, "Open!" but her eyelids refused to obey. Come to think of it, she couldn't hear her own voice, either.

"But I—" the man halted.

"Go! Now!" the black-skinned Jamaican woman pointed to the door. "Make sure you're not followed. And don't let on you was here, you understand? To *nobody*, you hear me? Not this girl, not Logan, nobody, you got that?" It was clear from Queen Esther's tone who was boss and the male voice stopped talking before Sarah heard a door slamming.

"Where am I?" Sarah made out the blurred image of Queen Esther's blue muumuu sitting in a rocking chair across the room.

"You at my place, child," the priestess explained, "sorry about that needle in your neck. I couldn't let you know where I live or how to get here. For my own safety, you understand."

"No, I don't understand," Sarah replied, "I don't understand any of this. I don't understand why people are hunting Dr. Logan and me, I don't understand why they killed his wife and daughters, and I sure as hell don't understand why you led me here and drugged me. No, I don't understand."

"There are people. Like you said, people who want you and Dr. Logan dead. Forever silenced. But they's also people who want to keep you and the professor alive. The bad ones catch you first, and they'll be sure to pay me a visit after they done with you and Logan. They'll torture you before they kill you; make you tell them everything they want to know—like where I live. Cain't take that chance." The rocking chair squeaked each time it reached the midpoint of its cycle. "You hungry?"

"No! I'm not hungry! I want answers! I want to find Ruby and Dr. Logan!" Sarah was sitting up, trying to stand, but her legs weren't listening to her brain.

"Yeah, you hungry, child. I'll put up a pot of coffee and fry you up some beignets." Queen Esther rose from the creaking chair and thumped her way across the two-room apartment to the cupboard. She huffed as she worked her way around the kitchen, melting lard into a cast iron pan and assembling a tin, drip-style coffee pot.

Sarah had managed to make it to her feet but she was still woozy. She tried to gain her equilibrium before attempting to navigate the room.

Panting, the voodoo priestess motioned to the kitchen table covered by a red-and-white plastic tablecloth, "Sit. Sit yo'self-down. We gonna' stay here till nighttime. Get comfy."

Sarah could hear the sound of her own blood pumping through her body. She didn't ignore the Queen's instructions to sit down; she simply couldn't follow them. She stood paralyzed beside the couch.

Tears welled up and blurred her vision as Sarah watched Queen Esther lift a yellow can from her kitchen shelf. She measured chicory coffee into the tin percolator and stirred the beignet batter. Sarah had learned to trust no one and pay heed to the hair on her neck. So far, the plan had kept her alive. Now, despite her neck hair screaming danger, she was standing in the living room of a street hustler with nobody else to trust.

Sarah had felt scared before—just never *this* scared. Suddenly, a blast of cold wind swirled through the living room, peeling doilies off the Victorian couch and knocking a vase of plastic flowers onto the floor.

"Sweet Jesus!" the priestess exclaimed, "Where did that come from? Close dat window, dear, will you please?"

Sarah leaned over the back of the couch and touched the window frame. "It *is* closed," she reported, retreating clumsily to the center of the room, "and Jesus had nothing to do with it."

"Well, mercy, me. I cain't imagine how that breeze blew through here with de window shut."

"I can." She knew what caused it. It wasn't weather balloons or swamp gas. It was the reason she and Dr. Logan were being hunted.

"Come, sit," Queen Esther patted a chair beside the kitchen table as she rattled on between gulps of air. Every instinct told Sarah not to trust this woman, to run as fast and as far as she could, but she needed the priestess' help. Cautiously, she sat down on the red vinyl and chrome chair at the table.

Queen Esther sucked in air after every sentence, "Two hundred years ago, dis was de slave house for all the white folks what lived around the courtyard here. They's only one window on each floor, and there weren't no air conditioning," she said as she scooped beignets from the hot grease and doused them with powdered sugar, "musta' stank somethin' horrible. That's how it was in the slave days. Weren't no privacy." She placed the pastries and a mug of fresh-brewed chicory coffee on the table in front of Sarah. "These'll

88

warm yo' insides up real good, child." Queen Esther ordered, "Fill your belly."

Sarah wasn't hungry. She sipped from the steaming mug. "Queen Esther, may I ask you a question?"

"Ruby," she interrupted, "call me Ruby. Queen Esther is my street name. My friends call me Ruby."

"But I—you told me—" Sarah recalled their exchange on the street.

"No, I din't tell you nuthin'. I aksed you what da sign say. You bin callin' me Queen Esther ever since."

"So, you *are* Ruby. The Ruby that Dr. Logan knows. The Ruby he told me to look up, is that right?"

"Might be you could say that."

"So, if your friends call you Ruby and Dr. Logan calls you Ruby, then you must be his friend?" Sarah probed.

Ruby didn't answer.

"And you're asking me to call you Ruby, so I'm supposed to believe I'm your friend, too?"

"You kin believe as you like."

"How did you know my name?"

Ruby held her finger to her lips and leaned close to Sarah's ear, pointed toward the ceiling, and whispered in perfect English, "Shhh, be quiet. We don't know who is listening in. Dr. Logan said you would come looking for him. He said that if you did, the world is in a lot bigger trouble than anybody is letting on. He told me what you look like and to keep a lookout for you."

Sarah, "So you *do* know Dr. Logan?"

"I never said I didn't."

Sarah leaned forward eagerly, "Can you take me to him? Where is he?"

Resuming her conversation in street dialect, Ruby explained, "I din't know you wuz *lookin'* for the professor. I jes' thought he sent you to me for a Tarot reading. Don't have no idea what the professor has got hisself to."

"I see," Sarah continued softly, "I thought you might know where I could find him. I'm sorry if I was wrong. My apologies."

"Don't have no clue," Ruby's eyes sparkled as she looked again at the ceiling, then sat down across from Sarah. "You got business with the professor?"

"I suppose not," Sarah followed Ruby's lead. She'd been on the run for more than a week now and suddenly, she was feeling its effects.

"Have you ever seen a Carnival parade, child?"

"No," Sarah replied drowsily. She didn't care about Carnival, or Mardi Gras, or Bourbon Street, or voodoo. She just wanted to be at home, in her own bed.

"Well, it's high time you did," Ruby clattered about the kitchen, washing the cast iron fry pan and wiping the countertop. Ruby pointed at the flour pastries and coffee getting cold, "For now, you finish those beignets. You want more coffee?"

"Thank you, but no," Sarah answered slowly. Her voice was an echo now. Her radar had been on high alert since she left New Jersey for Detroit, and her 24-hour drive from Pennsylvania, and bus ride to New Orleans. Despite just waking up, she fought against falling back to sleep. She was losing.

"How long's it been since you slept?"

"Are we counting the little nap you gave me earlier?" Despite being groggy, Sarah's tone was sharp. She didn't trust Ruby. She wanted her to know it.

"You were only out about an hour," Ruby said as she guided Sarah to the couch beneath the room's only window. She placed the yellow can back on the shelf. Ruby kept the morphine-laced coffee for times like this. "So, not counting the last hour, how long has it been since you got some shuteye?"

"I'm not sure. I stopped in a rest area outside Macon somewhere—slept a half hour maybe—I don't know." Her brain wasn't working now. She would sleep. Just a nap. She would sleep for just a minute.

Ruby sat back in her rocking chair, reached under her loose dress, pulled out a ringing cell phone, and accepted the call. The caller asked, "Is she with you?"

"Yes. She's with me. What is it you want?" Ruby's street accent had again disappeared. "No, she has no phone, no tablet, GPS, nothing. No transmitters." She paused before saying, "Fine. Tomorrow then." She listened for a moment before responding sternly, "I told you I will bring her to you tomorrow, and that's what I am going to do. Take it or leave it." Ruby jabbed the end-call button and threw the phone onto the oval side table next to her armchair. She knew she had to act fast.

Ruby pulled her computer onto her lap and typed in Sarah's name in the Google search bar. She studied Sarah's Facebook page and Instagram photos. Ten days had passed since Sarah had posted anything. It was clear that Sarah had begun eliminating her digital footprint weeks ago.

Ruby rocked slowly in the chair until daylight disappeared. Only the glow of the television lighted the dark room when Ruby gently shook Sarah awake.

"C'mon, child, time to go."

Disoriented from the opioid, Sarah felt another adrenaline rush as she struggled to gain her wits. "How long have I been sleeping?" Nowadays, she always awoke terrified that something terrible had happened while she was sleeping. Usually, she was right.

"That don't matter. What matters is, it is time for you to go with me. They saw us both earlier. Got to change outa' these clothes." Ruby handed Sarah a purple plantation dress and Mardi Gras mask made of purple sequins and feathers. "Put these on. We gonna' blend right in with the folks struttin' down Bourbon Street." Ruby slipped on a larger, turquoise version of the same dress and matching mask.

Ruby led her into the residence's only bedroom and slid open a back closet shelf, opening a gap in the wall leading into a tunnel.

"Let me guess," Sarah muttered. "Underground Railroad."

Ruby nodded. "Back in Civil War times, some white folks were slave sympathizers. Made tunnels like this so black folks could escape to the North. If ennybody'd caught 'em, they'da been strung up from the nearest tree." Ruby stopped and held Sarah's arm to reassure her, "We walk out my front door where we came in, ennybody been followin' us pick right up again. Dis way, you and me, we gonna slip out into the street and act like we's jes' part o' de parade, you got that?"

Sarah nodded; she understood. Sarah wasn't very good at trusting strangers, especially doing so might get her killed. She didn't like not being in complete control of her faculties. Her mouth was dry and an incessant ringing in her ears was annoying.

Ruby and Sarah followed the throng of revelers through the Quarter, passing Preservation Hall as they worked their way toward Jackson Square.

Without warning, Ruby body-checked Sarah into the dark alley behind St. Louis Cathedral. She pushed her into the shadows and tightly up against a heavy oak door. Sarah struggled but Ruby pressed her body's full weight against her. Ruby knocked on the door twice with a tarnished brass knocker, paused, then knocked three more times.

Where had she gone wrong? Sarah was frantic as she wrestled to free herself. Her mind raced and she couldn't breathe. She had followed Dr. Logan's instructions to the letter but now was being kidnapped by a woman Dr. Logan trusted.

91

As she opened her mouth to scream, the door opened a crack. Ruby elbowed it open wider and shoved Sarah inside.

Sarah felt the sting of another needle being jabbed into her neck. Her head throbbed as she began to lose consciousness again.

"You gotta be kidding," Sarah slurred as she faded to black, "not again."

14

Staring out the bay window, the silhouette of the portly man from the limousine didn't move. Those nearby stood silent, one in particular twitching nervously.

"You lost him," the portly man spoke. "Tremendous. You're supposed to be the experts. You can read a license plate from outer space but you can't find a college teacher?"

"Professor, sir," the twitching subordinate corrected. His hair was white. One would assume he was prematurely grey unless one understood how many years he'd worked for the portly man.

Slowly, the silhouette turned and stared hard at the man bold enough to speak.

"You think this is funny? Is that it? This is some kind of joke to you?" The thick man didn't raise his voice. He didn't need to. All of those in the room knew the danger he posed. They had witnessed his ruthlessness before. More accurately, they had witnessed what his ruthlessness had wreaked; his fingerprints were never left behind. He hired people for that sort of thing. At one time or another, each one in the room had done his dirty work. They knew, if he went down, he'd take all of them down with him. Those who were still breathing.

"Where's the girl?" he asked, turning back to stare across a garden of roses.

"The girl, sir?" the twitching one asked. The silhouette turned slowly back to glare at the man whose mild twitching now bordered on an epileptic seizure.

"The girl," he repeated, "tallish, dark hair, attractive—"

"She is—the last time we saw her—there was—we had a drone, sir—it was in the air, sir—"

"Isn't that where drones are supposed to be?" The thick man's voice dripped with sarcasm.

"Yes, sir, of course, sir," twitchy man continued. "The drone—there were actually several drones, sir—you see, we had to recharge them, sir—"

"Stop!" The silhouette held up his hand. "I don't care how many drones you used. I don't care how many batteries you charged. I want to know one thing. Just one thing, where is the girl?"

"Umm, well, sir, that's just it. We're not exactly sure, sir."

"You've lost her, too, is that what you are telling me?"

"As a matter of fact, yes, sir."

"Did you run out of batteries? Is that it? Is that your excuse? Please tell me we can afford drone batteries. How are our flashlights? Do we still use flashlights? You know, those things we use to see at night? Do we buy batteries for them or must we recharge them, too?"

"Yes, sir. We still use flashlights, sir." The man's convulsions paused for a moment before he realized the man was still staring at him. "Drone batteries. Yes, sir, we had—we now have—plenty of drone batteries."

"We don't know where she is, sir," a second voice interrupted. His body was still but his voice cracked in mid-sentence. "She disappeared. She went off the grid, sir."

"Off the grid. Off the grid," the thick man repeated, "I keep hearing those words. Like that should mean something to me, as if it is a legitimate reason that you can't find her. You see, back in my day, there was no 'grid.' There were no cyber footprints, no internet trails. Why? Because there was no internet. You see how that works? You're telling me she can disappear because she went 'off the grid'?"

Eight terrified people in the room—seven men and one woman—all spoke at once: "No, sir, that's not what I mean, we'll find her, sir, we promise, rest assured, sir."

"Rest assured," the man turned to stare out the window again. "That's an odd phrase, don't you think? Have you ever thought of that? Any of you? Have you? Do you really think, under the current circumstances, that I should 'rest assured'?"

A jumble of replies blurred "Yes, sir, no, sir, and I suppose not, sir" into an unintelligible babble.

"You see," the man went on, "to rest—that is, to experience a truly peaceful, rejuvenating repose—one must feel assured. Safe, you might say. Don't you agree? Think of it this way, if you think a knife will be plunged into your back at any moment, are you really able to get fitful sleep?" The thick man clasped his hands behind his back and rocked on his heels as he waited for an answer.

"I guess I never thought of it that way, sir," replied the one who earlier had chosen his words poorly.

"No, I imagine not," the man agreed. "But it is time you do. I will not rest—assured or otherwise—until we have them both. Neither should you. To do so could be a fatal mistake."

"I—we—understand, sir," the twitchy one muttered as he began to back out of the room.

"I hope you do."

"Sir, if I may ask, sir," the cracking voice spoke. "When you say you want us to bring them both to you, do you mean as in, here, *alive* so we can question them?"

"Alive?" the man replied. "Not necessarily."

15

Sarah was dreaming she was awake. Or she was dreaming that she was dreaming she was awake—she couldn't be sure. The smells, however, were real. Nauseatingly real.

Why, if she was awake, was her world completely black? She reached for her face to remove the blindfold she assumed covering her eyes but her hands met nothing but sweaty skin. She opened her eyes as wide as possible. Still, there was nothing to see.

Am I blind? she wondered. What had happened to her after Ruby pushed her into the cathedral? *Why would someone blind me? Why would they do that?* Her bloodstream felt the shock of more adrenaline. She was being fueled by self-pity and terror.

It stank. Wherever they had left her, the air was filled with an olfactory cocktail of rotting fish, diesel fuel, and sweet incense. Not the kind people burned to cover up the smell of smoking weed but more like incense Catholics used for funerals. The odor triggered the memory of her mother's funeral twenty years earlier and Dr. Logan's family only months ago.

She focused on what her other senses told her. The rotting fish caused her to gag and the taste of diesel fuel hanging in the air settled thick on her tongue. Croaking like giant frogs, river tugs' horns talked to one another as barge captains plied their way through The Big Easy. Heavy chains rattled against metal, and whirring motors hinted she was near the Port of New Orleans.

Then, the terrifying thought hit her. She may not be in New Orleans at all. She may have been kidnapped for the international sex slave trade. She could be anywhere.

Sarah prayed she was still in New Orleans, close to where shrimp boats, tugboats, and ocean freighters docked.

Relieved when she heard a radio in the distance, she heard what sounded like a talk show; two people having a conversation.

Her head throbbed. She wanted the talk show to stop but knew that as long as she still heard it, people may be nearby. The way things had gone so far, people being nearby may not a good thing. Right now, she was still too drugged to care or do anything about it.

The radio's volume grew. There were two voices, possibly three. They were arguing. Eventually, her addled brain realized the sounds were not from a radio but the voices of people coming toward her. Panicked, she again felt the burn in her arteries again. She was wide awake now. She was sure of it, even though she couldn't see.

She tried to sit up but slammed the top of her skull against the wooden railing above her. Stars sparkled in her brain and she yelped with pain as she fell back onto the pillow.

Sarah fought back tears as the lump on her head grew. "Shit!" she shouted. Where is she?

The radio people were close enough now to make out two voices. She recognized Ruby's. The second was that of the nervous man who had visited Ruby's townhouse while Sarah was semi-conscious. She listened for the third voice to speak again.

"Hush your mouth!" Ruby barked. "How about before you get bat-nasty crazy, we find out if she's still alive? The juice you put in that hypodermic was twice what she should have had, the little slip of a thing that she is and all. It's by the Grace of God she's not dead."

All along, Ruby was in on the plan to kidnap her; that much was clear. Sarah was disappointed but not surprised.

The door to Sarah's hell opened slowly. Gradually, the darkness turned to dim light and her eyes fought to adjust.

"You okay, child?" Ruby's voice dripped with a lilt of Southern charm and Jamaican rhythm.

"Don't give me that crap! Who the hell are you? What the hell did you do to me?" Sarah charged at the woman who was three times her size. Still woozy, she slammed into Ruby's cushy frame before trying to escape around her. Ruby's shadow filled the doorway. Sarah had no chance to get past.

"You're fine, Sarah. We've just got to be careful, you understand? We needed to be sure you weren't followed, you understand? You're safe now."

Now Sarah could see that the room she was in was small.

"Where am I?" Sarah stumbled back to the bottom bunk of the bed. Unlike the cathedral, a well-maintained tourist attraction, this place was dingy and smelled like fermenting seafood. Sarah guessed her captors had carried her through the secret passageways of the French Quarter.

As her pupils adjusted to the dim light, Sarah could make out the craggy face and warm smile of a willowy, aging priest. The waist of his black cassock was wrapped in a fuchsia-colored cincture. The tails of the cincture hung neatly down the front of the cassock.

"A Bishop," Sarah recognized his regalia. "The Archbishop of the New Orleans Diocese? *How is he involved in this?* Sarah wondered. She had no idea how long she'd been unconscious.

From behind the bishop, the third voice spoke gently. "Are you okay, Sarah?"

Sarah's immediate feeling of relief gave way to confusion. "Dr. Logan?"

John Logan, PhD in Astrophysics and former Princeton professor, moved between Ruby and the bishop and walked directly to Sarah.

"I'm sorry, Sarah. They had to do that. They were just being careful. People are trying to kill you. And me."

Ruby leaned close to the Archbishop's ear and whispered, "Is he sober?"

"More or less." The Bishop beckoned Logan and Sarah, "Come. Come, follow me, please." He led them through the dark sacristy and motioned toward the pew facing the church's marble altar.

"Blessed Sacrament Church has been closed since Hurricane Katrina," the Bishop apologized, "the flood waters damaged much of the sanctuary and the diocese didn't have the money to repair it. Only a handful of the congregation returned to the neighborhood so we saw no cause to re-open it." He held out his hand toward Sarah, "I'm Archbishop Joseph O'Donnell, by the way. My friends call me Bishop Joe."

"I'm not your friend," Sarah fired back.

"Bishop Joe gave me a place to hide, Sarah," Dr. Logan interjected. He grabbed the shop rag sticking out of his back pocket and wiped the pew to clean a spot for the two of them to sit. Dressed in a faded blue work uniform, Dr. Logan's once plump, reddish cheeks were hollow. His complexion was pale. It was obvious he had seen no sunlight in the past several months.

Ruby and the Bishop gave the two some space to talk privately, moving across the altar to the marble fountain where generations of babies had been baptized.

"Come, sit down," he patted the oak pew beside him, "call me Tom, Sarah. It's best nobody knows me as anything other than a church janitor named Tom."

"A janitor? For a church that doesn't have any parishioners?"

"The Bishop took me in. He put a bed in the closet off the organ room and gave me a roof over my head. When there's enough daylight coming through the windows, I mop the floors and wash the windows. I never get through with the dusting, though. When the sun goes down, I stay in the organ room closet with the door closed, and I light a candle for reading or doing my calculations. I can't take the risk somebody might see light coming from the church and start asking questions. The Bishop gives me a few dollars out of the collection plate at the Basilica on Sunday to pay for toothpaste and a couple bottles of Bourbon."

"I'm sorry," Sarah touched her mentor's hand. Pain pierced her heart, remembering how he was once a lively, gregarious man who easily, naturally, drew people to him. Now, he was a decaying prisoner in a decaying church.

"I'm surprised you were able to find me," Dr. Logan said, "or that you bothered, considering the circumstances."

"The circumstances?"

"Me disappearing. Not saying goodbye. Not trusting anyone. It was for your own good."

"With all due respect, Doctor Logan, that's a load of horse dung. Do you really believe that not telling me made it better for me? Not knowing if someone had slit your throat or dumped you in a wood chipper? You think it stopped anyone from following me just like they'd been following you? I was in just as much danger as you were—as much danger as we both are in now."

"Still, you went looking for the package I showed you in the basement." Dr. Logan observed. "You even went to the house with your friend but the Feds were already swarming the place."

"How did you know that? How? Where were you?"

"Across the street in the attic. The neighbors were gone for the week. I watched the whole thing. It was pretty crazy, wasn't it?"

"You sonofabitch! You watched me? My guts were retching and you've got a ringside seat to your own disappearance? You sonofabitch!"

"I'm sorry. I didn't think of it that way."

"No! You didn't think at all! You have no idea, do you? The agony I went through."

"I'm sorry. It didn't turn out the way I planned. I got a phone call—I didn't recognize the voice—but it told me to run for my life *now!* I left without grabbing so much as a sweater. I ran to my neighbor's garage to borrow his car. I heard a loud thud, looked out the garage window and saw two armed men kick open my sunroom door. When I heard sirens coming from every direction, I knew they were headed to my house. Whoever called me probably called the cops. I don't know who or why they did it, but that phone call saved my life. If I hadn't run before the killers showed up, the police would have found my bloody corpse. I climbed into my neighbor's attic and watched as the local police and the Feds argued with one another about who had jurisdiction over a murder which never happened. When the locals drove off, I figured the Feds won the debate. It was obvious I hadn't been murdered, but I might have been kidnapped. So the Feds claimed jurisdiction."

"Did the cops catch the killers?"

"No, of course not. Their getaway driveways kept their car running in the alley. As soon as they heard sirens, they were gone."

Sarah crossed her arms. She staring curiously toward the baptismal font. She watched Ruby's and the Archbishop's interaction, the way they talked to one another. Observing people was more than a hobby; it helped Sarah survive. Several minutes passed before she was calm enough to ask, "How'd you get into my townhouse? And why did you put the brass plate under my pillow?"

"I didn't. I knew Mr. Landon, your neighbor, had a key to your place. You told everyone he loves your grandma's chocolate brownies. So I bought some chocolate brownies for him and told him it was important that you get that brass plate; it was part of a homework assignment. I told him to promise to put it somewhere you couldn't miss it." Logan paused. "So, he put it under your pillow, did he? Well, I guess that worked."

"You need to say a crap load of Hail Mary's for that one, Buster."

Dr. John Logan—Tom the Janitor—faced the altar as his eyes now shifted to watch the Bishop and Ruby talking by the baptismal font. Occasionally, the two glanced toward Sarah and the professor.

Sarah's eyes followed her professor's, her head rigid. She would ask Dr. Logan about it later—if they weren't dead. 'Tom' beat her to it.

"You see anything odd about a Bishop in the Roman Catholic Church being friends with a Voodoo High Priestess?"

Before Sarah could reply, the sanctuary rumbled and creaked, its pews vibrated and the flames from a few votive candles on the altar were extinguished. Sarah and Logan locked eyes on one another. Ruby stared at the Bishop. Bishop Joe turned toward the Crucifix and made the Sign of the Cross.

"That was a—" Sarah began.

"Gravitational anomaly," Logan interrupted.

Sarah struggled to regain her composure; there was no time for distractions like earthquakes inside a musty church. Her eyes focused again on the Bishop and Ruby.

"What are you saying? I thought they are your friends—that they are protecting you."

"It seems that way. But I ask myself why. Why would they protect me? I really don't know either of them very well. There's a missing piece in all of this."

"Do you trust them?"

"No. I trust no one." Logan paused, then added, "When Julius Caesar led his rebels over the Rubicon River and into battle, he knew he was committing treason against the Roman Republic. It was an act of war. He stood in front of his troops and proclaimed, 'We have crossed the Rubicon.' It was his way of saying there was no turning back. There were only two possible outcomes—victory or death."

Sarah was about to ask Dr. Logan if he trusted her when the world erupted.

The explosion was deafening. Thick wooden entry doors at the back of the church were ripped from their hinges and spun as deadly projectiles through the sanctuary of the old church. Acrid smoke smelled of burning plastic and once-blessed debris filled the vestibule. Bishop Joe and Ruby collapsed onto the marble floor.

Dr. Logan yanked Sarah's hand, pulling her into the sacristy behind the altar ahead of shouting voices and beams of light poking through the haze.

"*Da-vai, ee-dyem!*" a voice moving through the smoke shouted. Whatever he was saying sounded urgent.

"Russians!" Dr. Logan confirmed as he opened a cupboard door and pushed her toward it. "Crawl!" he ordered. "Hurry!" He followed her, latching the cupboard door behind him, then squeezing past her shouting, "Follow me!"

Hours before, Ruby had told Sarah about the Underground Railroad. "Slave sympathizers used these passages to smuggle slaves out of the South," Dr. Logan explained as he scrambled through the tunnels and around corners. The tunnel snaked through the bowels of buildings on the fringe of the French Quarter, along Tchoupitoulas Street and into New Orleans' sewer and floodwater system.

Sarah's ears were still ringing from the blast. She could barely hear what Dr. Logan was saying. With her heart pounding, she raced on her knees and hands in pitch darkness. She charged face-first through spider webs and slimy sludge in the nauseating tunnels and municipal sewer. Sarah had heard rumors about alligators and poisonous water moccasins living in the sewers of Detroit and New Jersey; she knew they were far more likely in Louisiana. One way or another, there was a good chance she would die today. Odor from the explosion was nothing compared to the stench of human waste, dead, rotting fish and decomposing garbage. Sarah gagged nonstop until the tunnel opened to thick air along the levy bordering the Mississippi River.

"Stay low. Keep your head down," Dr. Logan grunted between his own retches.

Gulping fresh air, she tried in vain to cleanse her lungs and sinuses. When she'd collected enough air to speak, she asked, "Is Ruby—the Bishop—did they—are they dead?"

"Probably. Maybe. I don't know. Whoever just blew up the church is more interested in killing you and me than them. If the explosion didn't kill them, Ruby and Bishop Joe may still be alive."

"How did they find us?"

"I don't know but that's not important right now. The important thing is to keep moving fast."

"You mean, before they catch us and kill us, right?"

"Exactly. We have crossed the Rubicon, Sarah."

16

"I told you! I said you would lead them right to us, didn't I?" Ruby's face was covered in thick ash with trickles of blood forming red streams through the ash. Ruby had survived the blast healthy enough to curse the Archbishop. "Dammit, Joe, you just had to show up at my house. Just couldn't help your damn old self, could you? They've been following you ever since."

The Archbishop didn't respond. He just lay beside the baptismal font, his right arm twisted unnaturally behind his back, and blood, thickened by grey soot, flowed slowly across his forehead.

"Joe? Bishop Joe? Talk to me, you saggy old man." Ruby reached over to softly caress the priest's face, "Talk to me, you damned old fool."

Despite the ringing in her ears, Ruby heard voices approaching, moving through the cloud of debris. One was the leader. She recognized his voice. It wasn't the first time she and Dmitri had met.

"*Poisk! Poisk vezde!*" She knew enough Russian to know he was telling his troops to fan out, search everywhere. She didn't know how many soldiers were searching the church but she knew the leader was standing in front of her.

The barrel of Dmitri's Russian-made AK-47 was just inches from Ruby's nose.

"Help him, please," Ruby pointed to the unconscious priest. "He's hurt. Please help him."

"*Oh yMep.*" The Russian poked the priest with the muzzle of the AK, probing for any signs of life.

Maybe Dmitri was right; the Bishop certainly looked dead. She wasn't going to argue. She knew if the Bishop wasn't already dead; the Russian would make sure he was. Besides, staring into the business end of an assault rifle, she was helpless to ease the Archbishop's pain.

"*Gde oni?*" Leaning over her, Dmitri pointed the AK at Ruby's face as he spoke.

"Speak English. My Russian's a little rusty."

"Where they go? The Professor and girl?"

"Technically, she's more like a woman…"

The butt end of the gun landed on Ruby's cheekbone with a thud, and she felt an egg swell on her cheek. The Russian pointed the gun at her face once more, then turned and aimed it at the Archbishop's leg. The blast deafened Ruby to the point she almost didn't hear the priest's grunt as the bullet disintegrated his knee. The Archbishop's lower leg remained attached to his upper only by a thick tendon and skin.

He's still alive, Ruby thought, but she knew he wouldn't be for long if the Russian kept shooting off body parts. She knew Dmitri well enough to know that this would be his only warning. The next time, the Russian would put a round through his head.

Dmitri spoke, "You told me you would to bring her to me. We had deal."

"She said she wanted to see a few of the tourist traps in New Orleans before she got carted off to Kissmyassestan."

"You a comedian, yes? We make deal and you take her to Dr. Logan." The Russian pressed the barrel of the assault rifle against Ruby's forehead. "You didn't tell me you knew where Dr. Logan was. You knew the whole time but never mentioned it. I ask myself, 'Why is that so? Why is it you keep secret from me?'"

The Russian pointed his rifle at the Bishop's head. "I end his misery or maybe you can answer some questions."

"What do you want to know?"

"Who is Logan working for? Which government? Or is it somebody else? One of your American billionaires, maybe? Why do the priest and professor know each other? Since I'm asking, why do you know them both?"

"Slow your roll, Nikita. That's a lot of questions in one breath."

"My name is Dmitri. Dmitri Sokolov. You remember it, I'm sure."

"Like the hockey player?"

"Ees common Russian name. You know, like John Smith here in U.S. Are you CIA?"

"You know a lot of voodoo priests working in the CIA, do you?"

"Eet could make a good cover. Same with priest here. Is he really a priest?"

"Bishop?" Ruby touched the priest's shoulder, trying to nudge him conscious. "Bishop Joe? Can you hear me? Dr. Logan. Who is he working for? Is he working for the United States or some other government? The Chinese, maybe? Or North Koreans?"

The Russian's eyes bulged at the possibility that Logan was working for the Chinese or, worse yet, the North Koreans.

"Iran." It was all the priest could mumble before passing out again.

Damn old fool, Ruby thought. He had to say 'Iran.' Improvising a story about North Korea would have been much easier.

"Iran. See there? Iran! Now, he told you what you want to know. Just, now, let him die peacefully." Ruby struggled to her knees, breathing heavily.

"Iran?" Dmitri confirmed.

"Iran! Yes, of course, Iran. It makes perfect sense doesn't it? That's why they've been trying to get their hands on weapons-grade plutonium. It's not to build nuclear weapons; no, it's to provide the amount of electricity a massive supercollider requires. See, they figure instead of just powering a supercollider by electricity and magnets, they would create a nuclear-powered one and multiply the supercollider speed, and the energy it creates, tenfold, twentyfold, who knows? That's why NATO and every sane country in the world has been trying to keep them from getting it."

"Iran?" the Russian repeated. "North Korea? They are building supercolliders? How do you know this?" He knew why China would build a supercollider; they needed cheaper fuel for manufacturing.

The Asians are dangerous, Dmitri thought, *but the Iranians are unpredictable.*

"Nikita, have you ever heard of Nikola Tesla? Back in the 1920s and '30s, Nikola Tesla created a weapon he called 'the teleforce.' Others called it the death beam or death ray. The weapon created an electromagnetic field which could destroy anything in the sky—a rocket, a jet fighter, a weaponized drone—by aiming its particle beam at the incoming object. Even objects 250 miles away. Tesla's invention is what Ronald Reagan based his Strategic Defense Initiative—Star Wars, remember?—and it is the same technology the U.S. Navy presently uses in its Laser Weapons System. Hell, Nikita, the Israelis tested their version of this weapon in 2003. You need to read more, Niki."

"My name is Dmitri," the Russian growled. "Thees ees for comic book, thees talk. Ees nonsense." Secretly, Dmitri knew it made sense. If North Korea built a supercollider, the electromagnetic energy it could generate would create an impenetrable defense against any nation attempting to invade the country.

More importantly, considering the power of a supercollider, the range of the theoretical death ray's magnetic beam would increase exponentially.

"North Korea could blast a jumbo jet filled with passengers out of the sky halfway between Los Angeles and Tokyo. Or between Moscow and Beijing," Ruby conjured.

Dmitri rubbed his jaw as he pondered the consequences. If Ruby was telling the truth and Iran built a supercollider, Iran would strengthen its position as one of the most powerful players in the world energy game. Not only would Iran continue as a major force in the global fossil fuel supply but they would position themselves in the business of proton-based nuclear power as well. Plus, Iran could develop an electro-magnetic death ray of its own. *North Korea wants to destroy the U.S.A.,* Dmitri contemplated, *but Iranians want the global destruction of infidels.* Most of the world, including Russia, is inhabited by infidels. Ruby needed a diversion; some way to persuade Dmitri to take her away from Bishop Joe so he didn't kill the old man.

"Hey, Nikita, are your ears ringing, too? It's kinda hard to hear anything when your ears are ringing, isn't it? I'll say it one more time. Two syllables: 'I-damn-ran.'"

"Ees three syllables how you say it. I tell you once more, my name is Dmitri. You Americans show no respect."

"Dmitri Suck... something. Got it."

"Sokolov. Dmitri Sokolov."

Ruby watched Dmitri's face redden. "Dmitri, do you remember when Obama paid $400 million to Iran?" Ruby asked. "Some said it was ransom for the release of U.S. prisoners and others said it was a settlement going back to the Iran Hostage Crisis. Neither one made a whole lot of sense but did you notice the nightly news didn't mention that the actual amount was $1.7 billion? Are you following me? The $400 million figure was all over the news but the real amount was more than four times that amount. Does that make sense to you?" Ruby crawled across the ash-covered floor and pulled herself up into a pew.

"*Nyet.*"

"Both governments said it was the original $400 million for the money the U.S. owed Iran back in 1979, plus additional interest of $1.3 billion. The way I figure it, that's about 10% interest per year, compounded annually. Now, doesn't that seem a little convenient to you? Can you tell me any bank account you could get 10% on your money guaranteed for the past forty years? Oh, c'mon, Nikita, even you ought to be able to figure out that payoff wasn't about the Hostage Crisis or paying ransom for prisoners."

"My name is Dmitri." Dmitri reared back with the butt of his gun again. One gun butt to the face per day was enough for Ruby.

"Right. I forget. My apologies. You see, we Americans, we are capitalists first and foremost. We like a good investment but we also like to hedge our bets. What better way to protect our interests in the Middle East than to invest in an extra-strength supercollider right smack-dab in the Iranian desert? You know, right in Mother Russia's backyard?"

"Dirmo!"

"'Shit' is right! But that $1.7 billion is just a down payment. They figure they'll need at least another six or seven billion, maybe more, what with the overruns and all. You know Americans. They never finish anything under budget."

"The Americans are building a supercollider in Iran? That would mean the Americans and Iranians are allies, not enemies." Ruby watched Dmitri's face contort with confusion.

"Well, Nikita," Ruby laughed, "you just never really know who your friends are, do you? I mean, look at you and me. I thought we were tight. Then you come in, blowing shit up and smacking me in the face with the butt of your gun—"

"Zat-knis'! Shut up! My name is Dmitri. You will call me by my name or I will shoot you in your head." The Russian aimed his AK-47 at Ruby's head.

"You shoot me, and you'll be dead within twenty four hours. Your handler wants you to bring me in alive." Ruby looked at the unconscious priest. His breathing was shallow and labored.

"You see, N—Dmitri." Ruby spun her tale, buying as much time as she could get before the Russian turned the rifle toward the Bishop's skull. "It looks like the Americans are giving money to Iran, and who knows, maybe helping them build a supercollider there. Think about that, Dmitri. Think about how much money the U.S. owes China. Maybe—now I'm just spit-balling here—the U.S. is cooperating with China on their supercollider plans, too? One thing for sure, it doesn't look like the ol' U.S. of A. is helping Russia build its supercollider, does it?"

"What is this spit-balling you speak of?"

"You know, tossing out ideas, kicking them around. Seeing if two and two add up to four. You with me now?"

"How much do you know about what we are doing in Russia?"

"You tell me, Dmitri. You boys have been hacking our e-mail accounts over here. But those boys and girls trained at CalTech and MIT, they're the best hackers in the world, you know that, don't you? You know that we know everything you're doing in Russia."

"You're a comedian again, yes?"

"Let me put it this way. I heard some buzz about earthmovers digging around west of Moscow. Between Moscow and Minsk. Think about it, Dmitri. Do you have any idea how many satellites the U.S.A. has trained on Russia from outer space? The NSA probably knows whose windows you like peeking in to get your jollies on Saturday night." Ruby baited the Russian.

"You know about the supercollider in Ukraine?" the Russian blurted.

Bingo. "Oh, Dmitri. Nice try, but it's not in Ukraine. It is in Belarus. In Minsk."

"Ees not Minsk!" Dimitri spit his denial. Realizing she knew more than he did, he said quietly, "Could be Minsk. I don't recall." Ruby's fishing paid off. Yesterday, a Russian supercollider in Minsk was nothing more than a rumor.

Dmitri's news wasn't too surprising, though. Every world power was in the supercollider race, ever since Professor Peter Higgs' theory was proven. *But why Belarus, not Russia*? Ruby wondered. Why would the Russians build a supercollider in a neighboring country?

"So Russia is building a supercollider," Ruby pressed. "Why in Belarus?"

Dmitri puffed out his chest. "Because we needed lots of open land. Da' world will see! It will be biggest, most powerful supercollider ever built! Gorbachev started making the plans and confiscating land when we were still the Soviet Union. Soviet Union had thousands of square miles of open land between Minsk and Moscow. So, they put it there." He stopped himself again, "But I won't say where exactly. Ees not Minsk. Maybe eet ees somewhere else. Nobody thought Gorbachev would listen to President Reagan, 'Mr. Gorbachev, take down that wall,' but he did. He was weak. Weak president."

"Reagan?"

"No, Gorbachev."

Ruby let Dmitri keep talking.

"Boris Yeltsin didn't care about it; Yeltsin didn't understand the science. It sat rusting for ten years. When Russia got a strong leader, we started construction again. He is making Russia great again!

When supercollider is complete, Mother Russia will have the most powerful supercollider ever. It will have the power of 12 TeV, *twelve* teraelectronvolts!"

"Well, well, well, my, my, my, Dmitri. That's pretty impressive. Do you even know what a teraelectronvolt is?"

"Big. Very powerful. This is what I know."

"So that's why you need the girl and Dr. Logan. You need to test the professor's theories on your new, big-boy toy, is that about it?"

"*Da*," the Russian shrugged.

"I hate to be the one to tell you the bad news, Dmitri," Ruby twisted a metaphorical knife, "but your powerful leader has been telling you Russkies bedtime stories. The Iranians are way ahead of you. Their supercollider will be half again that capacity. And China has $6 billion budgeted for one that is nearly twice the capacity of the Hadron Collider outside Geneva, the very supercollider which confirmed Professor Higgs' theory of the Higgs boson particle. Just one more little tidbit in case you missed it: they just upgraded the Hadron Collider to 14 TeV. Russia is a lap behind the rest of the countries building supercolliders."

"*Nyet! Lozhnyy!*"

"No, it's not false, Dmitri. It's true." Ruby's creativity had nearly run dry when rapid-fire explosions from automatic weapons erupted in the rear foyer of the abandoned church. A gunfight in the church sacristy grew steadily closer to the sanctuary.

"Get up! Come with me! *Ckopee!*"

"Hurry up?" Ruby struggled to her feet. "You want me to hurry the hell up? You come in here, blow the place up, start shooting people in their kneecaps and shit, and I'm supposed to hurry up? You go on now, you in such a big-assed hurry. I'll catch up with you. I'll be right behind your Russki ass."

"*Zat-knis!*" Dmitri grabbed Ruby's arm and tried to pull her toward the street, forgetting the size of this voodoo priestess. She yanked her arm away, straightened her shoulders, and dusted off her turquoise plantation dress as her weight pounded down the aisle.

"Give me just a damn minute! Tell me to shut the hell up. We're in America now! I got my First Amendment rights! Shut up, you say? How about this? *Pa-shol na-rooy!*"

Dmitri nudged her with his rifle, urging her to move faster. "Your Russian ees not so rusty as you say. What you suggest, however, I think it is not physically possible for me to do."

"That's okay. We'll find you a nice American prison. I know some people be happy to help you with that."

Dmitri pushed Ruby into the back seat of a waiting SUV, then scrambled into the front passenger seat, shouting, "Go! Go! *Cko-pee!*"

Inside the church, the guns went silent as six soldiers in black nylon uniforms and Kevlar-reinforced gear surrounded the Archbishop.

"Ruby?" the Archbishop groaned. The medic of the squad knelt beside the Archbishop, squeezed a dose of morphine into the Archbishop's arm and smelling salts under his nose. Another squad member tightened a tourniquet around the Bishop's leg. They couldn't save the leg; they knew that. They had to settle for saving his life.

"No, sir. British Foreign Intelligence Service, sir. At your service."

"MI-6?" The Archbishop grimaced as they lifted him onto a stretcher.

"We've been called that, yes, sir."

"You're conducting operations in the United States?" Bishop Joe was dazed, falling in and out of consciousness.

"Well, yes, sir. Always wanted to visit the States. Thought we might like to do a bit of sightseeing here in the Crescent City, you might say. Joint operation, really, with the Yanks." The soldiers loaded the Archbishop into an ambulance without a siren or emergency markings. It was black as a coroner's hearse on the outside but, inside, it was loaded with state-of-the-art emergency medical equipment.

"Sight-seeing. You see any Russians in your sight-seeing so far?"

"As a matter of fact, we did, sir. Chaps seemed a tad unfriendly, they did."

"Unfriendly?"

"Yes, sir. Quite."

"Where's Ruby?"

"Sokolov and his driver got away. They took her."

"Find her before they make her talk."

"Yes, sir. I know, sir. Come, let's get you to a hospital."

"Thank you." The Archbishop peered at his name badge and rank. "Maycroft. Well, Commander Maycroft, are any of the other quite unfriendly Russians still alive?"

"No, sir."

"I suspected as much." The Bishop paused, then asked, "Maycroft. That's Irish, isn't it?"

"Yes, sir. My family hails from County Kilkenny."

Bishop Joe exclaimed, "Lord in heaven! An Irish lad working for Her Majesty's Secret Service, running a covert operation in the United States, killing Russians in the House of the Lord. The world is coming to an end after all, isn't it?"

"Not if we can help it, sir."

17

Passing Tulane's campus, Ruby yelled from the back seat, "Hey, Dmitri, if you're taking me to a party or somethin', could you get me a pretty dress and a nice up-do? A manicure and a pedi, too, maybe? You think you could arrange that?"

"You like to toy with me, don't you, Ruby?" Dmitri snarled. "You make jokes, think this is funny. I promise you, we're not funny."

"Oh, I agree. You not the least damn bit funny. Got no sense o' humor at all. But if we goin' somewheres, chances are they don't want me to get their pretty couch dirty, you see what I'm saying? Leastways, you might want to get me a change of clothes and a shower."

"*Poverni napravo!*" Dmitri ordered the driver to turn right. Passing familiar buildings, Ruby knew they were heading in the direction of the French Quarter. She also knew that Dmitri wasn't the brains of whatever operation was trying to find Dr. Logan and Sarah. She had learned one thing so far: the Russians didn't want the doctor and Sarah dead. They needed both of them for experiments on the supercollider the Russians were building in Belarus.

They no longer needed Ruby; she knew that. For now, all she had was the story about the Iranians she'd woven when she was trying to save the Archbishop's life. Any slip, any inconsistency which made her story less than credible, and she would not see the bullet coming before it shattered her skull.

Two quick turns off Tulane Avenue before they stopped in the alley behind the Hotel Monteleone, a few feet from the employee entrance. Ruby smiled and mumbled, "Oh please, Br'er Fox, don't throw me in dat Briar patch."

"What are you jabbering?" Dmitri didn't really care, he was just tired of Ruby's incessant chatter. He held a walkie-talkie in front of his mouth and spoke Russian. "*Da, ona zdes'.*"

"Yeah, tha's right. We all here. Right here. What you gonna' do now? Ah'm all bloody and dirty an' you got me here."

"*Zat-knis'! Poydem!*" Dmitri yelled as he brandished his pistol.

Ruby understood the first part; it wasn't the first time he'd told her to shut up, and she understood the general meaning of the second part when Dmitri opened her door and motioned her to get out. She stepped down from the SUV, pulled her shoulders back, and strutted proudly through the screened back door of the hotel. Inside, she walked through the hotel kitchen and past the commercial dishwasher, its plumes of steam filling the room. Hidden in his jacket pocket, Dmitri pressed his semi-auto Sig Sauer against her back, propelling her through the room. The driver led the way, talking into the microphone attached to his lapel and opening doors for Dmitri and Ruby.

A skinny black man stood bent over the hotel's expansive stainless steel dishwashing machine, rinsing dishes and placing them on the conveyor racks. He stopped abruptly when he saw Ruby's dust-covered face caked with dried blood.

Ruby stared hard at him, widely opening her pit viper eyes to accentuate her point, "You got an eye problem, mister?"

"No, no, ma'am," the worker jerked his head away and tended to the business of cleaning plates that were accustomed to serving five star recipes, now caked with diners' garbage. He waited until the two Russians and the very large black woman had passed through the kitchen into the service hallway before he straightened.

He dried his hands with a towel and casually reached for the kitchen's house phone on the nearby wall.

"She's here," the dishwasher whispered into the phone. "Yes, Ruby. She's here. She just came through the kitchen at gunpoint. She looked a little beat up. They're getting on the service elevator right now."

Dmitri's driver waited at the service elevator, holding the door open for Dmitri and Ruby.

"*Zalezay!*" Dmitri pushed Ruby into the elevator and made sure he and the driver were the only other passengers.

Dmitri waved the gun at the panel of buttons, pointing toward which one he wanted the driver to push.

"Fifteenth floor? Why are we stopping here? I thought maybe we'd go up to the Sky Deck for a few cocktails and some calypso music." Ruby hoped her associates were monitoring the elevator's microphones.

Dmitri pointed the gun menacingly under Ruby's nose, "If you call me Nikita one more time, I will blow your head off." Dmitri gritted his yellow teeth as he spoke. Ruby could smell the garlic from last night's jambalaya and the stench of the filter-less cigarettes Dmitri chain-smoked.

"No, as much as you'd like to, I don't think you will, Dmitri. You're not the one giving the orders. If you kill your only lead to Logan and the girl, somebody's going to be real upset. You coulda' had a backup hostage—the Archbishop—but you had to get all trigger-happy on him and kill the old man." Silently, Ruby prayed Bishop Joe was still alive.

"What makes you think he is a he? He could be a she."

Ruby threw her head back, laughing. "You saying he is a she? Well, Russia has come a long way, hasn't it, Dmitri? You sure your president knows he has a transgender spy on his payroll?"

Dmitri foundered, "No, ees not what I mean to say, ees not that a man that is now a girl. Our leader here in the United States, she is already a girl."

It was no surprise that her old nemesis, Mavra, was running this Russian operation. What was a surprise is that Mavra was still alive. Ruby thought she had killed her the last time they met.

"You will see very soon."

"Yes, I imagine so," Ruby muttered. "I imagine we are going to see some interesting things very soon."

"When she's done with you, I hope she tells me to finish you. I will promise to take my time."

Ruby was sure he would keep his promise. She knew, too, the Russian woman would tell him to kill her as painfully as possible. Before she would give that order, though, she would try to get as much information as possible from Ruby—by any means necessary. Ruby knew, firsthand, of Mavra's fondness for inflicting torture, especially by clipping battery cables to a person's most sensitive body parts and shocking her victims until their jaws locked. There were more effective ways to persuade people to talk; Mavra just enjoyed watching them writhe in pain for a time.

The elevator bell dinged at the 15th floor, and the driver held the door open as Dmitri pushed Ruby into the hotel's luxurious hallway. Her hands were grimy from the explosion, and Ruby pressed her fingertips against the smooth brass of the elevator's door as she waited for the driver to again take the lead.

"My old bones are getting tired, Dmitri," Ruby wheezed as she stopped to rest for a moment, pressing her sooty arm against the hotel's freshly painted wall. A few steps more and she stopped again. Her life depended on her team being able to follow her smudge trail.

"Hurry up!" Dmitri shouted. "*Zhirnaya svin'ya!*"

"Oh, you gonna pay for that one, you little Russki peckerwood," Ruby muttered beneath her breath.

"*Kakiye?*" Dmitri asked what she was mumbling.

"Nothing. Never mind." Ruby hobbled along the hallway behind the Russian.

Dmitri's driver stopped at Room 1501 at the end of the beige-and-burgundy-checked carpeted hallway.

"Room 1501?" Ruby quipped. "Whatsa' matter; your boss can't afford the penthouse suite, Nikita?"

He knocked once, then followed with two quick knocks. An ape-sized bodyguard in a blue sharkskin Brioni suit opened the door, and Dmitri pushed her inside. Ruby had seen more luxurious hotel suites, just not in the United States.

Seated near the window was a neatly dressed woman, her posture straight in the Queen Anne chair. A second bodyguard in a suit that matched the man-ape's positioned himself beside her chair, staring out the window. His head robotically panned from one side to the other, then up to down. Ruby observed that both bodyguards were heavily armed with automatic weapons. On the other side of the chair, her assistant stood, wearing a pinstriped business suit, low heels, carrying a notepad.

"*Zakryt' shtory!*" the sitting woman directed her orders to the pinstriped assistant who immediately drew the drapes closed behind Mavra's chair. Ruby's chances were just cut in half. She knew her team's sniper had his crosshairs fixed on the back of the chair, about where Mavra's head would be. Now his vision was blocked.

"It's a pleasure to see you again, Ruby," the woman greeted.

"It's a *surprise* to see you again, Mavra." When they last met, Ruby had suffered a concussion, two broken ribs, and a dislocated shoulder in their melee. Despite her injuries, Ruby jerked Mavra off her feet and tossed her over the balustrade bordering the Ritz Paris' fourth floor balcony. Ruby added, "I thought you were dead."

"Yes, well, it was an unfortunate turn of events. But we are professionals, yes? These things happen. I bear no grudge toward you, Ruby."

The hell you say, Ruby thought. Dmitri stood behind Ruby, eager for Mavra's approval, waiting like a dog begging for a bone. Mavra ignored him.

"Please accept my apologies for Dmitri's rude behavior. He is not, so—sophisticated, shall we say?—as we would like him to be." Dmitri clenched his jaw.

"Got some mouth on him, too." Ruby added.

"Excuse me?" Dmitri pressed his Sig Sauer into Ruby's side. Mavra waved him off.

"As you can see, I'm still covered in dirt from Dmitri's sacrilegious entrance into the House of God. Would you allow me to freshen up a bit?"

"Of course." The woman motioned to her assistant. "Please, take our guest to the adjoining room so she can shower. She nodded to Ruby, "We'll find fresh clothes for you in the meanwhile. We have some lovely Russian tea and cakes. May we brew a fresh pot for you while you're freshening up?" Ruby knew better than to trust Mavra's graciousness.

"Mountain Dew."

"Pardon me?"

"Mountain Dew. You can get me a 22-ounce Mountain Dew. Diet. Don't open it. I'll do that."

"Of course." Mavra waved one of the blue-suited apes off to fetch a bottle of Diet Mountain Dew.

Ruby stood in the steam-filled, marble-and-glass shower for several minutes, wishing it could be longer. Ruby always marveled at the conveniences luxury hotels like the Monteleone provided—it even had a retractable clothesline. She was pleased with how poorly the contraption was constructed and how easily the line snapped from its coil. Scrunched tightly into the plump crevice between her thigh and belly, the white cord was invisible as she stepped from the shower.

She cleaned the caked blood from around the edges of the head wound. The cut was not serious as she first thought. Outside the bathroom, the plain-dressed assistant stood guard over a dark green muumuu laid out on the bed. "We called the hotel's concierge to find something for you. We hope it is right size."

"Oh, you are so polite. How thoughtful. I'm a big beautiful girl; I know that. It's perfect. It's a lovely choice. Thank you." Ruby smiled as she slipped the silk gown over her body. Her team knew exactly where she was. Between her smudge trail and the concierge's delivery, Room 1501 was surrounded.

She returned to the suite's living room and sat in a wing chair opposite Mavra's. Ruby's Diet Mountain Dew sat on a table beside her next to an ice-filled glass. Ruby twisted off the screw top and sipped from the bottle.

"Comfortable?" Mavra asked.

"Mm-hmmm," Ruby wiggled her ample bottom deeper into the wing chair. "Snug as a bug in a rug."

"*Khorosho*. Good. Now, let's get down to business. Where are Dr. Logan and Sarah Carmichael?"

Ruby's robust laugh startled the ape-men. Dmitri pointed his pistol at her briefly before Mavra snapped her fingers. Dimitri dropped his weapon limply to his side as Ruby spoke, "We had them contained. We knew exactly where they both were before your goon squad, led by Goofy here," Ruby nodded in Dmitri's direction, "crashed our party. Now they are in the wind; they could be anywhere—Des Moines, Tokyo, Paris. Hell, for all I know, they're riding Magic Mountain at Disneyland."

"Disneyland. Goofy. You're very funny, Ruby," Mavra feigned laughter before turning deadly serious. "My patience is very thin."

"So are your lips, Mavra. You should get some Botox injections, girl. Your lips would plump up like a strawberry after a June rain." Ruby stretched her neck, visually sweeping the room. She scanned the far wall, past the air vent above the room's mirror, then back to the players in the room. There were six of them—Dmitri, two designer—suited apes, Dmitri's driver, and an assistant in low heels who might be as dangerous as any of them. Lastly, Mavra, whose reputation for savagery was legendary.

"Logan is smart," Ruby continued. "But the girl is smarter. She's got more street smarts than the professor. So, much as I would love to tell you where they are, I, too, am at a loss."

"I see. Then you are not much use to me, are you, Ruby?"

"None at all. I expect you will dispose of me now, but before you do, may I ask a question: why do the Russians want Logan and Sarah Carmichael?"

"We simply want to talk with them. Nothing more." Mavra had a 'tell,' like poker players who unconsciously reveal the strength or weakness of their hand with their body language. Mavra's tell was her tight, weasel-like smile. Presently, she resembled a giddy ferret.

"Oh, Mavra, I know you. But you know me, too. Do you really think you can pee on my slippers and try to convince me it's raining? You can do better than that."

Mavra fed Ruby a crumb. "Logan, he has a theory about these, what shall I call them—?"

"Anomalies."

"Ah, yes, anomalies. Gravitational anomalies, to be exact, yes? Things which are happening that we can't explain. You know, two months ago, in Ukraine, a crack in the earth opened up and an entire village disappeared. All the houses, the church, even the factory which made the petrol, it all just disappeared. It was sucked right into the earth."

"I'm sorry for those families' losses," Ruby replied sincerely, "but somehow, I think Russia's concern was more about the petroleum. Yes?"

Mavra shrugged. "Ees possible."

Ruby went on, "Besides, it didn't happen in the Ukraine. It happened in Liozna Raion on the border of Belarus and Russia. Like I told Nikita here, we have better hackers. It was in Belarus, wasn't it, Mavra?"

"My name is Dmitri!" the ineffectual tough guy spit through gritted teeth.

Mavra ignored Dmitri and Ruby's question but her weasel smile was gone and her lips were drawn. "You see, Dr. Logan, he has studied Dr. Hawking's theory about the vacuum bubble—that the earth and all of its Milky Way galaxy could be pulled into the gravitational suction of such an event. But why, we wonder, why are these strange events happening here on earth, not in outer space?"

Mavra had a good question. It was a question Ruby was prepared to ask the professor, too. She had planned to do just that before the doors blew off Blessed Sacrament Church.

"We wonder, too," Mavra, continued. "We wonder why we have a deal for you to bring Miss Carmichael to us and then, to our surprise, you double-cross us. You and the Archbishop take her to the Professor."

"Those are really good questions, Mavra. Think about it. If I'd brought the girl to you without showing her the professor was alive, she never would have come. My God, woman, the girl has been through hell; she's not about to trust just anybody. But your thugs—the dead ones, mostly—they come in, blasting the place apart with way too much enthusiasm and enough C-4 to take out a city block. They damned-near got us all killed. It was pure luck the pew Logan and the girl were sitting in was beside a marble pillar. It blocked them from the explosion. It is a damn wonder a shard of wood didn't pierce my skull and splatter my brains all over the altar."

"I'm sure your death would have been a terrible loss—" Mavra said flatly, "—to someone."

Mavra shifted slightly in her chair and bent slightly forward. Ruby could see Mavra flinch in pain with the slightest movement. "Back to the professor. He knows something. We know he knows something he hasn't told anyone. He was going to tell someone, maybe the world, but he stopped. They killed his family, and he ran away with his secrets. We must find him. For the protection of the world, don't you agree?"

Ruby's belly shook as she laughed, tossing her head back to distract Mavra from noticing her right hand slip into her muumuu. In a sudden epiphany, Ruby tilted her head toward Mavra. "*You* didn't kill his wife and daughters, did you?"

"No, of course not; why would we do that? What good would that do anyone? Now he has disappeared and by the time anyone finds him, it might be too late." Ruby couldn't disagree. In fact, Mavra's point had been troubling Ruby for some time: what was in the professor's theory which was so dangerous he never told anyone? What could be so important it got his family killed?

Mavra waved to the dapper-dressed missing link who had been watching the window and motioned him toward Ruby. From his pocket, he removed a syringe, pointed it toward the ceiling, and tapped the barrel of the needle.

"Now, my dear Ruby," Mavra dripped, "as much as I love our little conversations and as much as I admire your threshold for pain, I cannot indulge myself in play time today. Today, I must get the information I need quickly."

Ruby suspected the vial was filled with ethyl alcohol. Injected into the bloodstream in its purest form, its effects mimicked getting drunk instantly, eliminating good judgment and discretion. Ruby would talk whether she wanted to or not. Worse, the morning headache and dry-heaving would be excruciating. Ruby knew there would not be a next morning for her. By then, Dmitri would have already delighted in torturing her to death.

"We have some theories," Ruby feigned, "we think it may not be about something happening in outer space at all. It could be, maybe, you know, something went wrong with all these countries who are trying to build a supercollider. Like the one you were building between Minsk and Moscow. Just eight miles from the town that disappeared into a sinkhole. Are you connecting the dots, yet, Mavra? Something went wrong—I'm not sure what—at your supercollider site in Belarus and a whole town got sucked into oblivion."

Mavra scowled at Dmitri. Dmitri shrugged, "I thought she knew."

Calmly, Ruby panned the wall above the room's mirror. This time, she smiled. "I just love the colors in this room, don't you, Mavra? So warm. Soothing, even. Don't you feel soothed?"

The hardened Russian spy nodded toward the syringe-toting bodyguard. "Do it. We do not have time for such games."

Almost silently, the puff of the blowgun sticking through the air vent delivered the tranquilizer dart into the bodyguard's neck. As he collapsed, the other Russians went to his aid, except for Mavra. Startled but steady, Mavra reached between the outside of her thigh and the chair's cushion. As her hand reappeared, Ruby recognized Mavra's trademark weapon; a .380 caliber Walther PPK—James Bond's iconic pistol.

"Go! Go! Go!" a voice from behind the air vent shouted as the vent cover crashed into the center of the room followed by two flash-bang grenades. Dmitri's driver was bent over, trying to lift the drugged bodyguard. Pulling her hand from her muumuu, Ruby gripped each end of the clothesline as a garrote, and wrapped it around the driver's neck. She crossed her hands and tugged back hard, her knee firmly planted between his shoulder blades. As Ruby suffocated the driver, she twisted his body toward Mavra, just in time for him to be the unintended recipient of 95 grains of hollow-pointed lead from the PPK. Despite devastating injuries from the fall two years ago, Mavra was still a crack shot, and the bullet struck the driver center mass. A third flash-bang grenade accompanied a smoke bomb, and was followed by a battering ram destroying the Monteleone's lovely, freshly painted doorjamb.

"Weapons down! Drop your weapons!" Ruby's assault team leader shouted as the Russians realized they were outmanned and outgunned. Except for Dmitri. In defiance, he turned his weapon toward Ruby's assault team. Ruby reached him first, twisting the Sig Sauer from his grip, then tucking his head into her armpit, her thick arms tightening the headlock by degrees. Dmitri pleaded for mercy.

"You say it again, you hear me?" Ruby demanded. "Say it again."

"Say what? Vaht is it you want me to say?" Dmitri gasped for air between words.

"*Zhirnaya svin'ya*, remember? Say it again. Say it so we can all hear you."

Dmitri paused, then muttered softly, "*Zhirnaya svin'ya*." The sound of his spine cracking was followed by his lifeless body falling to the floor.

"I give up. Don't shoot." Mavra raised her hands from her wing chair.

"Get on the ground! Everyone! On the ground!" the assault team leader commanded.

Everyone complied except Mavra. "I cannot. I am a cripple."

"Well, well, well, well," Ruby smiled. "That trip I gave you over the railing in Paris didn't end so well, did it?"

"The hotel's awning broke my fall. My pelvis was crushed. I cannot walk."

Ruby's assault leader stood beside Ruby, looking down at Dmitri's motionless lump of flesh.

"Did you have to kill him?"

"'*Zhirnaya svin'ya!*' He called me a fat pig."

The assault leader glanced at Dmitri's corpse. "A poor choice of words, obviously."

Ruby pulled her team leader aside as the Russians were handcuffed and led from the room. The pinstriped assistant rolled Mavra's wheelchair into the living from the main bedroom and helped her into it. Then, both were handcuffed and led from the hotel room.

Ruby leaned close to her team leader and whispered, "It's not about Hawking's theory; I'm certain of it. It's something about the supercolliders being built in China, Russia, and God-knows-where-else. The professor knows one of them is causing these anomalies."

"And the girl?"

"I think she knows which one."

The team leader stared at Ruby's snake-like eyes, "What the hell happened to your eyes?"

"Contact lenses. I bought 'em on eBay. You like them?"

"They scare the hell out of me."

18

The muck-slime was turning into a crusty layer on Sarah's skin as they ducked in and out of the shadows along the levy and raced across Tchoupitoulas to another slave passage. A scrim of humidity filtered the Delta moonlight.

"Where are we going?" Sarah panted as she followed Dr. Logan. Still feeling the effects of her latest drugging, her mouth was dry as cotton. Darting through dark streets abandoned since Katrina made it worse. *She trusted Dr. Logan, she did. Didn't she? Sure, she did.* Nevertheless, she wasn't eager to be rendered unconscious for a fourth time in one day. He knew where they were going; she didn't. She hated not knowing.

Dr. Logan stopped short in front of a garage door. He gripped the padlock on the door's steel latch and twisted a key. As the lock fell open, Logan slipped it from the garage's latch and lifted a rotting wooden door. Inside, a plain beige car was collecting a layer of dust.

"I hope it starts," Dr. Logan muttered. Logan lifted the hood and reconnected the starter cables to the battery's terminals. He saw Sarah staring at him. "The battery lasts longer that way," he explained.

"I know." Sarah's dad taught her how to do an oil change when she was eight. Only 72 hours had passed since she watched her dad tapping the alternator of the SS with a ball peen hammer; it seemed as if it was weeks ago.

Logan popped the trunk, grabbed a faded blanket, and tossed it in Sarah's direction, "Here, cover the seats with this." Then, he handed her a bottle of water and a towel, "You can clean your hands off with this."

"Why do you have? How the…? Whose car is this?"

Sarah had a lot of questions for Tom the Janitor; that much was clear. Come to think of it, the manner in which he acquired the car may not be at the top of the list.

She wiped as much of the festering muck from her hands, arms, and legs as she could. Dr. Logan wiped his hands, then plopped into the driver's seat. He turned the key and the beige Chevy's motor sputtered to life.

"Get in. It's a long story. We'll have plenty of time for it on the drive." Sarah jumped into the passenger side and Dr. Logan pulled into the street before jerking to a stop. He got out, closed and padlocked the garage door, then pulled a handkerchief from his pocket and wiped down everything he might have touched.

"What in the world?" Sarah wondered if her mentor had completely lost his mind. She wouldn't blame him if he had.

Dr. Logan returned to the Chevy, shifted into drive, and pulled away. "You probably think I've lost my mind, stopping to lock up, right? It's best nobody sees anything out of the ordinary. If somebody comes by tomorrow and asks the neighbors, 'Did you see anything unusual here last night?' and some do-gooder says, 'Yeah, that garage door's been shut and locked up for long as I can remember but it's wide open today.' It's sure to get their attention."

Sarah remembered the package she had left in the Greyhound terminal. "Wait! Stop! How close are we to the bus station?"

"Two miles, maybe less. Why?"

"We need to make a quick stop."

"For what?"

"Please. Just go to the bust station."

Logan steered the car into a passenger pick-up parking spot.

"Wait here." Sarah hurried toward the main terminal entrance, ignoring the looks she got from being covered with putrid grime. She reached under the hibiscus flower planted outside the terminal door and dug down into the dirt, retrieving the bus locker key she had planted two days earlier.

Logan watched people moving into and out of the terminal to see if any made eye contact with Sarah or followed her as she walked through the concourse.

Within three minutes, Sarah retrieved the package and returned to the car.

"The envelope, remember? We're going to need this, aren't we?"

"Yes, we will. It was pretty risky to plant the key under a hibiscus, wasn't it?"

"Hibiscus aren't that dangerous," Sarah said. "People with guns are."

The Chevy turned onto the entrance ramp to eastbound I-10. Sarah watched her mentor repeatedly check the rearview mirror above the dashboard, then the speedometer, look toward the mirror outside the driver's window, then across to the passenger-side mirror. He'd cycle back to the rearview mirror, and the sequence began anew.

"Where are we going?" Sarah asked again. The remaining sewer crust on her skin was beginning to itch.

"There's a truck stop a few miles east of town. It has showers; we'll stop there."

Logan parked the Chevy at the backside of the building and behind a jacked-up pickup truck with a Rebel flag painted on the side.

"I checked this place out a few months ago. It has security cameras on only one side of the building. The cameras are aimed at the fuel pumps and parked semis. Act normal but keep your cap on and your head low. Be back here in fifteen minutes. No more." He opened the trunk and grabbed a pair of gray sweatpants and a University of Texas t-shirt. "These are mine. They might be baggy but they'll do till we can buy you some clothes."

"Fifteen minutes," Sarah muttered as the hot spray washed the slime off her body. She wished she could stay in the shower for fifteen hours, not minutes. She knew, though, how important it was to keep moving fast.

Back in the inconspicuous car, Logan accelerated onto the entrance ramp to eastbound I-10. Sarah had never known Dr. Logan to be anything but kind but, right now, he was tense. Scared. Judging the number of cars zipping past them, Sarah guessed Dr. Logan was driving ten miles an hour under the speed limit.

"Dr. Logan?"

"Tom!" Dr. Logan barked with uncharacteristic sharpness.

"Right. Tom." Sarah paused, "Tom?"

"What?"

"Everybody's passing you. Driving this slowly, the police will notice you."

Logan—Tom—pursed his lips as if to say something, then held back. He stared at the stretch of concrete ahead. "You're right," he answered softly. Sarah felt the car's speed increase gradually. "I'm sorry. I've just never done this sort of thing before."

As if I have, Sarah thought.

Crossing Lake Pontchartrain, Logan finally turned his head in Sarah's direction. "Maybe you should drive. They probably wouldn't recognize you as quickly as me."

"You know the roads better, Doctor—Tom. Besides, it's night time. It will be easier for the police to see who is driving in the daytime. I'll drive after sunup. Or will we have arrived where ever it is we're going by morning?"

"I'm not sure."

Before, Sarah would not have questioned her mentor. After hopscotching across the country to find him, then being rendered unconscious repeatedly, and crawling through waste-filled sewers, Sarah was wary of everyone and everything.

"Does that mean that where we're going is far away or you're not sure we'll reach it by morning?"

"It means I don't how long it will take to get there. It means I don't know if we'll still be alive in the morning."

"Ah. Good to know. Good to know. Good talk." Sarah's head bobbed as she stared out the passenger window toward the south, where the night's black sky cloaked the Mississippi Delta. The Delta held secrets. Deadly secrets. Secrets of slaves, interracial breeding, a Cajun culture, and its mysterious society. Sarah stared into the Delta's blackness and wondered if any of its inhabitants suspected what Tom the Janitor and Sarah knew.

No, they're just living their lives, Sarah thought, waking up in the morning, meeting with their friends at the coffee shop and talking about the strange events as if they'd read them in the National Enquirer. They couldn't explain the odd goings-on any more than the next guy. She imagined one of them saying, "It's just swamp gas. If you've ever been in a swamp at night, it gets real spooky in there. Anyhow, the government says it's just swamp gas and I, for one, believe the government."

But Sarah knew the anomalies were happening throughout the country. She could imagine a conversation in a coffee shop south of Fort Wayne. "Swamp gas, my ass. We live in a friggin' cornfield in Indiana. Where the hell is the closest swamp? Two hundred miles!"

An hour passed before Sarah spoke. "So, about that Texas plate on the back of the car. You said we'd have plenty of time for the story on the drive. Was it *this* drive you were talking about?"

Sarah counted four mile markers before Logan finally spoke, slowly at first.

"When I left Princeton—Princeton, the town, not the university—I knew I would be watched. I knew they—the 'authorities,' I'll call them, I don't know who they actually are—would follow me for the rest of my life. That is, unless I disappeared. They had everything they needed to find me—my email address, phone number, the IP addresses of my laptops and desk computer. The university has had my fingerprints on file for 15 years. As do the police, FBI, and God-knows-who-else. For all I know, they planted a tracking device someplace in my body—under my skin, in a tooth or bone marrow, in one of my organs, who knows? What they apparently didn't know is that my college roommate was—or still is—a U.S. spy. He left college and went missing for years. Eventually, I put two and two together and figured out he worked covert intelligence for the NSA or CIA. I'm not sure which."

"Covert? You mean, like, undercover? If he was undercover, how did you know?"

"I didn't. Not for sure. We lost touch after undergrad. I was getting my doctorate, and I heard he was running an office in Paris for an advertising agency. One day, after I had finished teaching a class, he casually walked into my office at Princeton and said, 'Hey, Johnny, you up for a beer?' like it was any other Thursday. I hadn't seen him in ten years. He'd moved back to the states to head up the creative department for a New York agency, making commercials for fast food burgers and dog food. He said that most of the time, he couldn't tell one from another."

Logan breathed deeply before continuing, "He'd come and he'd go. He'd disappear for years at a time. I had my suspicions but I never asked outright. When he learned of Beth's and the girls' murder, he sent me a note: 'My deepest condolences. If you need anything, call me.' On the note was a handwritten Virginia phone number. I thought it odd he had a Virginia phone number when he lived in the city. When the time came to run, I knew there was nobody I trusted more. So I called him."

Sarah felt her skin twitch. It was as if she was listening to a scary story around a campfire at midnight. But this was real.

"He told me to meet him in the parking lot of the boat ramp at Round Valley Reservoir, an hour's drive from Princeton. He launched the boat and aimed it at the middle of the lake. I told him I was getting the hell out of Dodge."

"Yes?"

"I told him I needed to know how go off the grid completely. I didn't want to leave any trace. No forwarding address, no smart phone with GPS, nothing." Dr. Logan's eyes welled up as he added, "I didn't have anyone who needed to find me—"

"I know," Sarah said.

"It was only a matter of time they'd come looking for me. I remember him nodding as if he already knew. There, in the middle of the lake, he took out a pencil and a little spiral pad and started writing. He didn't speak a word as he scribbled. I asked him what he was writing, and he just held his finger to his lips then looked up at the sky."

Sarah remembered Ruby looking up at the sky when she shushed her.

"Satellites," Tom the Janitor went on, "whoever was tracking me has satellite surveillance. Of course! Why didn't I think of that? So he writes down, on his little notepad, a list of instructions, step-by-step, and hands the piece of paper to me. Then he pulls out a lighter and burns the rest of the notepad, leaving no impressions of the pencil on its paper, no fingerprints, nothing. There, drifting in a ten-foot aluminum fishing boat, it dawned on me how much trouble I was in. They have satellites—freakin' billion dollar satellites—tracking me in the middle of a reservoir."

Janitor Tom paused, "He told me to memorize the list, to do everything he wrote down, in *order,* with no exceptions, and—"

"And—?"

"After I memorized it, he told me to burn the note."

Sarah noticed the Delta's night sky seemed more ominous than any other sky she'd ever seen. The line separating Louisiana from Mississippi was invisible. Sarah stared into the darkness and Tom was zipping along with freeway traffic at 72 miles per hour, as unremarkable as the Chevy itself.

"So, how'd you wind up in Texas?" Sarah pressed.

"On the list of things he told me to do, one of them was to travel around the country. Iowa, California, Nebraska. Fast. Unpredictably. He told me to keep changing directions and modes of transportation. "Drop your phone in a lake, preferably a deep one like Lake Tahoe," he said. "Then, get on a jet and fly to the other side of the country. Post a picture of yourself on Facebook standing on the Observation Deck at the Empire State Building, then rent a car and drive through New York to Canada. When I reached the Montréal-Trudeau Airport, I put my laptop in a locker off the main concourse. Unlike you, I didn't hide the key in the roots of a hibiscus plant; I threw it in the trash can."

"Then what?"

"I drove west through Canada and re-entered the U.S. in Minnesota. Charlie had a resource in Edina—just outside Minneapolis—who knew what to do if I made it that far."

"A resource?"

"A plastic surgeon. He assured me the doctor was somebody I could trust."

Sarah forced a slight smile. "I thought you looked a little different."

"Not that much. He did a little rhinoplasty and a tuck on my wrinkles. It didn't seem to make much difference in my appearance but that isn't why I went to him; I went to him to get a complete examination of my skin, teeth, and all my organs. I wanted to find out if there was a bug planted in my body. He ran a CT scan and MRI, x-rays—he even bought a transmitter detector from Best Buy in the strip mall and checked me over. Then he handed me some guy's wallet with his social security card and birth certificate."

"He gave you someone's ID? Whose?"

"Hang on. I'm getting to that. The plastic surgeon told me to wait until the swelling went down, then drive to the little town of Effie, just south of the Canadian border. Tell the clerk I lost my wallet, he said, and that I needed to replace my driver's license. He told me if I showed up around 4:00 p.m., the clerk would rush me through because she likes to close up shop and be sitting on her personal barstool at the Neighborhood Tavern by 4:30."

"Go on."

"Finally, he said to drop the rental car and take a bus to Texas. Texas doesn't ask a lot of questions, he tells me. Trade the Minnesota driver's license in for a Texas license when you get there."

"Whose license was it?"

"Somebody named Tom Moore."

"Hence, Tom the Janitor. Who is he, really?"

"A dead guy. Died in a bird-hunting accident a year ago. Somebody in his hunting party blasted him with a turkey load between the eyes. The doctor had the birth certificate and Social Security card because he moonlights for the Coroner's office. He said that I looked enough like the guy that nobody would question me and my nose job would make it difficult for facial recognition software at airports or to identify me by the Texas driver's license."

"So, now you're in Texas." Sarah pressed on. "Houston? Dallas?"

"Longview."

"What? Why Longview?"

"Longview, Texas. It was where the last bank the Dalton Gang robbed was located. It seemed poetic, being on the run and all. I bought the car for cash at a corner car lot. I parked it in a storage unit and rented a room for two weeks until the title showed up in the mail. As soon as it came, I drove to New Orleans. It's been parked in that garage ever since."

Sarah cocked her head, trying to make sense of everything Tom the Janitor was telling her. "Weren't you worried about security cameras at airports and bus terminals?"

"Of course. Charlie assured me they would be so busy chasing the electronic trails, it would be a day or so before they sat through hours of watching security tapes. I knew the risk. If an airport had high-speed facial recognition software, my face could pop up instantly and my escape would be over. Charlie gambled that the airports I chose wouldn't have my face loaded onto the software just yet."

"Why didn't you throw your laptop into a lake like your phone?"

"Two reasons: one, misdirection. The people looking for me would assume I was coming back to retrieve it at some point. At least some of their manpower would be wasted camping out in the Montreal terminal. It might be weeks before they realized I wasn't coming back."

"And the second reason?"

"There is information on it I want the Canadians to have," Logan looked into the greenish hue of the dashboard gauges, then to the rearview mirror, before shifting his eyes to each side mirror.

"You wanted the authorities to find your laptop?"

"Not the United States authorities; the Canadian ones. I knew they would search every bit of data before turning it over to anyone, and even then they would only share it with Her Majesty's Secret Service in London. With U.S. and British relations as strained as they are right now, I was sure they wouldn't give it to the United States' intelligence agencies once they saw what is on it. It was better in the hands of the Canadians."

"You don't trust the U.S. Government?"

"It's not that I don't trust our government; it is that I don't know *who* in our government to trust. I was certain Canadian intelligence would turn over any information to the Brits. The Queen would see it and decide what, if anything, should be shared with American intel."

"How could you be so sure?"

"Have you heard of the Five Eyes Accord?"

"No."

"In 1946, a secret treaty was signed between the U.S. and Great Britain to share military intelligence. It has been expanded to include Canada, Australia, and New Zealand. However, the United States botched its relationship with the four other countries' intelligence communities in the past several of years, and the current administration has made it worse. So, the five other signatories to the accord are extremely cautious about sharing their intelligence findings with anyone in the United States government, including the President and the Department of Justice."

"Go on."

"The Queen and other world leaders are not isolationists; they see the world as one global civilization and one global economy. They understand we can fly to the other side of the world in less than a day and satellites circle the globe every day. An intercontinental missile could land in Russia in about 30 minutes."

"What is your point?"

"The Queen wields power through quiet diplomacy with world leaders—sitting in embroidered chairs and sipping tea—not grand-standing before bright lights and television cameras. The Queen is too savvy to bully other nations into thinking the way she does about our future as a planet. The United States, historically, has been seen as a superpower because of its military arsenal, not because of its diplomatic skills."

It was clear to Sarah there were more worldwide players in this chess game than she thought. Germany, Japan, Saudi Arabia, Israel, India, China, and, of course, Russia. How much did they know? How many gravitational anomalies had each country experienced? Which countries were forming alliances with another?

"So, your laptop has information on it you don't want certain people to know. Am I understanding that right?"

Logan nodded.

A stream of fireballs blazed across their path through the night sky.

"Did you see *that*!" It wasn't a question; she knew he couldn't have missed it.

"Yes, I saw that."

"I've never see a meteor shower like that before!" Sarah exclaimed.

"Neither have I," Tom agreed. "That's because it wasn't a meteor shower."

"It wasn't?"

"Have you ever seen a meteor shower traveling east to west, countering the rotation of the earth? Opposing the sun's gravitational pull?"

"Oh, shit."

"Yep. Shit."

"What is doing this?" Sarah asked.

"I don't know but I am believing more and more that it has to do with experiments scientists are doing."

Logan's knuckles had turned white gripping the steering wheel as he stared through the windshield. His face was drawn; he looked twenty years older than a year ago.

"Your friend, your old college roommate," Sarah probed, "have you spoken with him at all since he wrote his instructions down?"

"No, that was the first thing on this list. Never contact him and he would never contact me. No matter what. It doesn't make much difference now, anyway."

"Why is that?"

"He's dead. I was walking through the Montreal airport; a TV news report of a fiery crash caught my eye. It was on the Jersey Turnpike. They showed a ball of flames and then Charlie's name and picture popped up on the screen, saying the police believed he was the lone fatality. I was stunned and heartbroken. I searched a New York station online and they were still streaming live video of the crash scene. 'Manhattan man dies in a fiery crash,' the reporter said, and they showed the flames.

"Apparently, he rear-ended a tanker carrying benzene and it exploded, engulfing his car in a ball of fire. Benzene burns at 3,000 degrees Fahrenheit. What's worse, a double-bottom tanker hauling a full load of diesel fuel plowed into the crash from behind. It burned so hot and so long the highway was destroyed. He was cremated at the scene. The only thing they found to identify him were two small surgical screws from the time he broke his wrist playing soccer in college, and those were warped from the heat. I sat, paralyzed for a moment. In a daze, I put it the laptop in a locker and headed back to my rental car."

"Do you think it was an accident?" Sarah forced the words out of a cotton-dry mouth as her skin went cold.

"I don't know," Logan replied. "I suppose it's possible he fell asleep at the wheel and rear-ended the truck. Or, someone forced his car in between the two trucks and the front one slammed on its brakes. He wouldn't have any place to go when the double-bottom rammed him from behind."

"'Someone?' You mean the people who are looking for us?"

"There are lots of people looking for us. You'll need to narrow that down a bit."

Sarah's blood felt like razors coursing through her arteries. Her face flushed hot, then it drained till her complexion resembled a ghost's. Logan was right; they'd probably both be dead by morning.

East of Pensacola, Tom the Janitor turned south, guiding the car onto US 98 toward the Gulf of Mexico's northern coastline and its barrier islands.

19

Archbishop Joseph James O'Donnell, once the leader of the Archdiocese of New Orleans, lay in a private room, in a private wing of a secret military hospital outside Bluemont, Virginia. Four stone-faced men in black suits stood beside Bishop Joe's bed. "You know, they say after you lose a limb," the Archbishop chuckled nervously, "you can still feel it—you know, like it is still there. I tell you, it's true. I swear I can feel a hangnail on my big toe—" The four faces didn't smile.

The white-haired leader of the group spoke first, "This is quite a facility. It doesn't show up on our satellites."

The Western Virginia Office of Controlled Conflict Operations, nicknamed 'Mt. Weather,' is the nerve center of FEMA, the Federal Emergency Management Administration. It is one of many rabbit holes built to protect the President and the United States' most essential political and military leaders as well as FEMA's emergency strategists. The hospital within the complex would rival the best medical facilities in the world.

"Archbishop O'Donnell," the leader continued in a clipped British accent, "we're sorry for the loss of your leg. It was regrettable that we did not reach you in time."

"Please, George. Call me Joe," the Archbishop replied. "We've known each other too long for your British formality. Besides, 'regrettable' hardly describes it. Bloody painful might. I'm just lucky your MI-6 lads showed up before I bled to death. They cut it damn close, by the way."

The group of men in tight-fitting suits stared blankly at the gangly priest who lay on white sheets in front of them. Three days after surgery to remove Bishop Joe's leg below the knee, British agents interrogated him deep inside Mt. Weather.

"What happened, Joe?" George asked.

"I was hiding Dr. Logan in the organ room of an abandoned church. The girl, Sarah, found Ruby. Then I buggered it up. I went to Ruby's home and the Russians followed me. After drugging her,

Ruby stashed the girl in a broom closet of the church. When the drug wore off, she and Logan were sitting in a pew when the explosion blew everything to bits."

"Tell me about the girl," the Brit said.

"Feisty, she is. She didn't look the part of a scientist; that was my first impression. But then, I'm a bit of a codger. I didn't get any time to talk with her before the Russians showed up." Joe paused for a moment and asked, "How's your family, George?"

"Mum and Dad passed, and we sold Lazenby Castle, Joe. It was a sad day. What the hell is going on, Joe?"

"I wish I knew," Bishop Joe shook his head. "One day I'm the Archbishop of New Orleans. The next day I'm hiding a fugitive in an abandoned church, and Russians are blowing the place up. They took the time to shoot off my knee, you might have noticed. Then they took Ruby."

Forty years. It had been all of that since he'd graduated from the seminary at St. Patrick's College in Maynooth. His first cover was as a Presbyterian minister in Jamaica. Then he reappeared as a Catholic priest in the United States. If the Vatican had known, he would most certainly have been defrocked.

"Tell me everything."

"That's just it, George. I don't know anything. It's strange, bizarre, beyond imagination. There are these things; Logan calls them anomalies. A table moves across a kitchen with nobody near it. A wind blows through a closed room. The earth trembles in one spot but, just ten feet away, it's perfectly still."

George nodded, "I've heard. A city in Belarus disappeared into a sinkhole. There was no trace of the petrol refinery which had stood there. Oil derricks and sixteen million gallons of oil disappeared without any remnants of oil in the soil, no pipeline, no debris, nothing. Even the river which flowed through the town is gone."

"Logan was trying to figure that one out, George. Every night, before he drank himself stupid, he would sit in the organ room of the church with a small lamp, a pencil, paper, and calculator."

"Where is he, Joe?"

"Until a few days ago, he was at the church. Now he and the girl are in the wind. He was getting worried she wouldn't show up; he was preparing to go on the run by himself."

"Why did he think she would try to find him?"

"She has his research papers. Stopping the anomalies will take every ounce of grey matter they have between them." Bishop Joe paused and asked, "George, who sent you here? And why?"

George didn't flinch. Nor did he answer Bishop Joe's question.

Bishop Joe pressed. "Okay then, let me guess. If it is as important as I think it is, you are here on Her Majesty's orders. The Royal Family owns 51% of British Petroleum. The Queen is a key player in the world's fossil-fuel game. She's protecting her interests. That doesn't take much thought. But there's more, isn't there, George?"

"BP is the backbone of the British economy, Joe," George replied. "The British pound will be rendered worthless in the world market if the oil industry collapsed."

"George, does Homeland Security know you are here in the U.S.?"

"No."

Bishop Joe grabbed his friend's collar and pulled his ear close to his lips, whispering, "Bloody hell, George! You're running a covert operation on U.S. soil, and the President of the United States has no idea? You know what the consequences are, don't you?"

"Yes, Joe, I do."

Bishop Joe clung to his friend's collar, "You'd face a feckin' firing squad. You know that?"

"If so, the Yanks would need two firing squads."

"Two? You have two spy teams operating without the United States' government's knowledge and permission?"

"One sanctioned by the Queen. One freelance."

Bishop Joe looked to the ceiling, made the Sign of the Cross, and whispered, "Jesus, Mary, and Joseph, what the devil have you gotten yourself into? You're completely off the rails."

"Joe, you've been at this a long time. As have I. I know a rotten cod when I smell one. This fish has been sitting in the sun too long."

George leaned over and whispered, "The Yanks don't trust their own people. The CIA doesn't trust the NSA; the NSA doesn't trust the FBI; and nobody trusts the politicians on either side of the aisle, let alone the President. The U.S. British Ambassador brought us in. He's a member of Bavarian Grove. You see, one small leak, and whatever is happening will be on today's evening news, with both political parties blaming the other. It'll be a feckin' circus."

"I can't argue that."

"As Commander-in-Chief, the United States President has the entire U.S. military under his direct orders. They report to no one but him. He won't think twice about running end around Congress and starting a war if it serves his purpose."

"And you and I report directly to Her Majesty," Bishop Joe murmured. The Bishop pulled George's lapel again. "Wait. Wait a minute. You said 'freelance.' Is Ruby working for you?"

"She didn't tell you?"

"No, once she left MI-6 and went freelance, we agreed to never talk about our assignments. We couldn't cross that line. Now it makes sense why MI-6 showed up when the church was bombed. They were Ruby's backup."

George shrugged, "I can't confirm nor deny."

"Do you have any word on her whereabouts?"

"No, Joe, nothing yet. We know it was Dmitri Sokolov's team who took her from the church which suggests Mavra may be in charge. When they kidnapped her, telecommunications chatter went silent for several days. Today, we heard there was quite the melee at the Hotel Monteleone two nights ago. Signs that the Russians—the FSB, the Federal Security Service of the Russian Federation—or one of the Russian mobs had been there, we're not sure."

"Hah! The FSB," the Archbishop scoffed. "That's just a new name for the KGB."

"Yes and no. There are some FSB agents who are still loyal to the KGB. They do have a tendency to go rogue and follow the orders of one particular Russian."

"What did you find at the Monteleone?"

"A couple dead Russians and a lot of blood. One was strangled with a garrote and shot in the chest with a .380 hollow point. I've never seen that before."

Bishop Joe smiled. "That was Ruby."

"She carries a .380 caliber?" George asked.

"No. She's an expert with a garrote. I don't know who had the .380."

"The other dead Russian, it looked like his neck had been snapped."

Sighing in relief, the bishop laughed, "She's alive—and somebody pissed her off."

20

The Archbishop's eyes grew heavy once he knew Ruby was alive. Bishop Joe knew Ruby could take care of herself and pitied the poor bastard who crossed her. They'd worked together for years. He'd known her a lifetime. As he fell asleep, he dreamed of Jamaica decades ago.

"You! Mon!" the booming voice of a carnival barker ricocheted off buildings' walls along the Kingston tourist street. Two hours past sunrise, the busy courtyard beside Holy Trinity Cathedral was bustling with sightseers. His eyes scanned the crowd till he saw a sturdy black woman in a satin muumuu. She nodded and waved. "Come! I see you future. Here. In the cards. Come. Sit." She was a head taller than the average tourist and almost as tall as the lanky, young clergyman.

He laughed at the idea that a Presbyterian minister would be gullible enough to get hustled for a Tarot Card reading by a street con in a Jamaican alley. She was convincing, though, as much by her charming smile as her persistence.

"Come. Sit. Sit down. I see danger ahead. Heed my warning. Sit." In 1982, Father Joseph Roberts was still new to his ministry at the edge of downtown Kingston, near the harbor in Tivoli Gardens. The Kingston slum was well known in the ganja trade, and the blood of rival drug gangs flowed freely beneath the tarp-roofed huts, through the brick and seeping into the dirt streets of the Gardens.

Father Roberts slid the metal folding chair from beneath the card table and sat as the Tarot Reader shuffled her cards and chanted in a language Father Roberts didn't understand. "So, you're going to tell me my future?" he asked. She smiled as if she was charming a cobra.

"Dat what de sign say?" The street con nodded toward the sandwich board beside the card table. 'Queen *Esther's Tarot Card Reading, $5*,' it read.

"Five dollars? That's a bit rich for a man of the cloth," Father Roberts protested. "If I had an extra five dollars, I'd put it in my Sunday collection plate."

"You sitting down. On my chair. You not going to lay five dollars down, then get up and move along. Let somebody else sit in that chair."

Father Roberts looked around. There was nobody waiting to sit down. "Queen Esther? That's your name, eh? Or just Esther? Are you royalty?"

"You ask a lot of questions, don't you? You like asking questions?" The fortuneteller kept moving cards around the table, strategically interjecting a chant for authenticity.

"Just curious. Curious about someone I might give the money I had set aside for the poor."

"No might about it. Wouldn'ta' sat yo' white ass down if you wasn't gonna pay. I saw you look at the sign before you came over here."

"Ah, yes, well," Father Roberts smiled as he reached to his back pocket.

"Stop! Stop!"

Father Roberts froze, unsure why he trusted this woman's order, but he did.

"Now ever'body on the street knows where you keep your money. Stupid Americans. You all carry your wallets in your back pockets where you can't watch it or see who's sneakin' up behind you to take it." She paused, then added, "Might as well take it out now. Just don't make a big show of it. They's people on rooftops with binoculars, watching to see how much money you carrying."

Father Roberts carefully plucked a five from his wallet, not too worried that the $15 he had left would attract much attention.

"Now stuff it down your pants." Father Roberts began to slide the wallet into his front pocket when she stopped him again. "No, not your pocket! Stuff it in the crotch of your tighty-whities. Ain't nobody—man or woman—gonna be reachin' into your jiggly bits to steal your wallet. He did as she told him as he slid the five across the table and looked around to see who was watching.

"Oh don't worry about me. I kin take care of myself. Well, me and three bodyguards you cain't see."

Father Roberts believed her. He certainly wasn't going to challenge her statement. He sat silently, scanning the alley and street bazaar surrounding them. The card reader regained his attention when she spoke. "It was my grandmother's name."

"What?"

"Esther. It was my grandmother's name. She was queen of her Creole clan."

"So, you are Creole?" Father Roberts knew very little about Creoles but he knew some practiced Voodoo and spoke their own language.

"Far as I kin tell," Queen Esther moved the cards around and chanted again. "We Creoles are like gumbo. You take a big cast iron pot, toss in a bunch of Spaniards, French, Africans and Indians, and we're what you get."

"Indians?"

"American Indians, not the ones from Bombay. You bring that pot o' gumbo to a boil and you get all kinda funny talk going. Kréyol La Lwizyàn, it's called."

"What is?"

"Our language. Got its own name. But you kin jes' call it Creole."

"Is that Creole you're speaking now?"

The snake-oil sales woman threw her head back and laughed, "Nah, that's just somethin' I made up. Sounds sorta' voodooey, though, don't it?"

"Yes, I guess so. I don't know the Voodoo language but I suppose it might sound like that."

Tivoli Gardens smelled a mixture of both fresh-slaughtered and rotting fish, rancid corn oil bubbling over a fire, and pungent incense. Puffs of marijuana smoke floated past and a cacophony of noise merged into a dissonant symphony serenading the Presbyterian minister and a Jamaican con artist.

"Esther was your grandmother's name. What is your name?" the minister asked.

"That's not your business," she retorted bluntly, then smiled broadly, "any more than your business is being a minister."

Father Roberts stopped. He stared at her quietly for a moment, then another, before speaking slowly, "Have you had lunch yet today?"

"Why you asking?" Queen Esther shuffled the cards again, laying them flat on the rickety card table and moving them around, in between one another, all the while uttering something authentic but unintelligible in any language.

"I'd like to have lunch with you."

"Why? So you kin ask me a buncha' questions? About stuff I don't know nothing about?"

"That's a double negative."

"What is?"

"Don't know nothing. It means you know something. But then, you already knew that."

"I don't understand one thing you jabberin' about."

"Yes, you do," Father Roberts replied and laughed, "anybody smart enough to see that I'm not a Presbyterian minister is smart enough to know what a double negative is and how to use it to tell the truth and make it sound as if they are lying."

The sun was reaching its highest point, and the day's heat was beginning to build.

"I suppose I could eat something," she replied as she gathered up the cards, shoved them into a big bag, and folded her table.

"Wait! What about my reading?" Father Roberts objected. "Don't I get my reading?"

"No. Be a waste of time, the way I see it. You don't believe me, and I sure as hell don't believe you."

"So, you're done for the day?"

"No, I'll be back when the sun goes behind the buildings. Just too hot and sticky out here in the afternoon. Even the tourists find shade during the heat of the day." Father Roberts grabbed her chair, folded it, and held out his hand for the table.

"Why, you're a real gentleman, thank you," Queen Esther handed him the table, slung her bag over her shoulder, and marched ahead of him. Passing a doorway filled with a muscular, stern-faced black man, Queen Esther nodded. *That's one of her bodyguards*, the minister thought. Seeing him, he wasn't quite sure why she needed three.

As their path narrowed, tarp roofs closed in and the smell of spicy Jamaican recipes enveloped him. The rough stone alley had turned to hardened clay. Esther's pace was steady and strong and, despite his long legs, Father Roberts struggled to keep up.

His hair stood on his neck but he knew, soon, he would be asking these people to be his parishioners at his St. Andrews Scots Kirk Presbyterian Church on Duke Street. He'd better get used to it. The church was a Kingston landmark; its white stone exterior and blue trim had stood on the same piece of land since the early 1800s.

"Where are we going?" Father Roberts panted, mostly out of fear, partly from exhaustion.

"Special place." Esther didn't look back. "You like it just fine. You'll see." The smell of ocean water was stronger than it had minutes earlier, and the sound of seagulls mewing and cawing drowned out the sounds of humans.

"In here." Esther pulled back a flap of canvas and nodded toward the inside of the lean-to.

A leathery-skinned, jet-black, and elderly Jamaican man was inside. Wearing what appeared to Father Roberts to be a diaper, he sat on his haunches leaning over hot coals. The tent filled with a cloud of sweet, white smoke—a mixture of dried mesquite limbs and grapevine wood. Layers of woven palm fronds were stacked one on top of another, each one laid with thin strips of flesh—chicken, lamb, salmon, and grouper. The aroma swirled its way up through the honeycomb of meats, adding its flavor to that of the Jamaican jerk seasonings—Scotch bonnet, paprika, cumin, cinnamon, garlic, nutmeg, and thyme.

Queen Esther grabbed two bowls from the counter and spooned in a dollop of rice into each one. She picked a variety of pieces from the smoking meat—fish, chicken, and lamb—and tossed them on top of the rice before ladling the rich brown sauce over each bowl. Father Brown leaned over for a whiff of the mixture, then reeled back, his eyes instantly filled with tears.

"Jerk," Esther announced.

"What? I meant no offense. I just smelled it—"

"No. Jerk. Jamaican Jerk. It's what they call it. Like your American chili, 'cept it's got flavor."

"Flavor?" Father Roberts stared at the concoction as if he was looking through a fish bowl, "I think my skin is melting."

"Your eyes, they'll clear up in a minute or two," Esther reassured, "or twenty."

Father Roberts muttered, "Good Lord! How in Jesus' name do you eat this?"

"I don't know about Jesus but, the taste, you get used to it. Makes you sweat on a hot day. Makes the little wind we get seem like a northern breeze."

"You eat this nuclear waste to cool off? That makes no sense."

"It does if you live in a place so hot it's like living on the sun."

Father Roberts dipped the tip of his spoon into the bowl and touched it to the end of his tongue. It was flavorful, that much was certain. The seasonings ravaged his taste buds in an overwhelming, masochistic assault. His eyes filled with tears, his nose dripped, and sweat flooded his brow. Nothing, though, described the pain.

"Ah, ah, oh, this is good." At once, Father Roberts lied and spoke the truth.

"You get used to the heat," Esther promised. The priest nodded as if he actually believed her. He didn't.

"What do you do after lunch? You know, once your mouth recovers and before the sun sets behind the buildings?" Father Roberts watched as the Tarot reader rolled a joint, touched a flame to it, and sucked in hard.

She held the ganja smoke in her lungs as she spoke. "Some folks make love and take a nap," Queen Esther replied directly. She held her lungs for nearly a minute before exhaling. "The others take a nap." She held the joint out to Father Roberts.

"But I, no, I didn't mean, I wasn't trying to—"

"Take a hit," Queen Esther said. "It'll relax you."

"But I mean, about the sex," he stammered, "I wasn't—I didn't—that wasn't why I came with you."

Queen Esther tossed her head back and answered with her throaty laugh. "You're funny, you Father Roberts, or whatever your real name is."

"My real name?"

"Oh, hush, it don't matter," Esther touched her finger to his lips, "It don't matter to me if you the Queen of England. You just seem nice. Like you need somebody to look out for you, make sure you didn't get knocked in the head while you got your bearings here on the island. Wasn't plannin' to get frisky with you, neither." Esther pointed to the corner. "Grab a couple pillows there and stretch yourself out. Get comfy. I imagine you've had a long trip. You got a few hours to catch a few winks." On the other side of the lean-to, Esther tucked a large, yellow pillow beneath her head and lay on her side, her back to Father Roberts.

Father Roberts stared at the handmade cigarette he held, put it between his lips, and sucked in deeply. He closed his eyes and felt the buzz of the drug as the sounds from beyond the lean-to slowed and mingled into an odd symphony.

"Adriana," her voice muttered from across the room.

"What?" Father Roberts replied, still holding his breath.

"Adriana. My real name's Adriana. Means dark and rich. They got it half right."

Father Roberts had never met a darksome woman; at least not one to whom he was attracted.

She didn't care if he was the Queen of England. If she only knew.

In his trance, images ran through Roberts' brain as parallel tracks in a railroad yard. Her smile beckoned him and her body moved in an agile, seductive dance. Frames of her face rolled through his head even after he drifted off to sleep. He tried to wake up. He wanted to know more about this entrancing con artist.

"Joe? Bishop Joe?" The Archbishop felt his shoulder being rustled till he began to awaken.

"Adriana?"

"No, Joe. It's Aedain," the voice repeated, "Aedain Maycroft, Joe. We're trying to find Ruby, Sarah, and the Professor."

"Ruby? How is she? How's my little Ruby? Is Adriana here?" Bishop Joe mumbled incoherently.

Now was not the time to talk about Adriana, Aedain knew. Not now. As for Ruby, Aedain had no answer. Sarah and Logan were off the grid, and Aedain's MI-6 team needed to find them fast.

"Wake up, Joe. C'mon, Joe, wake up," Aedain slapped his cheek, gently at first, then more firmly. "Nurse!" Aedain shouted over his shoulder, "is there anything you can give him to wake him?"

21

Mavra rarely showed fear. She did once, two years earlier, as Mavra clung to the balcony in Paris just before she fell. She knew her fingers would grow weak and slip from the wrought iron spindles; it was only a matter of time.

Bloodied and near death herself, Ruby fought to remain conscious. Sprawled across the hotel balcony, she slowly peeled each of Mavra's fingers from the iron until she plummeted toward the sidewalk. Ruby remembered Mavra's eyes as she fell; they seemed to plead to Ruby for mercy.

Ruby had no choice. If Mavra survived, she would eventually kill Ruby. Ruby couldn't have guessed the hotel canopy would break Mavra's fall. Today, Ruby discovered Mavra's pelvis had been crushed in the fall. Despite being unable to walk, she was still a deadly enemy.

Now, Mavra sat in her wheelchair, staring calmly at Ruby. She was in the United States, with all its protections of civil rights. She felt safe. She trusted Ruby as her respected adversary. Mavra seldom made mistakes but she'd just made a big one.

Across a plywood table laid over saw horses, in a seafood shipping room, Ruby stared back at Mavra. The air was stale and smelled like day-old boiled shrimp. There were no windows, but a large mirror covered one wall. Mavra knew she was being watched by people on the other side of the mirror.

"So, tell me, Mavra, why do you want Dr. Logan and his student?"

"I'm not the one who wants them. I follow orders," Mavra answered smugly.

"Mm-hmmm," Ruby nodded as she listened, "yes, I suppose so. Your orders come from very high up, I presume?"

"You may presume as you like," Mavra dodged.

"The Kremlin?" Ruby probed.

Mavra shrugged.

"Let's play a game, shall we, Mavra? I ask a question. You say 'warm' if I am close. Or 'cold' if I am incorrect. 'Warmer' if I am getting closer. You know this game, don't you, Mavra?"

"Ees child's game. I will not play child's game with you."

"Ah, yes, I see," Ruby replied. "How, then, do you suggest my friends and I get the answers to all the questions we have?" Ruby nodded toward the one-way mirror.

Wearing a pastel pillbox hat matching her suit, an elderly woman rose from the oval table on the other side of the mirror. She walked toward the conference room doors, as two of her four bodyguards held the doors open for her. Pivoting to face the others in the room, she said, "Do what you must. *Whatever* you must." Toddling past the double doors, she added, "I have a plane to catch."

Instantly, the room's door flung open and two members of Ruby's assault team wrangled Mavra's assistant into the room, still wearing her pinstripe suit and low heels.

Ruby held out her hand and the team member standing beside Ruby handed over his .40 caliber Sig Sauer. "Maybe this will help." The pistol's explosion was followed by the assistant's agonizing scream and her body writhing in pain. Blood poured down the assistant's leg from her shattered knee.

"Geneva Convention!" Mavra shouted, stone-faced. Ruby nodded, "We'll call that payback for the Archbishop." Ruby paused, then waved her team to take Mavra's injured assistant from the interrogation room. "Drop her off at the Emergency Room. Come right back."

Mavra seemed relieved her assistant would not be tortured further.

"You know, Mavra, it is interesting that you feel entitled to invoke the Geneva Convention when it suits you but you make it your common practice to violate it. I wish we could talk more about this but I am pressed for time." Ruby waved toward the mirror as she drew the blade of a nine-inch Bowie knife back and forth across a leather strop until it was razor-sharp. She sat beside Mavra, tracing her carotid artery with the point of her blade.

"Too bad. We were having such an enlightening conversation," Mavra sneered.

"Ah, yes, but now it's time for you to share your secrets," Ruby said. "Mavra, if I fail to convince you to share your information, I will put you on a plane to Syria and you can have a nice visit with the Syrian National Coalition. I'm sure they will enjoy meeting a Russian responsible for killing their children with bombing raids."

Mavra clenched her jaw.

"Now, which interrogation technique should I use? Pure alcohol injection, sodium pentathol, or should I use my carving skills? Maybe I should scribble each one on a piece of paper and draw them from a hat. This will be fun! It will be such a surprise, don't you think?"

"I already tell you, I won't play your childish games. The first two are not reliable, you know that, and the third? You already know how much pain I can endure."

"Fair enough. Then let's get you packed for your flight to Syria." Ruby rose and started for the door. Mavra knew if she left, she wouldn't come back.

"Wait." Mavra sucked in a deep breath. "What is it you want to know?"

"Let's start at the beginning," Ruby laid her Bowie knife on the table and picked up her .40 caliber pistol as she settled into a worn vinyl chair in front of Mavra. "Who are you working for? Why do you want Logan and the girl?"

"You know who I work for—Russia's FSB. You Westerners still think of it as the KGB."

"No, you don't," Ruby said quietly, "your cover is that you work for Russia's Federal Security Service as a spy. But the KGB still exists, doesn't it?"

"*Nyet.*"

Boom! The sound of the explosion of the .40 caliber round reverberated off the walls. Mavra ducked her head as she heard the bullet whistle past her left ear.

"The next one will be between your eyes," Ruby warned softly. "Our conversation is almost over."

Staring down the smoking end of Ruby's .40 caliber, Mavra was terrified. Mavra knew Ruby would make sure she was dead with the next shot.

"*Da.* KGB still exists. But not as government agency. It was disbanded after KGB Chairman Vladimir Kryuchkov led the coup against Gorbachev in 1991."

"It never really ceased operations, though, did it?" Ruby probed.

"*Nyet.* The FSB was formed as a new… how you say… transparent intelligence organization of the Russian government. But loyal KGB operatives still work in the shadows."

"You have always been loyal to the KGB, haven't you, Mavra?"

"*Da.*"

"And you have been loyal to those who have remained loyal to the KGB, yes?"

"*Da.*"

"So you work for the KGB but the KGB doesn't work for Russia. Am I understanding you?" Mavra nodded.

"The KGB works for certain individuals, isn't that right? One in particular? How am I doing?"

Mavra shrugged and turned away, realizing if the video being recorded reached certain hands, her life would end within hours. When she heard the hammer click on the Sig Sauer, she had even less time if Ruby chose to pull the trigger.

"Look at me," Ruby whispered as her pit-viper eyes bore into Mavra. The semi-auto pointed at the Russian spy's nose spoke clearly. "You look at me when I talk to you. Do you understand?"

"*Da.*"

"Let me guess. You tell me when I go wrong. Someone very high up in the Russian government wants to gain control of two things: one, a new, inexhaustible energy source which could destroy the value of fossil fuel—coal, oil, and natural gas; and, two, a spacecraft propulsion system which could open the Milky Way to exploration within our lifetimes. How am I doing so far?"

"Ees possible."

"If this person—let's just pretend for now it is a man—if he can control twenty percent of the oil supply, he can manipulate the world's price per barrel, yes? He could withhold supply and drive prices up, or flood the market to drive prices down, yes?"

"*Da.*"

"Now imagine if he could manipulate the oil market, but, as an added bonus, he also had an ace-in-the-hole?"

"I don't know what this means—ace-in-the-hole?"

"In cards—poker, for example—you keep the ace you've been dealt a secret. You have a secret weapon. Now do you understand?"

"Da. Secret weapon I understand."

"I thought you might. In this case, the ace-in-the-hole is a weapon of war capable of nuclear destruction but with laser-guided accuracy. Such a weapon could destroy an enemy air base sitting next to a hospital without so much as rattling the glass in the nursery's windows."

Mavra shifted in her chair.

"A person who had a new source of energy, a new, more predictable weapon of war, and a propulsion system to explore the planets, would become a very powerful person, wouldn't he?

"*Da*. Yes. Very powerful."

"Just for fun, let's give him a name. You pick."

"Ees child's game again."

"Or, wait, maybe it's not just one person but two—maybe even a group of people. Does the group have a name?"

"I told you, I don't play children's games."

"Okay, that was your turn. I'll give this secret partnership a name: The Montana Project."

"Who told you about the partnership?" Mavra blurted.

Ruby leaned back and smiled. "You did. Just now. We heard rumors of a shell corporation involving Russians and other world players, but you just confirmed it."

"Eees stupid name." Mavra shifted again. Mavra knew she had said too much. "Ees nonsense."

"Isn't this fun? This girl time we're having together? Now, let's say that someone, a professor at a college maybe, discovers that the experiments this shell corporation is conducting threaten the stability of dark matter and dark energy on Earth right now?"

Mavra shrugged. "What ees your point?"

"Today, I will find out who is conspiring to control the world's economy. You're going to tell me."

22

Handcuffed, Mavra squirmed uncomfortably in the chair as Ruby rested her plump bottom on the corner of a credenza against the wall facing her. Two of Ruby's team stood guard inside the room and two more were in the hallway.

"We've been at this too long, you and I, haven't we, Ruby?" Mavra's face appeared worn as she spoke.

"Not long enough," Ruby replied, "you are still alive. When you are dead, then, maybe I will think about retiring. Not before."

Ruby rose from the credenza and stood facing her long-time enemy. "Well, Mavra, catching up has been great fun but it is time to get back to the matter at hand."

Sweat began to collect on Mavra's forehead and upper lip. Mavra knew her options. If she talked, Ruby would leak the video to the KGB and Mavra would be dealt a particularly gruesome death. A Polonium-210 cocktail would cause the traitor agonizing suffering. She might be beaten to death with a hammer or shot in the head on a Moscow sidewalk in broad daylight. The more gruesome murder, the more powerful the message to others who may foolishly consider betraying their oaths.

"You think I will help you follow the money. I won't," Mavra asserted.

"I've been given permission to do whatever is necessary."

Mavra blinked. She knew the degree of excruciating pain Ruby could inflict.

On the other side of the mirrored glass, the conference room's oblong pecan-veneer table was ringed with thick, leather chairs. The room's soft lighting belied the harshness of its purpose.

"So, these people behind the glass, do they know what you are capable of, Ruby? Have they ever witnessed a human being tortured?" Mavra didn't wait for an answer before adding, "Will you violate the Geneva Convention again?"

"I thought we already talked about this Geneva Convention matter," Ruby replied. "Torture? I suppose that's one description.

Yes, I expect I will need to use extreme measures to get the information I want. You see, Mavra, I see the Geneva Convention more as a guideline..."

"You. You people. You are so smug," Mavra spit her words. "You think you are above the law when it suits you. You will break the law to protect one religion while you vilify another. You are hypocrites. You think you are better than we are but you are not. We are no different. We just work for different people. We are fighting for opposite outcomes, that's all."

"I suppose there is some truth in what you say," Ruby replied. Deep down, she *knew* Mavra was right. Ruby, her assault team, and those watching from the other side of the glass had gone rogue. They were operating outside conventional rules. In a world where other nations unleash chemical weapons on its own citizens, torture them to get information, and resort to genocide for ethnic cleansing, Ruby and those behind the glass believed they were leveling the playing field—accomplishing what civilized governments were unable to do. They were freelancers—a band of ideologues with the power to stage a coup against a misguided third-world dictator. Around the oval table sat billionaires, government leaders, retired generals from several nations, celebrities, and entrepreneurs. Together, they controlled a war chest of money, weapons, and mercenaries—enough to influence the outcome of elections in hundreds of nations.

"You see, Mavra, there is a difference." Ruby continued, "Without seeming too Machiavellian, we believe our goals justify the methods we employ. If our violation of the Geneva Convention prevents one dictator from starving his citizens into slavery, we've done well. If we live by fair play, we will not allow the world's economy to be destroyed for one man's pursuit of wealth and power. If we fail, millions will die, and those who don't die will work for food scraps thrown onto the ground in front of them. No, Mavra, our methods may be the same but our purposes are not."

Mavra screamed, "Remember this! Before Russia could rise up from the ashes, it had to be destroyed. It was planned. Our economy was reduced to rubble. The Soviet Union was disassembled and the Berlin Wall was demolished. It was all part of the plan. *Our* plan! The people who now control Russia."

"KGB loyalists?"

"*Da!*" Mavra confirmed. "We knew our Soviet leaders were weak. We knew we could not remain a superpower with people who believed in democracy running our government. Everything was planned. As it is planned for your country. Your country is weak. It is being destroyed from within. And Russia is now in control of what you do."

The interrogation room doors opened and four men in MI-6 assault gear calmly entered the room. The leader of the MI-6 team walked easily toward Ruby. His fully automatic, short-stock rifle hung casually against his thigh. Ruby smiled and wrapped her fleshy arms around him.

"Aedain."

"Ruby," he said, the man's body nearly disappeared into Ruby's muumuu.

"Aedain, Aedain, Aedain," she repeated as she squeezed him, "excuse me. I should say, Commander," as she straightened and stood tall. "Forgive my familiarity, sir."

"No apologies necessary, Ruby. It's good to see you, too." He pulled her back into his embrace. "It's been a long time," Commander Aedain Maycroft replied.

"Too long," Ruby agreed. Wiping her tears, she returned to business. "I was just about to begin my interrogation," she explained. "I doubt you will want to watch. You know, British rules of engagement and all—"

"Who the hell are you people?" Blood drained from Mavra's already-porcelain face. Ruby and Aedain ignored her interruption.

"I see. Yes, of course, I understand," Aedain said, "but first, Ruby, I have news."

"News?"

"Not here," Aedain said as he led Ruby into the hall. Aedain whispered into her ear, "Ruby, he's alive."

Ruby fell limp with joy. "He's alive? Bishop Joe is alive?" She was certain she had left him for dead back at the church, bleeding out on the marble altar. "That tough old bird. You sure he's alive?"

"Yes."

Ruby's knees wobbled and Aedain helped her to a nearby chair.

"May I see him?" Ruby asked.

"Of course. Gather your things. We have transportation waiting."

"Where is he?"

"I'll tell you once we're en route."

"But—my interrogation—"

"Ruby, there are people in Kingston who remember your mother and Father John. Even after all these years, they're still loyal. They remember your mother being murdered and then Father John disappearing. They never knew what happened to their beloved Father John when the CIA changed his dossier to one Father Joe O'Donnell in New York City."

"He faked a Catholic priest so well they made him Archbishop." Ruby laughed. "He's alive?" Ruby repeated.

"Yes, he's alive, but he's going to have one helluva' limp for the rest of his life."

"But, about Mavra—"

"Oh, don't worry. We took the liberty of inviting some of your family's Jamaican friends to fill in. But let's keep that information between us and the folks in the conference room here, shall we?"

Ruby watched three Jamaican men walk past her into the room. They wore tan uniforms and chevrons made up of Jamaica's colors—green, yellow, and black. The island nation's military intelligence had adopted its interrogation methods from the notoriously brutal Jamaican drug cartels. The three interrogators smiled widely, white teeth glistening against jet-black canvases.

"Dees should be fun, Mon." The Jamaican leader smiled at Mavra. Mavra fainted.

With lights and sirens, the Queen's specially appointed diplomatic detail raced toward the New Orleans airport.

"Where is he?" Ruby asked.

"He's at the CIA hospital at Bluemont, Virginia, outside D.C."

"How did he get to Virginia from New Orleans?"

"British Airways."

Confused, Ruby replied, "British Airways doesn't fly out of New Orleans."

"When the Queen of England sends a jet to New Orleans, British Airways flies out of New Orleans."

"You mean," Ruby cocked her head, letting it sink it, "you mean to say that British Airways is an arm of the British Secret Service?"

"I didn't say that." Aedain leaned back in the front passenger seat of the speeding Range Rover and tilted his ball cap over his eyes. It had been a long day.

Ruby sat in back, pondering the scope of the organization for whom she worked. Today, she learned its members were sheiks, billionaires, Jamaica's military intelligence, a country singer heavily invested in ethanol, and the Queen of England. She knew there were more.

Today, the most important thing was learning her father was still alive.

23

"Wake up, Mavra, the Jamaican leader said as he waved smelling salts under her nose. Time to have a little talk. I've got you a little something for you."

Groggy, Mavra mumbled, "You cannot make me talk."

"Ooooh, I think maybe I can, Mavra. I do believe we will make you talk. First, we will inject you with alcohol straight into your veins."

"That's nothing. I have done this before, remember? I am a trained professional."

"Yes, of course, forgive me. I meant no insult. So, should we just skip that and go right to sodium pentothal? Truth serum, you know?"

"It's not reliable, you know that. You'll get mumbling gibberish, nothing more."

"Oh, you are so right. I am happy we agree. Since that is case, let's forego the kindergarten play and proceed to the advanced class. Mavra. Do you know what I find is the most effective? In fact, for me, it has never failed."

"Enlighten me," Mavra said dully, unimpressed by the Jamaican's threats.

"Extract of Carolina Reaper. The world's hottest pepper. On the Scoville scale, more than 2 million SHU—Scoville Heat Units. First, we squeeze the juice from the peppers, then evaporate the water to concentrate it into an oily extract five times more powerful than the pepper juice itself.

"So you're going to make my lips and tongue burn." Mavra's voice dripped. "How terrifying."

"Ah, well, yes, there is that. Your lips, your tongue, your eyes. Can you imagine if it is not just your mouth and eyes but your whole body on fire?" The Jamaican held up a small, glass vial with thin, red-tinted liquid for Mavra to see.

Mavra's jaw clenched.

"I am going to inject the extract into your spine. Your body will feel like your blood is boiling you alive." The Jamaican smiled gleefully.

Mavra's body stiffened as the three Jamaicans surrounded her. "Let's begin." Two Jamaicans held her arms while the third man's fingers located the soft, cushiony disc between her C3 and C4 vertebrae.

"One last chance?" The Jamaican offered. "No? So be it."

Those sitting at the long, oval conference table on the other side of the one-way mirror shuddered in horror at Mavra's agonizing screams.

In gulps of air between her shrieks, Mavra told the Jamaicans she didn't know the whole story—she is on a need-to-know basis, as any spy would be. She said Russia had nothing to do with murdering the professor's family, that it was a contract hit ordered by someone in the United States. She heard through the grapevine it was a botched job; they didn't intend to kill her. When the professor disappeared, the Russians' only lead was Charlie, the former U.S. covert operative. The next day, though, he died in a car accident. Russian agents scoured Charlie's home and office. They found a clue: a sticky-note pad. Beneath the missing top page, the words Queen Esther left an impression in the pages below. She was surprised such an experienced spy would make an amateurish mistake. In fact, she assumed it was done intentionally to throw them off Logan's trail. Mavra, though, remembered 'Queen Esther' as Ruby's alias from years before. Mavra recalled their throw-down in the Ritz Paris—the last time Mavra could use her legs—and she believed she knew where she could find Ruby—on Bourbon Street.

Day after day, Mavra's team surveilled New Orleans' tourist haunts—Bourbon Street, Jackson Square, and the French Market. She was shocked when she saw Sarah. Mavra knew Sarah hadn't come to the Big Easy for the Grayline tour; she was nervous, and glancing over her shoulder as if she was certain someone was following her.

"She led us right to Ruby—*Queen Esther's Tarot Card Reading* sign on Bourbon and St. Anne," Mavra gasped between spasms of pain. "It was clear Sarah was searching the French Quarter for Ruby, too." Sarah was a bonus, Mavra explained; her team would get a two-fer—both Ruby and Sarah. Two of Mavra's accomplices ducked into a tourist shop to buy Hawaiian shirts, donning them in an attempt to disguise themselves as tourists. They lost them, though, Mavra said, when Ruby pulled Sarah out the back door of

Marie Laveau's Voodoo Shop and disappeared into the bowels of the French Quarter. "How did you manage to find Logan and Sarah?"

"Please," Mavra screamed. "Please stop this pain! I'll tell you whatever you want to know!"

"Just a little longer. You're almost done." The Jamaican patted her on the shoulder.

"Russia wants Logan and the girl—"

"The girl? Sarah?" The Jamaican interrupted.

"Yes, of course, Sarah. They believe Sarah and Logan know why supercolliders are creating gravitational anomalies in the universe, even within Earth's atmosphere."

"And why would they think that?"

"Because Logan said so." Mavra dug her fingernails into her burning skin as she writhed. "He talked in his lectures about how the acceleration and collision of protons could affect Earth's dark matter and dark energy, especially Earth's gravity. He as much as told the world he knew what was causing them and he knew how to stop them."

"He said that?" the Jamaican asked. "It makes perfect sense, then, for your employers to send you here to kidnap them. Dr. Logan knows how to make this new source of energy viable. Is that it?"

"And the girl," Mavra said, nodding her head rapidly. "They needed the girl, too. We needed both of them alive."

"So you weren't tracking her—Sarah? You didn't put the transmitter in her shoe?"

"No, of course not. We had no idea she was wearing a transmitter."

"But you recognized her. How did you know it was Sarah, Logan's teaching assistant?"

"We had a dossier on all of them—Ruby, Sarah, Logan—photos, descriptions."

"So when you saw Sarah, you figured she could lead you to Logan, yes?"

Mavra jerked her head. "*Da.*"

"After your comrades lost her, how did you find her?"

"We called Ruby. Our intelligence had intercepted her phone calls so we knew her phone number. We said if she didn't bring the girl to us the next day, we would murder everyone she loved."

"Including the Archbishop."

"Da. Yes. We'd been watching him, too. We knew he and Ruby went way back for some reason; we didn't know why until recently.

When we saw him duck in and out of Ruby's townhouse after Sarah and Ruby escaped from Madam Laveau's. We were certain she was in there. So we waited."

The concentrated capsaicin of the Carolina Reaper poison caused Mavra's muscles to twitch and spasm grotesquely. She gulped for air between sentences. "We lost Ruby and Sarah later that night but we knew the Archbishop would lead us to them eventually, and to Logan."

"What else can you tell me?" The Jamaican leaned in close, "Remember, your life depends on it. You need the antidote soon, before your flesh melts from your bones."

"Nothing, I swear. Nothing." Mavra gasped. "That's everything I know. Now, please, I beg of you, please stop this pain. Please, I beg of you, the antidote."

The Jamaican paused then asked, "Why did you shoot off the Archbishop's leg?"

"No reason in particular," Mavra panted, her body now thrashing wildly in a futile attempt to eliminate the poison.

"I see," the Jamaican replied as he tapped the refilled barrel of the hypodermic needle. He stuck it into her arm and watched her eyes bulge in horror.

Instantly, Mavra's body convulsed. "Why? Why would you do this? I told you everything I know."

"No reason in particular." The Jamaican smiled wickedly as he drew the curtains across the one-way mirror. He leaned across the table, speaking slowly. "Oh, about that antidote thing. You see... I lied. There is no antidote. But I have this for you." Beside her, he laid a 9mm semi-automatic with its clip removed. The chamber held one bullet. Mavra grabbed the gun and pointed it at the Jamaican. Her eyes were blinded by tears and her hand trembled.

"Ah-ah, choose wisely," the Jamaican admonished Mavra as he shook his finger. "Your vision is blurry; you can barely see me. Your hands are trembling. You may fire the gun but you will probably miss. Or, the bullet may hit me but not kill me. If you are very lucky, you will succeed. You will kill me and you will have exacted your revenge. But you will be out of bullets. You must ask yourself: 'How long will you suffer with your burning, disintegrating flesh before you die? Is vengeance more important than stopping your own misery?'"

Mavra tried to steady her arm and take aim at the Jamaican but it was impossible. She watched with blurry eyes as the Jamaican backed out the door and clicked the latch behind him.

At the oval table, a single, muffled gunshot was heard from the room beyond the drapes.

24

Thirty-six hours of sleeplessness causes tricks in one's head. Sarah passed that mark yesterday; now, she was nearing the 48-hours mark without sleep. By the time Logan turned onto the shell road in Apalachicola, Florida's Gulf Coast night air turned into salty fog. It clung to the Chevy, turning its finish whitish grey. 'Room to Rent' blinked in faded pink neon, then to black and back to pink.

At best, Sarah calculated, she would get three hours' sleep before sunrise. That was two hours ago. Now, as Sarah lay on her back, she stared at the sign's reflection blinking off the particle board ceiling. Beside her, Tom Moore sucked in air, making a raspy sound, then snorted it out. The empty bottle of Ten High he'd bought a liquor store on U.S. 98 sat on the nightstand.

Her mind raced. Sarah reached for the TV remote and scrolled through channels.

She stopped at the History Channel. A middle-aged TV journalist stood in the middle of sand and scrub, holding a 1960s-era microphone as he looked into the camera.

"On July 8, 1947, Walter Haut, the public information officer for the Roswell Army Air Field, issued a press release. A flying disc had been recovered from a nearby ranch." The reporter's tone then turned suspicious, hinting the Army intentionally covered up a more nefarious event, "Within 24 hours, the military's story had changed. Decades later, the Army clung to its story that the disc was nothing more than a weather balloon which had crashed."

Sarah sat upright on the bed; she just heard a clue about the legendary Roswell incident she'd never heard before. Maybe, she'd just never had a reason to hear it before.

"Years later, the Air Force admitted that the weather balloons were part of Project Mogul. The balloons were equipped with microphones to detect Russian atomic bomb tests from halfway around the world." The government's story about harmless weather balloons had just been exposed. The weather balloons were an integral weapon in the United States' Cold War with Russia. The weather balloons collected information on Russia's atomic bomb tests.

It appeared to be a slip of the tongue by the Army. Sarah paused and wondered, *Why would the Army even mention weather balloons if they were being used for intelligence gathering?*

"Despite the Army debunking the UFO version with the weather balloon story," the narrator continued, "many local residents, tourists, and citizens throughout the world still believe today that the Army covered up the real truth. Since the incident occurred in 1947, the base has been under tight security. Follow me."

Sarah stared at the TV. The reporter moved from the desert two-track bordering the base's perimeter toward a fence at the top of a man-made earthen berm.

He explained his findings as he huffed up the small hill which crested fifty yards away. "Even though twenty years after the incident, in 1967, the base was transferred to the General Services Administration, it is still very active. It is also very secretive, as you can tell by its electrically charged fencing you see there," he said, stopping to catch his breath and point to the berm's crest, "as you saw when we were driving in, this levy and fencing surrounds this former Air Force base, even though, according to military sources, there have been no Air Force operations underway here in a half-century." The camera panned the fence as the reporter explained, "There are 'No Trespassing' signs, video cameras and, I suspect, satellite surveillance." The reporter looked and pointed up into the sky. "Watch what happens when we get too close to the fence."

The reporter closed to within 20 feet of the fence and stood, waiting. Barely 90 seconds passed before two speeding trucks approached, one from each direction, on the desert road where the news van was parked. Four beefy men exited each of the four-door extended cab pickups, all of them heavily armed with automatic weapons. Neither the trucks nor the men's uniforms showed any military indicia; their trucks were plain white and their desert camo fatigues appeared to be more from a sporting-goods store than a quartermaster's inventory. The leader stood at the base of the hill with his hands on his hips and shouted to the reporter. "Sir, will you please come down here?"

"Maybe we can get some answers from these gentlemen," the reporter huffed as made his way down the hill. His hopes faded when the first man ordered, "Please turn the camera off or we will confiscate it." There was no insignia above their pockets or name patches on their fatigues—not even an American flag on the shoulder. The cameraman shut the video feed down immediately but the audio engineer continued recording.

Over a black TV, screen, Sarah heard the reporter ask, "May I ask you who you are?"

"No, sir." the leader replied evenly. "Please leave."

"But we have a right to be here," the reporter protested, "we are standing on public land."

"Actually, no, it is private land, sir. The landowner has simply granted us the use of this road for convenience in securing the base. This is not negotiable. You have sixty seconds to get into your van and leave." The sounds of automatic weapons being cocked could be heard on the recording.

Five miles away, the reporter was on-screen again. His face was pale and drawn. "They told us we had sixty seconds to leave, then all eight of them pointed their weapons at our heads." The microphone shook in his trembling hand as he spoke.

The base? Sarah's ears pricked up. The base hasn't been a base in fifty years but the machine-toting alpha male just called it a base. She replayed his statement in her head. He claimed the landowner had given them permission to use his land as a security buffer for a base that was no longer a base and which never—even when it was a base—was supposed to hold any secrets.

She clicked the remote, turning off the TV. It wasn't the first time she'd been suspicious of the government's accounts of the Roswell mystery, she compared the accounts of the military to those of local residents and visitors.

There was no shortage of fervent believers who were certain an alien spaceship had landed or crashed on the Army base. They, too, believed that a real alien was found in the wreckage. Nobody was certain if the spaceman lived through the crash.

Any hope of sleep vanished. Sarah sat on the bed scribbling notes until daylight shone through the grimy motel window. She threw on her jacket, grabbed her backpack, and ran to find the nearest library.

For three days, Sarah scrolled through decades of microfiche archives. She followed the extraterrestrial trail from the Roswell military base to Nevada, then to Wright-Patterson Air Force Base in Dayton, Ohio. Rumors hinted the spaceman was being preserved in the basement of the Ohio air base's main hanger. *But why?* Sarah wondered. Why would the Army ship everything pertaining to the UFO halfway across the country?

Sarah's dad had always been skeptical of the government explanation of the Roswell incident. Now, Sarah was, too. It seemed clear the Roswell Army Air Force Base had been keeping secrets well before 1947.

Until today, Sarah and most UFO believers thought that the crash occurred on the base's land. But they were wrong. The crash occurred on a nearby ranch. Sarah wondered if it be the same ranch as the one adjacent to the GSA's secretive, non-military property? Was it the same ranch whose owner is generous enough to maintain a road and private security for the safety of the non-military, no-secrets base? Who were these guards? Were they private security or secret military operatives?

From Florida's Franklin County library, Sarah hacked into New Mexico and Nevada property records and discovered not one, but two nearby ranches. One of them was 85,000 acres, another 55,000. The Chaves County aerial photo blacked out the base but showed the two parcels, totaling 140,000 acres, adjacent to one another. The larger of the two shared the base's eastern border. All told, the military and private parcels represented 200 uninterrupted square miles.

El Chapo's escape tunnel was nearly a mile long, 30 feet underground and built in one year. The government has had nearly seventy years—The possibilities of what was being hidden on the heavily guarded Roswell land sent shivers down Sarah's spine.

But it was nothing compared to what she would discover about another closely held secret.

Unable to sleep, she stared at ceiling tiles of the inglorious motel room as the blinking neon reflected from them. Sarah and Dr. Logan were in more danger than she could possibly imagine.

25

Five days and six nights in a cramped Gulf Coast room to rent was wearing on Sarah's nerves. So, too, was sleeping beside a man she once respected, posing as the wife of a janitor who self-medicated every night with cheap whiskey and Xanax. The rhythmic pulse of the faded pink reflection on the ceiling had nearly soothed her to sleep when the intermittent reflection stopped.

Sarah jolted upright, then dove beside the bed before crawling to the window. She peeked through the gap in the motel's vinyl curtains.

"What the—?"

Two black SUVs idled in the parking lot below, in front of the motel office's open door. Sarah strained make sense of unintelligible shouting just before the night clerk bolted into the parking lot.

Simultaneously, Sarah saw the muzzle flash of a rifle. The motel clerk collapsed to the tarmac in a lifeless heap.

"Shit." Sarah muttered and repeated, "Shit. Shit, shit, shit, shit!" She looked toward the bed and saw Dr. Logan unconscious. He would be no help. Sarah didn't know who these killers were but she knew her life and Logan's were in danger.

It was clear they had found the motel because they were tracking *her*, not Tom the janitor. If she was in the room when the gang of men kicked through the door, they would both be kidnapped, tortured, and eventually murdered. Dr. Logan had a better chance alone. Maybe he could make them believe he was a lonely, drunken janitor from Texas if the car and Sarah were gone.

It wouldn't take them long to check the motel's records and find the registration for couple in Room 206, driving a plain, beige Chevy. Eventually, they would find the car parked behind the laundromat next door to the motel—if they didn't make a beeline for the motel room first.

She slipped on her jeans and shoes, grabbed her backpack, the car keys, and her sweatshirt. She opened the door a crack and peeked into the hallway. Stepping quickly to the back entrance of the hotel,

162

she ran out the door and toward the car. Even in the middle of the night, the laundromat buzzed with activity. Customers sat on flimsy plastic chairs and stared at their smartphones as they waited for their washer loads to finish, oblivious to the murder in the parking lot. Sarah realized that she saw muzzle flash in the darkness, but, like the laundromat customers, she never heard gunshots. "Silencers," she muttered as she twisted the ignition. She was running from men with automatic weapons fitted with silencers. They were professional killers.

Sarah didn't look back as she floored the beige sedan east on Highway 98. *He'll be alright*, she convinced herself. In his near-comatose state, maybe Dr. Logan wouldn't wake up when they burst through the door.

She was wrong. The men from the SUVs wasted no time finding the hotel records, matching up the license plates and descriptions with the room registrations. The leader pulled the motel's master key off the dead clerk's belt then waved a circle above his head, ordering two of them to search the nearby area for the couple's car.

Weapons drawn, four others ran toward room 206—the only room registration whose car listed out-of-state plates. Pointing their short-barreled rifles at the doorknob, they blasted the lock off before kicking in the door. The gang leader shoved the muzzle of an Uzi into Dr. Logan's face as another turned on the room's lights.

"Wake up!" the leader shouted. Dr. Logan didn't budge. "Logan! Wake up!"

They tore Logan's belongings apart, ripping his wallet open and pulling out his ID. "Hey, Boss, I'm not sure this is Logan. His license says he's somebody named Tom Moore from Effie, Texas. He's got an ID card says he works at a church as a janitor. This guy is skinnier than Logan. He looks like hell, too."

"Search the place!" the leader ordered. "See if there's any sign a woman was here. Says here he registered with his wife, Nancy Moore." He peeked behind every doorway, asking over and over, "Where are you, Nancy?"

"Nancy? Is that you, Baby? Did you come back, Baby?" Tom Moore suddenly moved, slurring his speech and feigning semi-consciousness.

"Wake up!" the leader shouted and shook the Professor.

"Who… wha'? Who are you? Where's Nancy? I told her I was sorry." The professor's gibberish sounded plausible as he gained consciousness and looked around the room. The car keys were gone and Sarah's sweatshirt was missing from the closet. Logan prayed she grabbed her backpack, too.

The leader's voice shifted to friendly, helpful. "Yeah, that's right. Where's Nancy? Tell us where Nancy is. Let's help you find Nancy."

"She left me, I guess. I don't know. She got tired of my drinking. She told me she was leaving."

"When did she leave?"

"Yesterday. No, the day before yesterday, maybe, I'm not sure. What day is it today? I said I was sorry. I promised I'd stop drinking."

"Yes, and you're doing real well at that," the leader reassured Tom Moore. "Yeah, Nancy's going to come back, you can bet on that. Real soon. You got any idea where she might have run off to? She got a sister, a best friend, maybe?"

"Do you work for the motel?"

"Yeah, yeah, sure, we work for the motel. You know, we help, we uh, we clean up messes, you know? Kinda' like you, Tom, we're a sorta' like janitors."

The clerk's murderers weren't paying much attention to the laundromat's customers or the bloody lump of flesh in the middle of the lot but the customer who had just arrived at the laundromat did. He dropped his plastic clothes basket in the lot and called 9-1-1.

One gang member, guarding Room 206's open door, heard distant sirens approaching.

"Boss, we gotta' go. Cops."

"Sonofabitch!"

"You wanna' take him with us?"

"No, he'll slow us down."

"I could just shoot him, you know? In the head."

"If this is Logan, we need him alive and we need the girl, too. We kill him and we've got no chance of him leading us to the girl." The leader pushed the others through the door of Room 206 and waved for the drivers of the two black Escalades to pick them up at the bottom of the stairs.

Four Florida State Trooper cars whizzed past Sarah, heading west toward the motel, their lights flashing and sirens blaring. She couldn't tell if it was a good sign or a bad one. If Logan wasn't already dead, the cops might get there in time to save his life. Or they could be too late. Sarah cut the steering wheel hard, turning onto a shell road leading toward the Gulf, then cut another hard right to circle back toward the motel on the deserted road parallel to Highway 98. She clicked the headlights off a half mile east of the motel. Jogging, then running beside the gator-infested marshland between the road and the highway, she wondered how the killers had found them. Were they the same ones who murdered Logan's family? Were they an assassination team who had orders to kill her and Logan on sight? Sarah's sweat drew the attention of hundreds of mosquitos who called the swamp home. Swatting constantly, Sarah watched as the four Trooper cars were joined by the county sheriff, and the Apalachicola police chief. She saw a bedraggled but breathing Tom Moore, wrapped in a blanket, sitting on a curb as he was interrogated by the police.

Sarah breathed a sigh of relief. She couldn't go to him but at least he was alive. Despite evading the police, the killers weren't far away; Sarah knew that. They would be watching for a 2005 Chevy with Texas plates.

How did they find them? Sarah pondered. It had to be a tracking device on her. Somewhere. It wasn't the car, and Dr. Logan told her that Ruby had checked her for electronic tracking transmitters. Ruby said she was clean. Could Ruby have missed something? Her backpack, maybe? Her purse? She could sit by the marsh being eaten alive by mosquitoes or even an alligator, weighing the possibilities till the sun came up, but that wouldn't give her answers. More important, driving after daylight would be dangerous. She had two hours of darkness to get as far away from the motel as possible.

More than an hour away, Panama City Beach was the closest town with an electronics store. She knew that she needed to buy a transmitter signal detector and check herself for electronic bugs. Until she identified where the bugging device was, the thugs would be able to follow them anywhere. Doing so, though, meant leaving Logan in police custody, or worse, back at the motel.

Sarah looked west down the shell road and guessed how long she could drive parallel to U.S. 98. She glanced back across the marsh to the highway and knew she had to move fast. The shell road was not built for speed. She ran back to the Chevy, sped west, and turned toward the highway at the first intersection.

It's better to get stopped by the Florida Troopers than the killers in the black trucks, Sarah thought. Once westbound on the tarmac U.S. 98 again, she pressed the accelerator to the floor and coaxed underpowered car to more than ninety miles an hour. With the murder weapon in their SUV, she hoped the killers might think twice about driving fast enough to catch her.

Just east of Destin, Florida, and now pushing a hundred miles an hour, Sarah used her free hand to pull the burn phone from her backpack. She bit the corner of the blister pack to open it, then loaded the battery and powered it up. Sarah punched in ten numbers. A voice answered.

Sarah trembled, "I need your help." The conversation was short. As she crossed over East Pass, a channel leading to the Gulf of Mexico, Sarah rolled down her window and threw the phone over the railing into the water a hundred feet below.

Her fingers wrapped tightly around the steering wheel, Sarah watched for signs of headlights following her, an SUV hiding behind a tree, or parked down a two-track just off the highway. She watched for anything which looked like the black trucks of the murderers.

As the sun rose over the east horizon, sunlight reflected off the city limits sign over the highway, making her squint to read: 'Welcome to Panama City Beach.' A mile into town, a Best Buy store was on the far end of the strip mall anchored by a Target store in the middle. Sarah parked the Chevy in the parking lot close to the highway and walked a hundred yards to the electronics store. It wouldn't open for another hour. Sweat streamed down her back but it wasn't because the temperature was already 80 degrees with humidity to match.

"Do you have scanners?" Sarah nervously asked the clerk once the store opened.

Annoyed by Sarah's interruption, the clerk lazily turned in her direction. "What kind of scanners you want? We got barcode scanners, copier scanners, police scanners, radio signal scanners—"

"That one!" Sarah blurted. "Do you have scanners that can find a bugging device planted on someone?"

"A transmitter detection scanner?"

"Sure." The clerk stopped, looked Sarah up and down, and then said, "This way. Follow me. Aisle seven. We only carry two brands—a cheap one that isn't worth shit and one that's four hundred bucks. Which one you want?"

Sarah reached into her backpack and pulled out the roll of hundreds. "The good one," she replied. She restrained herself from yelling at the teenager to hurry as he ambled toward the cash register. Right now, she didn't want him to remember anything about her— her appearance, how she talked, nothing. Remembering her could get them both killed.

"That one will find any electronic bugs on you or in a room from twenty feet away. Plus, it detects radiation like a Geiger counter, magnetic fields, hell, you can even use it at the beach as a metal detector. There's real money in finding jewelry people lose in the sand," he rambled on as he took her cash. Sarah bit her lip as he scrawled a highlighter across each bill to verify its authenticity, then punched the buttons on the cash register one at a time with his index finger until the drawer popped open and the receipt printed.

"Do you have a bathroom?" Sarah asked.

"Well, it's not really for the public," the irritating young man drawled, "Now, Target, down the mall there, they got a public toilet."

"Fine," Sarah muttered. It wasn't fine but she was in too big a hurry to argue. She ran to the Target store, ducked into the rest room near the entrance, and unwrapped the scanner from its packaging. When she passed it over her body, she discovered a signal was being transmitted from her left running shoe. She remembered Dr. Logan telling her that Ruby had checked her for tracking devices. Somehow, this one got past her. *Or did it?* Sarah couldn't help but wonder.

She grabbed a pair of $4 flip-flops from the end cap by the nearest cash register, paid for them, and dumped her shoes in the trashcan in the store's lobby. She started toward the Chevy but stopped short. Instead, she ran back into the store, to the Electronics Department, grabbed a handful of burn phones, and threw them onto the counter.

At the far edge of the strip mall parking lot, the same black Escalades she'd seen at the motel were parked beside Dr. Logan's car. Eight men surrounded the Chevy, jiggling the door handle and checking the trunk to see if it was locked. Walking around it, they felt the hood for warmth, then peeked inside the car's passenger cabin, before the leader of the group shouted toward one of the others standing beside one of the black SUVs. He reached into the SUV and pulled out a slim jim—a tool for unlocking car doors. The leader jimmied the car open and motioned to three of the men to tear it apart searching for clues. The other four paired off and headed for the strip of stores on the other side of the parking lot.

"May I help you?" the chirpy Electronics Department clerk asked Sarah in a syrupy Southern drawl.

"I want to pay for these phones," Sarah blurted, no longer able to contain her urgency. She peeled two hundreds off the roll and laid them on the counter. "Is there an exit to the back parking lot?"

"Why, yes, there is, but it sets off an alarm when we open it. It's for emergencies only." The bubbly clerk tilted her head as if to say, *I'm sure you understand.*

"Will that be paper or plastic?"

Sarah growled, "This *is* an emergency! Is there any way to shut the alarm off?"

"Only with the manager's code and she won't be in till noon today. Sorry." She tilted her head to the opposite side. "Paper or plastic?"

"What?" Sarah asked.

"Paper or plastic?"

"Oh, for Christ's sake. Plastic. Listen, the truth is: look out there. Across the parking lot. The tan car. That's my ex-boyfriend, rifling through my car with three of his buddies. See those four walking this way? You see what they are carrying? Those are machine guns. They'll be inside this store in two minutes and, if I'm still here, you'll get to witness a murder. My murder. Then they'll kill you so there are no witnesses."

"Oh, Sweet Jesus!" the girl exclaimed. "Do you want me to call the police?" The vacuous smile had disappeared from the clerk's face. Sarah held the store clerk back from getting too close to the window.

"Oh no, no, no," Sarah improvised, "you see, they *are* the police. If he and his cop friends find me, I won't make it to jail. If they don't shoot me in the head right in front of you, they'll cut me up with a chainsaw and dump me in the swamp for alligator food. Now, you have three choices: one, watch them kill me—and be found in a pool of your own blood. Or two, live with knowing they cut me up and dumped me in a swamp."

"Noooo," the terrified girl was shaking.

"Okay then, three. Turn the back door alarm off and tell them I was never here—and make it convincing. Now, which is it going to be?" The clerk saw the terror in Sarah's eyes and knew she was telling her the truth. "Please, can you turn off the alarm?"

"I—" The girl twitched nervously.

"My life depends on it."

The girl started pressing keys on the cash register. "The manager, she sets the code to turn off the alarm. I know what her code was last week. She changes it every week, though," the girl mumbled as she pressed the keys faster, "If she hasn't changed her passcode yet—" She turned to Sarah, "It says I just turned it off! I can't be 100 percent sure. Hurry!"

The chirpy girl had succeeded. Without setting off a blaring exit alarm, Sarah stepped into the morning sunlight and edged along the block building's rear wall till she reached the street at the opposite end of the strip mall from the Best Buy store.

Mobile was four hours away by bus but that wasn't an option. The men in the SUVs would find her waiting at the bus station before the bus to Mobile arrived.

Sarah crossed to the northbound side of State Road 79 and stuck her thumb into the air. She prayed a black Escalade wasn't the first to offer her a ride.

26

Oyster boat captains don't ask questions for good reason. Most of the men hiring on are running from something. Usually the law.

Apalachicola Bay, an inlet from the Gulf renowned for its small, sweet oysters, is a magnet for vagrants from around the world during oyster-harvesting season. The City of Apalachicola's Police Department is tucked into the back corner of the first floor in City Hall's two-story red brick building. Its two cells sit empty most days, except Fridays and Saturdays when the shrimp and oyster boats are in port.

Logan lay on the sagging cotton mattress sinking into the box-spring bed frame. It stunk of stale beer, vomit, and chlorine bleach. The only window was across the hall and Logan stared into darkness through the bars of his cell. When the Apalachicola Police Chief fingerprinted him, he discovered John Logan wasn't Tom Moore, a janitor, but instead, a renowned astrophysicist, and a person of interest in the murder of his wife and children in Princeton, New Jersey. The New Jersey State Police immediately dispatched a transport vehicle to extradite him from the sleepy Florida oyster town. The van with two New Jersey troopers was speeding through the night on I-95. They'd arrive in Apalachicola by early morning.

Watching thick fog settle over the Delta, Logan hoped the New Jersey troopers arrived before the black Escalades returned. The Franklin County Sheriff and the Florida State Police had left the scene. Logan knew these knuckle-busters wouldn't give up.

The retired Chicago beat cop—a now pot-bellied police chief who would be no match for full-auto machine guns.

An hour before dawn, the Escalades eased in front of the red brick building. The Police Chief was napping when the explosion blew the door open and eight men rushed in. The old cop went down in a hail of bullets before his hand reached his .38 revolver. Snatching the cell keys from a peg on the wall, the killers charged down the hall toward Dr. Logan.

I'm a dead man, Logan thought as his body went cold.

Yanking him from the cell, they pushed him down the hall corridor toward the street. Logan struggled but was easily overpowered. They dragged him across the asphalt parking lot, tugging him toward the black trucks.

Logan watched as, one by one, each of the killers fell to the ground, a pool of blood encircling their heads. In the bedlam, the remaining killers fired randomly into the dark sky but hit nothing. They saw nothing. There was no sound, only a phantom sniper. Every kill shot found its mark.

"What the hell?" Logan muttered, surrounded at his feet by eight corpses. The shooter had one target left: him. He dove beneath the closest Escalade and pulled a dead body in front of him for protection.

Then Logan heard a roaring engine rounding the corner. The black and tan Chevy SS screeched to a stop.

"Get in!" Sarah shouted. He scrambled into the passenger seat as Sarah slammed the four-speed into first gear and popped the clutch. The tires howled and smoked, and the car's rear end fishtailed as she left the parking lot. She was headed west on Highway 98 and wasn't going to let anyone catch her.

Twenty miles down the road, they both stopped trembling enough for their mouths to form words.

Logan spoke first, "Wha'—what the hell happened back there?"

"You were drunk. Passed out cold." Sarah described Logan's barbiturate-laced stupor. "When the motel sign stopped blinking, I knew something was wrong. I jumped out of bed and looked outside. I heard shouting and saw the night clerk make a run for it. They shot him in cold blood."

"I know," Logan nodded, "I saw him being loaded into the Coroner's wagon. Where were you? How—" Logan looked at the car, "Where did you get this car? Where did you go?" He paused, touching his blood-spattered shirt and jeans.

He didn't wait for an answer. "What the hell happened? One second, I'm out cold, these goons wake me up and ask me where you are. I play dumb but they're dragging me out of the room. When they hear sirens coming from every direction, they haul ass out of there. Next thing I know, the Police Chief is questioning me as I'm trying to sober up. He drags me past the dead guy and throws me in jail. 'For my own good,' he says. The next morning, I watch the Police Chief get sprayed with bullets, and blood flying everywhere. They nab me; I'm sure I'm dead. They're pushing me toward their trucks when they start dropping like flies. What the hell was happening? Who killed them?"

"A sniper, maybe?" Sarah muttered.

"And you would know this—how?" Logan stared at his protégé. She didn't answer. Sarah's eyes were busy darting back and forth from one side of the road to the other.

"Where did you go after you ducked out of the motel?" Logan asked.

"When the black trucks showed up, the night clerk must have sensed something was wrong. He shut off the motel sign. Thank God he did; if he hadn't, I wouldn't have had any warning. I saw them kill the clerk. I knew they would find us and, if we were both there, we'd be dead for sure. Our only chance was for me to run out the back door. I had to get the car away from the motel before they found it. I hoped they wouldn't kill either of us until they had us both."

"You *hoped?*"

"Well, yeah. What did you want me to do? Try to lug your drunk ass off the bed and carry you with me?"

"No, I suppose not." Logan's head was still pounding from his bender. "Where did you go?"

"When the Florida Troopers and the Sheriff showed up, I was across the road on the other side of the barrier island when they hauled you to jail. I knew I had to get my hands on a transmitter signal detector to find out how they were tracking us. At first I thought they were tracking the car's GPS signal but they didn't install GPS as standard equipment until 2009."

"They install GPS on all cars now? I didn't know that—"

"Most people don't but that's not important. Stay focused."

Logan saw the white and red Target bag at his feet. "What's this?" He reached into it and pulled out a blister-packaged cell phone."

"It's a burn phone. Almost impossible to track with GPS unless you screw up."

"You bought a burn phone? I thought those were just on TV."

"I bought three; there are two more in the bag. I dropped the one my dad gave me into the Gulf of Mexico when I was driving to Panama City."

"You drove to Panama City? For what?"

"It was the closest town with a Best Buy. I needed to buy a transmitter signal detector and scan myself for bugs."

"Your dad gave you a burn phone? When did he do that?"

"When he gave me this car."

"Your dad gave you this car? What the—? Where has it been?"

"In long-term parking at the Mobile airport. I left it there on the way down from Detroit and bought a bus ticket to New Orleans. I thought we might need a Plan B. It's not like we had a lot of time to talk about this before the Russians blew up the church, did we?"

"We've been hiding out in the motel for a week. You might have brought it up then."

"You were drunk most of the time. The rest of the time you were having a hangover. So, you'd start drinking again to stop your head from hurting. Nothing else mattered."

"So, last night, you drove to Panama City, then to Alabama and back all in one night?"

"Actually, Dr. Logan, it's been thirty hours since the night clerk was shot. You were passed out most of the time."

Dazed, Logan asked, "It has?"

"The killers caught up with me in the Best Buy parking lot. I left your car in the parking lot, hitched a ride headed west and made my way to Mobile."

"You left my car in a parking lot?"

"Sorry. The Feds probably have it by now. If I were you, I wouldn't plan on getting it back."

"No, I suppose not." Logan agreed. "Three burn phones? Why three?"

Sarah laughed. "We're going to need them. We don't know whose phones they have tapped. As soon as we call one number, we destroy the burner. We don't use one twice. Ever. Got it?" Sarah's face was drawn from fatigue.

"Who did you call?" Logan asked pointedly.

"With the phone I threw over the bridge?"

"Yes, that one."

Sarah paused several moments. "My dad."

"Uh-huh." Dr. Logan pieced the puzzle together in his brain. "The ex-Army Ranger sniper. He got all the way from Detroit the Florida Panhandle in six hours? How'd he manage that?"

"I didn't ask. He just said he would and I believed him." Sarah said matter-of-factly. "He said he had plenty of time to scout a spot, get into his Ghillie suit, and dial in his rifle."

"I didn't hear any gunfire. Where was he?" Dr. Logan observed.

"He used a silencer. He was on the roof of the Episcopal Church across the street, behind the cypress tree. I couldn't see him, either, until he started shooting. I was parked at the corner watching for muzzle flash. He told me to wait till he stood up; that was my signal he had neutralized all of them. I hit the gas and came around the corner to pick you up and escape."

"Neutralized," the Professor noted, "as in killed."

"Yes." The car's wide tires gripped the asphalt as Sarah pushed the speedometer to 120 miles per hour. Logan stared through the windshield, trying to mentally digest the last twenty minutes. One puzzle piece which was still missing was how the assassin squad knew where they were.

"How did they find us?"

"They tracked us. Ruby must have missed a transmitter some-one planted in my shoe. I don't know why it took five days to find us, though. Maybe the transmitter's signal was weak, who knows? But they came for both of us."

"Who planted a transmitter in your shoe?"

"That's the million dollar question. It could have been anybody. Even somebody back at Princeton. How do you know Ruby?" Sarah asked suspiciously.

"My friend, Charlie, gave me her name, God rest his soul. When he gave me the instructions on how to go off the grid, he said to leave a breadcrumb trail that only someone who knew me well could find me. Ruby could be trusted, he said."

"Maybe she can. Maybe she can't," Sarah countered. "Why would he tell you to leave clues for someone to find you if you wanted to disappear?"

"Not just someone." Logan swallowed hard. "They were for you. In case you wanted to find me."

"Oh."

Peering into the rear view mirror, she saw the sun's reflection from the windshield of a distant vehicle. She wasn't sure if it was a car, a truck, or Escalade. She wasn't taking any chances.

"Hang on," Sarah instructed as she pushed the accelerator to the floor, and buried the speedometer at 140. Logan looked over his shoulder and saw the reflection, too.

"How fast does this thing go?"

"I'm not sure. My dad thought about 150 but that was just a guess."

"Try for 160." Logan gripped the dashboard and pushed himself deeper into the passenger seat. "Speaking of your dad, I wonder what he will tell the New Jersey Troopers when they show up."

"Nothing. He won't be there to tell them. He's halfway to De-troit by now."

"Did he give you anything else besides a burn phone and a hot rod?"

"Maybe." Sarah's gripped the steering wheel and focused on the road ahead.

Logan watched telephone poles flash past as if they stood beside one another. The questions he had racing through his brains would need to wait. At 160 mph, any distraction would be their last.

27

Just east of Port St. Joe, along Florida's Panhandle Gulf Coast, Sarah jammed both feet onto the brake pedal as she saw the upcoming bend in U.S. 98. Careful not to leave black skid marks in the highway's pavement, Sarah cut the wheel hard to the right and headed north on desolate Highway 71.

Port St. Joe, a fishing village on Saint Joseph Bay, is the first sign of civilization west of Apalachicola. Just off U.S. 98, Sarah slid the car to a stop behind a small sand dune. Sarah and Dr. Logan ran to the crest of the dune and peered through a stand of sea oats, waiting for the car in the mirror to appear. Sarah and Logan watched, hoping it would keep going straight on U.S. 98. In unison, they breathed a sigh of relief when a station wagon with a family on vacation breezed past.

As Logan and Sarah stood to leave, three plain-colored Crown Victorias flew around the station wagon and passed it, bumper-to-bumper, at more than a hundred miles per hour.

Logan spoke first, "What the f—? Who are these people? They just keep coming!"

"BAU," Sarah replied, recalling her conversation with Aedain.

"B.A. what?"

"Behavioral Analysis Unit of the FBI," Sarah explained.

"You mean like on TV? Penelope and Rossi?" Logan asked.

"Yes, them."

"I thought they only investigated kidnappings."

"They've branched out."

"How do you know this?"

"You remember that morning you were hiding in your neighbor's attic and your place was surrounded with police cars?"

"Yes."

"And you remember how I was supposed to retrieve the envelope you left in the basement safe, right?"

"Yes."

"You know, the one you had already removed and stashed in my locker? Remember? Right after you bribed poor Mr. Landon with a plate of brownies to put the brass plate with my locker combinations scratched into it someplace I'd be sure to find it? You remember that, right? By the way, who the hell gave you my locker combination?"

"You're still pissed. I can tell."

Sarah scowled at her mentor. "I was there, outside your house with Aedain, one of the students in your class. He explained the whole FBI BAU thing to me."

"Aedain who? A student in my class? How would he know?"

"He's a Criminal Justice Major. A couple of years back, he did an internship with the BAU."

"What is he doing in my class?" Dr. Logan's brow scrunched tightly.

"Cosmology is his hobby, he says. He says he passed the prerequisites by taking a waiver exam."

"Bullshit. There's no such thing." Logan hunched his shoulders. "He snuck into my class—or worse, he was planted with the university's permission."

Sarah felt the now-familiar burn surge up her spine. "No, I don't think he was planted by the university. He was planted by someone though." Sarah's heart sank, knowing that Aedain, someone she had grown fond of, had lied to her. It stung, but she'd gone off the grid and would likely never see Aedain again. Right now, staying alive was her first priority.

"So," Sarah said after composing herself, "Aedain told me that many of the federal intelligence and law enforcement agencies drive certain kinds of cars. The Treasury—the Secret Service and ATF people—they usually drive big, black SUVs. The NSA is unpredictable; their cars are very normal. They might drive a sporty little red Nissan Sentra one day or a rusted-out pickup truck the next. But the FBI's Behavioral Analysis Unit, they almost always drive plain-colored Crown Vics."

"Crown Vics?"

"Ford sedans that old men drive. Come on, let's go."

Sarah put the SS in Drive and pulled onto the deserted highway. "When you were peeking out of the roof vent from across the street, did you notice anything peculiar?"

"Yes, my house had yellow tape all around it and there were cop cars everywhere. Like I said before, it looked like the cops were arguing over who had jurisdiction."

"Think carefully. Did you see any local police cars at the scene?"

"Well, I—uh, I don't know. How would I know?"

"Local police cars would have a shield or insignia on the doors and light bars on top."

"Now that you mention it, no, I don't remember seeing police cars there."

"Exactly. The locals got pushed out by the Feds before they even got to the neighborhood. Homeland must have handed the whole investigation over to the FBI who put the BAU on it."

"So now the FBI is chasing us?"

"They have been all along. It's just that these hired assassins caught up to us first. The gang in the church sounded like they were speaking Russian. They could be FSB or the Ukrainian Mob. The men in black suits who murdered the night clerk and police chief, we don't know who they are, either."

"They sounded like New Yorkers." Logan had spent enough time on the East Coast to recognize a New York accent.

"Great. The FBI, the Mob, Russian spies, and Ukrainians. Anyone else?"

"The KGB, maybe?"

"The KGB? I thought the KGB was disbanded after the Soviet Bloc fell apart."

"Not entirely. Many of those loyal to the Soviet Union remained loyal to the KGB. The ones who blew up the church are more likely to be KGB. They do not pledge loyalty Russia but to just one man."

"How reassuring," Sarah said, her voice cracking.

The black and tan muscle car rumbled north on Florida Highway 71 toward Interstate 10. Sarah knew the authorities would be camped on I-10 overpasses and entrance ramps. Sarah navigated country roads north until they reached Alabama before she crossed over to I-20. She'd go through Dallas but doubted they'd make it that far.

Two miles east of Longview, Texas, the fuel gauge dropped to empty. Sarah parked across the street from the one-pump station and waited until nightfall before pulling up to the street side of the single pump, hoping to block the view of their car from the building. Sarah went inside and paid in cash, grabbed a couple of bologna subs from the cooler, two Styrofoam cups filled with hot coffee, a handful of jerky, Doritos, a Mountain Dew, and a bottle of water.

"Living large," Sarah smiled at Logan as she waved the plastic bag of food. "Isn't this where you got your car?"

"That's just it. I don't think th"Just down the road, in fact." Logan pointed west.

"Do you mind if I give you a little break from the driving?" Logan asked as he slid into the driver's seat and switched on the ignition.

"Thanks. Are you sure you know how to drive a stick?" Sarah asked as he took the wheel.

"I used to. We'll see." He was a bit rusty at first but as they rumbled slowly through a quiet evening in Longview, the choreography of pushing the clutch and shifting at the same time came back to him.

Sarah unwrapped the cellophane-wrapped cold sub made with half-stale bread. "Mustard or Mayo?"

"Mayo."

Sarah bit the edge of the foil condiment packet and tore it open, squeezed the contents onto the sub and handed it to Logan.

"Why did you leave the university?" Sarah asked as she handed him a cup of coffee.

Logan paused, then spoke. "It was only a matter of time. After Beth and the girls were murdered, the police suspected me of something—a person of interest, they called me. It was a death sentence for my career. The administration began losing the university's big donors. As you know, endowments from very wealthy families, philanthropic foundations, and grants are the lifeblood of any university, especially when it comes to science. Government grants were leaving faster than rats could jump ship. Corporations funding our research suddenly diverted their support to, as they put it, 'more viable research.' Once the money ran out, the University had no reason to keep me on. Their plan was to let me sit in my office and collect a salary till my contract ran out."

"When did the drinking start?"

"The night they were murdered. The doctor gave me a sedative—Xanax, I think—but I decided that washing it down with a 12-ounce tumbler of Bourbon was a really good idea. It's a miracle and a curse that I woke up at all. Within a week my drug-laced cocktail was an evening ritual."

Cruising west on I-20, Sarah watched every exit and entrance ramp for law enforcement vehicles. By now, the authorities would have seen the surveillance video from the police station and the laundromat. They would certainly have noticed the black & tan

Chevy SS speeding away. Sarah watched the map and ordered Logan to turn left or right, seemingly without logic, as the two fugitives hopscotched across Texas through the night.

Logan continued his story about leaving the university. "I was hoping I would die before my contract ran out but the corporate purse strings and donors' pocketbooks closed up quicker than the university expected. The university saw my drug and alcohol addiction as less than appropriate decorum for a professor at their renowned institution. Once word spread that I was unfit to teach, the accusations became part of my personnel file. They said I was crazy, unstable, entertained wild conspiracy theories, was a Russian spy, and was trying to ruin America…and a pill-popping drunk."

Sarah's angst increased with each passing minute. She leaned toward the windshield to peer into the sky, looking for a helicopter. Logan rattled on.

"Whoever killed my family expected me to quit teaching and run for my life. I kept trying to teach so they turned up the heat. One morning when I woke up—it might have been afternoon—I booted up my home computer and it made a funny little glitch in the startup screen. Just for a second, you know? I thought the computer may have caught a virus so I did a scan. I found over 8 gigs of image files. *That's weird*, I thought. I only had a handful of photos in my pictures file, so I switched to command prompts—"

"Command prompts?"

"The way we made computers work in the 80s, before Macs and Windows."

"Uh-huh."

"Before you were born. Anyway, someone had planted a ton of incriminating evidence on my computer, everything from child porn to state secrets. They had framed me and were getting ready to take me down. I would have never seen the light of day again."

"Holy shit."

"I'd look out my window, and it was as if they were working in shifts. Coordinated, you know?" Logan laughed and impersonated a police shift sergeant's gravelly voice, "'Okay, listen up. The Logan house. Let's see. Israeli Mossad, you've got from six to nine p.m. Iranian Ministry of Intelligence, you're on deck. Russian FSB, you'll take over at midnight. Be careful out there. Dismissed.' I mean, can you imagine? All these people, all these countries, wanting me dead?"

ey want us dead," Sarah nervously scanned the side roads and sky as she spoke. "At least, death isn't their first choice. If they did, they wouldn't have taken turns watching you."

"Ultimately, their plan worked. My family was murdered in the most heinous, brutal way, and, eventually, I ran for my own life."

"That wasn't the reason they were killed."

"What? What do you know?" The steering wheel followed Logan's shoulders as he spun in Sarah's direction.

"Watch out!" Sarah shouted. Logan steered the car back into the westbound lane.

"What do you know about their deaths?"

"I don't *know* anything for sure," Sarah stated. "I don't think the person in charge intended for your family to be killed. I think they planned to kidnap them and blackmail you into working for them. Something went wrong and they panicked. They couldn't leave any witnesses."

"Go on." A lump formed in Logan's throat as he clung to the steering and forced the words from his mouth. He *needed* to know but he didn't *want* to know.

Dawn was rising as Sarah continued, "They never expected you'd go off the grid, or that you would be successful doing so. They need you and they need me. Killing Beth, Lisa, and Lucy was counterproductive."

"So—why are they dead?"

Sarah's finger jabbed toward the green highway sign along the shoulder, "Take this exit!"

"Why?"

"Just do it. It looks like a good place." Sarah read the green highway sign, 'The Brock Junction.'

The SS veered onto a flat exit ramp 70 miles west of Dallas.

"Stop," Sarah ordered. Logan pulled to the side of the road. "Pop the trunk."

"What are you doing?"

"Just watch." Sarah reached into the trunk, pulled out the tire iron and smashed the rear passenger window, then threw the iron back into the trunk. "Drive," Sarah instructed, pointing toward the main street of the one-horse town. "There! Pull in there!"

"Ted's Body Shop?" Logan read the sign.

Sarah did the talking, in a remarkably convincing Southern drawl. "Mr. Ted, dahlin', this is gonna' break my daddy's heart," she explained as her eyes welled with tears, "this here cawr is his baby, and somebody smashed its window last night at the motor hotel. They stole my purse and phone, too. I cain't bring it back to him like this. Kin you fix it for me, shuga?"

"Sure, no problem," the body shop owner babbled, "I'll get right on it. Should be done tomorrow if we can find the right glass. You know, being a '69 and all. You okay with that?"

"Why, sure, of course, I understand," Sarah looked up at a clear, blue sky, "I just—you see, I'm worried about the weather. Or somebody doing more damage through the open window—I jes' couldn't forgive myself if somethin' else—"

"Oh no, ma'am! We'll put this baby right inside our body shop till we got 'er done! Keep her nice and safe, you see? I sure wouldn't want to see that paint job scratched, neither. Check with me day after tomorrow, and it should be ready."

"That would be so kind of you. So, is there a place we can rent a car here in town?"

"No, but they's a Greyhound bus stop down yonder in front of Maggie's diner. Next scheduled stop is 2 o'clock. Maybe three. Depends on which driver is on duty today. Now, Bill—we call him Wild Bill a' cuz he drives like a maniac—he's liable to roll in about 1:30 with passengers ready to pee their draw's. The other driver, Daryl, he drives like a grammaw and stops every time a passenger tugs on the string. Sometimes, he don't get here till after we close up shop. Maggie's has some real good chicken n' grits and a pretty fair burger."

Great, Sarah thought, *we're stuck sitting in a diner booth till God-knows-when.* She and Logan would be sitting ducks until the bus arrived. Southern fried chicken sounded good, though. She was hungry. She could hear Logan's stomach growling.

She slung her backpack over her shoulder and started down the street, then turned back toward Ted.

"Oh, forgive me, shuga, just one more little thing. You think you might throw a little paint job on that thing before we come back for it?"

"You want me to paint over a rare black and tan Chevy SS? It's in mint condition. Your Daddy's not gonna' be happy about that."

"Oh, darlin', Ah'm his sugar plum. He don't never get mad at me. Besides, he's always wanted a hot rod in candy apple red."

"Yeah, sure, but this—this paint is original."

"Oh, I know. But it's so boring. Red would be real perty, don'tja' think?"

"It's your money, lady but for something like that, I need payment upfront."

Sarah reached into her backpack and pulled out a thick roll of $100 bills. She peeled off forty of them and handed them to the body shop owner. "Will this get me a good paint job?" The owner stared at the $4,000 as Sarah read his reaction. "You think this covers the window repair, too, or do you need more for that?"

The owner stammered, worried she would come to her senses any moment. He grabbed the money as he muttered, "No, this will be fine. I'll spray a coat of clear coat on it, too; make it real shiny for ya. Candy apple red, huh? You want any striping or anything?"

"Surprise me," Sarah batted what lashes she had, and turned toward Maggie's Diner. Logan tried to keep up, alternately looking back at the body shop owner standing in the driveway, counting and recounting the C-notes in his hands.

"Where the—? How did you get your hands on all that money?"

"I found it."

"Where did you find a wad of money like that?"

"Same place I found this." Sarah reached into her backpack and pulled out the butt of a .40 caliber Glock. "Found it under the spare tire in the SS." Sarah stuffed the handgun into the bottom of her backpack.

"Oh, Jesus."

Sarah reached the bare metal door of Maggie's and pulled it open. The Brock Junction is hardly a town—just a pit stop along the old highway separated by worn telephone poles and shallow ditch. The town didn't need curbs; there wasn't enough rain in the county all year to add up to one good gully washer.

Sarah and Logan had two, maybe three, hours to kill until the next bus stopped in town. The 'Please Seat Yourself' sign stood just inside Maggie's entrance, so they did. Logan led the way toward a booth in the back of the diner. Sarah faced the door. Across the street from Maggie's, a worn, green rectangle sign with 'Ed's Hardware,' printed in faded white letters, hung above a door. A Five & Dime wrapped around the end of the block.

Staring at the two retail shops, Sarah barely noticed when the waitress delivered two glasses of water. Now hovering beside the table, she asked if they were ready to order.

"Give us a minute, if you would be so kind," Logan said.

The waitress turned in a huff, "Ain't all that much to think about. Only things worth eating are the burgers and the fried chicken. Only side orders we got is onion rings or grits." She pushed through the swinging doors to the kitchen and disappeared.

"Do you mind if I go do some shopping?" Sarah asked. It wasn't a question. Sarah was already sliding out of the booth.

"Shopping? Now? Did you see the waitress scowl when we weren't ready to order? And you want to leave and go shopping?"

"I'll be right back. Won't be but a minute."

Logan watched her jog across the empty main street; it was Sarah's big-city habit to look both ways for oncoming traffic. Here in Brock Junction, the only traffic was a dusty Ford F-150 headed east on Main.

Sarah stopped to see if anyone was watching as she ducked into Ed's Hardware. Five minutes later, she exited out the back door, carrying a brown paper shopping bag. She followed a makeshift alley behind the row of downtown stores to the Five & Dime, adding more items to the hardware store bag. Once more, she looked both ways crossing Main Street. Sliding into the booth, she re-joined Logan.

"What did you buy?"

"Just some craft things to keep my mind occupied while we're riding the bus."

"You about ready to order sumthin' now?" The waitress seemed to appear from nowhere and scowled at Sarah.

"Ah am *so* sorry," Sarah drawled as she read the waitress' nametag. "I'm so terrible sorry, Laura-Lee. I was desperate to get a few lady things, you see, personals. It's going to be a long bus ride and, well, I'm sure you know when we ladies need our—"

"Don't you worry none, honey," the waitress's sudden compassion shocked Logan. "I understand completely. Wouldn't want you needing your necessities halfway between here and Abilene, and you don't got no place to buy 'em. Now, what kin I git you from the kitchen, darlin'? The deep-fried chicken is real good with a side o' gooey cheese grits. Maggie plops a little spoonful o' sour cream on top just to add a little somethin' special."

"That sounds perfect," Sarah chirped. Having forgiven Sarah for her impromptu shopping trip, Laura-Lee started toward the kitchen, then turned back and peered over her glasses at Logan. "You made up yer mind yet, mister?"

"Ah, yeah, sure," Logan replied. "A burger—and the onion rings."

"Ketchup, onion, pickle, mustard on that?" Laura-Lee asked.

Logan nodded. Laura-Lee pushed through the saloon doors into the kitchen.

"So which is it?" Dr. Logan stared at Sarah.

"Which is what?" Sarah looked confused.

"You said you wanted to buy craft supplies. You told Laura-Lee there you bought lady things. Now, which is it?" Logan asked, as confused as he was perturbed.

Sarah tucked her shopping bags tightly against her side. "Neither."

"Neither?"

"That's what I said." She looked out the window of the diner, hoping that Wild Bill was driving the bus today. She didn't want to sit in the booth with a target on her ass any longer than necessary.

28

Shredding meat from chicken bones at Maggie's Diner, Sarah glanced out the window, then leaned across the table and spoke in a whisper, "Have you ever heard about an organization called Bohemian Grove?" Sarah looked down at her greasy fingers and plate of food. "Oh my goodness, this fried chicken is good." Sarah shoved a large chunk of moist breast meat into her mouth.

"Well, yes, I heard bits and pieces about it years back. Charlie —"

"The spy," Sarah mumbled through her food. Logan nodded. "Yes. He told me a little about it. Where it is located. Somewhere in California, if I remember right. The people who went there, what they talked about. Nothing specific, of course, just general stuff."

"Tell me about the general stuff."

"Bohemian Grove is a social club, so they say. It's a bunch of rich old men, politicians, and intellectuals who go skinny dipping, and sit around the fireplace in their boxer shorts, smoking cigars, scratching themselves, and telling dirty jokes."

Sarah pressed her hand against her lips to suppress a gag, "I'm eating, for God's sake."

"Yeah, not a pretty image inside my head, either. Anyway, it started in 1872, long before Kennedy was president. There have been several presidents who have belonged to Bohemian Grove. Kennedy was a regular, even when he was a Senator. His dad, Joe Kennedy, made his fortune in the stock market, Hollywood movies and booze, especially Scotch. Can you imagine an Irishman getting rich on Scotch?"

"Focus." Sarah scooped her fork full of the thickening grits and shoveled them into her mouth. "JFK, he was good-looking, a Navy Lieutenant and war hero. He went to Princeton and Harvard. He was destined to be President. There was almost no way he could have avoided it. His father and his brothers—Bobby and Teddy—they knew it, too. JFK's father died after two of his sons had been assassinated and four months to the day after Teddy drove off the Chappaquiddick Bridge."

"What's your point?"

"It was no accident JFK became president when he did. And it was no accident he died the way he did."

A chill ran down Sarah's back. She glanced out the window and stopped cold, staring at the dusty F-150 parked across the street at Ed's Hardware. It was the same truck she had seen half an hour earlier as she crossed Main Street.

Oblivious to Sarah's growing fear, Logan continued, "Long before he became president, John Kennedy was part of the conversation in California at Bohemian Grove. Politicians are pawns. They are the gatekeepers. They get a chip in the big game for keeping the rich folks safe and the masses looking the other way while they make themselves richer."

"Yeah, well, we know that much," Sarah whispered, her eyes alternating between the pickup truck and Dr. Logan. "What does that have to do with the people who are chasing us?"

"Kennedy was different. He saw a threat to the United States—even the world—and he started to do something about it. He and some of his Bohemian Grove pals secretly created another organization. Back then, they worried that nobody took the threat of extraterrestrials seriously and he believed that space aliens posed a greater threat even than Russia. It's no coincidence that 10 days before JFK was murdered, he asked for a report on extraterrestrial activity."

"What on earth are you talking about?" Sarah asked.

"I'm not talking about anything on earth. That's the point. Bohemian Grove is made up of the most brilliant academicians—scientists, politicians, the smartest military minds, millionaires and billionaires. They were talking about stuff far beyond this earth. Growing up, JFK heard them talk about Nikola Tesla's electromagnetic death ray and discussed propulsion theories with scientists who designed V-2 rockets for Hitler. He drank whiskey with the Defence Minister of Canada, who has evidence of UFOs. He hobnobbed with NASA engineers sketching the Saturn 5 rocket which would eventually propel astronauts to the moon. Do you think it was coincidence that he proclaimed the United States would land a man on the moon before 1970? It wasn't a challenge. It wasn't an ultimatum. He already knew it was going to happen. The propulsion system had already been invented. The flight was already scheduled."

Sarah's head tilted in curiosity.

"He made the announcement solely for the purpose of political grandstanding," Logan explained. "He stole NASA's thunder by taking credit for their decades of work. Kennedy winds up dead, lying on a hospital gurney beside a pristine bullet."

"You're saying Oswald had help."

"I'm saying Oswald had nothing to do with it. Shooting a moving target at that distance, with a notoriously unreliable rifle and no scope, impossible."

Sarah eyes widened and she held up her hand. "Wait! What do the Kennedy Assassination and the Moon Launch have to do with the Higgs boson theory and supercolliders?"

"They have everything to do with it, Sarah. The potential energy in the collision of protons in a supercollider is exponentially greater than the power of a Saturn 5 rocket. For thousands of years, human transportation has been by wind, animals—like horses and camels—and the natural movement of water."

Sarah's head turned and her eyes locked on the Ford F-150 and the man opening its door. Logan mumbled through a mouthful of ground beef.

"Then, along came hot air balloons, steam engines, airplanes, and the gasoline engine. The Industrial Revolution expanded our ability to traverse the globe. Over a span of twenty-five years, we developed rocket technology which could propel a bomb from Germany to England. But then what happens? Scientific evolution speeds up. In twenty years, we take a huge leap. Just two decades later, how we are able to thrust humans into space traveling at 25,000 miles an hour?"

"That's simple. We made bigger rockets."

"Exactly." Logan smiled as he spoke. "Then, this same civilization, who invented rocket ships capable of reaching speeds of 25,000 miles an hour, decides to halt the invention of new, more powerful propulsion systems? Does that seem logical?"

"Does what seem logical?" Sarah's eyes watched the western boots of the F-150 driver as they touched the dusty street.

"Does it seem logical that these brilliant minds would stop at 25,000 miles per hour, knowing it would require much greater speed to travel to Mars and back, for example?"

Her eyes hardened as the cowboy exited the truck and entered Ed's Hardware.

"They didn't stop. They kept on searching, discovering. I'm certain of it, but I can't prove it. They didn't stop inventing. They just stopped *telling* us about it. For all we know, our government has already visited Mars."

Turning briefly from staring across the street, Sarah spoke slowly. "Supercolliders. That's why the United States is keeping its supercollider secret. NASA scientists have already found the way to harness and deliver the energy generated in proton collisions. They already know its potential for the global energy but they also know it is key to exploring our universe and beyond. Am I getting this right?"

"Yes, it's the reason Elon Musk can make a prediction that he will send people to Mars within the next eight years. It's the reason he launched a car into orbit. He's probably a regular at Bohemian Grove, sitting around in his Jockeys—"

"Stop!" Sarah interrupted. "I get it. I don't need any more visuals."

"Don't forget its potential to be turned into the electromagnetic death ray that Nikola Tesla envisioned…on steroids."

The man from the pickup truck walked out of Ed's Hardware, carrying a small brown bag. He tossed the bag into the bed of his truck as he strode toward Maggie's Diner. His western boots were conspicuously shiny. Filled with Maggie's chicken and grits, Sarah's stomach twisted.

"Quick! We need to get out of here!" Sarah nearly shouted as she started to slide from the booth. She tossed two twenties onto the table and waved a thank you to Laura-Lee.

"But—my milkshake," Logan protested, "and onion rings—"

"They're bad for your cholesterol," Sarah said as she dragged him from the booth

"What you rushin' off for?" Laura-Lee crossed the dining room to their booth. "The bus ain't even here yet. It could show up at any time but—"

"Saht-seein'," Sarah lied, "we're gonna' take a little walk around town," she drawled. "You mind if we go out the back door, Laura-Lee?"

Laura-Lee spotted the $40 on the table, more than half of it was her tip. "No, of course not, y'all go on out through the kitchen if you like, but—" Laura-Lee's head snapped up as she saw the Greyhound sliding to a stop in front of the diner. "Looky there, here comes the bus now. Wild Bill must be driving. They's ten minutes early."

Sarah turned on her heel, pulled Logan behind her, and headed straight for the bus's front door. Sarah calculated the shiny-booted man would reach them first, though. He wouldn't do anything in front of witnesses, would he? She couldn't take the risk to trust that he wouldn't. She reached into her backpack and wrapped her hand around the molded rubber grip of the Glock. The man reached behind his back as Sarah aimed her semi-auto, preparing to fire the 15-round clip through the backpack's canvas.

"Wait! Stop!" Laura-Lee hollered as she ran into the line of fire between Sarah and the man. Laura-Lee had bagged Logan's leftover onion rings and poured his milkshake into a Styrofoam cup. "Here, shuga, you kin take these on the bus with you."

The man stopped, then started toward them again. Inside the backpack, Sarah raised the gun into position as the stranger pulled a pouch of Mail Pouch chaw from his back pocket.

"You 'bout ready to get offa' work, Laura-Lee?" the man asked as he wrapped his arm around the waitress.

"Ah sure am, dahlin'." Laura-Lee smiled and kissed his cheek. "C'mon in. I'll have Maggie whip up something special for ya." Laura-Lee gazed adoringly up and down her strapping cowboy. "You get yerself some new boots? They look real shiny. You been needin' new boots." Laura-Lee pulled him toward the diner.

Sarah collapsed, her backside landing the bottom step of the bus's open door. She had just raised her gun to kill a man for wearing new boots and biting off a chunk of chewing tobacco. Cold sweat gushed from every pore.

"That was nice of her," Logan looked down at his bag of leftovers, then saw Laura-Lee hug her man as they walked through Maggie's front door. "That was really nice of her, don't you think?"

"Uh-huh," Sarah nodded. "Yeah, nice. Real nice."

"Now, where were we?" Logan asked as he squeezed past Sarah and walked up the stairs of the bus.

29

Following Logan up the steps of the Greyhound, Sarah noticed the nametag of the driver. "You're Bill, huh? I've heard about you."

"Most people have." The craggy-faced driver said as he pulled the door shut behind her.

"Thanks for getting here early," Sarah said. Bill tipped his straw cowboy hat.

Sarah pushed Logan to the back of the Greyhound and found a seat next to the window, as far away from other passengers as possible. She donned sunglasses, tucked her hair up under a low ballcap, and pulled him close so they could talk quietly. Fourteen hours into their trip from Apalachicola, they had only begun talking about why they were being hunted.

"So," Sarah started, "you're saying that someone, maybe NASA, knows how much energy is generated in a proton collision as well as its properties for magnetic propulsion in space exploration?"

"Yes, but not 'maybe NASA.' There is no question that NASA knows all about it and are keeping the technology secret until the United States perfects its methods of using it. They are testing the effects, working out the kinks. But somebody else knows, too, and they are the ones who are dangerous."

"Let me guess, the ones who are not working for NASA need a couple of astrophysicists with specific knowledge of accelerated proton collision science to 'work out the kinks,' as you put it. Right?"

Dr. Logan nodded. "Yes. They need both of us, not just one of us."

"I see," Sarah said. "Somebody thinks that, together, we can figure out the answer. That's why they haven't killed either of us. But once they've extracted all the information we know, we're dead."

"Yes, but their presumption is flawed. We know the anomalies are not Stephen Hawking's theory coming to life. I believe they are caused by humans unwittingly tinkering with Earth's dark energy and dark matter."

"They think we know how to correct it but we don't," Sarah interjected.

"If they knew how little we know about the effects of proton collisions on dark energy, they wouldn't be chasing us. Once they find out that we don't know—"

"Got it," Sarah said, "dead."

"We're running out of time. The anomalies are occurring more frequently and they are more extreme. As more people experience them, they won't keep falling for the 'swamp gas' or 'weather balloon' explanation our government has been feeding them."

"You mean Project Blue Book," Sarah blurted.

"Right. Environmental experts began poking holes in the study's findings and the government shut down Project Blue Book in 1969. Today, the government attributes the earth's odd behaviors to naturally occurring geological phenomena—sinkholes, global warming, and, believe it or not, swamp gas. They say it's just part of the earth's climate cycle. The truth is, those explanations are misdirection to keep the people from discovering the truth."

"Go on." Sarah listened intently as she subconsciously reached for Logan's Styrofoam cup and sipped what was left of his milkshake.

"The media has been a willing pawn; they want to sell air time; that is their product. They want to focus on airing broadcast commercials for beer and basketball shoes; causing mass hysteria will not help their bottom line. So the media parrots whatever the government says. The only ones speaking out are a few Cosmologists and Astrophysicists who aren't afraid of losing their jobs or seeing their families murdered. After Beth and the girls were killed, those who were thinking about blowing the whistle clammed up."

The Greyhound swayed and rattled as Wild Bill tried to beat his personal best from The Brock Junction to Abilene. Logan grabbed the seat back to steady himself as the bus lurched through a curve in the highway.

"So your hypothesis is?" Sarah asked.

"Remember what I said about dark matter and dark energy? We don't understand most of what happens in our universe, including within Earth's atmosphere. We don't know how dark matter and energy will react to the massive amount of energy released in a subatomic particle collision, do we?"

"No," Sarah said. "But there have never been any anomalies caused by the Hadron Collider in Switzerland."

"Are you sure? How do we know that? Has any scientific research been conducted to determine what impact the Hadron Collider has had on our environment?"

"None that I know," Sarah replied. "So you're saying anomalies might have happened but they were simply not reported."

"Very possibly, yes. But remember: The Hadron Collider is small by comparison to others which are currently operating or are being built throughout the world."

"True. But how would supercolliders in other countries be causing gravitational anomalies here in the United States?"

"First, we don't know the full impact they are causing in their own countries; all of the countries involved are highly secretive. But it is a good question: if we believe what the government is telling us—that the United States *doesn't* have a supercollider—then why are we witnessing so many of these anomalies in North America?"

"You think the government is lying."

"Yes, I do."

"That's why you were so scared the night we were having coffee at The Small World. You know the United States has built an extreme supercollider which will compete against anything else in the world, and has the capability of wreaking far more havoc."

"I believe my exact words were, 'I think the United States *might* be building one—'"

"Stop! Think!" Sarah interrupted. "Have you ever known our government to sit by and do nothing while other countries threaten our national security? What did we do in the arms race? The space race? The technology race? The Middle East oil grab? Look at how competitive we are with the Olympics. Name one thing where the United States has settled for second place or not even played the game? As a nation, we live to be the firstest with the mostest, don't we? There is no way our government officials would have willingly taken a back seat in a supercollider race, would they?"

Traveling through the dark night on a bus bound for Abilene, Logan pondered Sarah's question carefully. "No, I suppose not. So you're saying my suspicions were right? The United States has a supercollider?"

Sarah nodded. "I'm certain of it. The NRC—the United States Nuclear Regulatory Commission—has kept it under wraps since it was built."

Logan paused to let what Sarah was saying sink in. "They stopped construction on the Waxahachie accelerator in 1993. The Fermi Supercollider west of Chicago could only generate two teraelectronvolts so it became obsolete long before it was closed in 2011."

"Precisely," Sarah confirmed. "With Waxahachie, politicians said the reason we stopped construction was to reallocate the national budget to provide money for the Manned Space Station Program. Most Americans didn't even blink when they quit building in Waxahachie because they have no idea how the government spends their money. If our politicians made decisions based on a budget, we wouldn't be 20 trillion dollars in debt, would we?"

"You're convinced the government has already built a supercollider somewhere in the Continental United States?"

"Of course. Yes. The United States would never sit still for Russia and China having the upper hand militarily or economically, would it?"

"No." Logan shook his head. "No, they wouldn't. So, where would the U.S. build a supercollider?"

"Where is the most secure place in the world?"

"The White House?"

"Try again."

"The Kremlin."

"Not even close. Keep trying."

"NORAD?" Logan was sure this guess was right. "It's built into the side of a mountain."

"Warmer, but not quite. What has 550 square miles of land, a no-fly zone fifty miles around its perimeter, and even satellites can be blocked from photographing it?"

"They can do that?"

"Focus."

"But how—?"

"Satellite cross-jamming technology, but that's not the point. I did a lot of research after you went off the grid. You see, if the Chinese, the Americans, or the Russians don't want another nation taking pictures of their nuclear facilities from outer space, they jam the satellite feeds with radio frequencies, microwaves, and infrared rays. Didn't you ever wonder how Iraq was able to move all those weapons of mass destruction we claimed were the reason we invaded Iraq without our satellites recording them being moved?"

"I thought the CIA said there weren't any."

"No, there were. The CIA just didn't want Americans to know our satellite surveillance had been rendered impotent by a despot they assumed was too stupid understand technology."

"You're talking about Saddam Hussein?"

"Yes, he figured out that if he could intercept Russian porn by satellite, he knew, for the right price, he could find somebody tech-savvy enough to jam satellite surveillance of his WMDs. So he did. Guess who it was? The United States! We gave the SOB the technology! It was part of a weapons deal. We had no idea he would use it to hide chemical weapons."

"So-o-o-o-o-o, you're saying," Logan breathed the words out slowly, "you're saying Iraq has a supercollider, too?"

Sarah shook her head. "Wait. Yes, I believe they do, maybe, but we're way down a squirrel trail. Let's get back to the point. What has 550 square miles of desert, a no-fly zone above it, and satellite surveillance blocked?"

Dr. Logan sat silent for several minutes before answering, "Area 51."

"Winner, winner, chicken dinner. Area 51."

"What about it?"

"That's where the United States' secret supercollider is. It's perfect. And it's huge! Imagine, you can fit twenty supercolliders the size of the Hadron Collider into Area 51. Or, you could build a supercollider with twenty times the power of the Hadron Collider."

"But if they were building one in Area 51, why did they build one in Waxahachie?"

"Misdirection. The US government wanted everyone to believe we had started building a modest supercollider in Waxahachie. It was nothing more than a decoy. The government never intended to finish building it; they already had the Area 51 collider on the drawing table and had begun construction. The goal was to get the Russians and Chinese to point their surveillance satellites at Waxahachie rather than Area 51."

Logan stared out the bus window into the darkness.

"As recently as 2016, satellite images of Area 51 were compared in time-lapse animation." Sarah continued, "Those studying the animation reached the conclusion that the site has been under construction since 1984. I believe the U.S government was already building a supercollider with at least ten times the capacity of the world's next-largest collider when they shut down Waxahachie."

"And it was all being built underground. Oh my." Dr. Logan leaned against the headrest.

"Exactly," Sarah agreed, "going back to the 1940s, Area 51 was a secret testing facility for military equipment and secret aircraft. Like back in the days of the X-15 and Chuck Yeager, breaking the sound barrier, then the development of a rocket to the moon, the landing module, it was all tested in Area 51. When the Roswell Man was stored in Area 51, it became the highest security location in the world, even more secure than the White House or the Pentagon."

"How do you know about Chuck Yeager? You're too young."

"Focus, squirrel," Sarah, explained, "my dad told me about Chuck Yeager. Anyway, when Professor Higgs presented his theory about the Higgs boson particle in 1964, the government knew they had to investigate it, to be on the cutting edge of the science, right? But they had no idea what that meant. They had no idea what his discovery would mean to the planet."

"I don't get it."

"All they knew is the Higgs boson particle is the subatomic particle which holds all mass together. Like everyone else, they thought supercolliders would answer whether the Higgs boson was real and what happened in the zillionth of a second after the Big Bang. That's what the scientists wanted to learn from proton acceleration and collision, right?"

"Yes."

"Scientists are still talking about supercolliders as if they hold the secret to evolution. But that is their misdirection—or naiveté. I don't believe that all these brilliant scientists are ignorant of the enormous potential supercolliders offer in space exploration as well as a viable nuclear energy source. As you pointed out in your lecture, the proton collisions themselves could produce enough energy to eliminate worldwide dependence on fossil fuel."

"Elimination of fossil fuel would destroy our global economy." Logan's forehead was coated with a layer of sweat.

"But wait. There's more. A supercollider the size that Area 51 could hide would have the potential of becoming a military weapon far more devastating than a hydrogen bomb."

"It would multiply the killing range of Tesla's electromagnetic death ray to the hundredth power," Logan mumbled.

"Easily." Sarah reached for the shopping bags she had gotten in The Brock Junction.

Dr. Logan continued to stare into the darkness, hoping to see a sliver of light. His voice trembled. "A supercollider has the potential to be used as a killing machine, as a new, safer atomic energy source, and it holds the key to space exploration. Any one of those would be worth killing for. It is a deadly hat trick."

"Can you imagine the global chaos one madman could cause if he got his hands on a supercollider which could generate that much energy?" Sarah looked over her shoulder to see if anyone on the bus was listening.

"Such a global threat would create more mass hysteria than the gravitational anomalies themselves," Logan said as reality sank in.

"Yes, it would. Now, stay with me here," Sarah continued. "Get this. The Hadron Collider is 17 miles in circumference at a depth of 50 meters below the earth's surface to 175 meters at the deepest point. Think of downtown buildings. The top of the underground tunnel is five stories beneath the earth's surface, less a third of a football field. At its deepest, the tunnel is about 20 stories deep, or about two football fields."

"That's a mid-sized city."

"Exactly. What's more, the Hadron Collider in Switzerland generates 14 teraelectronvolts."

"That's a lot of energy."

"I know, I remember you standing in front of class, saying, 'Imagine a gnat. One TeV is equivalent to the energy of a million gnats flapping their wings in space a million-million times smaller than a gnat."

Logan smiled, "I remember."

"It's like saying a car's motor has 200 million horsepower."

"Well, more than that, actually."

"Right. One teraelectronvolt has incomprehensible energy for the amount of space it occupies. The Hadron Collider has 14 TeV, fourteen times the energy of one teraelectronvolt. Imagine that my dad's muscle car we were driving had 2,800 million horsepower!"

"Back there on the highway, I wasn't sure it didn't."

"Sorry." Sarah was only a little sorry.

Logan did the math in his head. "So, in Area 51, the United States could be hiding a supercollider which is ten, fifteen, or even twenty times the size and power of the Hadron Collider."

"Yes," Sarah replied. "As the collider increases in size, it increases exponentially in its output."

"Like a car's motor."

"Bingo. A 200-horsepower motor is nearly as large as a 400-horsepower motor but the power generated is double. One more thing: I don't think we *might* be hiding a supercollider in Area 51; I

197

am *certain* we are. After you went off the grid, I did some digging into Project Blue Book and the dark files of the Montauk Project."

"The what?"

"The Montauk Project was a series of experiments in time travel and mind control conducted at the U.S. Air Force Base on Long Island, New York, during the 1970s and early '80s. Project Blue Book goes back further, into the 1950s, where the government conjured up experiments to refute the legitimacy of UFO's. As we know, the research findings were bogus; the research concluded that citizens' sightings were just swamp gas. My point is: the U.S. government has a long history of conducting secret experiments about space exploration and time travel. Why *wouldn't* they keep secret the fact that they built a supercollider under Area 51?"

"Oh my," Logan replied. "Can you imagine the power being generated by a collider of that magnitude? More important, can you imagine the havoc it could wreak in dark matter and dark energy? We have no idea what 280 teraelectronvolts unleashed into our universe would cause."

"Actually I think we are seeing some examples of what it can cause. It could explain the anomalies," Sarah replied.

"Yes, of course. These people who are chasing us?" Dr. Logan began, "They know it, too. That's why they are willing to kill to find us. They think we have the answer, but we don't. They believe we know how to eliminate the unpredictable effects the accelerated proton collisions have on the universe's dark matter and why those collisions are causing gravitational anomalies. They think you and I know how to make the collider safe, and if we are able to do so, they will control the world's most powerful economic and military weapon, as well as a propulsion system capable of space exploration beyond our universe."

"Yes." Sarah watched her mentor's complexion pale.

"Oh my, my, my, my. If the collision of protons can occur without the side effects of destabilizing dark matter and dark energy, supercolliders could—intentionally or unintentionally—target the Higgs boson subatomic particle and completely disassemble mass. Military installations, weapons, even cities and towns could be—" Logan's throat constricted. He couldn't finish his thought.

"Vaporized."

"Yes," Logan agreed. "Tesla knew his teleforce weapon could destabilize matter and interfere with the simplest electrical circuits. He knew it could destroy fighter planes, tanks, aircraft carriers, and buildings. Back then, we didn't know that dark matter and dark energy existed on earth so Tesla didn't fully understand why the death ray's magnetic force could destabilize all forms of matter, not only those which used electricity."

Sarah nodded as Logan continued. "If the U.S. Military had put research and development money behind Tesla's idea, World War II would have been over before Germany invaded France. Tesla's teleforce weapon could have wiped out Germany's Luftwaffe before its fighter planes and bombers crossed the Maginot Line. The teleforce would have had the atomic bomb's power to destroy combined with the pinpoint accuracy of a laser-guided missile."

"It would have caused zero collateral damage," Sarah interjected.

"Yes. It would have been unparalleled in its surgical-strike capability. It would have been capable of completely destroying a military target without so much as mussing the hair of the children playing in the sandbox twenty feet away."

"So why didn't the Army develop Tesla's weapon?" Sarah asked.

"Politicians didn't understand the science behind Tesla's invention. Military leaders wanted weapons of mass destruction—whatever would knock down the most buildings and kill the most people. Body count was the method of keeping score. As humans did when they witnessed the world as flat, military leaders believed in what they could see—buildings bombed, dead bodies, and cities in rubble. They couldn't comprehend a weapon that could disassemble matter and vaporize it. Roosevelt and Churchill were terrified by rumors that Hitler was months away from having an atom bomb which could obliterate Western Europe, and they already had V-2 rockets which could reach outer space. The U.S. Military poured all of its resources into the Manhattan Project—the United States' effort to beat the Germans in the race for the first atomic bomb."

"That's terrifying," Sarah muttered. She cocked her head and looked at Dr. Logan. "So, let's assume for the moment that a weapon like Tesla invented actually existed today and was powered by the world's strongest supercollider. It could destroy opposing armies and their weapons from thousands of miles away, couldn't it? A madman could dominate the world by the threat of vaporizing a nation's people and army, but the result is the ultimate end game. That is, if all the people are dead, who does he have power over?"

"Nobody."

"So, to have long-term power over the world, the madman must control the world through economic domination, don't you agree?"

"Long term, yes," Logan answered, "but how could a supercollider control a nation?"

"Again, you said it in your lecture, if we could harness that energy, if we could capture it consistently, if we could contain that zillion-zillionth-of-a-second surge in energy, one-zillionth of a second after another, we would create an inexhaustible energy source which could power the world without one drop of fossil fuel."

Logan listened to his pupil turned teacher. "You see, the supercollider race isn't about uncovering the secrets of the universe. It never was. It is about creating an energy source powerful enough to replace fossil fuels. The military and space exploration potential were discovered along the way. They are bonuses, secondary to the main objective: the supercollider race has always been about creating an energy source capable of demolishing the economies of oil-rich nations like Venezuela, Saudi Arabia, Iran, Canada, and Russia, to name a few. But it would also destroy the economies of countries who rely heavily on fossil fuels for manufacturing—the United States, China and South Korea, for examples. Oil and Gas commodity markets would crash."

"Most likely," Logan agreed.

"The people who are hunting us believe you and I already know how to harness the energy to make it safer. But they are running out of time. They must capture us before oil-producing and industrial nations realize how fragile their hold is on the world economy."

"Why?"

"Because the oil players would beat them to the punch."

"How so?"

"Once the world's Big Oil magnates realize they are the target of a scheme to destroy their industry, they will cut oil supplies and crash the global economy themselves. The world would spiral into an economic depression worse than any in history."

"Then we're screwed," Logan said. "Metaphorically speaking." Sarah's hands were tucked inside her backpack, working intently on what

Logan assumed was her craft project for which she'd bought materials at the hardware store and the Five & Dime.

"Jesus! Who are we up against?"

"Everyone. When Big Oil learns these supercolliders can destroy their hold on the global economy, they will do anything to destroy it first—along with you and me."

The Professor caught of glint of silver. At the opening of Sarah's backpack, the threaded end of a galvanized plumber's pipe stuck out.

"What the hell are you making?"

"Bombs," Sarah said matter-of-factly as she stuffed M-80 firecrackers and sparklers she'd bought at the Five & Dime into two, one-foot-long galvanized pipes and spun 2-inch plumbing caps onto the ends.

"*Bombs*, for God's sake? In case of what?"

"Shush! Not so loud!" Sarah shoved her hand over his mouth. Logan's head spun in every direction, certain that someone on the bus would see Sarah making a crude pipe bomb. She whispered, "Just in case we need it. You know, like if somebody's trying to kill us."

"How in the world did you learn how to make a bomb?" Logan shook his head in disbelief as he spoke, then stopped when he saw Sarah staring at him.

"*Forensic Files.* You ever watch that? It's really interesting. It was an episode about a guy running a Ponzi operation whose car was blown up when mobsters found out he had bilked them out of ten million dollars."

"Great," Logan mumbled.

Sarah stuffed the makeshift artillery deep into her pack as the top-heavy bus tilted through a curve. Wild Bill's grey work shirt was soaked with sweat as he wrangled the beast into the straightaway.

Logan shook his head, rubbed his hand over his face and looked out the window again, just in time to see the green highway sign, 'Abilene, 2 Miles.'

"Oh, by the way, we're switching buses in Abilene, Sarah said flatly. "We're going to catch one headed north to Amarillo."

Logan opened his mouth to speak but Sarah stopped him.

"Don't ask, okay? Just don't."

Logan's head was already spinning. Rockets. Death rays. Pipe bombs. He couldn't make sense of any of it. He just nodded and chose to trust Sarah.

30

Dr. Logan was able to count fence posts lining the highway now that he and Sarah were no longer on Wild Bill's roller coaster ride. Beyond the fences, cattle grazed in barren Texas fields. Logan wondered how a cow could grow fat eating scrub grass and turn it into milk and prime beef. "Where are we going?"

"West. Mostly." Sarah spoke in low tones although the rattle of the bus's lavatory fan behind her seat dampened conversation she and Logan were having.

"Funny." Logan added, "Explain."

"Our tickets are for Albuquerque, New Mexico. We'll pass through Amarillo on U.S. 287, then connect with I-40. There are fewer passengers on the buses traveling this route so we'll stay below the radar. That's assuming they know we're heading west. It's not like we gave them our itinerary."

"Didn't we lose them when they went blowing past the sand dunes?"

"We can't assume anything. By now they have figured out we didn't go to Panama City. If they are smart—and they are—they've commandeered highway camera footage from the state police and saw the SS headed north and west. Hell, they probably have satellite footage by now of us pulling into The Brock Junction and catching a bus. For all we know, the cameras on this bus are streaming to Greyhound's headquarters and they're just waiting for us to pull into the bus terminal in Albuquerque."

"Great. Now what?"

"We're not going to Albuquerque."

"But you just said—?"

"I said our *tickets* are for Albuquerque. This bus is scheduled for a driver change at a rest stop southeast of Amarillo. They'll switch drivers and let the passengers stretch their legs. We won't be getting back on the bus. The bus will head toward Albuquerque and leave us behind. The new driver won't miss us."

"What do we do after we get off the bus at the rest stop?"

"A grey Dodge Charger will be parked at the edge of the rest stop parking lot. The keys will be sitting on the top of the driver-side front tire."

"And you know this—how?"

"You didn't notice we're down to two burn phones, did you?"

"No. Where is the third one?"

"Somewhere in Arkansas by now. At the Abilene Greyhound station, I tossed it into the open luggage carrier in the belly of a bus bound for Chicago. By the time the Feds find it, they won't know which of the Windy City's nine and a half million people it belongs to."

"You called your father again, didn't you?"

Sarah shrugged. Logan took that as a yes. He stared at Sarah for several seconds before asking, "And what name is on the rental agreement?"

"Tom Moore. It was rented for you and charged to a credit card."

"Whose credit card?"

"Tom Moore's."

"How—who—where did they get my—Tom's—social security number to open a credit card account? Isn't that identity theft?"

Sarah looked at Logan dully. "He's a dead guy. Is anyone going to care if we stole a dead guy's ID to open a credit card? I mean, we're trying to save the world here."

Logan rolled his eyes and leaned back, "How *is* your dad, any-way?"

"Good. He's good. He said to say hello."

"I'd like to meet him someday."

"You already have."

"No, I don't mean from across the street while he's shooting people. I mean in person."

"Yes, in person," Sarah replied. "It was a long time ago."

Logan sat, stone-faced, before muttering, "How long ago?"

"Before I accepted the fellowship at Princeton; he wanted to make sure his little girl would be safe."

"Safe. Ha! Instead, I get you mixed up in this. Hardly what a father would consider safe."

"It's not your fault."

"You think your dad believes that?"

"You wouldn't be breathing if he didn't." Dr. Logan knew Sa-rah was telling the truth. If Tuffy thought Dr. Logan had put his daughter in harm's way, he would have made sure that Logan's death was slow and painful.

Logan sat silent for a time, then stammered, "I've been meaning to talk with you. I—umm—I know there's always been talk. Talk about you and I."

"You and me," Sarah corrected.

"Right. You and me." Logan continued, "I know people have said things. Mean, hateful things. They made assumptions because we talked so often, spent so much time together in the lab. When I invited to you to join the Small World Big Brains coffees, I got some looks, even from the other professors. They figured, well, you know what they figured. But I invited you because you are really smart. The others at the coffee shop knew it, too, once they got to know you. We talked about how you were someday going to be a superstar in the world of Astrophysics and Cosmology."

"Universe." Sarah corrected.

"What?"

"That I would be a superstar in the *universe* of Astrophysics and Cosmology, not just the world."

Logan smiled. "Touché. In the *universe* of Astrophysics and Cosmology. Anyway, I admired how you didn't allow others to suck you into their drama. Beth thought the world of you. So did Lisa and Lucy."

Sarah gritted her teeth but couldn't stop a sudden flood of tears. "I know. I felt the same way about them."

"This pretending to be husband and wife, at the motel and all, you know, I mean, I know that sharing a bed was just part of the ruse. It was nothing more than that." Logan swallowed the lump in his throat before asking, "Was it?"

Sarah didn't answer for a long minute. "I will admit, when I first met you, I had a crush on you. A schoolgirl crush. You were smart, funny, and—" Sarah paused, "not unattractive."

"Not unattractive? Well, thank goodness for that. That's a resounding endorsement. Not unattractive. I'll put that on my resume. 'Not terribly unattractive.'"

"It's the best you get. When you asked me if I could sit for your daughters, I met Beth and the girls, and they welcomed me like family. After that, you were more like my brother."

"Brother. Ah, yes," Logan said, smiling, "at least you didn't say uncle. Brother is good."

"I didn't expect you to turn into my drunk cousin."

"Ouch."

Sarah peered over the rows of seats to be certain nobody was listening in on their conversation. "I'm serious. I need you at the top of your game if we're going to figure out how to stop these gravitational anomalies and get supercollider energy under control. You aren't going to be any help if you're drugged out on Xanax and Bourbon. Get your shit together, Doctor. I mean it. I can't do this alone."

Logan arose from his seat, pulled the prescription bottle from his pocket and the half-full fifth of Ten High from his backpack. He walked to the bus's bathroom and dumped them down the toilet.

31

The thick man from the limousine sat in the middle of the Louis XV settee at the edge of the large room in the German convention center. Reigning dignitaries mingled throughout the room, shaking their heads, nodding and smiling at one another, even though most did not understand a word the other said.

"Shall we get you an interpreter?" asked the compactly built man sitting in the corner of the settee. His own interpreter, a hulk of a beast, filled the French provincial chair beside the settee. Hunched forward, he waited for an answer.

"No," the thick man replied to the Russian on the settee, "no, I'm fine. You speak perfect English. I understand every word. Beautiful English. I'm not so good at Russian."

"*Spasibo*," the man relaxed deeply into the cushions and spoke calmly, "thank you. We'll speak English then."

"*Pridurok*," the Russian interpreter muttered. His countryman on the settee scowled at him briefly, then turned back toward the thick American.

"What did he say?" the thick man asked.

The Russian paused before replying, "He was complimenting you on your English. It is very impressive. Right, Sergei?" He was certain that telling him the truth—that the Russian interpreter had just called the American a moron—would not strengthen diplomatic relations.

"*Da*. Yes. Very good English," Sergei replied, smirking.

The Russian on the settee continued, "Do you know that these rooms, the ones they use for such meetings between foreign dignitaries, are secure?"

"Well, I suppose, yes, I suppose they would be," the thick man answered, scanning the room. "There are a lot of soldiers with guns around, I can see that."

"*Nyet*. Forgive me, no," the man at the end of the settee replied. "I am not talking about guns. I am talking about the room being secure from listening devices. They use electronic jammers capable of rendering listening devices useless." The Russian interpreter stifled a snicker. The American turned toward him.

"Sergei, he has allergies," the Russian explained, then frowned at his interpreter. He turned back to the American and said, "As I was saying, the room is secure from eavesdropping."

"Good. That's good, right? It seems like it would be a good thing."

"*Da.* Yes, it is a good thing. We can speak freely. Quietly but freely."

"Sure. Of course. Why not? I can speak quietly."

"Let me get right to the point. Do you want to play, how you say, in the big leagues?"

"What are you talking about? I am already in the big leagues —"

The Russian put his finger to his lips. "Stop. No, you're not. Not even close. I came from nothing and I own 100% interest in an oil company worth 500 billion in U.S. Dollars. You owe hundreds of millions to Mother Russia but you live as if you are a billionaire. Remember, my intelligence agency has successfully hacked your IRS. We have seen your tax returns. You cannot pretend with me."

"Fine. Fine." The man stuck in the middle of the antique divan shifted his shoulders, belying his discomfort.

"Is that a yes?"

The man appeared befuddled, "Yes to what?"

"Do you want to be rich? Really rich?"

"Sure. Yes, sure. Of course. Who doesn't want to be rich?"

The Russian smiled and waved his hand as if to paint a picture. "Can you see what I see? You and me, looking out over the mountains of Montana; we would become investors together. Buy some land—in Colorado, Wyoming, and Montana. Like the Russian Navy officer in that movie about a submarine. Do you remember that scene? He always wanted to see Montana. Do you like Montana?"

"Sure. I like Montana. I don't usually watch movies. I can't sit still for that long. But Montana? Yes, I've heard it's nice. I haven't seen the mountains but I've been at the airport, you know, for a rally. Montana's tremendous. Great people."

"We could put up condominiums, maybe a golf course or two. Wouldn't that be fun?"

"I do that. I mean, I did. You know, before."

"Yes, yes, of course you did," the Russian said dismissively, "I'm sure you are very good at it. If we are fortunate, we could find some land where, possibly, the competition was, let's say, limited."

"I'm not following you."

"Of course not. Forgive me. Let me say this: America, it has so many beautiful places. Mountains, plains, deserts. You agree, yes, don't you?"

"Of course. We have a beautiful country. I own a lot of it—"

"Yes, you've told me, often," the Russian interrupted, "but please, let me finish."

"No, sure, of course. Go on. I'm listening." The thick man wrung his hands as he listened to the Russian.

"America has many riches in its lands. Lands your people do not use. National parks, Indian Reservations—forgive my manners—Native American Reservations."

"That's okay. I still call them Indians. We have a lot of sports teams they call Indians... or Redskins. Indians are great. I love the Indians."

"Da. Good. Then we understand. So mountains, deserts, and plains you Americans don't use, why don't you sell them? Foreign investors would pay billions for America's unwanted land."

"What investors?"

"Well, you and me, for example, through a joint venture company. It would be very hush-hush, of course."

"Of course."

"Nobody can know the company is owned by us, you understand?"

"No, of course not." The thick man smiled and nervously waved at the German woman wearing a plain suit and serviceable shoes as she walked past. She crooked her head quizzically but did not return his awkward greeting.

"These, these things. What do you call them? Executive orders? Is it possible you can privatize—is that a word?—your American lands with one of those?"

"Privatize? Yes, it's a word. I mean, I use it as a word. I think it's a word. I suppose I could privatize them with an executive order. Why not?"

The Russian leaned into the corner of the settee. "I—I mean 'we,' our joint venture—we want to buy Area 51."

"Area 51? I've heard of it. Is it in Montana?"

"Nevada."

"Nevada? The desert? Why would you want to buy a desert?"

"Look what Bugsy Siegel did for Las Vegas. Maybe we could build another Las Vegas. He was Jewish, you know?"

"Who?"

"Bugsy Siegel, the mob boss. Rumor has it that he and Meyer Lansky funneled millions through the Mormon Church to launder their blood money so they could build the city of Las Vegas."

"I didn't know that; I didn't know he was Jewish, either. I figured, you know, being a mob guy, he was Italian. I mean, not that it matters. I love the Jews."

"I'm sure you do. So, you think you could sign an executive order to make some land in Montana and Nevada available for a private investment company to purchase and develop? Maybe Wyoming, too. The mountains are beautiful."

"Sure, I don't see a problem with that. I understand Montana and Wyoming, but are you sure about the desert?"

The Russian laughed and tossed back his head.

"Oh yes, I'm sure. We could make a casino with little green men as waiters."

"Little green men?"

"You know? Like the spaceman?"

"I don't get it."

"You don't know about the flying saucer that crashed in your American desert?

"I heard something about it but I was just kid. I really didn't pay much attention." The thick man chuckled embarrassedly, "See how much I know?"

"I suspected as much," the Russian smiled with him.

"I could find out."

"No! *Nyet!* Ees not important. I was just curious. We wouldn't want to ask questions which could lead to other questions, would we?"

"No, of course not," the American agreed, not completely sure why.

The interpreter muttered, "*Pridurok.*"

"Thank you," the American replied and nodded to the Russian interpreter. "So you—we—want to buy Area 51, is that it? It's just a wasteland; there's no value there. I don't see a problem selling it."

"*Da.* Good. My company—forgive me, our company, yours and mine—we would offer fifty million U.S. dollars for that piece of desert."

"That's a lot of money for sand and rock. That sounds like a generous offer, but what if somebody discovers a Russian company is buying American land?"

209

"Oh no, no, no, it would be an American company, of course. I will have my lawyers draw up all the paperwork so it looks like it is owned entirely by Americans."

"Good. That's good. Everybody is watching me right now. I can't get my lawyers involved. I'll let your lawyers work something up."

"I would be happy to do so. And you will handle the executive order?"

The thick man shrugged, "My Chief of Staff drafts the executive orders. He writes something up; whatever I tell him. I just sign them."

"Of course. You leave the small things to your underlings, yes?"

"Exactly," the American said, puffing out his chest, "delegation is the sign of a great manager. My father taught me that."

"I'm sure he did. I'm sure he was a very wise man and taught you well."

The American held his hand out as he spoke, "We can't let the media get wind of this. They'll make up some stories. Fake stories."

The Russian gripped the American's hand and agreed, "No, of course not. We will keep this under wraps as much as possible."

"Do you really think we could make a killing building condos in the desert?"

"A killing? Oh yes, I am certain of it."

The thick man nodded and smiled broadly, knowing he had just bilked the Russian out of fifty million dollars for worthless desert land.

32

When he returned to his seat at the back of the Greyhound, Logan found Sarah eager to learn more about the Five Eyes Accord.

"So, if I understand, these five nations—the United States, Great Britain, Canada, Australia, and New Zealand—tell one another the secrets they discover about other countries. Am I right?"

"They did, but they don't nowadays."

"Why? Wait. Why did they share information in the first place?"

"To keep the world safe. Whether to acquire wealth and power, or to act upon some twisted ideology, there are people in the world who will risk the annihilation of Earth to achieve their objective. A Middle Eastern dictator or the chairman of a Russian oil cartel, a Czechoslovakian billionaire who made his money in human sex trafficking, the king of a Jamaican Drug Cartel, an Asian dictator with bad hair, or the Don of the Sicilian mob—they won't hesitate to murder and, to them, the concept of the earth being destroyed by their actions is nonsense. It's how they are wired. In their minds, the ends *do* justify the means. So, the madmen of the world are monitored daily by numerous intelligence organizations—Russia's FSB, Israel's Mossad, Germany's FIS, Interpol, you get the idea."

"How do you know which of them are madmen—ideologues who believe they have been sent by a higher power or the ones willing to destroy the world for wealth?"

"That's just it; you don't. They are all deadly in their own way. So the more powerful countries keep them in check. They handle situations which appear to be spiraling out of control with their own resources or those of their allies—Israel's Mossad, for example. The intelligence community—the spies—are really the people who control the balance of power in the world, not the superpower governments, NATO, or the United Nations. The political royalty of these countries strut about making threats and rattling sabers but the real power exists in knowing the other guy's secrets. Well, that, and having a lot of money."

"I don't follow." Sarah stuck her head into the bus's aisle to take a quick glance up and down the rows of seats, just in catch someone who had their ear tilted in Sarah's and Logan's direction.

"The intelligence network has the information. They get tons of new information each and every day. Those who subscribe to the Five Eyes Accord share it with one another. Some of the other intelligence agencies—like Mossad and the FIS—have historically shared information with other peace-loving nations. But they're all being much more cautious about what they share nowadays."

"Why?" Sarah noticed a pale-skinned woman two rows forward and across the aisle. It appeared to Sarah that she was pretending to read a book but she leaned so hard on her right elbow, her upper body partially blocked the aisle.

"Because they are worried about the safety of their secrets, and the consequences of sharing them. If sharing their secrets results in one of those countries starting a war, it may not be the outcome the nation who shared the information had intended. Even back when they were sharing intelligence, governments seldom did anything about the information they gathered unless and until it appeared one or two power-mad dictators were going to tip the delicate balance of global politics. They acted only if our human species faced imminent extinction by its own hand."

"That's frightening."

"Take Saddam Hussein. Every intelligence organization in the world knew he was exploiting his country's natural resources and murdering Kurds with mustard bombs. But they didn't do anything about it, did they? Why? Because they knew he was a stabilizing force in a very unstable region. Iran was afraid of him. Turkey was afraid of him. And the poor little Kuwaitis trembled in fear every morning they woke up. Kuwait knew he could and probably would cross the border any time he wanted, to rape its oil fields and its women. As long as he didn't do that, powerful European nations like Germany, Great Britain, and France turned a blind eye. As did the United States, Russia, and China. They rationalized his torture and exploitation as a justifiable means to keep the oil markets stable. The result of their non-intervention: the oil flowed regularly and oil prices didn't spike up and down. It was all about oil. Life was good."

Sarah stared as the pale woman walked slowly past their seats toward the lavatory. Sarah put her hand to Logan's mouth until the woman had locked the door and Sarah could hear the sound of the bathroom's fan whirring.

"What changed?"

"First, he crossed the line. He invaded Kuwait. The invasion threw oil futures into a tailspin. Industrial nations like Germany, Japan, the United States, and China knew, without Kuwait's reliable shipments of oil, the cost of making cars, televisions and refrigerators would bounce around like a pinball. Let's say Kia made a car one day, put it on a container ship in South Korea, and sent it on its way to America. Two weeks later, it is docked in the Port of Los Angeles, being offloaded. During those two weeks, though, the price of oil skyrocketed because Iraq invaded Kuwait. The oil commodity market had become completely unpredictable. Kia is forced to pay higher oil prices to keep making cars—as did Ford and GM—but they were not sure if or when their manufacturing costs would come back down. So they jacked up the prices of the cars being offloaded in Los Angeles. But Kia's competitor, Hyundai, rolled the dice and kept prices down, gambling that world powers would step in and free Kuwait, meaning oil prices would eventually stabilize. Do you remember what happened?"

"I was two years old."

"The United States led a coalition to take Kuwait back from Hussein."

"A coalition?"

Logan laughed. "We'll call it that for now. The coalition of 94% American soldiers charges across the sand, obliterating Hussein's army. Virtually unchallenged, they reached Baghdad's city limits and slammed on the brakes. This coalition wagged it finger at Hussein and said, 'Don't ever do that again.' Then they turned around and went home. They didn't finish Hussein when they had the chance, did they?"

"No."

"Do you really think President H. W. Bush didn't want to? Of course he wanted to end the Hussein regime but the intelligence communities of the world stopped him. They knew that removing Hussein completely would leave the political stability of the region in tatters. So they left him in power. Soon after, we saw the lowest oil prices in decades. Is this starting to make sense now?"

"Not really. What was the other reason?"

"What other reason?"

"You started out by saying, 'First.' That usually suggests there's a 'second.'"

"Oh yeah. Hussein threatened to kill H.W.—George W. Bush's daddy. In Texas, where Dubya grew up, you don't threaten cattle ranchers or oilmen and really think you'll live to see the end of the day. When America retaliated for September 11 by invading Afghanistan, George W. said, 'Since we're in the neighborhood, we might as well finish what we started back in 1991.' So we did. We took down Hussein and Baghdad. But that left a gaping hole in the power balance. It gave tribal leaders the chance to organize and wrest power from what was left of Hussein's regional government. Now we have ISIS and Al-Qaeda fighting for control."

"What does that have to do with what we're involved in?"

"It has everything to do with it. George W. ignored those in the world's intelligence network who warned him not to topple Hussein. What followed was a gradual disintegration of support for Bush and the Bush dynasty. Even Jeb Bush's popularity as Florida's governor began to plunge, and he couldn't even get his party's nomination for the governorship in 2006. By the time he ran for president, he never had a chance, even though he was probably the best qualified for the job. George W. had snubbed the wrong people."

"So, I still don't get it. Who are these people, and what are they trying to stop?"

"You've heard of the Deep State, right?"

"Yes, I've heard the phrase but I'm not sure what it means."

"In the United States, there are very powerful people—people far more powerful than the President, Congress and the Justice system. They are made up of people with extreme wealth or influence, or both—academicians, entrepreneurs, philanthropists, politicians and military leaders, past and present. Mostly, they advise, lobby, pressure, or influence the politicians in office to their way of thinking."

"Like the people who belong to Bohemian Grove."

"Yes, but Bohemian Grove is one of numerous similar organizations with political agendas and the means to achieve their goals."

"I've noticed many politicians don't have any net worth when they come into office, but three years later, they're millionaires."

"It's not because they've made wise investments, I assure you. It is because their vote is worth money."

"So that's who is pulling the strings behind the curtain?"

"It is much bigger than that. The United States' Deep State is just one dance partner in a global tango."

"France, Germany, Italy, Canada, Russia, they all have their own 'deep states' who manipulate their governments. It doesn't matter whether they are socialist governments, totalitarian dictatorships, democracies, or republics. They all have their agendas."

"So, the politicians we see on Capitol Hill are not really the people making decisions?"

"Nope. What's more, the politicians you see on television pretending to be in charge, aren't. The really powerful people stay in the shadows. They protect the world from self-destruction so they can continue to accrue billions of dollars in wealth. But even their powers are not without limits."

"Self-destruction? Limits?"

"Yes. Just like in the oil example, our global economy requires balance. Twenty-five years ago, it was necessary to restore balance to the flow of oil to manufacturing nations and the industrial-military complex throughout the world. The United States had the biggest stake in the game, of course, because Americans need a steady flow of black gold to slake their thirst. They need oil to refine into petroleum so they can fill their gas-chugging pickup trucks, recreational vehicles, and power boats."

"But this has nothing to do with oil."

"It has everything to do with oil. Rather, it has everything to do with consequences if the world falls out of balance. Can you imagine what would happen to our global economies and governments throughout the world if, suddenly, as if by magic, a cheaper alternative to fossil fuel appeared?"

"You're talking about energy produced by the collision of protons, aren't you?"

"Yes. Of course. Fossil fuels—coal, oil, and gas—have powered the world's economies for the past 200 years. Renewable energy—solar and wind energy, for example—haven't gained traction because lobbyists for coal, gas, oil, and pet coke have lined the pockets of Congressmen and women for decades. They actively thwart those who try to develop new sources of energy by passing laws which block the development of alternatives, regardless that they might be more powerful, safer, and efficient."

Logan talked faster as he unleashed his frustration. Sarah put her hand on his mouth again when she heard the bathroom fan stop and the pale woman open the lavatory door. She stood at the back of the bus until Sarah stuck her head out into the aisle and stared at her. She walked slowly past the two of them to her seat and resumed reading her novel.

Sarah spoke, "So these powerful people—the Deep State, let's call them—don't really want anyone to discover how to capture the energy produced in the collision of protons in a supercollider?"

"Yes."

The puzzle pieces began to fit for Sarah. "Because, if one private entity—a corporation, for example—could seize control of the world's largest supercollider, politicians, and even the Deep State would be powerless to stop the corporation's ability to market a new source of energy. How am I doing so far?" Sarah's brain reeled at the catastrophic consequences.

"Yes. Simply put, there would be a new sheriff in town. A private corporation could replace all the coal-generated electricity presently delivered through the world's electrical grid with a new energy so immensely powerful and so inexpensive to produce that it could eliminate the world's current dependence on fossil fuels."

"Is that realistic, though? Is it possible to harness, store and distribute the energy from supercolliders and their proton collisions?" Sarah asked.

"Not right now," Logan explained, "but long-term, yes, I believe it is. So do many others. The proof that they believe it is possible lies in the fact that there are so many countries involved in the supercollider race—China, Russia, Iran, Switzerland, and France, and, if we are correct about Area 51, the United States. Harnessing the energy from proton collisions may not be feasible yet but it's not far off."

"I'm listening."

"It is the reason Iran needs uranium and why the Russian nuclear agency, Rosatom, bought out controlling interest of UrAsia in 2010. It has nothing to do with the Higgs boson particle. They are not trying to discover the secrets of the universe or what happened in the zillionth of a second after the Big Bang. That's hogwash. It's all about oil or, in this case, the elimination of oil as Earth's primary fuel for manufacturing, heat, and transportation."

"Did you mean what you said? That the collisions of protons in a supercollider create more energy than the atomic bomb which was dropped on Hiroshima?"

"Yes. Proton collision generates considerably more energy but with considerably less radiation. It is more predictable and, by comparison to our current method of nuclear energy, its risks are slight."

"So, the oil companies would collapse—" Sarah felt sweat rolling down her back despite the bus's air conditioning.

"They wouldn't go down without a fight."

Sarah pondered what Logan said for a moment before saying, "No, they wouldn't, would they? That's what is happening right now, isn't it? Someone, we're not sure who, is trying to corner the market on proton collision energy with a goal to monopolize the world's energy supply. To do so, that someone would already be a major player in the world's fossil-fuel supply. If you're a large oil company with the power to gain control of the energy created by supercolliders, you could control both. Owning both would allow you to manipulate prices of oil by regulating the flow of proton-collision energy as well as fossil fuels."

"Bingo! Now you're catching on. What's more, how do you think the world's governments and oil companies will feel about being taken hostage by a worldwide monopoly controlled by one corporation; a corporation wholly owned by two of the world's most powerful people?"

"They'd be pretty pissed, I imagine. Wait. You just said two people. I thought we were talking about one."

"One corporation owned by two people. Let's stay focused on oil right now. The Queen of England's family owns fifty-one percent of British Petroleum, right?"

"I've heard that, yes."

"How do you think the Queen will feel if a collaboration to create a monopoly succeeds? Or the shareholders of Conoco and Shell? They will all be fighting for the crumbs of the oil market left behind by the super-conglomerate based in, let's pretend for now, Moscow?"

"Wait. Stop. What is it? Is it one madman or two? Is it a corporation or a rogue entrepreneur? Tell me what you know."

"I don't *know*. That's the whole point. If I knew, I'd blow the whistle myself. But if you are right about Area 51—that the United States is hiding the world's largest supercollider there—it makes perfect sense that there are two very powerful people involved. One with the brains to think of it and the other an unwitting pawn who thinks he's going to get rich. If they are successful, the result is the global imbalance I've mentioned. It will cause such an extreme imbalance that demand for the world's energy supply will be turned on its head."

"It's worth killing over, isn't it?" Sarah's back sweat soaked her t-shirt. Sarah turned toward the pale woman. She had stopped reading. A large cloth purse sat on her lap and her hand was tucked inside.

"Yes, of course," Logan replied. "But who is trying to kill us? That's the question. It could be anyone. It could be the FSB, working for the Russian president. I'm certain they are hunting us. Or it could be the Brits, whose sole interest is to protect the Queen's wealth and the economies of the British Commonwealth."

"The black trucks at the motel? Who do you think they were?"

"I can't say for sure. They did more shooting than talking and my ears were ringing so I didn't hear so well but I swear their accents sounded like they were from the Bronx or Brooklyn."

"New York City?"

"No, specifically, the Bronx and Brooklyn part of New York City, if you catch my meaning."

"The Mob?" Sarah asked, looking over her shoulder to see who in the bus might be watching them, "Why would the mob be trying to kill us?"

"Technically, they were trying to kidnap us. I don't know that they intended to kill us. Just yet."

"They want us to get the beast under control first. Right?"

"Yes. Let's say, and I'm just spit-balling here, that you are the one who thinks you're going to get rich in this little scheme. You know you are up to your eyeballs in a conspiracy with a foreign power. That's treason. You couldn't trust your own military or the intelligence community, could you? Are you with me so far?"

"Yes."

"Who do you send to kidnap the two people who know more about supercolliders, the energy produced from protons collisions, and the Higgs boson particle, than anyone else? Not your military or your CIA or FBI. No, you job it out to freelancers. You call some guy named Fat Tony who takes calls at a payphone outside a bodega in Bedford-Stuyvesant."

"Bedford-Stuyvesant," Sarah muttered, remembering Aedain's story about his father being a Bed-Stuy cop gunned down in the line of duty. "Shit. It could be anyone, couldn't it?"

Even Aedain.

33

Those seated at the oval table on the other side of the mirrored window barely flinched at the muffled sound of Mavra ending her suffering. The information she had provided proved it was time to act.

As the three Jamaicans passed through the conference room to leave, the woman seated at the head of the table asked, "Have you called the cleaning service?"

"Yes, ma'am," answered the man who had administered Mavra's final injection.

"Thank you." The woman turned to the others in the room. "Now that we know who the actors and their script, what do we do now?"

The man in the oil-stained cowboy hat and braids spoke first. "If they get control of the supercolliders, they will control the world's economy. All of our nations will be under their thumb."

A young, dark-haired man added, "The world economy will crash. We will see a global depression as we have never seen before. People will kill for a scrap of bread."

"*Oui*," the French man dressed in a well-tailored suit agreed. "*Nous devons agir de manière* decisive. We must take decisive action."

"We must tell the FBI or the Department of Justice," the young man said.

"No!" the Texan blurted. "Hell no! That damnable Congress couldn't pour water out of a boot with instructions on the heel. Some DOJ intern will leak it to some politician looking to get rich through insider information. They'll short oil futures and make a killing. They'll wind up richer than a Jersey bull's ass and we'll be the ones getting screwed. By the time our politicians get around to saving the world, we'll all be dead."

"Are you saying that nobody in Congress is suspicious about these gravitational events?" the Canadian asked.

"Oh no, I'm not saying that at all. I'm saying they don't give a shit," the Texan spewed. "They'll find a way to get rich from it.

They don't give an armadillo's nuts about their constituents. If they can't find a way to turn it into a million or two for themselves, they won't bother with it."

"Seriously," the Canadian probed, "they wouldn't believe the truth?"

"Why would they?" the Texan spewed. "They've been selling that swamp gas story for 70 years. American politicians don't give four bits and a crap about the people who vote for them. Most of them got elected because their family had money and they wanted to make sure any laws passed favored their family's interests. Ninety-seven percent of real scientists believe in global warming but more than half of America has chosen to believe the three percent of scientists who don't. They're the same ones who think the moon landing was faked and Columbus took a wrong goddamn turn. They'd rather put their faith in the dumbass who stood on the floor of the Senate and threw a snowball on the floor to prove global warming doesn't exist."

A diminutive Asian gentleman spoke in halting English, his words seasoned by a Mandarin accent. "With utmost respect, America's Achilles Heel has always been its arrogance. Americans believe they are too smart for such a thing to happen here; they don't believe an entire nation could be swindled by a man they trusted and voted for. They believe the democratic form of government will prevent such foolishness. But, as Mavra has told us, they are wrong."

The Texan added, "You know as well as I do, all they care about is who is lining their pockets today and making sure the money keeps flowing; they are the gatekeepers for the wealthy. They put on a three-ring circus to keep everybody lookin' in the wrong direction while they pick our pockets."

A German woman spoke slowly. "We—all of our nations—have a political agenda. Let's not be so naive as to think we don't. But what Mavra revealed today threatens the sovereignty of every nation on earth. The entire world will be held hostage to the manipulation of the world's supply of energy. All to satisfy the greed of two men."

"Would the United Nations intervene?" the Asian man asked.

"No. The UN would not become involved in such a matter without unanimous approval of its members," the German stated as she scanned those seated at the oval table. "We all know there are at least two 'no' votes."

"We, here at this table, are the nuclear option," she continued. "There are no laws which govern this committee—only our collective good conscience. This. This right here. This is the reason our group was formed. Our purpose is to stop a maniacal dictator and his adolescent sidekick from taking over the world."

The Asian man nodded. The others followed his lead.

"With the authority of the Queen, I can speak on behalf of England," a tall man whose British Royal Navy uniform was adorned with medals and ribbons, spoke in The King's English. "We must do whatever is necessary."

"The Queen made that perfectly clear earlier, but thank you for repeating Britain's commitment." The German woman then asked the graying military man, "Can you please articulate your thoughts on how we defeat them?"

"I assure you," he began, "they are prepared for a full frontal attack. They expect it. If they cannot take complete control of the media, they will attempt to discredit it. They will blind their people with nationalism; they will initiate a flag-waving propaganda campaign to bolster support when they send their young men and women into war. They, too, will do whatever is necessary to win and they will not hesitate to employ a military solution. If they act in concert, they will quickly quash any threat of insurgence. There will be no misgivings about employing nuclear and chemical weapons on their own people and their enemies."

Silence cloaked the room.

"You're saying we'll lose this bar fight," the Texan eventually drawled. "Am I hearing that right?"

"In a nut shell," the Commodore answered.

"Are there any American politicians we can trust?" The French man asked.

"Only three that we know of. Proposing military action against a sitting administration is an act of treason. Politicians are more motivated by getting rich than facing a firing squad. We'll have better luck with the intelligence agencies."

"What about a military coup?" the young man replied. "If we have proof of treason, the military may take over the government."

"What if they don't?" the cowboy asked. "They'd be just as likely to kill us as traitors and spies. It's a fifty-fifty shot." The cowboy tilted his hat farther back on his head. "Do you think they will believe what Mavra said on the video? She was, after all, being tortured."

"They will need corroboration. Mavra's forced confession isn't enough. If Logan and Sarah live, they might be able to corroborate Mavra's story. If not, then, no."

"*Je comprends*." The Frenchman nodded. "I understand. I thought as much." Then he rubbed his chin with his hand. "I have an idea."

"One that will work?" the Texan asked.

"If it doesn't," the French man replied, "*Préparer la guerre.* Prepare for world war. We will have no other choice."

34

"Use the back door," the front-seat passenger of the long, black limousine ordered the driver.

"Yes, sir," he nodded as he spoke into the microphone attached to his shirt cuff. "We'll be using the alley entrance," he radioed the man behind the black glass partition. A motorcade of black vehicles turned from Brooklyn's Halsey Avenue and pulled to a stop behind Salvatore's Little Sicily restaurant. Surrounded by a dozen bodyguards, the hulking man in a dark cashmere topcoat walked through the back entrance.

"This won't take long," he shouted to his entourage carrying automatic weapons, as they stood post in the alley.

"I hate it when he pulls one of his stunts," one of the bodyguards muttered to the one beside him. "We're stuck in an alley with no escape route. Some terrorist group can decide to block each end with a garbage truck and we'll be fish in a barrel."

"Zip it. I'm sure he has an escape plan for himself. I pity the terrorist who walks into Salvatore's looking for a gunfight. Frankly, it's not his job to worry about our safety. It's our job to protect his. You don't like the detail, I hear that mall security is hiring."

"Funny." The bodyguard scanned the buildings rising into the New York skyline, turning the alley into the bottom of an inescapable canyon.

"I wasn't joking."

"It's just that he does whatever pops into his head. No advance team. No plan. He doesn't get it that the bad guys have satellites, too, and are tracking our every move. Right now, there's a terrorist cell racing to get here so they can and take us all out."

"Then you better keep a sharp eye open—and your mouth shut."

Ever the gracious host, Salvatore welcomed his friend warmly, opening his arms to hug him and kiss his cheek.

"*Benvenuto, benvenuto, vecchio amico*," Salvatore gushed as he guided his guest to a private dining room, its walls covered in Romanesque wallpaper and straw-wrapped Chianti bottles recycled as candle holders on every table.

"Per Favor, please, come. Sit." Salvatore pulled a chair away from one table at the edge of the room. The portly man said, "Thank you, Sal," and nodded to Salvatore as he sat down. Those of the visitor's entourage which accompanied him inside quickly established an armed perimeter around him. Salvatore took a seat across from him.

"It's been a very long time," Salvatore began. "Last time you stopped by, it wasn't so—" Sal paused scanned the security detail wearing full tactical gear, then continued, "—it wasn't quite the spectacle it is today."

"My apologies, Sal," the man said, "I don't have a choice, you know? Things are different now."

"No, no, of course," Sal replied, "I understand completely. What can I do for my old friend today?"

"Your 'vecchio amico,' is that how you say it in Italian? You're my vecchio amico?"

"*Si.* Yes," Sal beamed as he spoke. A Sicilian immigrant, he never imagined one of his restaurant's regulars would reach the level of wealth, power, and influence his friend did. Yet he still called Salvatore 'friend.'

"Good, Sal. That's good to know. Do you still make your spaghetti and meatballs?" the man asked.

Fragrances of roasted garlic, Italian cheeses, basil, and oregano danced seductively with one another as the two men sat.

"Mama's linguine with red sauce and meatballs. Why yes, of course," Sal replied, turning toward a waiter standing beyond the protective perimeter of his entourage. He snapped his fingers and the waiter nodded knowingly. "Do you still like my Caesar salads, my friend? With anchovies?"

"Ah, no anchovies today, Sal," the man replied, pressing his fist against his chest, "I still love them but, at my age, we have our disagreements." Sal held up two fingers toward the waiter. The waiter nodded and turned on his heel toward the kitchen.

"Now, I am flattered that you still like Mama's linguine recipe," Sal looked into his friend's eyes, "but I know you didn't bring all these people here to my little restaurant for a plate of pasta."

"No, Sal, you're right," the man admitted. "I need your help."

Salvatore owed him. When Salvatore was a penniless, undocumented immigrant, the man hired him to cook in one of his hotel kitchens. Late one night, the kitchen had closed, but the man walked in through the service entrance with two bodyguards. Sal was cleaning the kitchen, preparing for the next day. The man told Sal to make him something, anything he could scrounge up. He was angry he had missed dinner. Sal whipped up his mother's linguine with red sauce recipe, and the man loved it. Days later, he fronted Sal the money to open Salvatore's Little Sicily restaurant in Brooklyn. He brought his friends and family to the restaurant and met his associated for business lunches in the booth next to the kitchen's swinging door. His restaurant prospered beyond Sal's wildest dreams.

Then, the man hired Sal's brother, Giuseppe—'Gary,' as his American friends call him—as a non-union scab to work on his construction projects. Gary became a general contractor and hired non-union, undocumented immigrants who worked for less than union laborers. Sal's brother, Vito—Vince—got seed money and contracts to start his garbage-hauling business for New York City restaurants and hotels. Sal's sister arrived in the City where a bag of money waited for her to start her non-union housekeeping and laundry business serving hotels and restaurants.

Sal owed him, alright. "Whatever you need, I can get it done for you."

This time, it was the man who reached above his head and snapped his fingers. The leader of his protection detail objected, "But, sir, our orders—" He didn't get the chance to finish his sentence before the man snapped his fingers and glared at him. "Yes, sir, understood, sir." The protective perimeter disbanded and the man's armed guards disappeared to the other side of the room's curtain.

Now it was just Sal and the tall, thick man from the black limousine. The man who, months before, had watched Dr. Logan and his wife, Beth, eat bagels and read the New York Times on a Sunday morning while their daughters, Lisa and Lucy, dug with spoons in the flower garden.

"They failed, Sal. They're dead. You know that, right?"

"Who is dead? Who failed?" Sal's face drained of color. The man shrugged confirmation. Dazed, Sal didn't want to believe it. "No, I, uh, no, I—they're dead? All of them? My sister's husband was one of the men I sent. Are you sure?"

"Yes, I'm sure. Sorry, I thought you knew," the man said nonchalantly. "All eight of them. Shot by a sniper hiding behind a tree across the street. Every pull of his trigger was a killshot. The guy was probably ex-military. A real pro. You gotta' admire his work."

"A sniper?" Sal struggled to understand. "A sniper? Who the hell—? You mean somebody in the Army killed my men? My best men? They're all gone?" Where in the hell did this college teacher get a sniper?

"Technically, he's a professor, but, yes, they're dead. The shooter picked them off one-by-one in the motel parking lot as they were dragging Logan to their SUVs. Dropped 'em like flies."

Choking back nausea, Sal tried to reject it as some sick joke, but he knew the story must be true. "What am I going to tell their families? What will I tell my sister?" Sal agonized.

"Tell them they died with honor, something like that, you know? Tell them they died as heroes. That usually makes them feel better."

"Honor," Sal scoffed. "What do you know of honor? There was no honor in sending my men to kidnap an innocent professor for you. But I did it. I did it because I owe you. That is honor. My family wasn't supposed to die. You said it was going to be easy. Overpower the police chief and kidnap the professor. Nobody gets hurt. That's what you told me. Heroes? No, there was nothing heroic about what they were doing. And you got them killed."

"Yes, well, things happen. Nobody knew it would be so complicated. It was supposed to be easy. The town had a fat-bellied retired cop as the police chief. But it's impossible to predict all the possibilities, you know. From what I heard, they killed the cop before he got his hand to his gun, but the sniper—nobody planned on a sniper waiting across the street. It just goes to show you can't predict everything, am I right or am I right?"

Sal arose from his chair, staring at a man he once believed was his friend, certain now that he was not. "You came here. In person. You said you needed my help. I gave it to you. I gave you eight of my best men and now they are dead."

"Like I said, things happen. They knew what they were getting into, though, right? Sometimes, things go badly. Not good, you know? Bad. But then, they knew the risks. Who puts an automatic rifle under his arm, goes into a police station to kidnap someone, and thinks nothing can go wrong, you see what I'm saying?"

"I see your mouth moving but I hear nothing. Only excuses for my men being slaughtered."

The man leaned back and inhaled through his nose, savoring the smells of garlic, basil, and oregano. "Ahh, Sal, it still smells great in here. I have always loved how this place smells."

"Salvatore." The restaurateur glared down at the man through bushy eyebrows.

"What?"

"You can call me Salvatore."

The visitor frowned before replying, "Yeah, sure, okay, if that's how you want it."

"Why are you here? What do you want?" Salvatore asked, "You come to my restaurant, you order spaghetti and meatballs, and you tell me my men have been murdered. What is it you want?"

"I need eight more of your men. We got word they're on the run—the professor and the girl. When they escaped from the jail in Apalachicola, they headed west, driving a late '60s muscle car. They ditched the hot rod somewhere along the way and boarded a Greyhound bus West of Dallas. Right now, it's heading northwest toward Wichita Falls. Once they pass through Wichita Falls, they'll be traveling on U.S. 287. The bus makes a couple stops along the way. It should be closing in on Amarillo in four, maybe five, hours."

"You want me to sacrifice eight more of my men for you? No! These men are my family. Their families are my family. You get that? I'm not giving you eight more to be slaughtered!" Salvatore scowled at the man as the waiter brought his Caesar salad to the table.

The man pointed toward Salvatore's chair and said, "Sit down." He waited for Salvatore to follow his orders, then the big man stood. He told the waiter, "Put that in a to-go box, will you? The spaghetti, too. It's gotten a bit chilly in here today."

As Salvatore sat, the man towered over him. He looked down and whispered coldly, "I didn't ask. It wasn't a request. You see, nobody, and I mean nobody, will find my fingerprints on this. You understand? This time, your men will bring them both to me—alive. You got it? If you refuse or your men fail, ICE will swarm your restaurant, your sister's laundry business, Vince's garbage trucks—am I making myself clear?"

Salvatore nodded. He understood what failure would mean to his family.

"Automatic rifles, ammunition and all the gear your men will need is loaded on a private jet at LaGuardia. There are two black Suburbans rented and waiting in Amarillo. Get moving. You don't have any time to spare. I understand there is a scheduled stop at a rest area twenty miles southeast of the I-40 junction."

"Yes, sir." Salvatore conceded, reaching for his phone. "I'll make the call."

His mission accomplished, the man reached out for cartons of food the waiter had bagged for him. "Good. Good man. Thank you. Come, give me a hug, old friend." Salvatore pulled back. There would be no more hugs for a man who got his friends and family killed and threatened to deport the rest. He stood in the dim room with Romanesque wallpaper and Chianti-bottle candleholders and watched the man pivot and disappear from the restaurant through the kitchen's saloon doors.

Sal held his phone in his hand. He pressed numbers on the keypad once he was sure the motorcade had left.

The waiter came to his side. "What was that all about, Papa?"

"That was about a man who thinks he is a lot smarter than he is, Son."

Sal reached for his shirt and pulled out the pen he used for taking orders. He held it for his son and clicked the top of the pen. The voice-activated digital recorder had captured their guest's every word. For ten minutes, Sal stood beside his son, listening to the thick man implicate himself in a conspiracy to kidnap the Logan and Sarah, the murder of the Apalachicola Police Chief, and the threat to expose Sal's family to Homeland Security and immigration authorities.

"You know, Papa, if you give that to the police, it will simply disappear," Sal's son commented. "The Attorney General will pretend the recording never existed. He will destroy you and the entire family."

"I know." Sal nodded. "I'm sure he's counting on that. But I know people, too."

"What do we do now?"

"For now, we send eight men. Call your Uncle Vince to make the arrangements. This time, be sure to send our most expendable people."

"There are some we think are skimming on drug sales. Others are confidential informants for NYPD or DEA." Sal, Jr. followed his father through the swinging doors separating the restaurants guest tables from its noisy kitchen.

"Send them. Hurry up. Call your uncle," Sal ordered his son calmly as he untied his white apron, pulled it over his head, and tossed it into the soiled laundry bag.

228

He grabbed his pork-pie straw hat from its hook. "While you're at it, find out who killed our family in Florida. I want a name. Get me a name, you hear me?"

"Where are you going?"

"To see someone."

Sal, Jr. watched his father disappear through the alley exit door. Over the years, when the family faced a threat, Sal, Sr. called a meeting of the family. Uncles, brothers, and cousins gathered around the table in the room with Romanesque wallpaper and Chianti-bottle candleholders. For decades, the family had warred with Jamaican, Asian and African-American gangs who tried to take over the family's drug trade, prostitution, bootleg booze, and cigarette businesses. But this was different. This was the government. The people who are supposed to be the good guys had suddenly became the bad guys, and the bad guys were being hired by those who are supposed to be the good guys.

Since coming to America, Sal had worn a permanent target on his back and, most days, he traveled with heavily armed Sicilians surrounding him. But not today.

Alone, Sal hurried down the alley, across Halsey toward a dimly lit viaduct beneath the subway tracks. He stopped and faced a lanky shadow cast leaning against the yellowed tiles of the tunnel walls.

"The bus will be stopping in a rest area southeast of Amarillo. My men will be there to apprehend them. This is for you. I don't want to see it again." Sal handed his pen with the recording to the man then turned back toward the restaurant.

He didn't look back.

35

As the sound of the Greyhound's tires hummed over the sticky tarmac of West Texas, Sarah asked the question which had been on her mind for days. She wasn't prepared for the answer.

"Why did we go to Apalachicola?"

Dr. Logan, a.k.a. Tom the Janitor, looked out the window of the bus, staring at the seemingly infinite stretch of flat, dry, brown land which stood still as the bus whizzed past. Framing the bottom of the panorama was the string of electrical wires connected to vertical wooden poles.

"Did you hear me?"

"Yes."

"Why did we go to Apalachicola? How did we end up there? It just seems so, I don't know, odd; an odd place to hide out."

"That was the point. Nobody goes there. What few tourists happen through Apalachicola are driving U.S. 98 from Tallahassee to Panama City Beach, taking the scenic route from Disneyworld or Cypress Springs."

"Cypress Springs?" Sarah furrowed her brow.

"Never mind. It was a long time ago. Apalachicola Bay is known for its oysters. Most of the oyster boat hire transient or seasonal laborers. Strangers passing through is no surprise to anyone; they don't give them a second glance."

"Go on," Sarah coaxed.

"Go on about what? Why does there have to be more?"

"Because there is. I feel it in my gut. There is something you're not telling me."

"Charlie told me to go there."

"Charlie? Your spy friend?"

"Yes. In his instructions, he told me about Apalachicola. He told me to go the motel. He knew the motel owner from his days, you know, with The Company."

"The CIA?"

Logan nodded. "Or NSA, I never knew which. He said he if I mentioned his name to the motel owner, I'd be safe. The motel owner would make sure nobody came snooping around. Or, if they did, he'd send them on a wild goose chase. It was supposed to be a safe hiding spot till it was time for the next step to get out of the country. Charlie told me to stay there until the motel owner told me the arrangements had been made."

"Arrangements? You had a plan? You were drugged up and drunk the whole time we were there. It didn't seem to be much of a plan."

Logan hung his head. "I know. Last week, I started to feel paranoid about hiding in the organ room of the church and was about to leave New Orleans for Apalachicola when you found me. My plan was to get a job on a shrimper or oyster boat, and make my way down the Florida Coast. When I reached Key West, I'd hop a merchant ship to Haiti or Cuba. When you showed up at the church, it changed everything. I couldn't take you on an oyster boat with me." Sarah didn't need for him to explain why.

The trip along the two-lane highway to Amarillo was smooth by comparison to Wild Bill's bucking bronco adventure. "When you arrived on Bourbon Street, looking for Ruby, she called the Archbishop. Bishop Joe came to the church and told me. I couldn't leave you alone in New Orleans; if the people chasing you had caught you, you'd be dead. There wasn't any other option; I had to take you with me. So I waited until Ruby brought you to the church."

"Unconscious."

"Yes. It was for your own good. If the Russians had nabbed you when you were wandering around the Quarter—" Logan's throat tightened as he thought the unthinkable. "Minutes after we meet, *boom!* The church doors blew open and shrapnel was flying everywhere. The only plan I had was to head for Apalachicola. I didn't have time to make another plan so I went with that one."

Sarah pictured the man murdered outside the motel, lying in his own blood. "Was the man who got shot in the parking lot the motel owner?"

"I don't know. When I saw him, he was face down on the blacktop. I didn't get a good look at him. It might've been his son."

"I had all I could do to keep from throwing up," Sarah said. "I knew I had to get out of there or they'd get us both."

"I know. It was a very close call," Logan replied. "So that's why we went to Apalachicola. It was supposed to be a safe harbor. Somehow, though, Ruby's scan missed a transmitter someone planted in

231

your shoe. That's the part that just doesn't make sense to me. Charlie wouldn't work with anyone who makes mistakes."

"It must have been working the whole time. It was transmitting because the wand I bought at Best Buy picked up a signal immediately."

"Right. That raises a lot of questions. Could Ruby have put it there? Who else had access to your shoes? Was it in your shoe the whole time since you left New Jersey? Most of all, if they were following a tracking device, why did it take four days for the guys in the black Escalades to show up at the motel?"

Sarah nodded as she added, "Or this one: if I had a transmitter in my shoe when I was held captive in the church, why didn't anyone come looking for me before you, the Archbishop, and Ruby?"

Logan rubbed his week-old chin-stubble as he pondered, "It's possible you had the chip in your shoe the whole time, and that's how the Russians found the church. They may have tracked you all the way from Princeton. But if that is true, why did they come into the church by blowing up the doors with explosives? They could have broken through the door when you were locked inside the mop closet. See, I've been thinking about that. Something's not adding up."

"Wait. What? It was a mop closet? You kidnapped me, and stored me with the mops, for God's sake?" Sarah's drugged-fogged memory of the dark room was sketchy. She knew it was small and smelled like mildew, but knowing she was held in a room full of rotting mop heads was nauseating.

"Yes, I'm sorry about that," Logan apologized briefly. "So, if your theory is correct—"

"Stop! I'm not done! Let me get this straight. You drugged me—not once, not twice, but three times—kidnapped me and held me captive in a *mop closet*?" Sarah's voice rose along with her blood pressure. "And you want me to *trust* you? I did trust you, you sonofabitch! I trusted you more than you know. You sonofabitch!"

"I said I was sorry. Besides, I mean, technically, it was Ruby who drugged you and locked you in the closet. The Archbishop figured that if Ruby was the only one who knew where you were, you wouldn't be able to connect the Archbishop and Ruby to me. No amount of torture could make you give up information you don't have, right?"

"No amount of torture—how comforting."

"But if you knew where I was, or even where you were, it might have led them to me, and you wouldn't be of any more use to them.

They would kill you, maybe me, and probably Bishop Joe. The mop closet had no windows. Nobody could see in and, when you awoke, you couldn't see out. We planned to get there before the tranquilizer wore off but you were already awake. Like I said, I'm sorry."

"A closet," Sarah grumbled. Sarah wasn't really sure what bothered her so much about being locked in a musty closet but it did.

"Nevertheless, it doesn't make sense that if the Russians were tracking you by the chip in your shoe because they didn't capture you when you were alone. Blowing up the church risked killing all of us."

"I don't think they were the ones using the chip to track me," Sarah said. "Someone else was. But who? And why?"

They both sat silently for several minutes before Logan spoke.

"Let's go back to what we believe is true: there are powerful people trying to gain control of the world's energy, from fossil fuel, to wind, solar, and, most important, energy created from nuclear fission or nuclear fusion. Anyone who can control a safer, more powerful and more predictable form of nuclear energy will hold unimaginable power and wealth. They can monopolize the world's energy grid and will have a stranglehold on the Gross Domestic Product of every nation on earth."

"To put it simply." Sarah's tongue felt thick and dry. She was no longer sweating despite the West Texas sun pouring through the windows of the Greyhound. She was cold.

"So, although I am sure Charlie believed his motel-owner friend would help us stay under the radar, he might have changed his mind if someone began waving dollar bills under his nose, especially if they were holding a gun to his head at the same time."

"Millions of dollars bills, I'm sure. How well do you know Ruby or the Archbishop?"

"Not well. Bishop Joe always seemed nice. He's been protective toward me, you know? Charlie gave me Ruby's name so I know he trusted her. Money can buy a lot of betrayal, though. What we know is that somebody planted a transmitter in your shoe, and a bunch of guys in black Escalades showed up at the motel, gunned down the clerk in cold blood, murdered a police chief, and came within inches of kidnapping both of us. That's what we know."

It was Sarah's turn to stare out at the flat, brown land. The landscape flew past the bus's window while Sarah saw it in slow motion. She was startled from her trance when the bus swayed to the right and onto an exit. Its brakes squeaked as it ground to a stop southeast of the junction with Interstate 10. The rest stop would be the last before Albuquerque. She looked for a Grey Charger parked at the edge of the parking lot. It was parked precisely where her dad said it would be.

"That about sums it up." Sarah hoisted her backpack onto her shoulder as she rose from her seat. "We're being chased by *people* we don't know, for *causes* we don't know, who want to kill us for reasons *they* don't know."

"Yep." Logan followed Sarah as they exited the bus's back door and strode briskly to the bathrooms. Sarah was the first to reach the women's bathroom.

As she left the bathroom, a hand grabbed her arm and pulled her hard against the wall.

"Shhhhh! Be quiet!" It was Dr. Logan. His face was ashen as he held his free hand over Sarah's mouth.

Sarah turned in the direction Logan was facing. "Oh, shit," Sarah muttered, her expletive muffled by Logan's hand.

Two black Suburbans with tinted windows were parked beside the Greyhound, one on each side, and directly in their path between them and the Charger. Inside the bus, men in dark suits, white shirts, and skinny black ties moved slowly down the aisle, examining every seat and passenger's personal belongings. What passengers remaining on the bus didn't dare object; stubby automatic rifles hung from the black-tied men's shoulders. The consequences of resisting was clear.

Two of the gangsters were approaching the restroom building, their automatic weapons raised.

"They have guns. Lots of guns." Logan was trembling. Sarah pulled Logan's hand from her mouth.

"Do exactly as I tell you," Sarah said calmly. Sarah wasn't sure she had ever seen a real member of the Mafia except in the movies, but these guys looked like characters in *Goodfellas*. They were calm and appeared certain Logan and Sarah were on the bus or in the rest rooms.

"How did they know we were riding this bus?" Logan whispered.

"Someone has known every step we've made. Someone very high up."

It was clear someone knew Sarah and Logan would stop at this rest area. What they didn't know is what Logan would do next. He stepped from the shadows beside the restroom's vanity wall, his hands raised, and offered himself to the two men approaching the building. He dropped to his knees and placed his hands on top of his head. One of the men reached down to pull him up when he heard Sarah's steady voice in the shadows.

"Make one move, and you're dead."

The brawnier of the two didn't look in her direction as he spoke, "Oh now, Missy, you're not going to shoot us—"

Baaam! The explosion of the .40 caliber round echoed against the building's cedar walls and cement floors. Only one second before, the brawnier one was taller. Now he was shorter, writhing in agony on the hot cement floor, gripping his bloody leg. The Glock was now pointed at the second mobster's forehead. Bus passengers poured from the bus and the rest rooms, scurrying in every direction, ducking behind cars, and running toward the freeway.

"I hate it when men call me Missy." She nodded toward the man still standing. "Get his gun." Before the gunman could react, the janitor named Tom ripped the M-4 carbine from the mobster's shoulder. "The one on the ground, too," Sarah ordered, and Logan complied.

The uninjured man spoke, "Now, what'd you go and do that for, M—?"

"Stop! You say 'Missy' and I'll drop you where you stand."

Instead, he put his hands up and said, "Now what are you going to do? There are six others who just heard a gunshot and they're running this way."

"Tell them to stop or you're dead."

"They don't care if I'm dead or alive. They're coming for you."

Baaam! The second shot sounded louder than the first. The man grabbed his right ear. Only half was still attached, and warm goo flowed down his face and neck.

"The next one is an inch higher and three inches to the right," Sarah said flatly, pointing the laser sight's red dot between his eyes.

"Stop! Hold up!" The second man waved off the remaining gang running toward the restroom building.

"She's going to kill us both if you come any closer."

"Lie on your stomach," Sarah told the man with one and a half ears. He knelt beside the man with the bloody leg, then lay prone on the cement.

"Your move," he said, "you can kill me and my friend here but what are you going to do about those other six other guys with machine guns? They won't let you get away alive."

"Frankly, I'm betting they will," Sarah said, "I'm betting you all are under strict orders to take us both alive. We're no good to anyone dead. Capturing only one of us is worth nothing. How am I doing?"

The man shrugged.

"How about we test my theory?" Sarah pressed, pointing the laser at his eye.

"Now, now, just calm down, okay? Killing me won't do you any good."

Sarah looked at her mentor holding two machine guns. "Do you know how to shoot one of those?"

"No, not a clue."

"Pull back on the bolt to make sure it's loaded."

"The bolt?"

"The little thingy sticking out on the side. Pull it back all the way and then release it."

Brrraaaaap! A volley of rounds ricocheted off the cement in all directions. The remaining six mobsters dropped to the ground and covered their heads. "Umm, take your finger off the trigger. Then pull back the bolt on the other one."

Logan carefully cocked the second M-4 and released it. "Okay, now what?"

"Keep it aimed at the ones on the ground. Tell them to throw their pistols out of reach and pull up their pants legs."

"Huh? Why?"

"I saw it on TV. Make sure they don't have a gun in an ankle holster." Cold sweat poured down Sarah's back. Minutes ago, she was parched in fear. Now she was sweating profusely for the same reason.

"Then what?"

"Pick up their guns. Bring me a rifle and a couple clips. Go see if they left their keys in one of the SUVs. If so, drive the truck up here." Logan followed Sarah's orders, telling their pursuers to lie on the ground and stay put, and firing a couple warning shots over their heads to show he meant business. He climbed into the first SUV and pushed the ignition button. It revved to life.

"Over here," Sarah waved as she cocked the hammer of the Glock and steadied her aim on the man's eye.

"Tell them to get in the women's bathroom." She waited until he did as he was told, then added, "Go! Move! That's it. Everybody into the ladies' room."

"You're a dead lady, you know that, right?" One of the tough guys snarled, his hands on his head, as he walked past her toward the women's restroom. His accent confirmed they were from Brooklyn. Maybe Logan was right. Once they were all inside the bathroom, Sarah motioned to Logan to park the truck against the door of the bathroom. "Push the front bumper right up against the door," she ordered. "Leave the motor running. Pop open the hood." Perplexed, Logan did as he was told.

"Now, put all their guns in the back of the truck. We don't want to leave them out where some kid can get his hands on one."

From her backpack, Sarah retrieved one of the galvanized pipes, popped the truck's hood, and placed the bomb on top of the truck motor's manifold. They turned to leave when they heard a female voice.

"Stop!" Sarah and Logan pivoted slowly to see the pale woman from the bus pointing a gun at them. Sarah had no play with either of her weapons; the woman had the drop on her.

"Funny how these things turn out, isn't it?" Sarah couldn't place her accent but Logan did. Sarah took a step back and pulled Logan with her. Then another.

"What brings you from Belarus?" he asked.

"Very good, Doctor," she replied. "If I'd known there were others here at the rest stop who wanted to capture you, we could have combined our efforts. Sadly though, I don't think we want to take you to the same place."

"No, I suppose not," Sarah said, trying to hide her trembling hands. Even if she could get one of the guns raised, she knew she was shaking too badly to hit the broad side of a barn. Sarah took another step back from the idling Suburban, positioning herself between the woman and Logan.

"I said stop!" the woman screamed as fixed the laser sight's red dot on Sarah's forehead.

"What are you going to do with us?" Sarah asked. "Put us back on the bus? How long do you think it will take for the police to catch that big old thing?" With her free hand, Sarah reached behind her back and signed to Logan, "Keep backing up, no matter what. The truck is going to explode any second."

"This is true," the Belarus woman replied as she moved closer to the SUV blocking the women's bathroom. "But I think we could all fit in this nice truck, don't you agree?" She ran her hand over the fender of the truck. "I said stop moving. Take one more stop and I will shoot you in the head."

"No, you won't," replied Sarah, "because somebody you work for wants both of us—Dr. Logan and me—alive. Besides, what are you going to do with all those angry men when you move that truck?"

"Kill them. I will kill them all first."

"Actually, I must admit," Sarah said, "that's not a bad plan. It's going to take a lot of bullets, though. We put their guns in the back of the truck. See for yourself. I'm sure there are enough bullets for you to kill them all." Sarah kept motioning for Logan to back away from the truck.

The pale woman lifted the back window to peek into the van. Sarah knew it was now or death.

"Run!" Sarah shouted as she turned and raced toward the parking lot.

"Run?" Logan tried to keep up with her.

"Run *fast!*"

"Stop!" was the last word the pale woman shouted before the explosion. Pieces of the windshield and motor were hurled as deadly projectiles, followed by a fireball which engulfed the cabin of the truck. When the flames reached the guns' ammunition, bullets discharged in all directions. The only bullet trajectories that mattered were the ones which carried the armor-piercing rounds through the pale woman's torso. She was dead before her body reached the tarmac.

Dodging shrapnel as they raced toward the remaining SUV, Sarah dug into her backpack, and pulled out the second makeshift bomb. Logan released the hood latch and Sarah positioned the pipe bomb on top of the second truck's manifold. She started the motor and ran toward the waiting rental car.

As they reached the end of the entrance ramp, they heard the second explosion. The 400-horsepower Hemi roared onto the highway as Logan turned back to see one plume of smoke billowing from the restroom and another from the parking lot.

Dr. Logan was still trembling when they crossed into New Mexico. Sarah had the charger running just over 100 mph. Driving fast helped calm her nerves.

"See why Laura-Lee was so understanding about a lady needing her necessities when she travels? You just never know what you're going to run into."

Logan's expression was grim. "What if they had called your bluff?"

Sarah shrugged. In that moment, serenity enveloped her. "I wasn't bluffing. I am tired of being chased like an animal. If they started shooting, I would have shot back until I ran out of bullets.

238

They had more ammunition so, it's likely we would both be dead right now."

"How could you be sure they'd stop when you told them to?"

"I wasn't sure. Until I shot the guy's ear off and the rest of them did what he told them to do. Then I knew he was the leader. If they had kept coming, well—"

"I got it. Dead."

"I knew they had orders to not kill either of us. Somebody wants us, alright, but they want us alive. The woman, though, wanted us dead."

Logan checked his pulse. It had dropped below 130 beats per second, barely. "Did your dad teach you to shoot like that?"

Sarah nodded. "Growing up, he took me shooting at life-size targets. After, we go for ice cream and he'd say, 'I hope you never need to, but if you do, aim small and shoot first.'"

More than an hour had passed since they'd left the rest area and Sarah had a sense that other pursuers were closing in. By now, whoever they were had found the eight mobsters in the women's toilet at the rest stop, and whatever was left of a shrapnel-riddled pale woman. They also knew the make, model, and color of the car they were driving, as well as which direction they were headed—hard west.

"Aren't you worried they'll track this car?" Dr. Logan asked.

"Nope. We've got twenty minutes of daylight left. Then we'll drive through the night. They won't hunt us at night. By the time the sun comes up, we'll have arrived at our destination. I hope."

"Do you have any of those burner phones left?"

"Yes, one. Why?"

"I have a hunch. Maybe a Hail Mary pass—"

"What? What are you going to do?"

"Well, you see, Charlie had friends—lots of them in powerful places. He talked about a back door, a way to send an emergency signal to the circle of people he trusted—military folks, politicians and, of course, other spies. Maybe if I can get a message through to one of them, they'll see that Charlie's friends are in trouble and come to help us. It's a long shot, I know."

"Or they could hand the message over to the very people who are hunting us down. It would give our location, direction, and it wouldn't take a rocket scientist to figure out where we're headed."

"Rocket scientist," he laughed through his teeth. "Under the circumstances, that's funny."

Shortly after nightfall, Logan took his turn in the driver's seat as he asked Sarah, "Why are you so sure America has a secret super-collider in Area 51?"

"Because it is suddenly, inexplicably, secret again," Sarah explained. "Why? According to the government, nothing secret has been going on in Area 51 since they were building and testing stealth bombers more than twenty-five years ago. But then in July of 2017, the United States *confiscated* 400 acres of mining land and mountains adjacent to Area 51 for pennies on the dollar, in a land-grab eminent domain lawsuit. Instead of paying the family more than $100 million—the real value of the land and mining—the government ripped off the owners by paying them a measly $5 million and change. The federal judge virtually handed over land which this family had owned for decades to the Air Force for next to nothing."

"How did they manage to pull that off?" Logan asked.

"Simple. They got away with it because they can. All the government needs to claim is that the land is a national security risk and they're 90% of the way there. In this case, it is too close to Area 51 for the government's comfort. The land overlooks a top-secret Air Force facility which has been a national mystery for more than a half century. The government wouldn't care if there was nothing to spy on in Area 51, would they? However, if there *is* something going on underground, the mining operation would be an ideal location to monitor anything and everything beneath the earth's surface.

"Any foreign government intent on spying on Area 51 could do it easily from the mining land and its network of tunnels. They could measure SONAR signals, seismic vibrations, and magnetic levels. If there is a supercollider hiding underground, a magnetometer will peg off the charts and prove the U.S. has a secret supercollider."

Logan stared out the Charger's windshield toward the vanishing point of the two-lane highway a separating a sea of brown dirt and sagebrush. He turned his head only enough to see Sarah in his periphery.

"That's where we're going, isn't it?"

Sarah nodded. Logan didn't need to ask a follow-up question but he couldn't stop the words from escaping his mouth.

"You have a magnetometer in your backpack, don't you?"

Sarah nodded.

"We're never going to get into Area 51, you know that, right?"

Sarah nodded again. "I don't need to get inside Area 51. Just close enough."

"Shit," Logan muttered softly. He knew what that meant.

36

Going on three hours, Sarah had been watching the headlights in the mirror. They stayed a half mile back, sometimes farther, but the car wasn't getting closer. Just east of Winslow, Sarah caught a glimpse of the green highway sign, 'Rest Area, Exit Here' with a white directional arrow.

"Take this exit! Now!" Sarah yelled at Logan, yanking the wheel hard to the right.

"Why? What? You could give me a little warning, for God's sake."

"Just do it. A car that has been following us for more than two hours."

"It's a highway. Cars do that; they follow one after another. It's not that unusual, you know."

"Stay in the front of the rest area, close to the highway, so I can get a good look at it as the car goes by." Logan did as Sarah asked. They waited. A half hour elapsed but the car behind them didn't pass.

Logan turned to Sarah, "Do you think we might have missed them? A few cars have gone by. How can you be sure the car you think was following us didn't go by?"

"It had those blue-tinted headlights that they install on expensive cars, like Audis and Mercedes. I think they stopped and shut off their headlights when we pulled off. I think they're still there. I'm going to get out and walk back down the road toward them."

"What? Are you nuts? What are you going to do? Wag your finger at them? Tell them to stop following us? Ask them to never do that again? Or get a bullet planted between your eyes? Whoever they are, you don't screw with these kinds of people."

"I could take the machine gun—" Sarah eyed the weapon she stole from the mobsters in the back seat.

"Great. You might as well just ask them to shoot you from a hundred yards away." Logan pulled into a diagonal parking spot and put the car in park. "Listen, you stay put. I've got to piss like a race-horse. I didn't before but I sure as hell do now. Stay with the car. You hear me? Don't move!"

Sarah watched Logan walk toward the restroom building, then reached into the back seat for the tactical automatic. She checked to make sure it was fully loaded then stepped out of the car and snuck into the shadows along the roadside. Hiding behind the brush line as she crept, she worked her way toward their pursuers. A half mile from the rest stop, she found nothing. No car, no tiretracks, and no sign of a car in the distance. The stalker had vanished.

Walking back to the rest area, she checked over her shoulder every few seconds, certain their pursuers would re-appear. When Sarah returned to the parking lot, Logan was pacing frantically.

"I told you! Didn't I tell you? I told you to stay put. I mean—where did you go? Stubborn. That's what you are. So flippin' stubborn it's going to get you killed one of these days." Sarah watched him pacing and sputtering until he turned toward the Charger and climbed into the driver's seat.

Sarah pulled open the door and plopped into the passenger's seat, wondering how long Logan would scold her.

"Hi, Johnny," came a voice front the back seat. "I got your message."

Logan jumped high enough to hit his head on the car's ceiling. Sarah grabbed the rifle.

"Charlie?" Logan squeaked. Sarah aimed the machine gun at the unwelcome stranger.

"Don't shoot, Sarah," Charlie said calmly, "I'm one of the good guys."

"How do I know that?" Sarah pointed the muzzle at the gap between his eyebrows.

"Because if I wasn't, you'd already be dead, like the people in the three cars that were following you for the past three hours."

"Wha—?"

"That's right. As soon as you pulled into the rest area, we—a few of my friends and me—neutralized the threat. My boys drove the cars away and dropped me off here so we could have a little talk, the three of us."

"Who were they?" Sarah mumbled.

"Iranians, maybe, or Pakistanis. They were screaming a lot so I couldn't make out if it was Urdu or Farsi. From the weapons they had in their cars, they were planning to make sure you were good and dead."

Sarah's blood flowed through her veins as ice water.

Logan muttered, "I thought you were dead. The car crash, remember?"

"Pretty good one, eh? I must say, it was one of my better death fakes. Do you know how hard it is to find a tanker truck full of benzene, a double-bottom carrying diesel and two truckers crazy enough to smash them into one another?"

"Who was in the car?"

"A corpse I stole from the morgue. It's not hard. They don't care if a vagrant's body goes missing. I saved the county the cost of burying one. Toss a couple of titanium screws I bought at the medical supply store into the middle of the wreckage, and nobody gives it a second thought."

Charlie let Logan and Sarah ruminate on what had just happened for a moment before adding, "Are you going to sit here jabbering all night or are you going to get this buggy headed toward Area 51?"

"How do you know we're going to Area 51?"

"I'm a spy, remember? Do you really think everybody hasn't figured out you're making a beeline for Area 51?"

"They have?" Sarah sounded surprised.

"Yep. The bet is who is going to stop you. Before you blew up the mobsters' trucks in the rest area and killed the KGB spy in the explosion, Vegas had even money between the Brooklyn and Russian mobs. Now it's a horse race."

Logan started the Charger's motor and rolled onto the westbound ramp of the interstate.

"Wake me an hour before daylight," Charlie said as he leaned against the headrest and closed his eyes.

"What happens an hour before daylight?" Logan asked.

"If we're still alive," Charlie replied, "then we're not dead."

37

Just outside Snicker's Gap and deep inside the Blue Ridge Mountains, Ruby's gold lamé slippers floated over the tile floor. Despite her imposing stature, Ruby appeared as if she was on a cushion of air as she raced to be at her father's bedside.

"Keep up, will you?" she shouted over her shoulder. Aedain never understood how anyone Ruby's size could move like a ballerina and a middle linebacker at the same time. He was doing his best but the faster he walked, the wider the gap grew between them. She reached the nurse's station a full 20 seconds ahead of her long-time friend.

"I'm here to see Bishop Joe," she told the charge nurse.

Neither confirming nor denying the Bishop's presence in the hospital, the charge nurse peered over her reading glasses up toward Ruby's face, then back to her chart. She studied the chart closely, then looked over her glasses at Ruby again. Her brow furrowed, she asked, "Are you family?"

"Yes, I'm family," Ruby replied. "Of course I am family. Can't you see the resemblance?"

"You're—"

"Tall. Yes, I know. I've been that way as long as I can remember. We're both tall."

"But he's, well, he's—"

"White. I'm black. I know that, too. We've both pretty much been that way our whole lives, too."

"I was going to say he is a priest. I thought priests couldn't marry."

"He was Presbyterian then. Well, he was pretending to be Presbyterian. He met my mother in Kingston."

The nurse looked at Bishop Joe's chart. "This says he is a Roman Catholic Archbishop."

"And I say he's a spy," Ruby planted her hand on her hip as she stared down at the charge nurse. "You just can't believe one damn thing anyone tells you nowadays, can you?"

Aedain interrupted. "She is the Archbishop's daughter. I vouch for her." He showed the nurse his British Intelligence identification.

"But you're Irish."

Aedain shook his head. "Yes, I'm Irish and I work for Her Majesty's Secret Service. She's Jamaican and the Archbishop's daughter."

"Who does she work for?"

"You don't want to know. Believe me."

"Stay there, I'll check into this." The nurse pivoted and walked down the shiny tiled hallway. Halfway to the end, she turned into a patient's room.

"Ruby!" the Archbishop's voice reverberated through the hospital hallway. "She's here? Get her in here!"

Ruby was already moving toward the room and Aedain again did his best to keep up. She was floating even faster as she hurried toward the door the nurse had entered.

"You saggy-assed old man! I'm coming!" she shouted as her eyes filled with tears. "Go and get yourself shot like that. Oughta' take you out back and give you a whoopin' with a hickory switch." Her satin muumuu momentarily served as a tissue as she wiped tears from her face.

Aedain reached the entry of the room to find Ruby bent over her father, hugging him hard enough to break every bone in his fragile body. Her father's arms were wrapped around her in return. The nurse stood in stunned silence.

"I thought you were dead, Tata." Ruby referred to him by her pet name for her father.

"I thought the Russians had killed you, Ruby."

"They couldn't get that lucky." They clung to one another for several minutes until the tears subsided.

"You," the Archbishop said when he saw Aedain. "You were at the church. The Irish lad working for the Queen, if I recall."

"Yes, sir," Aedain replied. "You recall well. Commander Aedain Maycroft, Her Majesty's Secret Service." He extended his hand to shake the Archbishop's.

Bishop Joe glanced from Ruby to Aedain and back again. "You two know each other?"

"Yes, sir," Aedain replied. "When your wife was murdered in Kingston, the Queen arranged for Ruby to be raised by a British foster family. You were able to see her as she was growing up but it was always arranged in secret. Remember?"

"Yes, I remember."

"Ruby was a teenager when she put all the pieces together—that you were a British spy posing as a cleric in the United States. In college, she decided to join the family business, so to speak, and that's where we met. We were in the same graduating class of British spies. We've been friends ever since."

The Archbishop turned to Ruby, "Why didn't you ever tell me about your friend here?"

"We're spies, Tata. All of us. We're all spies, remember?"

"Tata." The Archbishop smiled. "Your mother called me that the minute you were born. Now, you're the only one who calls me that." He held Ruby's hand tightly as he spoke. "And you," turning to Aedain, "it's good to see you again. I may have forgotten to thank you and your lads for saving my life."

"No thanks necessary, sir."

The Archbishop stared at Commander Aedain Maycroft intently before asking, "You're not really Irish, are you?"

"I am of Irish lineage, sir."

"You told me your family is from Kilkenny, as I recall."

"Yes, sir. You have a good memory, sir."

"This time, tell me the truth, Commander."

"Yes, tell me the truth, too," Ruby asked quizzically as she turned to face Aedain.

"The truth." Aedain sucked in a deep breath. "My father was a New York City cop. He went undercover in the Bedford-Stuyvesant neighborhood in Brooklyn as a mobster. A few years later, he was a made man in one of New York's biggest crime families. He was black Irish—wavy hair and olive skin, he could pass for Sicilian. His name was Tommy Varisco. When I was fourteen, he was murdered when the family's Don discovered he was a cop. The U.S. Marshals knew my mother and I would never be safe in the WitSec program here in the States. As long as we were in the country, the mob would find us. So they set us up in Ireland, in a small village west of Ballyfoyle, County Kilkenny."

The Archbishop nodded, "You're an American. You volunteered for this mission, didn't you?"

"I'm proud to say I am a citizen of both the United States and Ireland, although that's a secret to most people. I'd just as soon it stay so."

The Archbishop's fingers twisted at his lips as if he was turning a key, "Mum's the word."

"Are they treating you well, sir?" Aedain asked.

"I couldn't ask for more," the Archbishop replied. "I asked that nurse there if she could slip me a little holy water in a flask but she turned me down flat."

Aedain reached into his pocket and pulled out a pint of Irish whiskey and slipped it under the Archbishop's covers. "This isn't holy water but I think it'll do."

The Archbishop made a Sign of the Cross over the crisp bed-sheets. "It is now," then winked. "I'll save it for later."

Ruby kissed his forehead. "I'm glad you're alive, Tata."

"Me too, Ruby. Me too."

Aedain gripped the Archbishop's free hand. He kissed Ruby on the cheek. "I hate to run but I have a plane to catch. I have an urgent matter to attend to." He turned and left the room.

"Taking British Airways, by chance?" Ruby hollered after him.

"I didn't say that," Aedain said as his heels clicked down the tiled hallway.

38

The thick man from the limousine sat behind the Resolute Desk, holding the black plastic handle of a mid-century telephone. "Did you draw up that document for me? Good. Bring it down to my office. Yes, now. No, I don't want a White House photographer. No, no White House staff, either." He started to put the phone's handle in its cradle then pulled it back to his face. "No press, no politicians, nobody. You got it? Just you and me."

Minutes later, a White House aide stood at the President's side, holding the executive order he had written. The order reclassified numerous large tracts of national park and military real estate holdings. The reclassification would permit individuals or corporations to purchase the land for business or residential development. The President scrawled his signature, authorizing the Department of the Interior's Bureau of Land Management to sell the land to private investors.

"Should I share this with the White House Press Corps?"

"Hell no! What part of keep it to yourself do you not understand? I'm the President. I have the right to do this." The aide turned to leave but the President stopped him, "Get the Secretary of the Interior on the phone for me. Now!"

The phone rang seconds later, and the President waved the aide away, waiting for him to close the door behind him before instructing the Interior Secretary.

"Right. I just wanted to give you a heads up. I signed an EO on a couple hundred acres of worthless desert land in Montana, Wyoming, New Mexico, and Nevada a few minutes ago. I heard through the grapevine one of my old real estate investor friends wants to develop them into golf, casino, and condos like Las Vegas. He's going to bring in drinking water, air conditioning, irrigation, whatever it takes. He says he's already written up a terrific offer on the one in Nevada. Just terrific. Way over market value. We don't want to miss out on an offer of $50,000,000 for junk land worth one-tenth of that, do we? Get that offer inked ASAP, you got that?"

He paused as he listened to the Interior Secretary's misgivings, and retorted, "You're the head of the Bureau of Land Management. You have the right to sell it if I say you can sell it. You can accept any offer on it, at any time. That's an order. We don't need Congressional approval. We can just do this. Am I making myself clear? When you get that offer in your hands, I expect you to sign it immediately."

The President paused again as the Secretary asked another question. His face grew red in frustration as he spouted, "No! No White House Staff. No photographers! What is it with you people? Tell you what. We'll get a nice big picture of us standing with the check in hand. How's that? Till then, let's keep this under wraps. This is not open for discussion."

He slammed the black phone hand into the cradle then leaned back in his plush chair, his fleshy face morphing into a satisfied smile.

39

Logan checked his watch. It was two hours till sunup. He couldn't keep his secret any longer; it was time to come clean with Sarah. He looked into the mirror at his back seat passenger, confirming he was sleeping, then he turned to Sarah.

"I have a confession," Logan began.

"Really? Now?" Sarah asked, shaking her head. "Is this really a good time? Do I look like a priest?"

"No, no," he replied, "not that kind of confession. What I was going to say is that I am certain these strange events we've witnessed, and others have witnessed, are man-made. I am certain of it."

"You've said that already. Several times," Sarah's exasperation with Logan was beginning to show.

"The truth is, I don't know how to stop the anomalies. If we are captured and the bad guys discover that neither you nor I know how to get the supercolliders under control, we will be of no value to them."

"I know," Sarah answered, "then they will kill us. Got it."

"Exactly. I can't help them. We can't help them. When they find out, we're dead." Logan leaned back against the Charger's headrest and stared at the ceiling.

Sarah replied, "After you left New Jersey, I did some digging. I searched for all the information I could find about these gravitational anomalies occurring throughout the world. There appears to be a pattern. Follow me on this. The moon is magnetic, right? We've known that since Apollo astronauts brought back moon rocks fifty years ago."

"Yes." Logan nodded.

"We also know that the moon's gravitational pull on the earth is greatest when the moon is closer to the earth, right? The moon causes high tides and low tides, and the size of the tides is affected by the earth's distance to the moon at any moment, right?"

"Yes. Go on." Dr. Logan turned his complete attention to Sarah.

"It's the same with the supercolliders. These bigger, more powerful supercolliders have exceeded their maximum safety thresholds. When 20 or 30 teraelectronvolt accelerators began operating, the power of the proton collisions caused unexpected reactions in dark matter, dark energy, and the earth's magnetic field. The side effects of these super collisions increase exponentially when the moon is closer to the earth."

"I'm not getting your point."

Sarah continued, "If the proton collisions occur while the moon's gravitational pull is weak—that is, when the moon is farther from the earth—they have little or no effect on the earth's magnetic field or gravity. When the moon is closer, things go wacky."

"Wacky I understand." Logan chuckled at Sarah's non-science jargon before asking, "You have an idea how it can be fixed, don't you?"

Sarah nodded. "Yes, I think so. The anomalies might be prevented by dialing back the power of these super-supercolliders. At least temporarily. Once we can predict how proton collisions influence dark matter and dark energy, and what impact the moon has on them, we will be able to measure their side effects. We will be able to reassure the world that The Apocalypse is not imminent; it's not even close. As we learn more about proton collisions' interaction with the universe, we can begin to develop the positive uses of supercollider-generated energy."

"If we get the accelerators under control and we can prevent mass hysteria. Is that it?"

"Precisely. With teams of the world's best scientists working together, yes, I believe we can open new worlds of discovery and possibilities."

Logan rubbed his chin. "Hmm, a collaborative approach rather than one driven by profit or quest for world domination. This has some possibilities, doesn't it?"

Sarah laughed as she shook her head in agreement. "Imagine that! Altruism might save the world! Who-da' thunk it?" Sarah paused then added, "Who knows, with the most brilliant minds in the world working together, we may learn that Einstein was right: interstellar travel may be possible by using worm holes in the universe."

A slow clap came from the back seat. "Well done, Sarah. You're well on your way to solving the mystery."

Logan's head snapped around, "I thought you were sleeping."

"Of course you did."

251

"Tell me. Why are you here? How long have you been tailing us?" Logan's voice was edgier than Sarah had ever heard.

"Ever since I told you how to disappear. When I saw on the news that you had disappeared from Princeton and the cops were hunting for you as a person of interest, I faked the crash and made my way to New Orleans. I knew Sarah would find Ruby and the two of them would lead me to you. When the Russians blew up the church, I had the place staked out. I was just about to send in my team when the Brits rolled up and took care of business."

"The Brits?"

"Her Majesty's Secret Service. MI-6. Those lads are right up there with Navy Seals and Army Rangers; they took down most of the Russians, except Dmitri Sokolov and his driver, who kidnapped Ruby. But Ruby and I already knew Sokolov and his boss, Mavra, were staying at the Hotel Monteleone. Both Ruby's team and mine had been surveilling them for a week. Ruby already had her people planted in the hotel before the Russians kidnapped her and manhandled her through the hotel's back door. We knew Ruby could handle herself. We thought it best we not expose ourselves to the MI-6 crew or Ruby's team."

Sarah snapped her head around to face Charlie. "Wait. Team? What team?"

"Ruby's a spy. Been in the spy game a long time. The Archbishop is her father. He's a spy, too. You didn't realize you had so many spies in your life, did you, Johnny?"

Logan drove, staring through the windshield. He couldn't talk.

"Honestly, Johnny, after the church blast, I thought they'd carry you two out in plastic bags. By the time I had a chance to get into the church and snoop around, you were long gone. Apalachicola was in the instructions I gave you; I knew you'd wind up there eventually so I hung around the town for a few days. My crew and I were just down the road when we heard sirens the night the mob killed the motel clerk and tried to grab you. I had two men in Ghillie suits posted in the swamp across from the motel when they came back and killed the police chief." He turned to Sarah and added, "Your daddy wasn't the only one shooting that morning. He's one helluva' shot, though. Next thing we know, we're haulin' ass west on U.S. 98 trying to catch that damn hot rod of yours. How fast does that thing go?"

"150, maybe 160," Sarah said quietly. "The speedometer only goes to 140."

"We were running at more than 140 in three Crown Vic Interceptors and we were losing ground every mile."

"That was you we saw from the sand dune?"

"Yes. We knew we'd lost you again when we got to Panama City Beach."

Sarah's face was an unnatural shade of white. "The people who are chasing us, are they all planning to kill us?"

"Oh, no, not at all; only about half of them. The Russians don't give a rat's ass whether you can stop the gravitational anomalies. They don't care if a tiny village in the hinterlands gets sucked into the ground. It's collateral damage, that's all. But they want you alive so you can tell them how to harness the energy of the colliders and dominate the world. The whole space exploration thing is just a bonus."

"Who else is chasing us?" Logan's face showed his utter confusion.

"As I said, there were some Middle Easterners who were shadowing you until a few hours ago. I've seen a couple of Israel's Mossad agents, and, of course, the British Secret Service."

Logan paused and drew in deep breath before asking his next question. "You know what happened to Beth, Lucy, and Lisa, don't you?"

Charlie asked his friend of twenty years, "You sure you want to know the answer to that question, John?"

Logan exhaled slowly and said, "Yes. Yes, I do."

Charlie spoke slowly. He wasn't one to express emotion but this was different. "They thought threatening your wife and family would be enough to keep you quiet. They planned to rough them up good, make them bleed, to get your attention and scare the hell out of you, maybe even kidnap them to get your cooperation. But it went sideways. The gang they hired were street thugs, not disciplined professionals. They didn't like it when Beth fought back. She fought like mama bear. They killed her first, then they had no choice but to kill the witnesses, your daughters."

Logan's eyes flooded with tears. The road was just a blur now. His steering became erratic as he alternately glanced at the road and into the back seat. "My daughters watched their mother being murdered?"

"I'm sorry, John."

"How long have you known?"

"Since the day it happened," Charlie answered. "I knew it but I couldn't tell you. You would have been out for blood."

"You're damn right I would!" Logan screamed as tears flooded his cheeks.

"And you'd be dead now. What good would that have done?"

Sarah sat in stunned silence. If Charlie knew about Beth's and the girls' murders, and he already knew about her theory to stopping the anomalies, so did others. She realized that her life and Logan's life meant nothing to their pursuers.

Sarah spoke as Logan tried to control his rage. "Why, then, are we still alive? These people chasing us are professionals. They should have caught us and killed us by now."

"You're right. The only reason you are still alive is there are people who have been killing the people who are trying to kill you. Like Ruby, and me, for example, and the MI-6 folks."

Sarah had learned to pay attention to hair standing on her neck. "I knew it. I knew we were being followed. How long were you following them?"

"A couple of days, maybe more. I lost track. Ever since I got word from a friend I know through Bohemian Grove that Mavra had spilled her guts about the Russians' plans as well as who in the United States was conspiring with them. If I knew, then other spy agencies knew, too. The Middle Easterners who were following you were too obvious; they stayed too close to you for too long. When you stopped, they stopped, too, and it gave me the opportunity to take them out before they made their move."

"But why now? Why not an hour from now or an hour earlier?" Sarah's curiosity was burning inside her. It was that or hatred, she couldn't be sure.

"I can't say why they didn't kill you sooner. But as you got closer to Area 51, time was running out. If you got within magnetometer range of Area 51, it would be too late. They were having trouble keeping up with you, let alone catching you. When you stopped, it surprised them, I think. They weren't prepared for that. Thirty seconds later, they were dead."

"But we didn't hear any shooting..." Sarah muttered.

Charlie rolled his eyes and let out a long sigh.

"I know, you're a spy," Logan acknowledged.

"Thank you," Charlie answered. "We all have our talents. We used silencers, Sarah."

"So they were just going to kill us?" Sarah asked.

"Yep. That's my guess." Charlie rested his head again on the back of the seat.

"Great. Now what?" Dr. Logan asked.

"You keep driving. Sunrise isn't far off," Charlie said as Sarah turned to see him with his eyes closed once more.

"What happens at sunrise?" Sarah responded.

"That's when we all find out if we're going to live or we're going to die."

40

Nevada's Great Basin Desert is flat scrubland. Usually, you can see for miles in any direction, except for the section of U.S. Highway 95 just south of Jackass Flats and east of the Area 51 Alien Center tourist stop. A dip in the road is the perfect spot for an ambush.

Charlie pulled himself forward from his reclining position in the back seat and squared his shoulders over the console between Logan and Sarah. He checked his watch before asking, "See that ridge up ahead?"

Logan nodded. Sarah's body felt paralyzed.

Charlie told Logan, "Get ready to ease onto your brakes, Johnny, when you reach the top."

"But—why?"

"You'll see any second now."

Sarah's neck hair was rigid and goose flesh crept over her body. Logan gripped the steering wheel with both hands until his knuckles were white. Sarah drew the butt of the tactical automatic rifle to her right shoulder and pulled a round into the chamber. Charlie placed his hand on her left shoulder. He said softly, "That will get us all killed. Give me the gun." Sarah hesitated as a river of sweat ran down her back.

"Give me the gun," Charlie repeated calmly. Cautiously, Sarah cleared the bullet from the chamber, clicked on the gun's safety, and handed it to Charlie.

"Now, whatever you do, stay calm. No sudden moves. Do whatever they tell you. Do you understand?"

Logan looked into his rear view mirror. Four dark vehicles had appeared from nowhere. Running four abreast, they were a half mile back but closing in fast.

"What the hell is going on?" Logan's forehead was lathered with sweat as he nodded toward the mirror. His hands were embedded into the steering wheel but his forearms trembled. Charlie turned to look out the Charger's back window. "Oh, Lordy, I did not see this coming."

Even though the desert sun had barely risen, wavy lines of heat shimmer rose from the tar pavement. Cresting the hill, the Charger bore down on blurry objects blocking the highway ahead while it was being chased down from behind. Sarah saw what Charlie saw when he began to speak.

"Back her down easy, Johnny. Don't spook 'em. Let's not give them any reason to shoot first and ask questions later."

Eight police cars were parked in barricade formation across the road. Two armored Humvees were behind the police cars, each with a sniper lying prone on the top of the cabs, their rifles resting on bipods, and their scopes were dialed in on the two front seat passengers. From overhead, Charlie, Sarah and Dr. Logan heard the 'chop, chop, chop' of helicopter rotors.

"Stop your vehicle or we will open fire!" the orders came from a loudspeaker above them. Peering through the top edge of the Charger's windshield, Logan saw the word 'Sheriff' painted in tan block letters on the helicopter hovering above them.

"What the f—" Logan's voice trailed away as he pressed the brake evenly.

"Easy does it," Charlie reassured him. "You're doing just fine." Charlie knew they were not fine; the black vehicles would come barreling over the top of the hill at any second. With the Charger at a dead stop in the middle of the road, their lives depended on their pursuers stopping before smashing into the grey Charger rented by someone name Tom Moore.

"You seem pretty damn cavalier about this, Charlie," Sarah snipped, turning her head to face Charlie.

"Look straight ahead, Sarah. Don't look at me. Keep your cool for just for a few more seconds."

Logan stared into his rear view mirror as the four black Suburbans crested the hill. He saw smoke billow from their tires as they skidded and swerved on the sizzling tarmac. Glass blew out of all four trucks as their front seat passengers unleashed a volley of machine gun fire through their windshields.

"Get down!" Charlie yelled. Logan, Sarah, and Charlie dove for the car's floor as they listened to glass shattering above them. The sheriff blockade returned fire, snipers targeting the Suburbans' front passengers, killing the shooter in each vehicle.

Rifle and shotgun rounds pierced the Charger while others sizzled past; Logan, Sarah, and Charlie were stuck in the middle of a firefight and had no idea who was shooting at whom.

"Now what?" Sarah screamed over the sounds of gunfire.

"We wait for the Cavalry."

"Any idea just when that might be?" Dr. Logan yelled.

Charlie checked his watch again. "Four, three, two, one—"

The desert floor shook violently, as if an earthquake was erupting. The accompanying roar rattled the car as four A-10 fighter jets—warthogs—approached the Charger from the south, two hundred feet off the hard deck. Firing nearly four thousand 30mm rounds per minute, two of the jets' Gatling guns strafed the four black trucks, reducing them to blood-smeared scrap metal.

The other two warthogs aimed their guns at the Sheriff cars and fired a warning volley of 1,000 rounds each over the tops of the police vehicles as they flew past. Shotgun-wielding police ducked behind patrol cars and the snipers buried their faces in their arms as stinging desert sand whipped furiously around them. Caught in the jet wash, the sheriff helicopter's main rotor lost lift and the chopper spun in circles till it hit the tarmac three hundred yards past the roadblock.

Simultaneously, a wall of smoke exploded between the Charger and the Sheriff cars.

"They dropped smoke!" Charlie explained. "Go! Go! Go! Get out of the car! Dive for the ditch at the side of the road. Go! Go! This fog will lift in seconds!" Sarah grabbed her backpack and followed Charlie and Logan toward the ditch alongside the road.

Once again, Charlie was right. If the three of them had remained in the car a few seconds longer, they would be dead. The Sheriff shouted, "Fire! Open fire! Shoot those sons o' bitches!" Sarah, the Professor, and Charlie watched the Charger disintegrate as it was peppered with buckshot and armor-piercing bullets.

Still firing blindly, the Sheriff and his deputies watched the smoke clear. All four tires of the Charger were flat and steam hissed from its radiator. Its occupants were gone, but hovering above the vehicle were three U.S. Marine Super Cobra attack helicopters, fully loaded with combat ordinances, including Sidewinder missiles and 20mm Gatling guns capable of dismantling the Sheriff's patrol cars as well as the Humvees.

"Holy shit," several of the deputies chimed in unison.

"Stand down," a voice from the middle helicopter ordered through the chopper's exterior loudspeaker.

Raising a bullhorn toward the helicopter, the Sheriff replied, "I am acting under the direct orders of the President of the Yew-nited States. You boys better check with your commanding officer before you go shootin' at us."

"You have thirty seconds to put your weapons on the ground or we will commence firing. This is your final warning."

Turning to his deputy the Sheriff barked, "Get the White House on the blower. Pronto!" The aging Sheriff turned ashen as he looked at the combat helicopters, then back to the second hand on his watch. "What's taking so long?"

"I'm on hold, Sheriff, listening to music. I think… wait… now I'm being sent to voicemail."

"Oh, for Christ's sake! Give me that!" the Sheriff said, grabbing the phone as he turned to face the three helicopters. Their 3-barrel Gatling guns were moving into position, aiming at the Sheriff's blockade.

"Sonofabitch!" the Sheriff threw his trooper hat to the ground. "Stand down!" the Sheriff yelled into the bullhorn toward his deputies. "Put your weapons down. Put 'em down on the ground. Snipers, get off those Humvees. Weapons down." The Sheriff stood on the centerline of U.S. Highway 95, his clenched hands planted defiantly on his hips.

Sarah, Dr. Logan, and Charlie peeked over the mound of parched sand at the road's edge as two squads of U.S. Marines and a six-member tactical squad from MI-6 rappelled out of a Chinook Marine transport chopper hovering above.

The Sheriff's face told his anger as the Marine E-5 approached him. "You boys gonna' be sittin' in a barrel o' boilin' cow shit when the White House hears about your interference in a military operation sanctioned by the President hisself. You hear me, boy?"

"Yes, sir, I hear you loud and clear, sir. Now turn around and put your hands behind your back."

"You—you—you son of a bitch! You think you're going to arrest a Sheriff elected by the good people of Nevada? Who the hell do you think you are?"

"We're the real military, sir, and we're not going to charge you with anything quite yet. Let's just say we're going to detain you until we find out how much you know about what is going on, whether you're just being cussed ornery or you're guilty of treason. We'll have plenty of time to get acquainted. Now, everyone, we can do this the hard way or we can do it the easy way. Turn around. Put your hands behind your backs."

Bruised and bloodied from their hard landing, the Sheriff's chopper pilots turned around and placed their hands at the small of their backs, followed by the other deputies.

"Dr. Logan?" Sarah whispered.

"Yes?"

"Did you ever meet Aedain? Remember, the guy you swore should have never been allowed in your class because there was no such thing as a waiver test?"

"Yes, I remember, but no, I'm certain I never met him."

"See that one in the black tactical gear? The one standing behind the Marine sergeant?"

"Yes. What about him?"

"I'd swear that's Aedain. I can't be sure from this distance but it sure looks like him."

Charlie interrupted. "Aedain? Commander Aedain Maycroft? Yeah, that's him," Charlie confirmed as he pointed his forefinger at Aedain. "He's a bit of a legend, he is. Glad he's on our side."

Sarah's eyes bulged and her complexion went white before it turned red.

"That son of a bitch! He played me!" Sarah sprung from their hiding spot and charged across the tarmac, straight toward the British spy. Working her way through the maze of Marines and handcuffed deputies, Sarah approached Aedain.

"Sarah? Where do you think you're going?" Dr. Logan called after her.

"Aedain!" Sarah yelled. He spun around, his eyes met Sarah's, and he smiled. Sarah did not smile back.

"You son of a bitch! You played me! You lied to me!"

"Welcome to Area 51," he said, ignoring her anger.

"You think this is a joke? You've been playing me the whole time. I should have known. I did know. My gut told me but I didn't listen," Sarah spit her words as she paced back and forth in front of him. "I knew there was something off. I knew you didn't belong in that class. Oh, you were good. Real good. You had me hook, line and sinker."

Dr. Logan caught up to Sarah and held her backpack out to her. "Calm down. Isn't there something you want to do right now?"

"Right now? You're damn right there is!" Sarah pulled her fist back and aimed at Aedain's jaw. Dr. Logan grabbed her fist just in time.

"No, I'm talking about what is in your backpack. Your magnetometer, remember?"

"Oh. Yeah. Right." Sarah shrugged her shoulders and reached into her backpack. She held the magnetometer in her hand as she powered it up. Its needle pegged hard to the maximum positive reading accompanied by an ear-splitting alarm. It was proof that the

United States' secret supercollider was buried deep beneath the Grand Basin Desert surface.

"Yes, Sarah, there are magnets underground. Lots of them. Now will you please turn that thing off before we're all deaf?" Aedain cupped his hands over his ears until Sarah turned the meter off.

Sarah turned toward Dr. Logan, "I was right. There's a secret supercollider here."

"Pretty sure it's no longer a secret," Logan muttered.

Sarah's anger turned to hurt, then confusion. She turned to Aedain. "You. Why? You knew all along. You knew what Dr. Logan suspected. That's why you came to his class. That's why you got close to me; that's why you pretended to like me."

"I wasn't pretending."

Sarah stopped, unsure whether to believe him. "You lied to me."

"Yes, I did."

"I never lied to you."

"Ah, to the contrary, I seem to recall a time when you were in Pennsylvania but you said you were in Charlotte—"

Sarah stopped and squinted hard, "That was different."

"Was it?"

"Wait. What? You knew? You knew I was in Pennsylvania?"

"No, but I knew you weren't in Charlotte. Our drone followed you all the way to Detroit. There was no way you could have made it to Charlotte that fast."

"That's not fair. You knew I was lying to you but I didn't know you were lying to me." Sarah paused at the absurdity of her logic before adding, "Wait! That was *your* drone?"

"Her Majesty's drone, actually. The Queen only lets me borrow them."

"The Queen of England knows you're here?"

Aedain nodded. "I'm under her direct orders."

Aedain stuck out his hand to Sarah. "Let me formally introduce myself. I am Commander Aedain Maycroft, British MI6, Her Majesty's Secret Intelligence Service."

"You mean, like James Bond?"

"He's taller."

"Oh, shit. I'm seeing a spy."

"Seeing? You mean like dating? When did we start dating?"

Sarah's face flushed in embarrassment. "You know what I mean."

Dr. Logan held up a finger as if to speak.

Sarah held up her palm. "Not now! I'm trying to figure this out."

"What is there to figure out, Sarah?" Aedain replied. "I was doing my job. I didn't plan on, you know, liking you. It just happened. You lied to me, I lied to you. We had our jobs to do."

The Marine sergeant interrupted. "Ma'am—Commander—do you think you can work out your relationship issues someplace other than on a tarmac that's 140 degrees and we're surrounded by millions of dollars in U.S. Military armaments? Just a consideration."

Sarah looked at Aedain, then to Dr. Logan and Charlie. "I need a drink," Logan said.

The Marine replied, "About a mile down, there's a saloon that serves its beer ice cold." He motioned Sarah closer and whispered, "In fairness, ma'am, it was Commander Maycroft and his boys who discovered the Russians had colluded with several top people in our current government to privatize all of Area 51. Once it was privately owned, nobody could stop them. The United States would have lost one of its most valuable assets—one that is essential to our national security—and the world's."

"What about him?" Sarah asked as she pointed at Charlie. "I'm not sure I trust him."

"Charlie?" the Marine laughed. "I understand. Sometimes he gives me the creeps, too. But when Ruby and Aedain realized how much trouble you and Dr. Logan were in, Charlie called a few folks in the CIA or NSA—I'm not sure which—to invite us to this little party today."

Sarah turned to Aedain. "Ruby and the Archbishop? Are they still alive?"

"Bishop Joe lost his leg in the attack at the church. He's recovering, though."

"I'm so sorry to hear that. But he's going to live?" Aedain nodded as he guided Sarah toward the side of the road. "And Ruby?"

"She's feisty as ever. She sends her best."

Sarah panned the soldiers and military hardware in the middle of a remote desert highway and asked the Marine, "But—how? How did you know to come here? How did the Sheriff know to ambush us here? How did Charlie know we were headed to this exact spot?"

"Charlie," the sergeant answered. "He has his methods. I try not to ask too much. He had the Sheriff's phones, office, car, and home wiretapped. He knew exactly where the Sheriff was going to set up the roadblock. Like I told you, sometimes he gives me the creeps, too."

"I'm standing right here," Charlie interjected. "I can hear you."

"Wait!" Sarah held up her palm. "Just stop. Let me get this straight. The Sheriff says he's under direct orders from the President but the President is Commander-in-Chief. So why aren't you guys under the President's orders?"

"These are exceptional times, ma'am," the sergeant answered. "I am not permitted to divulge the circumstances which have resulted in our present chain of command but, I assure you, we are acting in the United States' national security interests. Now, if you don't mind, I would like to escort these law enforcement officers into a more comfortable environment for interrogation and get all these vehicles from blocking a U.S. highway."

Aedain took Sarah's arm, "It's hot out here. C'mon, I'll show you the supercollider if you promise to stop yelling at me. I hear there are some places it is air-conditioned really well, like 500 degrees below Fahrenheit. We've got some catching up to do."

"Really? Seriously? You've seen it?"

"No, but I figure the sergeant here knows exactly where it is and how to get there. Right, Sergeant?"

"Yes, Commander. Sheriff, you don't mind if he borrows one of your patrol cars, do you?"

"Go to hell." The feisty, pot-bellied Sheriff spat on the Marine's shiny boots.

"Looks like you'll need to find transportation," the Marine said to Sarah.

Logan appeared dazed and bewildered, wandering aimlessly toward the destroyed rented car. "Who is going to pay for the car? Did we get the insurance?"

"It was on a fake credit card, remember?" Sarah reminded him. "Besides, it was the Sheriff who shot it up."

"Are you going to the supercollider? I'd like to see it, too, if you don't mind."

"Of course we meant for you to come with us, Dr. Logan."

The lanky Charlie spoke up, "I suppose I wouldn't mind seeing it, too. Do you have directions?" Sarah was surprised by his interest.

"All we need is a car," Sarah muttered as the Marine sergeant stared south through the heat shimmer to see a single vehicle approaching fast.

"What the hell is that?"

All eyes turned to see a bright red muscle car braking from 130 miles an hour to a dead stop.

"That's my dad." Sarah said flatly. "I think I'm in trouble."

"Hey!" Tuffy's gravelly voice said as he jumped out of the driver's side door. "Was it your bright idea to paint my damn car red?"

Sarah grimaced and said, "Maybe. Do you like it?"

"Well, it's going to take some getting used to. That black and tan paint was original, you know."

"I know," Sarah wrapped her arms around her father's neck. "Why are you here? How did you get the car?"

"Ted at the body shop in The Brock Junction—wherever the hell that is—calls to tell me my car is ready. I ask, 'What car?' and he says, 'The Chevy SS with the broken window.' I hop a plane and a taxi, and he hands me the keys to this." Tuffy nodded toward the red muscle car with white pin stripes along the tops of the fenders.

"I'm sorry. I had to make sure he kept it inside so nobody would see it."

Tuffy hugged his daughter. "It's alright, I suppose. I always said I wanted a candy apple red hot rod."

Dr. Logan stuck out his hand to Tuffy. "Thanks for your help in Apalachicola. I thought for sure I was a goner."

"I had some help." Tuffy reached out his hand toward Charlie. "Your boys did some nice shooting."

"Back at ya," Charlie said as he pumped Tuffy's hand.

"Dad," Sarah interrupted, "you want to see the supercollider?"

"Sure."

"You drive," Tuffy said, handing the keys to Sarah." The five squeezed into the Chevy and maneuvered past the patrol cars.

The sergeant leaned into the driver's side window and spoke to Sarah, "Drive until they aim guns at you. Tell them I gave you clearance. I'll radio ahead. Try to keep it under 100."

Then he turned to Logan. "One more thing. When you're done with your little tour, we'll be taking all of you to the U.S. Marshals for debriefing, then we'll turn you over to WitSec until we think you're safe. Enjoy your tour."

Sarah crested a hill when Charlie said, "Stop. I need to take a leak. Now!"

"Who? What?" Logan protested as Charlie opened the door disappeared behind a dune. Several minutes passed.

"What's taking him so long?" Logan spoke aloud what the others were thinking. They all got out of the car and followed Charlie's path to find him.

Nothing. There was no sign that Charlie had ever been there. He was gone.

41

Pushing the button to activate the intercom, the man behind the desk spoke: "Get me a Cobb salad for lunch, will you? Bleu cheese. Two of those little containers. And two scoops of ice cream." He drummed his fingers on the desk as if he was waiting for something. He just wasn't sure what. He jumped at the sound of the black rotary telephone ringing.

"Hello, this is the President. Oh, yeah, right. You know that." He paused until the Secretary of the Interior finished speaking.

"You got the deal I told you about? It's great, right? I told you it would be great. I knew it would be a terrific offer. Bring it right down to my office so I can sign it. Oh, you've signed it already. Of course. You can do that. I told you to do that. Sure. Come down to my office. Bring the White House photographer and the staff. We'll take that photograph now."

Three minutes passed until the door to the Oval Office opened. The Secretary entered first, followed by several key aides and the White house photographer.

A smiling President addressed the Secretary of the Interior loudly, "Fifty million dollars, right? That's quite a victory for us. Great work! Great work!" he said, pumping the Secretary's hand. "Fifty million! That'll make the media stand up and salute!" He looked at the smiling faces in the room, all applauding his deal of the century.

"Excuse me, Mr. President," the Secretary whispered as he pulled him aside. The audience watched his face turn pale as the Secretary explained that the offer was considerably higher than fifty million. There had been two offers, he explained. The offer from the President's friend arrived in a plain envelope thirty minutes after the first offer, which had arrived on his desk within seconds of their conversation to sell Area 51.

"Sir, I assumed that the first offer was the one you wanted me to accept, so I signed it before the second offer was delivered."

The President leaned in close to the Secretary's ear and growled, "Who knew the land was for sale that quickly? Is my office wiretapped? How did they find out?"

"I can't answer that, sir, but we received a remarkable offer. You told me I should accept it; that we wouldn't want the American people to lose out. Do you remember?"

The thick man noticed his aides and the photographer watching his interaction with the Secretary. "No, of course, we always encourage competition, you know, competitive offers on public lands. That's what is best for America, right? Of course. Sure." He leaned and whispered to the Secretary again. "Who is this other buyer?"

Blood drained President's face as he heard the Secretary's reply.

"The offer was made by real estate conglomerate, sir—a joint venture between a French and a British company. They appear to have an exceptional position in cash and precious metals, sir. This purchase will barely make a dent in their liquid assets."

The President replied, "I've never heard of them. Who are these people? How do we know they are legitimate? How do we know they really have the money they say they have? There are a lot of scoundrels out there, you know."

"They wired the full amount of the purchase to an escrow account here in the States as security, sir."

"How much did they offer?"

"Five billion, sir."

"Five what? Five billion? That was their offer? Five billion dollars? That's 100 times more than..." The president stopped, realizing he would incriminate himself in collusion if he knew about and offer made by his partnership with the Russian. "Who the hell are these people? Are they nuts? Who pays five billion dollars for dirt in the middle of the desert?" He was pacing now.

"Actually, sir, they felt it was a steal for owning the world's largest, most powerful supercollider. They said it was a bargain."

"Supercollider?" the President's brow furrowed. "What's a supercollider? We have a supercollider? Where?"

"Underground in Area 51, sir. It's been there about ten years."

"Why didn't someone tell me that?"

"It was in the briefings, sir. The ones you didn't attend. Did you want us to take a photograph now? I had the Graphics Department mock up a big check you can hold."

"Are you trying to be funny now? You're making a joke, right?"

"No, sir."

"Who cares, anyway? Why does anyone need a supercollider?"

266

"Apparently, they have five billion reasons, sir."

"Go! Get out. All of you. I need to make a phone call."

The Secretary was the last to reach the door. "Sir, they extended an unusual offer. I can't explain why and I don't understand it myself. But they said they would be open to the idea of returning the land to the United States for the price they paid for it, once your term of office is over. They hoped a consortium of world renowned scientists could collaborate to discover answers the secrets the supercollider might hold."

The thick man waved him away. The President's hand had barely reached the phone's black handle when it rang. He listened for a full minute to an irate county Sheriff scream into his ear.

"They did what? U.S. Marines? Helicopters with rockets? On whose authority? Joint Chiefs of Staff? Is that what they said? I'll fire every damn one of them. The sons o' bitches! Who the hell do they think they are?"

He was interrupted as the door to the Oval Office opened. The House Speaker and the Leader of the Senate flanked the U.S. Attorney General and several Department of Justice lawyers. The President invited them to sit. They remained standing.

"Mr. President," the Attorney General began, "we'd like to ask you some questions. Of course, you have the right to remain silent."

42

"Good morning, Sal." A lanky shadow stretched across the tiled viaduct. Sal had left himself unguarded and, today, that was a bad decision.

Instinctively, Sal jumped away. He pushed his pork-pie hat up his forehead to see the shadow's face.

"Jesus, Charlie! You're like a damn ghost!" Sal felt his breath sucked out as he spoke, "You scared the hell out of me."

"I intended to, Sal. I came to return your pen." Charlie held out the tape-recording spy pen toward the Mob boss. Charlie's right hand remained in his pocket, gripping the handle of his trademarked kill weapon, a double-edged dagger with a 9-inch blade.

Sal stared at the pen a long moment before accepting it. "Yeah, uh, yeah sure, thanks," he stammered. "I told you that you didn't need to return it. You know that, right? You remember? I said you could keep it."

"I remember, Sal. But I wanted to return it in person. It gives me the chance to tell you this: let him be."

Sal squinted and his head tilted defiantly at Charlie. "I can't do that, Charlie. He killed eight of my people—eight of my family." Heartache was etched in Salvatore's eyes.

"I said, let him be. Your people, your family, was planning to kidnap, torture and probably murder his daughter if they caught her. It was a contract you shouldn't have taken. I promise you, Sal, if it had been my daughter, I wouldn't have stopped at eight. By now, I would have already hunted down each and every one of your family and they would have suffered the most gruesome deaths imaginable. And you, Sal? I'd save you for last, killing you slowly and with my bare hands. You got off easy. Let him be. Have I made myself clear?"

Sal's head jerked up and down as he weighed his chances of pulling his gun before Charlie plunged his frog sticker into his throat.

"You're not that fast, Sal."

Salvatore decided to keep his hands where Charlie could see them.

"Good. I'm glad we could reach an accord." Charlie turned and, ghost-like, he slipped away into the dark canyon of burned-out Bedford-Stuyvesant buildings.

43

On Inisheer Island, off the coast of Galway, the barman rapped the side of the TV mounted behind the bar and the TV crackled to life. Its picture was faded but the sound was still good.

"Sorry, it's all we've got," the barman said, "just one channel. Looks like the Evening News is on now."

To Sarah, the barkeep's brogue made his speech nearly unintelligible. "The Gaelic Football match between Dublin and Kilkenny is up next."

"That's fine," the good-smelling man sitting at the bar replied. The chestnut-haired scientist sat beside him, sipping a pint of Murphy's drawn from a fresh keg. Six other patrons in the bar waited patiently for the Gaelic football telecast from Dublin's Croke Park to begin.

"Today in Washington," the reporter said, "the Department of Justice argued in Federal Court that the former President, now impeached and convicted of treason, will be sentenced next month. Political insiders expect he will spend the rest of his life in prison."

The young man tipped his glass in the scientist's direction. She clinked his glass as he said, "Sláinte."

"Sláinte," she repeated. They sat silently until she whispered, "Did we win? Really? It doesn't feel like we won."

"We didn't lose," the man replied. "It was never a contest, really. It was a matter of life and death." The two spoke low. So far, nobody had paid much attention to these strangers in town. To the locals, they were just a couple of American tourists who had taken the wrong ferry and wound up on Inisheer. Sarah and Aedain would just as soon keep it that way.

This. This moment, Sarah thought. It was the first time Sarah had the chance to examine Aedain's face. He was older than she first thought. Now, as shadows fell across his countenance in the dimly lit bar, she saw the weathered complexion of a career soldier who had already seen too much bad in the world. Sarah wondered how he managed to find joy when so much evil had surrounded him.

"We did lose, Aedain," Sarah whispered. "We lost our faith in those in whom we placed our trust. The people we chose to protect us, failed us. We lost trust in the man who promised to lead our country and the politicians who were supposed to keep him in check."

"You're right, of course. At least we stopped him before he succeeded."

"Only by the grace of God."

"God, the FBI, you, Dr. Logan, Ruby, Charlie, and a few politicians whose consciences are still intact. Plus, if I may say, we Brits played a role."

"Yes, you did. Thank you." Sarah rested her hand on Aedain's arm. In the months since their argument standing in the middle of a Nevada highway, she and Aedain had gotten to know one another at the safe house the U.S. Marshals provided. All of their lives remained in danger—Logan's, Ruby's and Bishop Joe's—but Sarah and Aedain had grown tired of being cloistered.

Living free was worth the risk.

Together, they sat quietly and stared at the black and white TV with poor reception. Sarah felt numb, as if she was in a trance. She had survived months of terror and more attempts to kill her than she knew. She didn't want to know. Right now, she wanted to sit on a bar stool beside Aedain and sip Murphy's.

Twenty minutes of silence ended when Sarah spoke. "There's something that's been bothering me, Aedain. Charlie's a spy. Ruby's a spy. Bishop Joe is a spy, and you're a spy. Is Dr. Logan a spy, too?"

"No, he's an asset."

"An asset?"

"Early in his schooling at the Burnage Academy in Manchester, the Governor's Board recognized his talent in mathematics and science. They made sure he was accepted at Cambridge for his undergraduate studies and then Princeton for his PhD."

"Who is 'they'?"

"The Queen of England. Her Majesty's Secret Service, really. The Queen began a program in the 1950s to identify exceptional British minds who could be embedded throughout the world in a way which could provide valuable information to the British Empire."

"So, he is a spy."

"No, an asset."

"Why is Dr. Logan an asset but not a spy? He's been intentionally embedded, as you put it, to provide information which could be advantageous to Great Britain."

"The difference is: Logan never knew he was being groomed to be Chairperson of Princeton's Astrophysics and Cosmology Department. He never knowingly provided secrets to Mother England. He was doing research, learning, teaching, probing for answers, and sharing what he found in the lecture halls and in his publications."

"Go on."

"He never knew the Queen had a plan for him. He still doesn't. She even set up that amateur rugby league he played in. She wanted to make certain he didn't get homesick for England."

"I don't get it. Why didn't they just make him a spy, feeding secret information to Great Britain?"

"It would have been too obvious. Every intel agency in the world has been watching him for years. If he was a spy, they would have exposed him years ago or simply killed him. Besides, his personality profile told them he would never stand for it; his moral character wouldn't allow him to be a spy."

"I believe that." Sarah nodded as she agreed that Dr. Logan's sense of fairness, his integrity, wouldn't allow him to be a part of something underhanded.

Aedain continued, "He was given the freedom to study the Cosmos, Hawking's theory, Einstein's gravity, Tesla's work, and come up with his own thoughts about how they intersected."

"How does that make him an asset for British Intelligence?"

"A British agent was in the audience of every class Logan taught, just as I was. All of his research, dissertations, and magazine articles were sent to British Intelligence who then shared them under the Five Eyes Accord. It worked great; the United States was happy to have someone spying on Logan without being responsible for doing it illegally."

"When the Queen stopped sharing intelligence with the President, he got nervous, didn't he?"

"Terrified," Aedain said, "and paranoid. He became certain Logan was a British spy and knew all about his conspiracy with Russia's president. That's why he hired people to send him a warning."

"The President hired the men who murdered Beth and the girls?"

"No, his mob boss friend, Salvatore, did. Unfortunately, he hired amateurs. Street thugs who couldn't comprehend the strategy of simply scaring Logan to keep his mouth shut. When Beth fought back, the gangbangers murdered her and the girls. Logan got scared alright—so much so that he ran for his life."

"And then I tracked him down and they all followed me right to him."

"He wanted you to find him. He left a bread crumb trail that only you could decipher."

Sarah eyes welled as she whispered, "I miss them. I miss them terribly."

"Lisa and Lucy?" Aedain probed.

Sarah nodded, "And Beth." Someday, Sarah's heart would stop hurting for her beloved mentor and his family. To her, they were family. But today wasn't the day her heartache would stop, that much she knew.

"Aedain?" Sarah whispered. "Who does Charlie work for—the NSA or CIA? Nobody seems to know for sure."

"Neither," Aedain said, sipping his Murphy's again. "Never has."

Sarah waited for him to finish his sentence until she realized he already had. Maybe he knew. Maybe he didn't. Either way, he wasn't telling. Logan was eager to get to work at the Area 51 super-collider, trying to unlock the secret to the worldwide anomalies. Sarah would join him there, eventually, but not just yet. For now, she needed to breathe fresh air.

"Dr. Logan already figured out how to stop the gravitational events," Sarah said. "The circumference of the accelerator was causing the protons to smash together at more than 800 million miles an hour. He thinks that was affecting gravity somehow but he's not sure why just yet. He reduced the particle collision speed to 500 million and it appears the anomalies have stopped."

"That's good."

"He's still working on why they happened in the first place. The next step will be to see if we can make it a safe, predictable energy source. Beyond that, who knows?"

"You're planning to join him at Area 51, aren't you?"

"Of course," Sarah said, surprised Aedain would ask.

"I was hoping you'd take some time to consider my offer," Aedain replied. "I know we could use someone like you in our investigations. There is a great deal of ground to cover. These players, the ones we caught, they are the tip of the iceberg. I believe there is a much deeper, more complex organization behind it all."

"I don't know the first thing about being a spy," Sarah rebuffed then added. "I know. I know. You'll teach me." Sarah breathed in slowly, then out. "If this experience taught me anything, it is that there are very dangerous people in the world who operate in secret. They stay behind the Wizard's curtain while they rule Oz. They are the puppeteers of the politicians; I see that now. I never set out to be a spy. I trained to be a scientist."

"I know," Aedain replied. "But you handled yourself well. You're one helluva' shot. Smart, brave, tough as nails. Those are characteristics we look for. The offer is open if you ever change your mind. We have much to do if we are to expose those who pull the puppets' strings. We need all the help we can get."

As if choreographed, Aedain's and Sarah's heads jerked together toward the TV. The news reporter announced, "In other international news, Russia's Prime Minister issued a statement on the mysterious disappearance of Russia's president. The Prime Minister vehemently denied that the President was missing and suggested he was on a long-planned, extended vacation, possibly horseback riding in Montana. He assured the Russian people that he, the Prime Minister, was in charge of the nation's business with the full knowledge, cooperation, and support of the President. When asked if he knew when the President would return from his sabbatical, the Prime Minister simply replied, '*Nyet.*'"

Sarah turned to Aedain, "Do you think he'll ever turn up?"

"Of course," Aedain nodded as he said, "the day after they find Jimmy Hoffa."

The two sat in silence for several minutes, sipping stout and secretly wondering what the future held. The game between Kilkenny and Dublin had replaced the news and the six other patrons' stares were locked on the faded TV. Dublin was leading Kilkenny but it was still early.

"Watch what these lads can do with that football," Aedain said. "Quite amazing. I can only imagine what it takes to become that skilled."

"Practice," Sarah replied, stating the obvious. "I suppose they practice every day." Just then, a Dublin player toe-kicked the ball into the Kilkenny net.

"*Cul!*" the six shouted in unison, clapping and whistling.

"What did they say?" Sarah asked.

"'*Cul!*' It's Gaelic for 'Goal!' Like in World Cup Football. You Yanks call it soccer."

"I see." Today, the world was quiet. Looking out the tavern's window across North Atlantic toward Galway, Sarah was sure that if anyone was chasing them, she'd see them coming. The sea was calm and there were no boats plying their way through the saltwater toward the island.

"You know," Sarah said, "I never did find out who planted the transmitter in my shoe."

Aedain nodded and faced straight ahead, taking another sip of stout. "No, I suppose not," he responded. Sarah turned, studying his face. Aedain's stare was fixed on a Gaelic football match.

She watched his nodding head for a minute before the epiphany. She blurted, "You! It was you!"

Aedain's head bobbed up and down slightly as his eyes focused steadfastly on the TV. He took a gulp of Murphy's.

Flabbergasted, the only word Sarah could find was, "How?"

"You were asleep."

"When?"

"That night." Aedain blushed.

"*What* night?"

"That night your apartment was ransacked and you called me."

Sarah remembered back to that night. She blushed, too, and turned to stare at the TV, her head now nodding in rhythm with Aedain's, and said, "Oh, that night."

"You remember it, do you?"

"Uh, umm, yes, I, uh, I remember that night, yes." She swallowed a big gulp of Murphy's.

"It was a memorable night, as I recall."

"Yes, yes it was," Sarah stammered, then returned to her question, "But, but, why?"

"We had to keep tabs on you. You were our ticket to Logan. If the Russians or the Mob had found him first, the outcome would most likely have been very different."

"So the drone followed the transmitter in my shoe from Princeton to Detroit."

"Yes, until you left us in the dust with that beast of a car your dad gave you. We lost track of you for a time. Then you showed up in New Orleans looking for Ruby."

"Ah, Ruby. She didn't miss the transmitter when she scanned me, did she?"

Aedain shook his head. "Nope. She was scanning you to make sure you didn't have any *other* transmitters on you, and to make sure ours was still in place."

Now, Sarah stared at the curious game on the telly. It wasn't American football nor the British rugby Dr. Logan enjoyed, nor World Cup soccer. It seemed as if it was pieces and parts of each

275

one. It seemed much like the spy game; she would never know all the rules but at the end of each game, she hoped the good guys won.

"That *was* a memorable night," Sarah said, tasting another sip of the stout.

"Yes, it was. Probably the best night I'll ever live."

Sarah stared at the worn television. "Well, with some practice, who knows?"

Aedain's head snapped in Sarah's direction as he jumped up from his chair and tossed a 20-Euro note on the bar. "Keep the change," he told the barkeep. He led her from the bar and they swung their hands together as they walked to their rented cottage on Inisheer Island.

Sarah leaned in against Aedain's ear. "*Cul!*" she whispered.